Below Par

by Lane Cohen

2016, TWB Press
www.twbpress.com

Edited by Terry Wright

© Cover Art by Terry Wright
Images from Shutterstock.com

ISBN: 978-1-944045-07-4

For Abbey...

Not a shred of evidence exists in favor of the idea that life is serious. - Brendan Gill

Prelude

I just couldn't get warm.

Uncle Morgan cranked the heat up in the Escalade to the max, but my shivers didn't get any better. My early meditation session in the woods with Mrs. Morrison had passed slower than a Nova documentary about the life cycle of algae. And with each passing minute in the morning sleet, as acid-induced 60s music jolted endlessly in the frozen air, little by little I lost feeling in each and every part of my body.

Pinson Dill sat in the back seat, completely silent, maybe lost in his own thoughts, whatever they might be. He hadn't said a word since we left Glenwood Gardens. My mother raised me to respect my elders, but my session with Mrs. *Woodstock* Morrison had been a strain on every lesson about manners my mother ever taught me, since I had wanted to scream at Uncle Morgan and Pinson about the insanity of meditating on the wet ground in 34 degree weather.

And now, Uncle Morgan guided his SUV up Bonham Road toward a horse stable. Of course. It seemed the perfect place to begin golf lessons, certainly fitting with every other part of Uncle Morgan's demented plan to turn me into a celebrity golfer. At least the weather had improved somewhat. The freezing rain finally stopped and the skies cleared. The sun glistened on the wet streets and across the tops of roadside grasses. But the better weather didn't matter. I still couldn't get warm.

"We're about there," Uncle Morgan said.

Bonham Road ended. My uncle maneuvered the SUV through the intersection, immediately across the street and between two brick columns that framed a long, twisting driveway. We drove uphill for about a minute until a large stable came into view on a rise to our left. Just beyond, I saw an outdoor horse-training ring. The dirt inside the fenced area was dotted with puddles. Uncle Morgan slowed the Escalade in a gravel parking area. Sandy Carson's film van was parked at the end of the lot.

We all got out. The cool air smelled of horses. Pinson walked to the back of the SUV and opened the hatch.

"Ready?" Uncle Morgan said.

I nodded at him even though I knew my answer didn't make any difference. Pinson and Uncle Morgan walked together toward a rolling meadow. Pinson carried a golf club under one arm, a plastic bucket, an MP3 player, and a small speaker.

I squinted at the sky. The dark clouds had returned. A breeze returned, as well, and my face was freezing again. I wanted to go back inside the Escalade with the heater set to Warp-9 and my bare hands over the air vents.

"Charley," Uncle Morgan said over his shoulder at me. "You okay?"

"Peachy." I stuffed my hands inside the pockets of my jacket and willed my legs to move as I followed my uncle and Pinson into the meadow.

"Here." Pinson handed the golf club to me.

I let it hang by my side.

He reached into the plastic bucket and pulled out a little white ball, much smaller than a golf ball. He dropped the tiny sphere into the grass. "A bit closer, sir."

I moved closer.

"Now, take the club and hit the ball."

I looked down. "This little white speck in the grass is not a golf ball."

"No."

"It looks like a golf ball from Munchkin Land."

"Jawbreaker."

"Candy?"

"Yes."

"You want me to hit a *jawbreaker* with this *golf* club?"

Pinson blinked. "The candy is about one-third the size of a golf ball. For the next month, you will practice your tee shots and fairway shots using only jawbreakers."

I tilted my head at my uncle. "Seriously?"

Uncle Morgan shrugged.

Pinson said, "If you can hit a *jawbreaker* accurately..." He waited for me to think about it.

I groaned. "Let me guess. When I try to hit a ball three times larger, it will be much easier."

Pinson smiled. His moustache shifted at the corners of his mouth. "That is the plan, sir."

It made some kind of twisted sense, but also seemed funny, hitting jawbreakers into a horse pasture. I pictured the horses leaning against the fence and chewing on the spheres of sugar. Nice treat at my expense.

I looked down at the jawbreaker, white with red swirls. "Okay. Whatever. Which direction?"

Pinson pointed northwest. "Grip the club as you like, and approach the ball in any fashion."

"I've never played golf, Mr. Dill. I don't know the first thing about gripping, approaching, or swinging. Or putting, if we ever get around to that."

"We will, sir. Putting is more than half the game. Many golfers fail because they spend a great deal of time on their long game and their middle game, but little or no time on their short game."

"Why is that?"

"Hitting the ball a long distance is fun. That is why you see so many driving ranges, but few good opportunities to practice on greens, where championships are *really* won. Golfers typically practice putting only after they finish swinging a hundred times at full strength. They use putting as a method of cooling down."

I nodded. "Thanks. You've saved me a lot of reading with that synopsis." I pointed northwest. "So, that way?"

Pinson nodded at me.

"No problem." I wrapped both hands around the end of the club. The grip was rubber, or a synthetic tacky material. I had no idea how to hold it, so I just did what came naturally. "Like this?"

"As you like." Pinson pressed a button on his MP3 player and music blared from the little speaker.

I assumed this song was called *Incense and Peppermints*, and I assumed this was another 60s song, just like those Mrs. Morrison played this morning. They all seemed to have a fuzztone guitar and incomprehensible lyrics that sounded meaningful but really were not.

Thunder rumbled from a short distance away. It bounced across the meadow and echoed off the side of a nearby barn.

"Okay," I said. "The skies are about to open up. I'm holding the club. Now what?"

"Address the ball. That means to move as close as you wish, and plant your feet."

Rain in the form of slush drops spit from above.

I grabbed the end of the club with both hands, took one step forward, and stared down at the jawbreaker ball. "Any time limit?"

"Study the ball, study the grass, and adjust your grip, your stance, your attention."

"Does that mean there's no time limit?"

"None."

I thought for a moment. "You know, you're right."

Pinson looked at me. "Your meaning?"

"How hard can this be? The ball is just sitting there. Right?"

"Yes it is, sir. Yes it is."

I bit down on my bottom lip, wiggled my fingers a little along the club grip, brought the club back around my left shoulder, grunted and swung back around as hard as I could, aiming directly at one little white jawbreaker.

I missed. "Crap."

"Try again."

The rain turned to ice pellets.

"Can't we come back later when the storm passes?"

"A few more swings."

Sleet swept in on a gust of wind from the west. I was soaked in an instant. I tried to steady myself over the so-called *ball*. I stared at it, brought the club back, and swung.

I missed again. "Okay. That's it."

"Concentrate, aim, and swing."

I stared at Pinson with what must have been a wild look in my eyes. "You're crazy, too."

Something caught my eye and I glanced off to the side. A large black dog watched us in the grass near a stand of trees.

"Where did he come from?" I asked.

"She's staring at you, sir."

Uncle Morgan chimed in, "Ignore the beast and continue. The weather isn't getting any better."

I pointed at the dog. "Look."

The black canine trotted to us, stopped at my feet, sat and stared up at me.

"I can't see a collar," I said.

"Wouldn't get too close," Uncle Morgan warned.

"He came up to *me*, Uncle Morgan."

He shrugged. "Probably a stray. May be feral, living alone out here in these woods."

"She may belong to the stable," Pinson said.

"She?" I said. "How can you tell?"

Pinson chuckled. "I have a feeling."

The dog pushed her nose against my jacket pocket. I pulled out half a bagel wrapped in a napkin. I offered the bagel, and the dog took it. She sank to the ground and began to chew.

Uncle Morgan took a step toward me. "Charley? Our schedule?"

"Wait until she's finished."

The dog gulped down the bagel, stood up, and pressed her head into my shin.

"She likes me."

"Golf? *Soon*?" Uncle Morgan growled.

"This is ridiculous," I spat. "They're going to find us here in the spring, all frozen, like those woolly mammoths in Montana."

"Training does continue, sir, rain or shine," Pinson said. "That is the plan."

I felt a jolt of anger punch the center of my chest. "Not today it doesn't."

"If the rain persists, we'll change our schedule."

"I can't believe I ever decided to..." I pushed the golf club into Pinson's hands. "I'm through."

"Okay, okay," Uncle Morgan said. "You're right. It's time we got out of the rain."

"Sleet," I insisted. "*Sleet*, Uncle Morgan."

"Pinson has a video to show you. Let's go to the condo and

do that now. Maybe we'll get a break in the weather in a little while and come back."

The dog shook. Water sprayed everywhere.

I took a step closer to my uncle and shook my head. "I'm through, Uncle Morgan. I quit. And not just for today."

He extended his hand and touched my shoulder.

The dog growled.

Uncle Morgan flinched and dropped his hand.

The dog became silent. She pressed against the side of my leg and glared at Uncle Morgan.

Uncle Morgan huffed. "Seems you have found a friend."

I looked down at her. "I know we just met, but you may be the one good thing that's come out of this." I turned and started back to the car.

"Charley," Uncle Morgan said. "This isn't you, Charley. You're not a quitter. Charley!"

I walked faster, heading for the shelter of the Escalade through swirling waves of sleet. I didn't look back to see if they were following. The black dog walked beside me, never more than one foot away. I could barely feel my fingers or my feet. My nose and cheeks were utterly frozen.

As I neared the black SUV, I wondered what it was like right now in Bolivia, where people didn't take golf lessons amid bullets of ice, where *hippie* music wasn't played constantly from every doorstep, and where golfers never shared their fairways with horses. It must be quite special in Bolivia, amid the banana plantations and banana barges, where I'd heard the average temperature was 82 degrees.

I reached for the door handle, pulled the door open, and slumped inside. Sleet popped on the metal and glass all around. My new canine friend jumped in and just managed to fit on the floor in front of me. I still couldn't feel my fingers, but I grabbed a towel and rubbed it through her fur. She stared at me with what must have been an expression of canine appreciation.

Maybe tomorrow I could research trips to La Paz. It sounded good there. Bright sun, palm trees, and sparkling, white beaches. It sounded like just the right place to spend a long, warm vacation.

My new fur-ball friend might like it there, too.

Eight Days Ago...
Part I

Chapter 1

Submitted For My Approval

"Quit your job," Uncle Morgan said. "And do nothing but play golf for nine months."

I stopped chewing a mouthful of turkey Reuben and gazed at him across the small countertop in my studio apartment. "What was that?"

"Golf. Nine months."

I swallowed. "Thought that's what you said."

"Thirty-six weeks. Exactly."

"It's too early in the day for this."

"Two hundred seventy days, Charley."

I dabbed at my mouth with a napkin. "Nah."

"Of course, I'll furnish all you need."

"Uncle Morgan-"

"Trainers, equipment. Living expenses."

I set the half-eaten sandwich on a paper plate, my last one, and shook my head. My uncle, Morgan Kinshaw, stood there in his plain dark suit and grinned, somehow pleased with himself. He was thin, about five-foot-nine, and reminded me a bit of Rod Serling, the host of *The Twilight Zone*, an early 60s TV show I watched sometimes on late-night reruns. The only thing missing was a lit cigarette.

"I'm not listening to this." I grabbed a Doritos chip, Cool Ranch flavor, popped it in my mouth, and took a long swallow from a bottle of Coors.

He squinted up at a water stain on the yellowed plaster ceiling. "We'll have to find you a more...suitable place, somewhere private, close to a good fitness center."

My stomach fluttered. "Enough."

Uncle Morgan began to pace.

I shuffled across the carpet and sank into a faded corduroy beanbag chair. From this angle I could see the coffee and spaghetti sauce stains on the threadbare carpet. "Want to go to a movie or something?"

I had to change the subject or my uncle would get lost in the moment and venture into his demented golf theory. Again.

He absently adjusted his solid black necktie. "The fitness center is for cardio health. You're still young, only twenty-four."

"Twenty-five." I leaned forward and put my head in my hands.

"But you never do anything physical. You sit on your butt at work, watch those classic black-and-white films or old *Star Trek* reruns, and you never lift anything heavier than a six-pack of beer."

"I don't watch *Star Trek* at work."

"Charley..."

"Besides, I think old-*Star-Trek*-reruns is double redundant." Pressure thumped at my temples.

"Not that physical conditioning should matter that much." Uncle Morgan charged right along. "Golfers come in all shapes, many are red-faced and way out of shape. Couldn't carry a bag of groceries up two flights of steps without getting winded. You're overweight, Charley, hardly any muscle to you at all, and you eat a horrible diet." He gestured at my abandoned Rueben and then pointed at the bottle of Coors in my hand. "We just have to firm you up and do some basic toning to allow for those powerful tee shots."

"Uncle Morgan, please. *Please?*" I squeezed my eyelids shut for a moment, and then opened them. "Every couple months you go on about your insane golf theories. I know your rant by heart."

"Oh, really?"

"But now you've added a new wrinkle. You've added me into the picture. And you know full well I've never played a round of golf in my life."

"Charley, listen. In order for my theory to be truly proven, the test subject needs to be of normal physical abilities and have just enough coordination to swing the club and make contact with a little white ball..."

"But-"

"And never have played a round of golf in his life." His eyes narrowed. "Just like you. Only then will I be able to prove golf is a game of practice, not a game of talent."

He seemed dead serious this time, and I knew it wouldn't be easy to make him drop the subject. "I have a job, you know."

"You call that a job?"

"Been there three years."

"You've moped about that dead-end job since you started."

"Yeah, I know, but–"

"You get a call from a dispatcher, drive the van, and fix somebody's broken computer. Fulfilling."

I nodded, my lips drawing tight. "Pays the bills."

He pushed the fingertips of one hand back across his short black hair. "How much are they paying you?"

"What does that matter?"

"Your salary."

I stared at him. "You've never asked me that before."

"I'm asking now."

"It's none of your business."

He shook his finger at me as if scolding a first-grader. "You are my business, Charley, especially after your dad died. And there's not a darn thing you and I haven't talked about over the years."

"Crap, Uncle Morgan, I can't tell you my salary."

"Of course you can."

I took a breath. "I know what you'll say."

He stood there with a glum look across his face, as if he were waiting in line to console a widow at a funeral. "What do you think I will say?"

My jaw dropped a fraction and held for a second. "That you'll pay me a lot of money to quit my job and play golf for nine months."

"Pay you?"

"Yes."

Uncle Morgan grinned. "How much?"

I thought for an amount even my uncle Morgan would never pay for this flight of fancy. "Double my salary."

"Double...how much?"

"Plus a signing bonus if I say yes."

"Is that all?"

"Plus season tickets for the Reds. Seats behind the plate." I figured those tickets would be impossible to get.

Uncle Morgan angled his brows. "So, if I agree..?"

"I'll quit my job and play golf for nine months." I shrugged. "I...I guess."

"And then you'll turn pro, right?"

"Or apply for a new job nine months from now."

He smiled again. "No. It's not going to end like that."

"And why nine months?"

"A metaphor. Rebirth."

"Ah. A golfing pregnancy."

"Your words, not mine."

The pounding in my head was getting worse. My uncle was either slipping into insanity or suffering the aftermath of an undercooked chicken dinner.

"So tell me, Charley..."

I squeezed my eyes shut and sighed.

"...How much does PC At-Your-Door pay you?"

For a second it was hard to breathe. I clenched my teeth and waited as long as I could, then I glared at him. "$34,000."

A light shimmered in his eyes. "Okay. I can double that, no problem."

Even though I suspected it was coming, those words hit me square in the chest like a wrestler jumping down from the turnbuckle. "You're serious?"

"As a PBS documentary about the Inquisition."

I shook my head. "I didn't think you would—"

"Yes you did."

I felt heat rise to my face. "No way."

"Charley?"

"If you're really serious, and you really want a serious answer, the answer is still no."

"Please listen to me, Charley. This isn't entirely about a middle-aged man with a nutty idea. Part of the reason this middle-aged man with his nutty idea has come to you is because of the personal stagnation he's seen in your eyes the last five years or so."

"That's ridiculous."

"You deserve better. Your life needs a change, Charley. I'm offering you a chance to start over."

"Can't see how."

Uncle Morgan took a step toward my door and looked back at me. "You know I'm right."

"No. I don't."

He smiled as he walked out the door.

The room began to sway, my stomach twisted, and I instantly realized it had been a dreadful mistake to try to eat a turkey Rueben slathered with Russian dressing when I knew Uncle Morgan was coming over for just a little conversation with his favorite nephew.

Chapter 2

The Allstate Code

A week later, I stood in front of my boss's desk like a good soldier.

He leaned forward in his high-backed chair. "It's November, Charley. The *holidays*." His eyes never left me. "How long have you been working here? Two years?"

"Three, Mr. Preston. Three."

"Bruce. It's *Bruce*, for God's sake. You've been with me for three years." The flab around his middle stretched his expensive white shirt and hung down over his belt. Bruce was about forty, wide as a Clydesdale, and didn't look much taller standing than sitting.

"What did you call me in here for, Bruce?"

"I wasn't going to break this to you until after the first of the year."

"Break what to me?"

"Your promotion."

"Promo..?" My breath hitched.

He smiled. "Area Director."

"The guys that service businesses?"

"Right."

"I thought they were called District Managers."

"This is bigger." A fine sheen of sweat coated Bruce's forehead all the way back into his receding hairline. "No more home appointments dealing with irate homeowners who whine, complain, and look over your shoulder. Now, you will go in style, more money, new truck, and work only businesses."

I couldn't believe what I was hearing.

He grinned showing perfectly even, unnaturally white rows of teeth, and leaned back in his chair. Framed award certificates mounted on the wall behind him surrounded his head. He was salesman of the year for about a decade at *Glenway Chevrolet* in Norwood before starting *PC At-Your-Door* a few years ago. Another photo showed Bruce posing from the deck of *Saboteur*, his forty-foot yacht. Bruce managed to sneak away to Kiawah Island at least two weekends per month in the summer and spend time bronzing in the South Carolina sun.

I figured that could be me someday. "More money, right?"

"Bigger salary, plus commission."

"Commission. From computer repairs?"

Bruce grinned like a boy who had just stolen a box of baseball cards from the corner store. "Yes."

When I didn't say anything, he stood and nodded. "Okay then. Secrets are completely and entirely confidential. Do you understand?"

"I know what a secret is."

"Do I have your solemn oath you can keep a secret?"

"I guess."

"No guesswork here. It's either yes or no."

"Sure. What for?"

"Columbus."

I tilted my head at him. "Excuse me?"

"The Columbus territory." He clapped his hands together. "Our next expansion region. I have you pegged to be Area Director for Columbus. Signing bonus, too. Company car. Chevy Avalanche."

I wondered what size yacht I'd be able to buy. My stomach was doing an entire gymnastics routine.

Bruce bent to the floor and flipped over a small rectangle of thick gray carpet. He shifted around, his back now to me.

My view was blocked, but it was obvious he was turning the combination in a floor safe.

"Here." Bruce straightened up and handed me a small leather-jacketed journal. "Go ahead."

I took the small book and stared at it.

"Open it."

I did.

Bruce smiled. "So?"

I examined the text. "It's code. Computer code."

"Yes. The *Allstate* Code." Bruce said it as if proudly announcing an answer on *Wheel of Fortune.*

"Allstate as in *insurance*?"

"Just my pet name for the code."

I looked down at the small journal. "What good is it?"

Bruce grinned. "Do you see any problem entering that code into a computer?"

"Looks simple enough. What's it for?"

"Basic insurance."

"Life, health? What?"

"No, Charley. Business insurance. *Repeat* business."

I stared down at the journal. "I don't get it."

"Computer reliability has been improving these past years. Less need for computer fix-it companies. So I did something about it."

I nodded even though I didn't understand.

Bruce gestured at the small journal I held in my hands. "Only our management team is privy to that code. And you're about to become part of that team."

I thought about that yacht again.

"Once the code is entered, the customer's PC or even the entire office network will crash...about once every six weeks." He grinned. "Then the call comes in to us, and you go fix the problem and rack up the commissions."

The air seemed to thicken around me. "We make the computers crash?"

"At companies only. Not home computers. Those folks ruin their equipment without our help."

Bruce stepped close to me and patted my shoulder. "Your commission is based on service calls to corporate accounts. If you're creative with the code, those commission dollars can add up quick."

"Ah. Commission...but—"

He extended his hand to me. "Glad to have you as part of the team."

It amazed me how much information the mind could process in a matter of only a few seconds. From the time Bruce extended his hand to me to the time I took his hand, about a thousand things careened through my brain.

For the past couple years, my life had really been a slow, fumbling dead-end journey. My job was boring, paid enough to cover the bills, but not much more, and certainly was nothing like I had hoped while growing up and attending college. Four years at Miami University ought to lead to something better than fixing PCs and just paying the rent.

All my friends had faded away. I hadn't had a serious female relationship since the single serious girlfriend of my life broke up with me during her sophomore year of college. She said she needed more time to concentrate on her filmmaking...if she ever wanted to succeed. I believed her at first, but later my suspicions grew. She broke up *because* of me. I was sure of it. She had finally discovered she didn't really love me.

But I never stopped loving her. I still saw her face whenever I met someone new, and probably because of that, my new relationships never went anywhere. Plus, I was too busy nursing my broken heart to have time for any real relationships. Maybe this had something to do with me declining my uncle's insane proposal to quit my job and subject myself to nine months of golf training. It might have interfered with my pity party. Maybe I didn't want to get over her. Hard to say.

But now there was the *illegality* of Bruce's perfect little scam. And from the look in his eyes, like a pit viper assessing his prey, Bruce might not be too comfortable with sharing his ingenious, reprehensible little secret with someone who wasn't part of the team. If I didn't shake Bruce's hand, here and now, I clearly envisioned a late-night visit from a company director, supervisor, or manager who would take a Louisville Slugger to the side of my head.

I grabbed Bruce's hand and shook it with little enthusiasm.

"Fabulous," Bruce said.

"Uh huh."

"Remember. Secrecy."

"No worries about that."

Bruce's eyes flicked to the small journal still in my hand. I reached over and placed it on his desk.

"Come in early tomorrow, Charley. I will personally run you through the code."

"Okay, Bruce."

Lane Cohen

I felt like saluting like a good soldier, but didn't, just turned and stepped through his office doorway. Once outside, I quickened my pace, jumped into my car, and sped out of the parking lot as if I were running in panic from a mob of knife-waving serial killers who had just escaped from an asylum. I needed to think about a future locked up in Leavenworth.

I needed a Coors.

Chapter 3

Arrested Development

"**I**'m uncomfortable about this," I said.

Uncle Morgan nodded. "You did the right thing."

"Bruce is going to be really mad."

"Even so, you should feel good about it."

"I guess."

"I was happy to get your call, Charley, about playing golf, even though you chose to tell my office voicemail in the middle of the night instead of telling me face to face. I'm glad you quit your job."

"I'm no crook."

"So you quit for the right reasons."

"Don't really know why I'm going to play golf, though, instead of getting another job."

Uncle Morgan tapped the dashboard and grinned at me. "It will become clear to you, in time. With enough space, with enough reflection."

"What's that supposed to mean?"

"Don't over think this, Charley."

I rubbed my temples. "I still feel pretty low about ratting on Bruce."

We sat in Uncle Morgan's black Cadillac Escalade, parked in the Amberley Village driveway of the same small English Tudor house he had lived in for all the years I had known him. He practiced civil law, but he made many friends in the prosecutor's office and the various police districts. And several of those friends owed him favors. After I squealed to Uncle Morgan about Bruce's criminal master plan, the authorities started their investigation.

I looked over and squinted at him. "I broke a promise to

secrecy."

"Charley—"

"A promise only an hour old by the time I told you, so recent I still smelled Bruce's cologne on my hand."

"Charley, you really had no other choice."

"I suppose."

A smile found its way across his face. "You're a good boy, Charley. You've always been a good boy."

"You sound like you're talking to a dog."

He chuckled.

"Look, you want to grab some breakfast?" I asked. "My treat. I could eat about fifteen eggs. Like Rocky Balboa."

"It's nearly lunchtime."

"Breakfast is a better *celebration* meal. No one celebrates at lunch."

His eyes sparkled. "Good." He patted my forearm twice. "You're smarter than you look."

"Thanks, I guess."

"I know a place on the way." He reached for his ignition key.

"On the way? Where?"

"And you don't have to worry about being late for work."

"That's a newsflash. Where are we going?"

"Your new condo. I want to show you."

"Oh. That's fine. I'll follow you in my car."

"Okay. Follow me, then."

"Sure." I stepped down from the Escalade and walked around to my Civic. The car was originally blue, but the paint had faded into a dull gray. I climbed inside and pulled the squeaky door closed.

I started the engine and noticed my hands shaking on the steering wheel. I exhaled, angled onto the road behind Uncle Morgan's enormous SUV, and pushed the radio button. Bob Seger blasted out speakers that were worth more than the car. I drove forward, traveling *against the wind*, toward my new condo and whatever else my crazy Uncle Morgan might have had in mind.

Chapter 4

Almost Heaven, Wyoming, Ohio

It took us only fifteen minutes to get across town to the old Victorian village of Wyoming. The condo on Bonham Road was great. Uncle Morgan bought it a few years ago and kept the place clean and furnished for the convenience of clients who might be in town for an extended period of time. The condo development was small and relatively new, set in a large grassy area on the outskirts of Wyoming, about eleven miles from downtown Cincinnati. Uncle Morgan showed me around, and he took so long we forgot all about breakfast. Afterward, Uncle Morgan and I stood together beside our cars in the condo parking lot.

"Fitness center is across the street." He pointed east. "Glenwood Gardens, a county park, is about a mile and a half north, right up Springfield Pike."

"Okay...so?"

"You'll be meeting one of your advisors there in a couple days."

I rubbed my temples again. "Advisor?"

"Her name is Mrs. Morrison. She's, well, a bit odd."

"Sounds about right."

"Oh, and she wants you to walk there."

"A mile and a half?"

"It'll be good for you."

"All right. Mrs. Morrison. Glenwood Gardens. Walk."

"I still haven't arranged a meeting with your other advisor, but that should happen within a few days, as well. Have you ever heard of Pinson Dill?"

Name recognition stirred in the back of my head. "Sounds vaguely familiar."

Uncle Morgan nodded again. "Movers will be at your apartment at 10:00 tomorrow morning. They will pack and bring all your personal effects, clothing, pictures and whatnot. The furniture will stay. No need to bring that junk over here. It's a furnished place."

"Yeah. It's nice."

"But you might want to get over there today for a toothbrush, a change of clothes, that sort of thing."

"I will."

"So." He smiled and extended his hand to me. "We start day after tomorrow."

I grasped his hand. "Sounds ominous."

He opened the door to the Escalade. "Oh, Charley. One more thing."

"Just one? Promise?"

"I've hired a crew to film your progress."

I couldn't talk for a second. "What for?"

"Your training, your advancement, from the first day to the last, nine months from now."

"A video camera in my face?"

"Actually, they work with film."

"Uh huh."

"I've instructed the production company to only film your training. They'll stay clear of your private life."

"What a relief. I'll be with advisors, playing golf, and working out. When will I have a private life, exactly?"

Uncle Morgan leaned into the Escalade. "The film crew will be here at the condo mid-afternoon today for introductions."

"I'll wear something nice."

"Oh, and Charley?"

"Yeah."

"Keep an open mind."

I just stared at him.

"Charley?"

"Sure. Yeah. Open mind."

He smiled at me, started the engine on the SUV, pulled out onto Bonham, and disappeared down the narrow tree-lined road. I waited a moment, and then jumped into my Civic.

Below Par

***

I drove across town to my apartment and picked up a few toiletries. Then I left *The Four Seasons*, my apartment complex that had nothing to do with Frankie Valli, and headed for the Kroger's grocery store in Woodlawn, down the road from my new accommodations, right beside Glenwood Gardens. Using some cash Uncle Morgan had given me, I bought three plastic bagsful of groceries and two golf magazines. I drove back to the condo, parked the car, opened the hatch, and retrieved the plastic bags. Then I walked through the grass to a concrete path. As I neared my condo, I looked around and tried to take in the quaint opulence.

I'd been suddenly removed from my relative urban squalor and dropped like a piece of space debris into a quiet section of suburban heaven. The day was unusually warm for November, about 55 degrees; the air was still and smelled of fallen leaves. The condos were centered in a rolling meadow that used to be acres of grazing pasture. The land still had that feel. And somehow it made me feel good to be here, as if a different phase of my life was about to begin, a good phase, as opposed to my last five years of going through the motions to nowhere.

I stepped inside my new kitchen and made a quick sandwich of shaved Sara Lee turkey breast. I ate in the kitchen and leaned against the countertop as I looked out the window, my kitchen window in a kitchen that had been mine for less than ten minutes. The sun was full and bright, warming the mid-November afternoon. I looked back into the room. A spread of sunshine beamed in across the floor.

As I returned my gaze outside, to the cars passing on the road in the distance, I wondered if my uncle was really crazy, or perhaps he was the smartest man on the planet.

Chapter 5

Close Encounters of the Ex-Girlfriend Kind

I'd fallen wildly in love with Sandy Carson the instant I first saw her.

It was my sophomore year at Miami University and I needed a four-hour elective. Film class sounded like a winner. I always liked movies and there was no exam. Our final film project would account for our entire grade, which I found a bit strange after I discovered we would not shoot our projects on film, but with video cameras.

It would be impossible to explain the numbness I felt that afternoon, the first day of film class. I was bored and didn't want to be there, but it was better than sitting through another pointless sociology lecture.

My life outside the classroom had been no life at all. When I did have a date during my horrible first year of college, the results were less than good. I had little hope this year would be any better, but a shot of pure electricity jolted my heart when Sandy Carson first spoke to me. She stood near the classroom window, searching for something in her backpack. I asked if anyone was sitting in the chair beside her, and she said, "Nope."

That was it. That was enough.

I sat in slow motion, unable to take my eyes from her. A guy stepped beside her and started talking. I was instantly jealous of a guy I didn't know who was talking to a girl I didn't know. He was good-looking in that rugged, unshaven scruffy appeal some guys have, and I was instantly jealous of that, too, since I was pale and gangly with the muscle tone of a noodle.

Sandy was stunning, and it was impossible not to stare. At five-foot-ten, she was taller than many of the guys in the room. A Cincinnati Reds ball cap, the newer black one, covered her short blond curls in a Tomboy sort of way. And when I looked into her eyes for the first time, I saw a deep, lustrous green, like dew reflected on leaves in an Amazon jungle.

We were teamed together, along with Ray Ford, that good-looking guy from the Abercrombie catalogue. The three of us had to write and produce a seven-minute film. Sandy already knew exactly what the film should be about. The shooting script was "percolating" in her head, she told us. Ray and I tagged along, since she was an unstoppable force of nature. Besides, neither Ray nor I had any film production experience at all.

We titled the film: *Nerves.*

The story was one evening in a woman's life in which an alien killer terrorizes her. It didn't sound like a new plot when she explained it, and I had watched a hundred DVDs with similar or better storylines. But Sandy was resolute, and eventually, she proved herself right.

I loved spending time on the project, just for the chance of being around Sandy. I asked her out about one month into the term and I couldn't believe it when she smiled at me and said "Yes," that most wonderful of all words. One date turned into two, then three. I started working out five times a week and put on pounds of lean muscle, just to look better for her.

Being with Sandy was wonderful. In fact, the only downside was keeping my composure and not correcting Sandy when she exhibited her one bad and truly irritating habit. She almost always misquoted lines from famous films, which seemed particularly odd coming from someone who was supposedly a film expert. But each time it happened, even though it got increasingly exasperating, I kept my mouth shut.

The three of us were genuinely excited when we met each day to resume filming. Sandy set up each shot and played the terrorized woman. Ray and I worked the equipment, built special tracks and booms for the camera, and we appeared in the film, as well. Ray was the alien killer and I was the campus security investigator. When the shooting finished, Sandy insisted she handle all the editing. It was her vision, she said, and she needed to put the pieces together. Neither Ray nor I ever considered any other approach. We knew she was right.

Each production crew presented their film to the class at

the end of the term. The showing was open to the campus, and the theatre was filled that night with an enthusiastic crowd of about two hundred. Some of the finished projects were pretty good and were received with genuine applause and appreciation. But the film from Team Carson was greeted by stunned silence.

From the opening shot, the crowd was mesmerized. The film was so disquieting, viewers watched in a terrified hush and came out of the theatre pale and speechless. They held hands, or hugged each other, *anything* to retain just a bit of human warmth. None of the audience, even our own classmates, would look us in the eye.

All of this flashed through my head as I turned my Civic into the condo driveway. A girl stood in the grassy meadow that bordered the front of the property. She was tall, wore a ball cap, and was adjusting a large camera poised atop a tripod. It took less than one second for me to realize it was Mr. and Mrs. Carson's little girl Sandy.

I slowed the car to a stop, switched off the engine, and sat there. I had to will my lungs to breathe.

"Charley?"

Her voice seemed to come from far away. My hands trembled on the steering wheel; I needed to be beamed up to the mother-ship immediately.

"Charley." She stood next to my car. "Hi."

I pushed the door open and managed to step out of the Civic without stumbling. "Hi, Sandy."

"God, Charley. You're all pasty."

"Pasty?"

"Spend all your time in a cave somewhere?"

"My membership at the tanning salon expired."

"And flabby. You stopped working out?"

"Didn't see much sense in it." I was trying to keep an open mind as Uncle Morgan had suggested.

She flashed a smile at me and I nearly melted. "Get in shape. You owe it to yourself, dummy."

I nodded. "My uncle hired you, huh?"

"Yeah. He made me an offer that I dare not refuse."

I cringed at the bungled movie quote. "Sounds like him."

"Someone at the station recommended me."

Sandy worked for Channel 19, the local Fox affiliate, for nearly two years. She produced and filmed short documentaries. A few of her projects won regional Emmys.

I had informally followed Sandy's career, even though I didn't like to admit to myself that I was still smitten. "How've you been?"

"Good. I've been good."

"Still with Ray?" I couldn't believe I asked about him.

She squeezed her eyes closed for a moment. "That romance ended a long time ago...but he's working for me now, part-time. He's doing some commercial work, too."

"Good for him."

"He uses his middle name, for professional reasons. Been doing some tire ads. Oh, and last month he did a Target flyer for the Sunday paper. Men's clothing."

"Sounds like his career is taking off."

"Charley-"

"Look," I motioned to the condo, "want to come in?"

"Sure."

I turned back to the car, leaned through the window, and grabbed two bags from the front seat.

She glanced around. "I need to get familiar with the locale."

"You and me both." I started walking. My legs felt numb, like my first day of film class.

Sandy chased after me. "Let me put my camera in the van."

I stopped.

She spun around and stepped across the lawn. Her Ford van was parked nearby. *Carson Industrial Films* was painted in royal blue letters across the side of the white truck.

I felt rooted to the ground, practically unable to move. I couldn't believe I was *watching* her. I also couldn't believe my crazy uncle was crazy enough to hire *Sandy Carson*...and not tell me.

"Nice place," she said as she came back to me.

"Thanks."

"How long have you been here?"

I looked at my watch. "Not long." I pushed the door open and we walked inside.

Sandy followed me into the kitchen. "Nice place."

"Yeah. You said that."

She squinted at me.

I saw her eyes moisten a bit. "What's wrong?"

She tossed her hair back. "We start next week. I'll be around all the time."

"I know."

"*All the time*," she said again, more forcefully.

"I heard you."

"Can we handle working together again?"

"Can you?"

"What I mean is...can *you* handle this?"

"Uh, sure? Sure."

Her lips grew tight. "Ray will be around, too. My assistant."

"Even better."

She shook her head. "Charley, I better get going now."

"You just got here. Haven't even seen the place."

She adjusted the brim of her ball cap, and faced me. "I'll do this for one week, contract or no contract."

"I thought—"

"Then we'll have a talk." She stepped back toward the door. "We used to talk all the time."

"It was the best thing we did."

She winked. "Second best."

The memory of first best thing shook me to the core.

"Get some rest," she said. "You look pasty."

"It's going around."

She gazed at me for a second, turned, and stood in the doorway. "Bye, Charley."

"Bye."

She walked away leaving the door open.

I watched until she disappeared around a corner then exhaled. My entire body started to shake. Sandy always did that to me. Today was no different, even though it had been five years since I had seen her.

I shook my head. *Sandy Carson*, exploding into my life again?

Uncle Morgan was even more devious than I had thought.

Chapter 6

Golfers Are Strange

After I pecked at a dinner of shaved turkey breast, I left the condo and drove a few miles to the Joseph-Beth bookstore in the Hyde Park area. I figured, if tomorrow I was to start playing golf every day for the next nine months, maybe I should learn something about the game.

The number of golf books on the shelves at Joseph-Beth overwhelmed me. There were books on practically any topic even remotely related to the game, including golf courses, strategies, clubs, balls, grips, swings, entire books on putting, humorous anecdotes, mental focus exercises, tournament histories, and photojournalistic essays on the golf courses of Scotland.

One book particularly appealed to me: *Weird Golf Legends*, written and edited by Marleigh Benford. This looked as though it would provide me with useful information, while being light enough to not force me asleep within the first few pages. I purchased the book, drove back to the condo, pulled out a kitchen chair, and sat at the table to read.

Weird Golf Legends contained chapter after chapter of either odd golfers, or good golfers who found themselves in the middle of terrible golfing breakdowns. One entire chapter was devoted to Greg Norman, who, according to this book, was one of the great golfers of the 90s. But one day on a golf course in Georgia, Greg Norman suffered a golfing catastrophe from which few men could ever recover.

At the time of Norman's incredible collapse, he was rated as the number one golfer in the world. He scored a sixty-three on the first day of the 1996 Masters tournament; the Masters, apparently, was the only reason people knew about Augusta,

Georgia, again, according to *WGL*. Shooting an unbelievable sixty-three at the end of that first day, Norman had a monumental six-shot lead over the golfer in second place.

But on the last round of the tournament, the skies fell in on Norman, and he couldn't hit anything right. He lost the Masters to someone named Faldo by five shots; that was an eleven-stroke shift from the first day of the tournament. Ms. Benford said this was the worst loss by a champion in a major tournament, ever. I took the editor's word for it.

One of my favorite stories, and I laughed aloud at this one, involved Bobby Cruickshank in the 1934 U.S. Open. Cruickshank was playing well that day. His shot on the 11th hole was not only spectacular but lucky as well. The shot sailed over a water hazard, bounced off the far edge of the rough, and miraculously rolled onto the green. Cruickshank was so overjoyed with the shot he threw his golf club into the air, only to be knocked out when the club came down and struck the unfortunate golfer right on his head.

Note to self: *If I throw my clubs into the air, watch their flight until they land. Or, be sure to wear a helmet.*

The book also contained a number of informational articles after all the weird golf stories, in a lengthy appendix. I scanned a list of golf clubs, which made my eyes glaze over. I had no idea there were clubs other than drivers and putters, but also a 3-wood, irons numbered 2 though 9, and three different wedges.

If I had to carry all those clubs, I would be in terrific shape in no time.

Chapter 7

Yellow Springs Lady

The next morning I overslept and panicked when I squinted at the clock. It took me a couple minutes to throw on some clothes and run outside to the Civic. I revved the engine and screeched out of the parking lot onto Springfield Pike.

Uncle Morgan had called last night and told me to meet Mrs. Morrison at 8:45 exactly, at a small stone bridge over a creek in Glenwood Gardens. And I was supposed to walk. I glanced at my old Casio watch I had worn since high school. It was 8:32. Uncle Morgan gave me directions to the creek, but at this point, I had no idea if I could make it there on time, even by car.

The access to the park came up on my left. I swerved into the entrance drive and slowed as I blinked the early morning sunlight from my eyes. I pulled into the first available space and glanced at my wristwatch. I had five minutes to get down to the creek.

I turned and began a quick pace toward a stone archway that marked the entrance to the Glenwood Gardens walking trails. The morning sun was at my back as I started down the wide concrete path. Although I was rushing along, it was hard to ignore the beauty of the place. Trees and wide stands of shrubbery lined the walkway. The fragrance of unspoiled forest wafted on the cool morning breeze.

I walked faster. The path angled left and flattened out. I could see a stone bridge about one hundred yards ahead. A figure stood motionless near the bridge. It was impossible to be sure, but I assumed it was Mrs. Morrison. I hoped she wasn't mad I was a few minutes late for our first meeting.

As I approached, I saw the lady more clearly. She was

about sixty-four and wore a faded, loose-fitting dress made of simple khaki material. She smiled, a wide grin across cheeks sprinkled with freckles. Her dark hair was peppered with gray and pulled back in a long ponytail. She extended a hand to me before I had stopped.

"You have your uncle's eyes," she said.

I took her hand. Her grip was warm and strong. "Mrs. Morrison?"

She nodded. "And you're tall."

Mrs. Morrison may have been over sixty, but she was in terrific shape. Despite the morning chill, her arms were bare, her muscles lean and strong. Her dark brown eyes studied me.

"Nice to meet you, Mrs. Morrison."

She moved a step closer and brought the definite scent of patchouli. I caught a glance of a faded red tattoo on the crest of her left bicep.

"Charley, let's talk for a few minutes about what you and I will be doing. Did Morgan tell you?"

"No."

She paused for a moment and closed her eyes. I waited. The soft chirp of morning birds came from the trees above. Then she opened her eyes and smiled at me. "We dated for a while, you know."

"We?"

"Morgan and I dated in college."

"You went to OU?"

"No. I was at Antioch."

"He never told me he dated anyone from Antioch."

Actually, Uncle Morgan never told me about his dating years at all, but the fact Mrs. Morrison attended Antioch explained quite a bit. Antioch College, in Yellow Springs, Ohio, was a small liberal arts college that shifted extremely left wing in the 60s. In fact, Antioch was so liberal then, and so completely populated by hard-core hippies, it made USC at Berkley look like the strategy room at the Republican National Committee.

Yellow Springs had retained its hippie character since then, as if 1968 stretched into five decades. I drove through there a few years ago, and it was an immediate time warp, head shops, tattoo parlors, and stores that sold everything as long as it was made of hemp.

"Morgan was interesting back then," she said. "Doesn't surprise me he came up with this golf project."

I raised an eyebrow.

"For now, all you will focus on is your training. We will start a week from today, as you know, and meet five days each week."

I didn't know but said, "Okay."

She turned and gripped what looked like a broom handle that had been leaning against the side of the stone bridge. Then she pulled a long black kerchief from her back pocket and held it out to me. "Here."

I took the cloth. She reached into a pocket on the front of her dress and pulled out a tennis ball with a long rubber band attached. She held the end of the rubber band and extended her arm out to her side. The tennis ball dangled in the air, about four feet from the ground.

"Now take this," she said, and held the broom handle out to me with her other hand.

I caught another whiff of patchouli as I took the wooden pole.

"Put on the cloth," she said.

"On where?"

"Over your eyes."

"You mean a blindfold?"

She smiled. "Yes."

"A *blindfold?*"

Her eyes narrowed. "Part of your training will be to listen and do exactly as I say."

"But I thought we didn't start until—"

"*The blindfold.*"

"Yeah, sure. Okay."

I balanced the stick against the front of my legs and fumbled with the long black cloth. I chuckled to myself as I wrapped it around my face and the light completely disappeared. Mrs. Morrison would have made a great trainer for Zorro, if she cut some eye slits in this stupid cloth.

"Charley, can you see anything?"

"Nada, Señora."

"Good. Take the stick."

I took it and held it in one hand at my side.

"Grip the stick as you would hold a baseball bat."

I did.

"Now take one step toward me and stop."

"Mrs. Morrison-"

"Charley."

"Okay. Okay." I stepped forward.

Mrs. Morrison remained silent. I stood blindfolded, holding a broom handle.

"What now?"

Silence.

"Mrs. Morrison?"

Nothing.

"Are you there?"

This was crazy.

And then the music started. It was *Purple Haze*, by Jimi Hendrix.

"What do you feel, Charley?"

"Ah, what?"

"Tell me what you feel." Her voice was even and soft, like those new-age singers must sound when they talked.

I considered her question. "The sun, I guess."

"And?"

"A breeze. It's a little chilly."

"Think about the sun on your face, Charley."

"Think about it?"

"Yes."

"I'm thinking." Well, not really. I didn't know what to think.

"And the breeze."

"You want me to think about feeling the breeze?"

"Yes."

"With this music playing."

"The music is meant to set the mood."

"Are we going to reminisce about Woodstock next?"

"I sense a sarcastic nature about you, Charley."

"Something I picked up a few years ago...when my girlfriend dumped me."

"Get over it." Her voice hardened. "Leave your sarcasm at home from now on. Understand? There's no place for that here."

I suddenly felt something else besides the sun and breeze on my face. I felt sick to my stomach that I was standing blindfolded in the woods, listening to Jimi Hendrix, with a broom handle in my hands, next to a sixty-four-year-old woman who had never matured beyond tie-dyed shirts and *The Grateful Dead.*

"Charley? You hear me?"

"Yes. Leave it at home. I understand."

"Good. Now, remember the hanging tennis ball?"

"Yes."

"Think about the tennis ball."

"Think about it how?"

"Just visualize it."

I tried to think about that tennis ball, but all I could visualize was an ice cooler filled with Coors.

"Do you have it?" she asked.

"Clear as can be."

The lid was propped open, the ice sparkly around the capped beer bottles.

"Perfect. Now, Charley, visualize the tennis ball and hit it with the broom handle."

"You're kidding, right?"

"Swing the broom handle. Hit the ball."

"Okay, sure. No problem."

I swung and missed. "Sorry, Mrs. Morrison."

"Again."

I bit my bottom lip until it hurt, and swung the broom handle one more time. I missed again. "Was I even close?"

"If you hit the ball the first time, there would be a great deal less for me to teach you."

"Can I take off the blindfold now?"

"Yes."

I removed the blindfold. Mrs. Morrison took it and broom handle from me. She backed up a step and lowered herself to the ground, her legs folded and crossed beneath. She inhaled and gazed across the green meadow toward the western horizon. "You were five minutes late this morning, Charley."

"Yeah. Sorry."

"And you drove here. You were instructed to walk."

"I know, but—"

"8:45 sharp, next Monday. Walk here."

"Uh, okay. Right. Walk. No problem."

She turned her head and stared at me. "Goodbye, Charley." She closed her eyes as if withdrawing into her own world.

"Goodbye." I shook my head and strode along the concrete path to the trailhead at the crest of the hill. I peered down when I reached the top. Mrs. Morrison was still on the ground in her spot by the stone bridge, like a troll waiting for her next victim.

8:45 sharp, next Monday. A morning in the woods with Hendrix and a broom-wielding old hippie.

Sounded *perfect*.

Chapter 8

Where the Wind Comes Sweepin' Down the Okinawan Plain

Uncle Morgan picked me up at 9:30 the next morning. I sat upright and still in the center of the leather seat. "I *Googled* Pinson Dill last night."

He tapped on the steering wheel. "That's not where we're headed."

"No?"

"Mr. Dill won't be available until next week."

I watched the drizzle inch down the glass. "Imagine not."

"Friday morning, Charley. I'm bringing him to meet you. Then, at his request, we're going to an open meadow at a nearby stable."

"Horses. *Horses* are involved?"

"Not involved. Just nearby."

"Uncle Morgan, why do we have all this drama and secrecy? You give me little bits of info to hook me, keep me interested, instead of a full explanation."

"What explanation would you like?"

"Why should I be kept in the dark at all? Aren't I the golfer, or the future golfer? I should know what's coming."

"You're right."

"I am?"

"Yes. Ask questions."

I considered that. "What is Mrs. Morrison supposed to teach me?"

"Hard to explain out of context."

"Try."

"Among other things, Mrs. Morrison is an expert at Combassa Combelbo."

"What's Combassa Combelbo?"

Lane Cohen

"It's the ancient art of Nigerian stick fighting."

"Exactly what does Combassa Combelbo mean in English?"

"Nigerian stick fighting."

I exhaled. "Fine. But in or out of context, how is she going to help me play golf?"

"She will guide you through the mental aspects of the game."

"Mental."

"Yes."

"That woman *is* mental."

"She sees things a bit differently, I agree."

"I don't know how I can learn about the *mental aspects of the game* from her and her Mongolian fighting sticks."

"Nigerian."

"Whatever."

I glanced through the window. We were approaching the Sharonville area, north of the city.

Uncle Morgan went on. "Mrs. Morrison's real name is Leslie Rae Frankel."

"She married a Morrison?"

"Sort of."

"How do you sort of get married, Uncle Morgan?"

"She has a tattoo on her arm: July 3, 1971."

"Yeah, I got a glimpse of it."

Uncle Morgan took a breath. "On July 3rd, 1971, *Jim* Morrison died in Paris."

"Jim Morrison?" A light clicked on in my head. "Oh my gosh. You don't mean *Jim Morrison* from The Doors? He was her husband?"

"Sort of."

Not again. "Make sense, will you?"

"You have to understand Leslie Rae was a hippie fanatic, and Jim Morrison was one of her icons. When he was found dead, she freaked out. So did a bunch of her friends. So, on August 30, 1971, she and six female classmates *married* Jim Morrison outdoors around a fire pit in a civil ceremony held in the Glen Helen nature preserve near the Antioch campus. Then the whole gaggle of them went into town and got those tattoos, on their left arms, close to their hearts."

I started to speak, but my throat felt glued shut.

"Charley, you have a strange look in your eyes."

"You know, you had me going."

"I'm not kidding."

"I didn't know you had this kind of imagination. You should write the script for the next *Indiana Jones* movie."

"Truth is stranger than fiction. Besides, what would be the point of making up a story like that?"

"Like Pinson Dill." I shook my head. "He's in prison, up in Lebanon."

"Yes."

"The same Pinson Dill you hired to train me."

"Of course."

"What don't you understand about *he's in prison*?"

"He's being released into my custody. A work release program I arranged."

"You don't have those kinds of connections."

"Why is that hard to believe?"

He had me there. "So golf is a new slant on community service?"

"His skills are better utilized beyond the walls of Lebanon Correctional."

I thought for a moment. "At least Pinson Dill was *a golfer.*"

"He shot a sixty-six at the Kenwood Country Club course when he was seventeen. The course record was sixty-four at that time."

"So, sixty-six is good?"

"Good for even a pro golfer on the tour."

I shook my head. "But there must be golf pros available who aren't currently imprisoned."

Uncle Morgan turned the Escalade into the parking lot of a two-story office complex. "Other pros would not teach you the same way. Pinson Dill has a special insight, Charley, and it is that insight that makes him a special golfer."

"*Made* him."

"Yes. It's hard to play from inside a cell."

"You still aren't giving me a *full* explanation about

anything."

"The pieces of the puzzle will fit together, but only after you study each piece, one at a time."

"What I thought. No answer. Again."

"I planned it this way for a reason."

He switched off the engine then turned to me. "Charley, if this is going to work, it must be done a certain way. Sorry for the mystery. But, and to be completely open about it, this is for me, as well. I've grown bored over the last few years. The names and faces change, but they also *remain the same*. I make the same arguments to the same judges against the same defense lawyers. Routine and dull. Now, I know for at least the next nine months, my life will be far from boring."

I smiled. "Careful what you wish for."

He smiled back. "Come on." He pushed his door open.

I put my hand on his forearm before he could get out. "Just a second. What about Sandy Carson?"

He sighed and shut the door. "Yes."

"You didn't tell me about her either."

"No."

"I'm not positive I want her to be a part of this."

"But you're not negative either?"

"I've changed my mind four hundred times."

He stared at me. "The film is important, but I can find another film crew. Someone else."

"That would be cool with you?"

"Not my preference. I chose Ms. Carson for two good reasons. First, she is a damn fine filmmaker."

"Second?"

He smiled. "That, Charley, will..."

"Become clear to me later?"

"Right."

I looked out the car window. "What are we doing here, Uncle Morgan?"

"Someone inside you have to meet."

"Who?"

"Do you trust me?"

"No."

"Come on in anyway." He pushed his door open.

I stepped out of the SUV and followed Uncle Morgan to a small storefront that looked as if it hadn't been remodeled since the 50s. Faded lettering on the door window read: *TAGAWA— Master Jeweler.*

Uncle Morgan pulled the door handle. A small bell jangled as we walked inside.

"Mr. Tagawa?" Uncle Morgan said.

We stood motionless. The inside of the store held four or five empty glass cases. A few small racks of cheap watchbands were placed atop a plain fiberglass countertop beside a terribly old-fashioned cash register. A sign on the wall, intricately hand lettered, stated: *Full Payment is Honorable.* A film of thin dust covered the sign.

I said, "Guess no one's home."

"Mr. Tagawa is *always* home. He may be upstairs in his workshop."

"Is he one of Santa's elves?"

"Mr. Kinshaw?" a voice called from somewhere.

"Hello, Mr. Tagawa," Uncle Morgan said.

"Please put the *Closed* sign on the door and join me upstairs. I apologize for not greeting you properly, but the years have not been kind to my knees."

"Be right up."

Uncle Morgan switched the door sign and we stepped into the next room, a dingy small office littered with stray papers, open ledgers, and at least ten fine ceramic cups, each containing a few ounces of what appeared to be very dark tea.

We maneuvered through the debris to a small stairway at the back of the room. The air grew a bit warmer as we moved higher. Uncle Morgan stopped near the top and turned back to look at me. "You have no idea what to expect, do you?"

"You're enjoying this part of it."

"Aren't you?"

"Immensely."

"What do you think we will see up there?"

"Maybe the heads of Sam Snead and Ben Hogan on ice?"

"Nice to know you are familiar with some golf lore."

"I bought a few magazines."

"Well, come on then."

We took the last two steps and reached the dark hardwood of the attic floor. My eyes widened to adjust to the dim light.

Uncle Morgan grinned.

A diminutive Japanese man shuffled toward us. "Always good to see you, Mr. Kinshaw." The elderly gentleman straightened his back with some effort and extended his hand.

"For me as well," Uncle Morgan said. "Charley, this is my old friend, Mr. Oh Tagawa."

"Where the wavin' wheat can sure smell sweet?" I joked.

"No, Charley."

"Sorry. Couldn't help it." I really couldn't. "Hello, Mr. Tagawa."

He turned to me with a smile. "And this must be Charley."

"Yes," Uncle Morgan said, "My nephew. We spoke about him last week."

I glanced around the attic. My eyes had now compensated for the low light. Swords hung everywhere on the walls, Japanese Samurai swords with intricate leather scabbards. There must have been more than a hundred of them. On the back wall I noticed some framed photos of vintage Japanese Zero aircraft, and old Japanese flags, circa World War II.

Mr. Tagawa gestured for us to follow. We walked with him across the room to a small square table. A vat was positioned in the center of the table, and a thick red liquid bubbled inside. Small wisps of steam floated in the air above the vat.

"Charley, Mr. Tagawa designed my wedding ring." Uncle Morgan extended his fingers to show me.

I looked at the beveled gold ring Uncle Morgan still wore, even though my Aunt Melissa died years ago. The ring shimmered with an inner light.

"I have done some legal work for Mr. Tagawa," Uncle Morgan said, "and now he has kindly offered to help."

I thought about a reason why. "Will I need a sword for protection from the adoring crowds?"

Mr. Tagawa smiled. The corners of his mouth pulled his wrinkles tight. "Come here please."

I stepped closer.

"Left-handed?" Mr. Tagawa asked me.

"Yes."

"Forget you are left-handed."

"Forget..?"

"Right-handed, left-handed, it will not matter."

Uncle Morgan stepped up beside me. "Mr. Tagawa will design your golf clubs."

I looked around at all the swords. "I don't get it."

"He'll construct them himself, here in this workshop."

"Your left hand, please," Mr. Tagawa said.

"What? No, I—"

"Charley, please cooperate," Uncle Morgan said.

Mr. Tagawa stood motionless with his palm extended.

It didn't take a genius to figure out he was planning to stick my hand in that vat of bubbling goo. "Do I really need to do this?"

Mr. Tagawa took my left wrist and plunged my hand into the tub. The red goo felt instantly hot and cold, totally confusing my nerve endings.

"At first the clubs won't matter," Uncle Morgan said. "The best clubs in the world will improve the game of only the top five percent of the world's finest golfers. The rest, the other ninety-five percent, will play just fine with any well-made set of clubs. Hand-made clubs are not unheard of, and some of the top pros have them."

"Feels weird," I said.

"Mr. Tagawa is a master Samurai sword craftsman. He has made his exquisite blades in this workshop for thirty-five years. He forges the metal, sharpens each blade by hand, and crafts the scabbards. Each scabbard is unique, made of rare leathers and silk."

"Your hand, bring it out, yes?" Mr. Tagawa said.

I stifled the urge to make some Yoda joke, and instead said, "Yes."

I removed my hand and Mr. Tagawa took my wrist. He grasped the red coating that had hardened quickly on my hand and pulled. A stiff red glove slid free. Mr. Tagawa placed it on the table and grabbed my other wrist. "Now. Other hand."

I shrugged and slipped my right hand into the vat of hot, thick liquid.

"So, if the clubs only matter to the top five percent... why do I need them?"

Uncle Morgan smiled. "At the end of nine months, starting from this Monday, you will be that good."

"And how could I fail, with Queen Hippie Morrison and The Golfman of Lebanon in my corner?"

"Your hand," Mr. Tagawa said. "Remove it."

I did.

He pulled off the other solidified red glove and set it on the table. Then Mr. Tagawa took a full breath, as if he were about to begin a speech at a college commencement ceremony. "I will now measure your body, arms, hands, fingers, shoulders, height, weight, and the distances between your shoulders and hands, your hips to the ground. Then, I will forge the weapons...er...clubs from Samurai steel, just six, created only for *your* body, *your* precise measurements."

"Six?" I remembered the lengthy list of clubs I read about the other night. "Only six?"

"One weapon is for driving off the tee," he said. "One for putting. And the other is for everything else."

"That's three."

"The clubs will cause quite a stir," Uncle Morgan put in. "Just imagine. You will be shooting scores comparable to the best players in the world, and you will use *only six clubs*. The media will eat it up. And golfers won't believe it."

"I don't believe it already."

"You should. Mr. Tagawa's craftsmanship will help make it happen."

"The weapons will become part of your body, indistinguishable from your own flesh," Mr. Tagawa said, "just as my blades are designed to assist the Samurai."

I felt queasy. Just when I thought there were no more weirdoes in the world, Uncle Morgan found another one. "Samurai?"

Mr. Tagawa waited a moment as if letting an ancient memory work its way to the surface. "Samurai. Yes."

"Lots of those guys running around these days?"

Mr. Tagawa turned and leveled his eyes at me. "Of course, the weapons will be for nothing if you are not properly trained."

I blinked at that. "My teachers. Right."

"Open mind, Charley," Uncle Morgan said. *"Open mind."*

"And your teachers will need to instruct you in *both directions*," Mr. Tagawa added.

I just stared. "I have no idea what that means."

"Six clubs, Charley," Uncle Morgan said. "Three right hand and three left hand."

It took a second to sink in. "No way."

"Yes."

"I've never played golf, Uncle Morgan."

"We've established that."

"And Pinson Dill is going to teach me how to play *both* right and left-handed?"

"He and Mrs. Morrison."

"Oh, yeah. She's probably home right now with a thousand records on the floor, selecting her play-list for our next session swinging broom handles at tennis balls."

"Charley..."

"Call Ingmar Bergman. He may be interested in this plot."

"Plus—"

"Are we sure Hitchcock is dead?"

"Plus, you will play blindfolded."

I stared at my uncle and my jaw dropped. "I'm sorry. My hearing must have been damaged from that Alice Cooper concert we went to last month."

"Blindfolded," Uncle Morgan said again. "It will be the ultimate demonstration of your training techniques."

"Uh huh." I didn't know what else to say.

"The weapons will be so constructed," Mr. Tagawa said. "Your teachers must do the rest."

We spent another thirty minutes or so in Mr. Tagawa's attic while Mr. Tagawa measured my body about four hundred different ways with an old cloth tape measure. The elderly Japanese man then escorted us downstairs to the door.

"One month," Mr. Tagawa said. "Come back in one month, just before 6:20 in the morning. The sun will break the horizon at 6:30. First light."

He bowed to us. We returned the bow and smiled at him as he disappeared behind the closed door to his shop. Uncle Morgan and I piled into the Escalade, and we pulled onto

Reading Road.

We were silent for a while, and then I collected my thoughts. "Swords. *He makes swords.* Not golf clubs. Does he even know what golf is?"

"Mr. Tagawa is an interesting character."

"Interesting to who?"

"Whom."

"I'm going to jump out of this car and roll into the bushes, Uncle Morgan."

"You may have noticed the photos of the old Japanese aircraft in his studio."

"Flags, medals, a few weapons. Think I saw a rifle and a small machine gun, too."

Uncle Morgan nodded. "Vintage. Mr. Tagawa was a hero back then."

"Hero. Back when?"

"More than thirty decorations."

I considered that. "And we're talking *World War II*?"

"Yes. Mr. Oh Tagawa is the last living Zero pilot who was in the air on December 7, 1941."

"You...he..."

"Yes."

"He attacked Pearl Harbor. The man who is making my clubs *attacked Pearl Harbor.*"

"Fought in all four years of the war. Was never shot down. Given a job with Fuji Heavy Industries in Tokyo after the war. Worked for them until he retired in the 80s. Moved here and he's been crafting swords since then."

I stared at him. "You have got to be kidding me."

"It's true."

"Where the wavin' wheat, can sure smell sweet..."

"Charley."

"Forget it."

I was quiet after that. During the twelve-minute drive home, I daydreamed about a squadron of Japanese fighter pilots in full flight and formation, dropping golf clubs on the paddleboats steaming their way along the Ohio River. It was all I could do not to scream.

Chapter 9

Dill Fought the Law and the Law Won

I stood inside the condo and watched Uncle Morgan's Escalade roll into the driveway. It was early, but for once I was awake, dressed, and alert.

Uncle Morgan told me he was bringing my second instructor to meet me this morning. When I ran the Google search on Pinson Dill a few days ago, *eight pages* of hits came up. Most of them referred to newspaper articles from about four years ago. When I scanned the articles, I realized why his name had sounded familiar. Mr. Pinson Dill was somewhat of a local anti-hero.

Pinson was the only son of Doris Mae and Pettus Dill, owners of the *Dill! Dill Pickles* factory in Carthage. *Dill! Dill Pickles* was the largest business in Carthage, only about a three-mile drive from my condo, employing more than sixty workers. *Dill! Dill Pickles* had a contract with the local Frisch's restaurant chain to supply sliced pickles for their Big Boy hamburger sandwiches. The Dills were so successful they lived in an enormous estate on Graves Road in Indian Hill, one of the most affluent sections around Cincinnati. People affectionately called the Dill's house, *Pickle Palace*. It was quite an upgrade. The family moved to Cincinnati about twenty years ago from Valdosta, Georgia, with not much more than a dilapidated Chevy truck full of cardboard boxes. Of course, Mama Dory Mae, as the family called her, also brought along her secret Georgia recipe for dill pickles.

Four years ago, Pinson Dill was twenty-six and still lived with his parents. He worked at *Dill! Dill Pickles* and stayed in a roomy guest cottage on the *Pickle Palace* grounds. One autumn morning, Pinson left the estate for work just before dawn.

According to public transcripts of Pinson's court testimony, it was still dark, and a light rain had just begun to fall. Pinson drove his Toyota Prius slowly along the unlit rural Indian Hill roads. He was listening to the radio traffic report as he followed a black Mercedes on Graves Road, about a quarter-mile from the intersection of Miami Road, when it happened.

A Golden Retriever darted out from the roadside shrubbery, took one quick glance at the Mercedes and took off in hot pursuit. The dog barked furiously, as Golden Retrievers often do when they are involved in hot pursuit. The Mercedes kept a steady course, straight ahead toward the stop sign at Miami. As the Mercedes slowed, the Golden caught up and sprinted to the front of the car. The Mercedes driver quickly applied his brakes even harder to avoid the dog, but the right front bumper caught the Golden in his left shoulder. The dog was flung into a small gulley of mud and rainwater by the side of the road.

Pinson Dill saw everything clearly. The Mercedes driver had done nothing wrong. The Golden was just being a Golden. Sometimes dogs chase cars and usually the cars win. But Pinson felt terrible for the dog. He liked dogs. They were loyal, giving, and fun. And that, more than anything else, was responsible for the cold knot of anger that blossomed inside Pinson's gut during the next few moments.

The Mercedes driver *knew* he'd hit the Golden. Pinson heard the *thump* from inside the Prius twenty yards behind. There was no mistaking that sickening sound. But instead of stopping, instead of at least getting out of the $100,000 car to check on the welfare of the injured canine, the Mercedes driver signaled a right turn and pulled onto the northbound lane of traffic on Miami, as if this were just another normal morning drive to work. Pinson watched in disbelief as the taillights disappeared in front of him.

Without another second of hesitation, as he testified in court, Pinson rushed to the dog and lifted him, with some difficulty, into the back seat of the Prius. The dog was big, even for a Golden, and soaking wet.

Pinson felt his lower back pull tight as he lowered and shifted the animal into the cushions of the dark cloth seats.

The Golden was breathing hard, and a splotch of red

streaked the long, rust-colored hair that covered his left shoulder. Pinson raced to a nearby animal hospital and stayed with the Golden until the vet was finished treating the dog's injuries.

Luckily, Goldens are naturally tough and resilient. This time, this Golden was only stunned and had a few surface scrapes. After a few hours of observation, the vet released the dog into Pinson's care.

As Pinson drove back toward Indian Hill with the dog asleep in his backseat, Pinson's lower back was on fire, twisted with a growing pain. But despite the ache, Pinson clearly recalled a series of numbers and letters *seared* into his brain: *100 DEM*, the plate number of the Mercedes.

With one call to a friend at the BMV in Columbus, Pinson was able to track the owner of the car, and was stunned to find it registered to Mr. Dudley Edward McGrath. It wasn't the name that surprised him, but rather McGrath lived on Graves Road in the residence right next door to his own. Pinson testified in court: *it goes to show people these days just don't get to know their neighbors.*

Pinson's further investigation revealed McGrath was a VP with Fifth Third Bank, the largest locally based bank in the Cincinnati area, and the McGrath family had started the bank more than ninety years before. Old money. Pinson hated old money, since, in his mind, it fostered an atmosphere of superiority, and a near visceral disrespect for those with an annual income of less than seven figures.

Just three weeks after McGrath struck the Golden, on October thirty-first, to be exact, Pinson donned a Jimmy Carter mask and strolled into the main Fifth Third branch on Fountain Square with the Golden at his side. Pinson held the dog's leash in one hand and a stack of red paper flyers in the other. A sawed-off Stoeger shotgun, the kind stagecoach drivers used in the old West, was tucked under the folds of Pinson's long dark raincoat. The gun was loaded with salt-pellet cartridges.

Pinson dropped a stack of red flyers on the counter in front of a petrified teller, withdrew the shotgun, pointed it at the ceiling and fired. Pinson wanted bank personnel to have no doubt he meant business. Then Pinson took another stack of red flyers from the back pocket of his jeans and tossed them over his head. The red flyers floated haphazardly in all directions.

Pinson slipped the shotgun back into a harness specially tailored inside of his coat, turned toward the door and casually walked out with the Golden still at his side.

The evening news made quite a fuss about the mysterious bank robber. The surveillance tape clearly showed the Jimmy Carter mask, which the news anchors reported with reluctant grins, especially since Jimmy Carter would probably be the least likely president to rob a bank.

The reporters also focused on the *dog* who accompanied the bank robber. One female reporter, again with a smile, but not a reluctant one this time, described the dog as "a graceful Golden Retriever." She was certain the perp was a dog lover for sure.

News personnel weren't able to categorize the *robber's* actions as even being a *robbery* since the person behind the presidential mask had neither demanded nor taken any money. This, they said, was a first in Cincinnati bank heist history. Police stated Jimmy would be caught and charged with various offenses, including some firearms violations.

But finally, and most newsworthy, as the news editors must have felt, the early evening broadcasts were teased with the red flyers the bank robber left behind. The flyers contained a message, or "Jimmy's Manifesto," a title coined by Jack Atherton, the anchor for Channel 5. In later weeks, all media outlets around the country adopted that catchy phrase to describe the bank robber and his mission, which lasted through six other appearances at branches of Fifth Third Bank in surrounding Cincinnati neighborhoods.

The single-spaced words on the legal-sized flyers were carefully typed on both sides in ten-point Impact font. The content was too lengthy to be repeated verbatim on either TV or radio news, but the newspapers gleefully reprinted the full version in specially detailed boxes. The national media picked up the text of "Jimmy's Manifesto," and the public reveled in each and every word:

#

Dudley Edward McGrath lives in Indian Hill. Dudley Edward McGrath's estate has a garage with spaces for 6 cars, and all the spaces are filled.

Being rich and owning 6 cars is neither bad nor evil. No doubt Dudley Edward McGrath and the McGrath family earned their riches honestly. Dudley Edward McGrath's great-grandfather, Franklin Peter McGrath, started the Fifth Third bank (I'm sure you've heard of it) more than 100 years ago, and the bank has thrived through four McGrath generations. There's a simple *balance of nature* to it - the McGraths operate honestly and reap the rewards of that honesty. Franklin Peter McGrath's business philosophy was to be open and forthright, to live by the strength and trust of his promises, to actually assist banking customers in their lives. Over time, the public would benefit, and the bank, in turn, would prosper. That's the *balance*, the give-and-take of it. What's that old saying? *Things come back around.* I think that's it. As far as the Fifth Third Bank is concerned, that old saying has proven true for the bank and the McGrath family.

The problem Dudley Edward McGrath has now, however, shows that old saying applies to our personal lives as well. Let's take this one example.

On October 7, Dudley Edward McGrath struck, *and knew he struck*, a helpless, loyal, and fun-loving stray dog I named Rusty, with the front bumper of his (Dudley's) Mercedes. Rusty was flung into a thicket, just down the road from Dudley Edward McGrath's estate. Rusty was hurt and needed help. Dudley Edward McGrath did not slow down, did not roll down his window to take a look, did not pick up his cell phone and call for help. Instead, Dudley Edward McGrath checked the cross traffic, and continued toward his office where he began one more work day, no different from the day before, probably no different than the day after, protected on all sides by bank walls, bank security, his money, and his prestigious Cincinnati family name.

As it turns out, however, there is a *balance* to all things, a *balance of nature*, which cannot be circumvented by ignorance, material possessions, or a callous disregard for canine life. I am here today as *nature's messenger*, to see this *balance of nature* is restored, and justice for both Rusty and for Dudley Edward McGrath, is properly accomplished.

You may have noticed I refer to Dudley Edward McGrath by his full name. I do this so we will never forget what this man has done, just as we always list presidential assassins by their full names. From this day forward, the name of Dudley Edward McGrath will be associated with someone who is so dispassionate and uncaring he cannot take a moment to stop and help a dog he had injured just seconds before. Such behavior might now be known as "pulling a McGrath." And maybe after the banking public considers this, the bank started by Franklin Peter McGrath nearly 100 years ago might begin to feel the ominous pressure of hundreds upon hundreds of bank accounts marching out the doors of Fifth Third Bank and straight into the vaults of other banks who are managed by people more passionate, caring, and who know the true value of a dog's life, a dog who, if given the chance, would love his owner unconditionally and forever. I am here today to see this is done.

I will keep visiting branches of Fifth Third Bank to deliver this message until Dudley Edward McGrath personally atones for his transgression by writing a check for $50,000 and then personally delivers that check to the Cincinnati SPCA shelter on Colerain, the place where stray dogs and cats live until they are adopted. Dudley Edward McGrath must alert the media before delivering the check. His repentance must be aired publicly. And it must be immediate.

Justice demands it.

A Concerned Citizen and Canine Rights Advocate

#

Pinson, as you might imagine, did not expect McGrath to easily cave in and comply with the demands of, "a deranged lunatic," as McGrath put it in a news interview with Jack Atherton. McGrath said his policy was not to negotiate with terrorists, a phrase he had no doubt heard on the old TV show *24,* where terrorists used to spring up on every corner. He further denied ever striking a dog with his car, at least as far as he knew, and he cared a great deal for dogs. His family owned two: Mona and Gumby, and he enjoyed having two Wiemeraners around the house. But in the spirit of "canine welfare," as McGrath said in that same interview with Jack Atherton, and the fact McGrath loved his own two dogs, he was willing to donate $500 to the animal shelter. To Pinson, this sounded like McGrath was indeed willing to negotiate with terrorists.

Of course, Pinson had a point to make and he continued to

make it, with Rusty at his side, six more times at other branches of the Fifth Third Bank.

McGrath may have held out indefinitely but for Jimmy Fallon using the phrase "pulling a McGrath" on *The Tonight Show*. The day after that, McGrath alerted the media and, in person, presented the animal shelter on Colerain with a check for $50,000. Ironically, at almost the exact moment, Pinson was arrested by mounted Cincinnati officers who easily ran Pinson down on horseback in a large wooded area behind the Fifth Third branch in Clifton. Unfortunately, Pinson hadn't seen or heard the reports earlier that day of McGrath's monetary submission.

All of this history flashed through my head in a single instant as I stood at the door and watched my crazy uncle escort Pinson Dill from the condo parking area up the walkway. Pinson Dill was pale, about five-foot-ten and thin. He wore a faded denim shirt with rolled up sleeves.

I opened the door. "Hi."

"Charley, this is Pinson Dill."

I extended my hand.

Pinson took it. "My pleasure, sir," he said with a southern drawl. He had muddy, hazel eyes, and a full mustache.

"Me too," I said. "Come on in."

They stepped into the kitchen. Pinson leaned back against a countertop, crossed his arms over his chest and gazed down at the floor. Bad body language. Uncle Morgan stared at me. The room was quiet for a moment.

I broke the silence. "Can I get anybody something to drink?"

Pinson shook his head. "Thank you anyway."

"Right." I stared at Uncle Morgan.

The room was silent again.

"Charley," Uncle Morgan said, "let's speak in the other room for a minute." He tilted his head toward the doorway that led to the study.

"Sure."

"Please excuse us both for a moment, Mr. Dill."

Pinson continued to stare at the floor as if attempting to memorize the pattern of ceramic tile. He raised one hand to his mouth to cover a raspy cough. Sounded like it came from deep in his chest. "I will be here when you return, sir."

"I know you will. Come on, Charley."

Uncle Morgan and I walked into the next room. Soft conversation from the TV filtered through the air.

"Charley, I need you to do something."

"Oh God."

"Pinson has refused to train you."

"Refused?"

"The plan won't work without Pinson Dill, and you're the only one who can convince him."

"Why has he changed his mind?"

"He said he only agreed in the first place because it would allow him the chance to be outside his prison walls for a great deal of time during the next year. But after he let the initial excitement of it wear off, he realized it wouldn't be right to train you in the 'special manner,' as he phrased it, of playing golf."

"What does that mean?"

"Something about upsetting the natural balance."

"That clears it up."

"I'm not sure I follow him either. But you've got to try to convince him anyway."

I shook my head at him. "And how..?"

"I don't know. *Talk* to him."

"About what?"

"Golf?"

"Golf. I know *nothing* about golf."

"I-"

"Wasn't that the whole idea?"

"Try to think of *something*." Uncle Morgan squinted at me.

I took a deep breath.

***

Pinson's eyes were still directed at the kitchen floor pattern when we re-entered the kitchen. It didn't take a genius at reading body language to know Mr. Pinson Dill wanted to be somewhere other than here.

"Charley has something to tell you," Uncle Morgan said to

Pinson.

I shot a sideways glare at Uncle Morgan. "Mr. Dill..."

He continued to stare at the floor.

"I've never played actual golf."

"That fact, sir, has already been made known to me."

Uncle Morgan stared at me from across the room.

"I've never played much of any sport, not even throwing a ball around with neighborhood kids. Or...or with my dad. He died when I was little."

Pinson looked up. "Sorry to hear that, sir."

"My mom and dad used to play golf together. They would leave me with my older brother and take off for the local golf course." I cleared my throat. "When they were gone, I'd go into the garage and take one of their old clubs and head out back. We had tons of pinecones on the lawn, and for twenty minutes or so, I'd swat at those pinecones and pretend I was playing golf with my dad. I was terrible at it, especially since the club was nearly as tall as I was."

Pinson straightened.

I thought I saw the outline of a back-brace under his denim shirt. "When my mom and dad returned, they would laugh and smile at each other, as if playing golf had made them closer. Golf made them *happy*, Mr. Dill. One of the reasons I decided to do this whole crazy mission, well, if my dad is up there somewhere watching, he might be proud of me. You know? I would like to carry on the good things golf brought to him, carrying on the *natural balance*, from father to son, from son to—"

"Natural balance?" Pinson interrupted.

"Something like that."

Pinson cleared his throat. His eyes locked with mine. "How long has your daddy been gone, if you don't mind me asking?"

"A long, long time, Mr. Dill."

He stared at me. "I lost my daddy, as well, Mr. Davis. When I was small, like you."

"Sorry to hear that, Mr. Dill."

He nodded. "Mr. Davis..?"

"Yeah?"

"I have changed my mind."

"What was that?" I could feel Uncle Morgan's warm smile

from across the room.

Pinson took a step closer to me and extended his hand. I looked at his hand for a second and then gripped it.

"It would be my privilege to instruct you, sir."

Uncle Morgan nodded.

I smiled but wasn't sure why. "Great. Great."

"Well then..." Uncle Morgan headed toward the door. "We start training tomorrow. 7:45, Glenwood Gardens."

"Tomorrow," I said.

"Rain or shine. Get some rest. It will be a long day."

He started to go and gestured for Pinson to follow.

"Wait a second," I said. "I know how much you like to surprise me, Uncle Morgan, but exactly what will be happening tomorrow?"

He studied my face for a few seconds. "Mrs. Morrison at 7:45. Allow enough time to get there since you must *walk* to Glenwood."

"Okay." I felt instantly numb at the thought of a morning in the woods with Mrs. Morrison.

"Don't be late."

"I won't."

"Wear loose-fitting clothing. Sweats, maybe."

"Fine."

"Your first session with Mr. Dill will be at 1:00. I'll pick you up for that."

"From..."

"From Glenwood. Mrs. Morrison won't be finished with you until 12:00."

I freaked for a second. "12:00? That means..."

"Yes. Your sessions with Mrs. Morrison will be about four hours."

I sank onto a kitchen chair.

"Give or take," he said. "At least at the beginning."

"*We who are about to die salute you.*"

"As I said, get some rest."

"Right."

Pinson tipped his hat at me as he walked by, even though he wasn't wearing a hat. I went to the door and watched him follow Uncle Morgan to the Escalade. After they were gone, I stayed in the doorway and stared outside at the brisk autumn morning. I glanced at the kitchen counter and noticed several golf books I had purchased the day before.

I picked up the stack of books, sat down at the table, and exhaled.

I began to read.

Chapter 10

Hamilton Ford and the Temple of Stupidity

November weather in Cincinnati was hard to predict. One day, like yesterday, we could be treated to crystal clear skies and balmy temperatures. Or, November in Cincinnati might be rotten, like today, where the temperature dropped to 35 degrees, the clouds sank to the treetops, and the air congested with a cold, mind-numbing mist.

The cloud cover wasn't the only thing that had sunk as I awoke and stepped to the window. The morning haze was so thick I couldn't see to the end of the condo walkway, and my stomach clenched with a special kind of nervous dread.

I dressed in layers, pulled on a black and gold knitted Pittsburg Steelers hat, near *heresy* in Cincinnati, grabbed a cold Pop-Tart, and stepped out the door. It wasn't officially raining, but the atmosphere was sodden with cold moisture. My face was immediately damp and freezing. I found the hood to my waterproof windbreaker and stretched it over my head.

Traffic was sparse on Springfield Pike as I trekked northward on the sidewalk. I ate half of the strawberry Pop-Tart, before it turned impermissibly soggy, and tossed the rest into bushes that framed a Dairy Queen driveway. I continued on, as fast as I could walk, past a florist shop housed in an old wooden building sorely in need of paint. I wiped the mist from my eyes and looked ahead. The outer woods of Glenwood lined the sidewalk to my left, and the park entrance was just beyond.

I glanced at my watch as I stepped along the Glenwood pathway. It was 7:35 and the stone bridge was just ahead. I was nearly ten minutes early.

I stopped at the bridge. It was deserted.

"Good morning, Charley," Mrs. Morrison said as she

appeared through the trees.

"Oh. Mrs. Morrison."

"I bid you welcome to your first day of training."

"I didn't see you."

Mrs. Morrison wore a thin gray rain parka, no hat and open sandals. Her face and hair seemed dry, despite the heavy mist. Maybe she was part spaniel.

"Shall we?" She gestured toward a barely visible path through the trees.

"Are we going somewhere?"

"Three minute walk. Your film crew is already there."

"Uh..."

I tried to ignore the fact that in three minutes or less I would see Sandy again. And I looked terrible. I took extra time this morning getting my hair to look at least halfway decent. But all that was for nothing with the cold rain, the parka, the hat, and the hood. Last night I even tried some of that self-tanning stuff on my face and neck, so I wouldn't look so *pasty*. But this morning, in the gray shadows, and with my hood pulled up, my face was barely visible anyway.

In a few minutes, we stopped at a clearing by a narrow bend in a creek. The running water made me shiver. If the temperature dropped another few degrees, the creek might be covered with a thin layer of ice.

Sandy stood across the clearing behind a tripod-mounted camera and looked through the lens. Ray Ford was next to her, crouched down and fumbling inside a huge black duffle bag. Mrs. Morrison didn't say anything. I guessed she was waiting for Sandy, Ray, and I to greet each other. I took a breath, swallowed what was left of my pride, and walked over to Ray.

"Hey," I said.

"Hey, man." Ray straightened up and smiled.

I extended my hand to him, but Ray ignored it and grabbed me in a hug like those given to soldiers who just returned from the front. I instantly smelled the Cool Water cologne Ray always wore. I pushed back from him and smiled involuntarily. His ultra-friendly greeting surprised me, but it really was good to see him again, even though it was kind of hard to admit it to myself. He looked as though he hadn't shaved in three days, as always, and was appropriately scruffy in his Hollister rain jacket and professionally faded and torn jeans.

I said, "You look the same."

"Thanks, bud." He studied my face. "And you've been spending a lot of time in the sun."

"Uh, no."

"Tanning salon?"

"Nope."

He smiled. "Neutrogena."

"Yep."

"Yeah. I see a few streaks on your neck, man."

"I'll be more careful next time."

Sandy watched me. "Hi, Charley."

I tried not to look interested. "Oh, hi."

She wore a black rain slicker. Her short blond curls stuck out from the sides of her Reds ball cap. Rain dripped from the brim of her cap, most of her face was hidden in shadow, and she was the most beautiful woman in the world.

"So," I said to Ray, "I hear you're doing well."

"Ups and downs."

"Yeah. Me too."

"Some decent commercial work. And I help Sandy out when she, you know, has a big project."

I gestured at the trees. "This project is big?"

"Man, it's a *nine month contract*. Monthly payments. They don't get much bigger. It's like PBS hired us to go shoot penguins in Belize."

"Ray, there are no penguins in Belize. At least, I don't think there are."

"I meant shoot with a camera."

"Yeah, I figured."

"Anyway, after the shoot is up, I'm thinking about going to Bolivia."

"What...like Butch Cassidy?"

"Or move to Montana and be a ski instructor. I'd like to see the Montana skies before it's too late."

"Wait a minute. *Bolivia?*"

"Who's Butch Cassidy?" Ray asked.

"Nobody. What's in Bolivia?"

"Bananas."

"Bananas?"

"Right."

"What's so special about bananas?"

"Heard on the grapevine they got a shortage of workers over there, to work on the banana plantations."

"You mean picking bananas?"

He nodded. "Planting, picking, packing. And we load the barges. They're shipped over here on barges."

"You're serious?"

"Hell yes, man. They use barges."

"No, I mean you're serious about going there?"

"Money's damn good. Do me wonders to get back into shape, six, seven months in Bolivia working outside in the average 82 degree heat. I've put on a couple pounds the last year or so."

"Ray, you haven't put on an ounce."

He hadn't, unless his hair gel weighed a few pounds.

Sandy gritted her teeth as she watched Ray and I talk. It seemed she wanted to say something and finally did. "Guys. Enough. You can catch up some other time. Okay?"

"Fine," I said, though I wanted to ask Ray if he could tell me the location of Bolivia. I was sure he would say it was somewhere in Africa.

"Okay. Here's the deal," Sandy said after a few seconds. "You and Mrs. Morrison will start in a minute. Ham and I will just be in the background."

I shook my head. "Who?"

"Oh, Ham, Hamilton." She pointed her thumb at Ray. "That's his middle name. I told you."

"Hamilton Ford," I said to myself.

"You don't look as pasty this morning. But you look tired, somehow older."

"It's not the years, honey. It's the mileage."

She paused for a second, then: "That's from a film, isn't it?"

"You're the expert."

My chest thumped in my ears. I just stared. Couldn't help it. Her green eyes glistened in the rain.

"Okay, so forget we're here," Sandy went on. "You train, we'll film. We won't ask you to do anything different."

"Okay."

"We can talk during your breaks, at the end of the day. Or, whenever."

"Yeah. I get it. You're not here. Neither is Ray...Hamilton."

"You're here, but we're not, man," Ray said.

"Very Zen, Ray."

He raised one fist to the sky. "Power to the people, man."

Sandy turned to me. "Are you okay?"

"Yeah. Yeah."

She shook her head. "I don't believe you."

"No, really."

She stared at me for a second. "Houston, there is a big problem here."

I cringed at her bungled movie quote.

"I see it all over your face."

"Sandy, nothing's wrong."

"Sure?"

"Yeah."

She titled her head at the ground. "It's good to see you, Charley."

Without waiting for me to respond, Sandy stepped back to her camera equipment. Ray smiled at me and raised another closed fist in the air. Then he followed Sandy and started checking the connections on a gray light pole.

Breath stuck in my throat. That was nothing new. Every day was like that when Sandy and I were together. The slightest glimpse of her could stop my breathing.

And then she walked away. Dumped me, for her career, or so she'd said. But that didn't stop her from hooking up with Ray a while later.

If nothing else, I always knew Ray was basically a good-hearted soul. However, when the looks and smarts were served about twenty-six years ago, Ray must have never found his way to the section of the buffet that contained the brains.

"Are we ready?" Mrs. Morrison asked.

"Yes." I tried to evacuate thoughts of Sandy from my head.

"Ready."

"Take off your boots."

"My boots."

"Yes." She folded her legs beneath her and removed her sandals. I caught the scent of damp patchouli.

"Okay." I glanced about for somewhere to sit that wasn't soaked, but found nothing even remotely dry. So I bent my knees and sank to the leaf-covered ground. I unlaced the low-cut Merrell hiking boots, pulled them off, and placed them under a short tree branch to my right. Maybe that would keep my boots dry, at least.

"And your socks," she said.

"Mrs. Morrison, it's really cold and wet." I didn't want to say that, especially with Sandy watching me through a telephoto lens and undoubtedly listening with enhanced audio equipment, but it really was cold and wet. I didn't like the cold and wet.

Mrs. Morrison's smiled vanished. "There is no wet, Charley."

"No wet?"

"No cold either. And now that we're all settled..." Mrs. Morrison stretched her arms. "Let's begin."

Chapter 11

Here's to you, Mrs. Morrison

The heat I generated from my walk to Glenwood had vanished and I was getting progressively colder. I wrapped my arms around my middle.

"Here's a simple explanation that should help you understand these exercises," Mrs. Morrison shifted her body and studied my face.

I wiped water droplets from my eyes.

The rain fell harder.

"Why do you think most golfers fail, Charley?"

"Don't practice enough?"

Mrs. Morrison nodded. "That is crucial. But practice is only one part of it. The *correct manner* of practice is the key."

"Makes sense." I tried to ignore a growing shiver.

"Thousands of amateur golfers, and professional golfers, for that matter, spend thousands of dollars and thousands of hours on golf lessons."

"I saw lessons, golf trips, and seminars advertised in some golf magazines."

"But while a player's game might improve somewhat, unless taught the proper techniques, he or she never improves enough to *master* any part of the game. Do you know why?"

"No."

She gazed at the ground. "Few golfers know the real answer. Only a select few have seen through the tangle of golf techniques, and then journeyed into the light."

"Sounds mystical."

"Much simpler than that."

"Simple is good."

"The secret, Charley," she leaned forward and began

speaking in her new-age voice, "is *clearing the mind.*"

"Clearing..?"

"Clearing the mind of *everything that fills it.*"

"Like..?"

"What was in your head this morning as you left your condo and walked down here?"

"A little of everything, I guess."

"Tell me."

"Locking the doors, where to put my keys so I wouldn't lose them in the woods, whether to take an umbrella, wondering if my change-of-address was effective yet, how much gas was in my car. You know. Stuff."

She nodded. "The typical content of the mind of any normal person. But now, you have to be *different.* You cannot be normal. And all that *stuff* has to go."

I raised a wet eyebrow. "*All* of it?"

"Our goal will be to *empty* your mind. Instantaneously. So when you step up to a shot, your mind is no longer in control."

"What is in control?"

She blinked. "Reflex."

"Reflex. So I will be thinking about...*nothing?*"

"Correct."

"Okay."

"Understand?"

"No."

She smiled at me as if I were a first-grader in tenth-grade algebra class. "Your training will allow you to empty your mind at will, at any time, under any conditions."

I just didn't get it and I was afraid she might get mad at me, but I chanced it and said, "Example?"

"Certainly. Golfers who cannot empty their minds fail when they focus on their grip, the straightness of their arms, the placement of their feet, the twinge in their shoulders, the heat, the rain, the wind, the stock market, their lovers, and everything else. They become distracted and their bodies react accordingly."

I thought about it and shrugged.

"So, instead of all that, when *you* approach the tee, or your ball on a fairway or at the edge of a green, here is what you will do. At first, your mind will *not* be empty, because you will have to plan your shot. Is there a wind? How is the cut and angle of the fairway grass? Do you want to hit a straight shot or have it dogleg, to the right or left? And the particulars of each shot on the green are of utmost importance. Is your ball uphill or downhill from the cup? Are there bends or angles to the turf? Does the grass have a layer of moisture? How much force will you need to putt the ball successfully? You will face all of these questions before you approach the ball and ready your shot. *Any* shot."

She stopped talking and looked at me.

"And that is when I empty my mind?"

She smiled. "Yes."

"I plan the shot, get it all in my head, and then *empty* my head."

"Yes."

"And *reflex* is supposed to take over."

Mrs. Morrison placed the back of her hands on each of her knees in some kind of meditation pose. She wore only a light rain jacket but was not shivering. "Pinson Dill is a master at clearing his mind."

I let that thought sink in. "Pinson?"

"Yes. I trained Pinson Dill when he was a kid."

"This does not surprise me."

"Even so, my training was just one of the reasons Pinson became such a great player. He has a special insight of his own." She looked away, into the trees. "Too bad his career was cut short."

"Yeah. I imagine jail can hurt your golf game."

She shook her head. "Pinson never played again *because of his back*. In fact, he hasn't played at all since that day he rescued Rusty."

I remembered the court records. "You mean when he hurt his back lifting Rusty into his car?"

"Ruptured a disc. It's inoperable."

"I thought I noticed a brace or something under his shirt when we met."

"Even though he can't play, Pinson knows the proper techniques. He can still teach you, show you correct form, golf procedures, get you in proper shape."

I'd read quite a bit about Pinson Dill. I saw no mention of a permanent back injury. He must be the kind of person who keeps that sort of thing private.

"So, let's get started," she said. "First lesson." She reached under a small blue tarp and pressed something. Music started. It was a 60s song, again, about drugs, or something. The drumbeat was a slow march and a fuzzy electric guitar led the way. The singer was either Janis Joplin or Grace Slick. My dad used to play and sing along with classic Broadway tunes while he was fiddling around with his car in our garage, but my mom used to play 60s music all the time, everywhere we went. Hits from the 60s filled my life when I was little.

"Assume this position," Mrs. Morrison said.

I tried to bend my legs and straighten my back. It was harder than it looked. "Like this?"

She nodded, but her eyes were closed and I wondered how she knew what I was doing.

"Now, listen to the music."

"I can't help but hear the music. It's pretty loud."

"Not just hear it, but *listen* to it. Let the words and the texture of the music fill you, overtake your senses, push everything else out."

I nodded, but I didn't know why, since Mrs. Morrison's eyes were still closed, and I had practically no idea what she was talking about. How was I supposed to clear my mind with drug-induced hippie music in the background? Maybe that was it. Maybe we were eventually going to take some peyote, or LSD, or something. That would help clear my mind. Permanently.

I glanced at Sandy and Ray across the clearing. They were working behind the camera, adjusting waterproof coverings, as if they had done this a thousand times. For some reason, I felt bad for them. Filming two people sitting motionless in the woods would have to be a creative challenge for any filmmaker, even one named Sandy Carson.

I took one last look at Mrs. Morrison, put my hands on my knees, and closed my eyes. I needed to try, at least, to do what she wanted.

The music buzzed on. Pills were making someone larger or smaller. I never wanted hot coffee so much in my life, and I think if I had a time machine right then, I would have gone back to that day in my apartment when Uncle Morgan first suggested this plan. Then I wouldn't be here, sitting on the cold, wet ground in the middle of November, taking some kind of new-age meditation seminar from a lady who no doubt thought *Aquarius* should be our national anthem.

I took a breath, let it out, and tried not to feel the chilling breeze that had just come up, or the BBs of ice that were now pelting my face. Instead, I concentrated on remembering the familiar glow of Sandy's incredible green eyes. It wasn't much, but seemed like a pretty good place to start.

Chapter 12

Present Day

Angelica Day Afternoon

On the way back from my first training session with Pinson Dill in the sleet-filled jawbreaker horse pasture, and after I had told Uncle Morgan, "I quit," I stopped at the nearby convenient store on the Pike and bought some dog food. If this nameless new friend was to stay in my condo, I had to supply something for her to eat. I bought a bag of what they had and returned home. Dutifully, the black dog followed me inside as if we had done this a thousand times.

When Uncle Morgan dropped me off, he suggested I call the dog pound to see if anyone reported this black furry beast with amber eyes missing. I didn't acknowledge him and just walked inside.

"Okay. Here." I placed a cereal bowl of dog food and another bowl of water on the white tile of the kitchen floor. "Eat. Drink."

The huge dog backed toward the door as if her bowls were somehow cursed.

"That's Purina One, Dog. Go ahead."

The dog watched me but did not answer. It was funny, but her expression was such I almost *expected* an answer. That was foolish, but perhaps no more foolish than me bringing a stray dog into my new home.

"Okay, Dog. Don't eat. But I'm making something for myself, if you don't mind, before I starve to death. And before I call the pound."

I made a quick sandwich of shaved Sara Lee turkey breast, oven roasted, not smoked. I remained in the kitchen and leaned against the countertop, shivering as I chewed. I had still not warmed up enough from my arctic morning. The dog watched me as she backed her body to the wall near the refrigerator. Her eyes seemed more open, and they were sending pointed waves of amber light in my direction.

"What?" I said.

She focused on my sandwich.

"This. You want this."

She continued to stare.

"Okay. I get it."

I opened the plastic bag of turkey breast and pinched a small clump with my fingers. The dog followed my every movement as I stepped closer, squatted down, and placed the treasure from Kroger's deli department into her food bowl. Then I backed away and waited.

She kept her gaze locked on my face as she stepped slowly toward her bowl. She stopped, blinked once, and dropped her nose straight into the tan ceramic. The turkey breast was gone in less than two seconds.

"I suppose this is progress."

She widened her eyes and walked right at me. She stopped at my side and pushed her massive, furry head against my right shin.

"Huh?"

The dog remained motionless, her head still pushed firmly against my leg.

"I'm your friend?"

I looked down at her mud-streaked fur.

"Yeah. Guess so."

I turned back to the kitchen counter. The dog moved with me, as if her head were sewed to my leg. I grabbed the bag of turkey breast.

"Here, Dog."

I emptied the bag into her bowl. She backed a step, tilted her head up at me, and extended her legs out in front, as if bowing. After a moment, she straightened up, turned, and gobbled the turkey breast. She then moved near the refrigerator and stretched out on the cool, white tile floor. She looked over at me. Her short bluish-pink tongue licked the last remnants of turkey flavor from her muzzle.

"Okay, look. I've got to take a shower. You can just...hang out. I'll be right back."

I slogged into the bathroom with the huge black dog on my heels. Guess she didn't feel like staying in the kitchen. My damp clothes dropped to the floor, and I turned the hot water in the shower up as far as it would go. It took nearly twenty minutes in the shower before feeling completely returned to all parts of my body. I was finally human again, and not a zombie Popsicle.

Ms. Dog was waiting for me at the foot of the bed when I got out of the shower. Her amber eyes followed my every move. I dried off, pulled on some flannel P.J. bottoms, found the bed, and collapsed. I stretched out on my back and pulled the bedcovers up to my chin. My skin still tingled, but I was warmer, the bed felt peaceful, and I wasn't standing frozen in the middle of an ice storm with a golf club in my shaking hands.

Uncle Morgan didn't say much on the way back to the condo from Jawbreaker Mountain. I think he was afraid I might shatter into four hundred pieces if he said anything. He just drove the Escalade into the parking lot, stopped the car, threw a glance at the dog, and said, "You should call the pound." Pinson Dill said nothing. That was it. And I rushed inside, anticipating the steamy embrace of the shower, which I never fully appreciated before.

The shower in this condo is a modern miracle. The water pressure is fierce and the temperature hotter than molten lava. Truly, this is a shower experience to be savored. I was going to miss this shower, now that I quit and would have to move out, back to my cardboard box at the Four Seasons.

I reached behind my head and switched on the electric blanket; I *desperately* needed to be even warmer. I heard somewhere electric blankets make you sterile. I'm not sure whether that applies to just men, women, or both. But right then, I would happily have traded sterility for the soothing comfort of 110 volts.

The heat from the blanket began to seep through the covers and surround me in a calming cocoon. The discomforts of the morning finally vanished. I closed my eyes, and exhaled a long breath.

Uncle Morgan expects a lot.

My eyes opened and I stared at the paint swirls on the bedroom ceiling.

I said, "Yes he does."

I slowly sat up and focused. The dog I had just rescued from the woods was seated like an ebony sphinx atop the quilt at the foot of the bed. She stared at me.

He barely explains a fraction of it.

The dog had not moved an inch.

"You understand."

Her amber eyes seemed to narrow.

Yes.

I pushed my hands back through my hair, still damp from my endless shower. "I wonder what your name might be."

What would you like to call me?

I considered a moment. "Angelica?"

Angelica, then.

I nodded. Why had that name come to me? "Angelica, I wonder how long you were alone in the woods."

Not a good judge of time.

"Well, how did you come to be there?"

Don't like to talk about that.

"Did you run away?"

I've never run away from anything.

I chuckled. "I bet you haven't."

Angelica inched closer to me and rested her chin on the quilt between her front paws.

Some questions for you?

"Questions?"

Do you mind?

"Uh, no. Go ahead."

Why so little self-confidence?

"I...I don't really know."

No reason for it.

"Must be some reason," I said.

You're stronger than that.

"Never thought of myself as being strong. And how would you know? We just met."

Giving up is for cowards. You're not a coward.

"You might be wrong about that one."

She licked the side of one paw a few times with her oddly discolored, mottled tongue. Then she settled down again.

Sandy is always on your mind.

I could barely breathe. Angelica's eyes pierced right through my skin. "It's...hard for me to talk about...her."

Maybe that's part of the problem.

"Problem?"

Why you still feel twisted inside.

"So, I should talk to you about it?"

Yes.

I took a few short breaths. "I didn't want to lay down and die when Sandy broke up with me. It wasn't like that."

Angelica rolled over onto her side.

You felt numb, as if you didn't want to do anything?

"Like it was all pointless after that."

That feeling is familiar.

She stretched her legs and sighed.

"I thought it would get better with time but I was wrong. It was a painful, open gash inside me that refused to heal."

Poetic.

"Yeah. And my themes are dark and sad. Like Poe."

Annabel Lee.

"You know that poem?"

Heard it somewhere.

"Yes." I shook my head. "Like Annabel Lee. I was tortured by the loss of..."

Angelica slowly closed her eyes.

Finish.

"She said she was too young. And she had a *career* to think about. She truly did care for me, but I was getting too serious. That it was the wrong time for her."

Angelica yawned.

Timing is important.

"Do you believe each person has only one true love? I never used to think so, I mean before Sandy. But when she left me, it felt as though part of my life was over. Instantly. And no matter what happened after that, no matter where I went, no matter who I met, no one would or could ever match the feelings

I had for her."

Angelica did not move.

"Angelica?"

She was snoring, a soft, regular, doggie snore. I gently stroked the thick fur behind one ear.

"No problem. Thanks for *listening*, even though you fell asleep in the middle of my monologue."

I leaned back and rested one arm across Angelica's side. It felt oddly good to have her there. And talking had given me a basket of issues to think about. I needed to clear my head, relax, and work things through.

I closed my eyes and tried to let the images come on their own, without forcing them. Tonight I had to call Uncle Morgan and tell him what I wanted to do, since I officially quit his mad plan during the sleet storm. Even though he hadn't said anything, I knew he would expect my call. After some thought, after a short afternoon siesta, I had to select a path that could change the direction of my life. But for some reason, I didn't feel like panicking, maybe because now, I didn't have to make this decision on my own.

I somehow *knew* Angelica would still be here later, by my side, and I could talk it out with her, since I never agreed to call the pound anyway. Maybe between the two of us, we could make some sense out of this life.

I patted her side softly as I felt myself drift off to sleep.

Chapter 13

Where Have You Gone, Dave Concepcion?

I sat on the edge of the sofa as Pinson inserted a disk into the DVD player. My new friend Angelica settled herself on the carpet beside my leg. I smiled at her; any guilty thoughts of not calling the pound had vanished, although at some point I would have to take her to a vet to check her out.

Uncle Morgan didn't sound surprised at all when I called him last night. I said I had changed my mind, *again*, and I was willing to resume my training. He'd waited a moment, then said, "Schedule is changed tomorrow. Pinson and I will be over at 8:00." I'd said, "Okay," and that was it. We hung up as if nothing unusual had happened.

The grainy image of a baseball player flickered on the TV screen.

"Charley," Pinson said, "do you know who this is?" He pointed at the screen.

I squinted. "Ballplayer from the 50s?"

"Correct, sir. This film is from that time period. And who are we looking at?"

"Willie Mays, I think."

Pinson smiled. "Correct again."

Willie Mays was in the batter's box at an old stadium. He was practice-swinging, eyeing the pitcher, preparing for his next pitch. After a moment, Willie shot a homer over the left field fence.

"I had the good fortune to meet Mr. Mays at a baseball card convention when I was about twelve," Pinson said. "He smiled at me and shook my hand. A real gentleman, sir. A real gentleman."

"Sounds like he made quite an impression."

"Do you know what I remember most about our meeting?"

"No."

"I was tall for my age, one of the tallest in my class."

I glanced at Uncle Morgan. He returned a blank look.

"What I remember most," Pinson went on, "is how I could nearly look Willie Mays in the eye. He is *not* a big man. In fact, he is of quite average height and build. He played at one hundred eighty pounds."

Pinson waited, as if I was supposed to finish his thought and make his point for him. But I had no idea what he was driving at, so I remained silent and watched Willie at the bat as he faced a series of pitchers in different ballparks. Abruptly, the TV image changed and a different player was at the plate.

"Roberto Clemente was not a big man either," Pinson said, as he pointed to the screen. "He played at one hundred eighty-two pounds and was of average build, as well."

I watched Clemente smack a line drive into center field. His swing was fluid and smooth.

"Now watch this man," Pinson said.

Tony Perez, a Reds player from the 70s, appeared on the screen. He pounded a homer, a double, and another homer. I knew Tony Perez quite well. He was one of my dad's favorite players, and because of that, Tony was one of *my* favorite players, too. My dad called him *Big Dog*. I thought that name was cool.

"Perez is slightly taller and heavier than these other men," Pinson said, "but he is not an unusually large individual either."

"I see that, Pinson. What's the point?"

"You want to know why we are watching baseball."

"I like baseball. I don't mind watching some of the old players."

Pinson chuckled. "Not that old. Mays is the oldest, and he stopped playing in the 60s."

"Right. And Tony Perez was part of the Big Red Machine of the 70s. I know."

"The point here," Pinson said, "is even though these ballplayers, and many others, are of quite normal stature, they were able to connect a rounded piece of wood, with a small hard sphere propelled at ninety miles-per-hour by other men who were trying to make them miss."

"Okay..?"

"These hitters *launched* the baseball. Watch again."

I did. Willie swung and connected. Dave Concepcion, a slim Reds shortstop from the 70s, swatted a towering double. Tony Perez planted himself and blasted one over the fence. His swing was large and powerful, and yet projected a fluid, graceful elegance.

"Observe and learn. Part of this is timing. That cannot be underestimated. But these men also knew the power of their swings rested in their legs and hips. Arm strength, upper body strength, is all well and good, but the best hitters know how to put their best *leg* forward, so to speak."

I watched again. I hadn't noticed it before, but Pinson was right.

"See how Perez shifts his hips forward before anything else happens?"

"I do."

"Our greatest physical strength rests within the power of our *lower body*. The trick is to harness that power and channel it into the swing of a baseball bat. Or..?"

I thought for a second. "Or a golf club."

"Yes. And, Charley, remember, baseball players must also rely upon incredible reflexes. They react in an instant to adjust their stance and swing a bat around without any time to think. In golf, however, the ball is just...*there*. Unmoving. Golfers have the luxury of time, to think, to plan, to adjust, focus, and then swing."

"Putting, too?"

He smiled. "We'll get to putting tomorrow." He paused the DVD. "And we'll watch a bit more of this later."

"It's interesting," I said. And I meant it.

Pinson started toward the kitchen. He halted his step for a second and stretched.

I could see the brace under his t-shirt.

"Excuse me for a moment. I'll be right back," he said. A few seconds later, I heard the outside door swing open and shut.

Uncle Morgan stepped across the room and sat on the other end of the sofa. Angelica turned her head and watched his every move. "Well, needless to say, Charley, I'm glad you changed your mind."

"Needless to say."

He stared at me. "You have not been happy."

"Uh, well..."

"And I don't mean for just the last week or so." His smile vanished. His serious lawyer look was back.

"Yeah. That's not really a secret."

I heard a door open. Angelica turned her head toward the kitchen.

"I think my first mistake here was not telling you enough."

"Uncle Morgan—"

"I should have explained the plan in more detail. All of it. Exactly how the pieces are supposed to fit together. I hadn't counted on causing you more personal stress than you were having already."

"Hey, it's okay. I overreacted."

He shook his head. "It's been too much pressure, not enough answers, and all of it my fault."

"Forget it."

"Let me make it up to you."

"Nothing to make up for."

"How about a movie tonight?"

"Have to check my calendar. I'm extraordinarily busy."

"More *Star Trek* reruns on the tube, no doubt."

I chuckled. "If I watch long enough, I'm sure I'll finally see an episode I missed."

"We'll get something to eat afterwards. And I'll fill you in on the master plan."

"Can I have a beer at dinner?"

"No."

Pinson walked into the room. He was carrying two chrome-plated weights at his sides.

"These, sir, are dumbbells." He set the weights on the carpet, and then straightened. "One day we will have to research how dumbbells got their name."

"Maybe I'll ask Ray to do that for us," I said.

Uncle Morgan raised his eyebrows at me.

"Your uncle has obtained a membership for you at the

YMCA at the bottom of the hill, just on the other side of Springfield Pike."

I nodded. "I've walked past it."

"Part of your fitness program will be cardio. Three times per week, more if you are motivated, you will work on a stair-master, treadmill, rowing machine, or whatever you choose. Again, this work is for your general health and has no application specifically toward preparing for golf."

"Okay." I hated exercise lately, and I avoided it like I had always avoided steamed vegetables in the school cafeteria.

Pinson took a breath and stretched his back again. His lips grew tight as he tried to suppress the pain that was obviously bothering him. "*These* dumbbells, sir, *do* indeed have a specific golf objective. I have three more sets to bring in, and tomorrow afternoon I will demonstrate the program I have designed for you. But, briefly, you will use these weights here in the condo, each day, every day, at specified times, to increase the strength of your hand, wrist, shoulder, and leg muscles."

I forced a smile.

Pinson retrieved the TV remote from a small marble table beside the sofa. "Enough baseball."

Angelica scooted next to me on the floor.

"Shall we watch some golfers?" Pinson suggested.

"Sure."

"I consider swinging a wood or a wedge to be athletic in nature. There is a style and rhythm to it that requires correct balance, power distribution, and timing. These men are masters. Watch. Learn from them. Pay particular attention to the movement of their legs, hips."

"Like the ballplayers."

"Yes."

"And putting?"

He stared at me for a second, as if to confirm I was smart enough to recognize the difference. "Putting is the opposite. Cerebral. Existential."

"I'm thinking of Mrs. Morrison."

He nodded. "Her methods may not make much sense to you at first, but eventually, sir, her teachings will overwhelm you in a sudden rush of enlightenment."

I glanced over at Uncle Morgan. He nodded, as if to reassure me Pinson's genius was understood.

Pinson pressed a button on the remote, and a full spread of lush green filled the screen.

I wasn't sure what golf course, or even what country was being shown, but I immediately realized why millions of fans remained glued to their TV screens in the dead of winter to watch golf. Whispering announcers described the play-by-play accounts, as the golfers sweated in the inevitable sunshine and hit balls around paradise-like surroundings. I supposed it must have been the ultimate dream of a couch potato to live the life of a professional golfer. Sun. Warmth. Adoring fans. Money. And all because they could hit the ball farther and straighter than most everyone else.

The TV film focused on a man I recognized as Arnold Palmer. He looked to be in his late thirties and was lining up a shot on a stretch of flat emerald grass. I was pleased I knew *something* about golf. At least I could recognize Arnold Palmer. I thought of a blend of iced-tea and lemonade and wondered how famous I had to be to permanently have a *drink* named after me.

I leaned forward and placed my elbows on my knees. I was intrigued, and watched with fascination as Arnold Palmer brought his club back, angled his hips forward, and absolutely smashed his golf ball into the next time zone.

I felt a smile broaden across my face as I anticipated his next incredible shot.

Chapter 14

My Dinner with Uncle Morgan

We had just watched *Raiders of the Lost Ark* at the Springdale multiplex. I had it on DVD, but nothing equaled the thrill of *Raiders* on the enormous screen with Dolby sound; the John Williams score was fantastic and impossible to get out of my head.

"I like that movie every time I see it," Uncle Morgan said as he drove away from the theater.

"Me too."

"The best of the trilogy."

"It's not really a trilogy." I grumped. "Each story stands alone. They don't fit together."

"Have you seen the fourth one?"

"Nope. And I don't intend to."

Uncle Morgan eased the Escalade through a four-way stop near the Tri-County Mall and pulled into the parking lot of a Skyline Chili restaurant. Skyline was one of the two best reasons to live in Cincinnati. The aroma outside the door sent my taste buds racing. We found a table, ordered right away without looking at menus, and waited for our mid-evening feast to be delivered.

Three minutes later, the waitress set steaming oblong plates piled with spaghetti, chili, cheese, and onions in front of us. That selection is called a *four-way*. Uncle Morgan and I never varied from ordering that special concoction.

The chili tasted wonderful. I dropped a few oyster crackers into the mixture and crushed them with my fork. "You know, *Raiders* is in my top-five favorite films."

"Terrific movie."

"I think you can tell a great deal about a person from their top-five films list."

He studied my face. "Is that really *your* theory or someone else's?"

I dabbed my mouth with a napkin. "Sure. Why?"

"It sounds like something Sandy might say."

That startled me. I forgot how insightful Uncle Morgan could be. "Yes it does."

We were both quiet for a while.

"It wasn't a mistake for me to bring her into this," Uncle Morgan said.

"Sandy? No."

"I thought it would make you happy to see her. Eventually."

"It did. I mean, it does."

"I didn't realize how distracting she would be."

"I'm dealing."

"*Struggling* is more like it."

I poked my fork into the mound of chili and spaghetti. "I'm okay with it, Uncle Morgan. Really. It was just a shock at first. That's all."

"If you change your mind—"

"No. No, it's all right."

He stared at the table for a moment. "Okay. Okay. Let's talk about the plan."

"Sure." I popped another oyster cracker into my mouth and waited for Uncle Morgan to start.

"First, Mrs. Morrison. As she told you, her lessons are meant to help you clear your mind of everything. You won't worry about how you stand, how you grip the club, or how you swing. No distractions."

I figured he was referring to Sandy again.

He waited until I returned his gaze. "So when you are ready to swing the club, you will do so by *complete reflex*, and nothing will interfere with the way you have been trained."

"Uncle Morgan, she teaches Nigerian pole vaulting."

"Stick fighting."

"Whatever."

"The martial arts will help your concentration and self-confidence."

"We'll see."

He nodded. "Pinson will supervise your exercise program, teach you to swing a club and putt correctly. He will show you the way around a golf course. His instruction will include the lore of golf, rules and strategy, clothing and equipment."

"Speaking of equipment..."

"Mr. Tagawa?"

"Uh huh."

"We get your clubs in a couple weeks."

I set my empty glass on the table. "A question, please."

He rolled his eyes. "Here it comes."

"Uncle Morgan, he can't be, no, *you* can't be serious about me playing left *and* right-handed."

"Do you have a problem with that?"

"No more of a problem than me picking up your giant Cadillac over my head."

"You can play both ways, Charley."

"How?"

"Give it a chance. Mrs. Morrison and Pinson will train you."

"Of course they will."

He shifted, put his elbows on the table and leaned toward me. "Think of it this way. You're left-handed."

"Right. I mean, yes."

"And you've never played golf."

"Right again."

"So, you'll be starting from scratch from *both* sides of the ball. You'll learn both sides at once before you're stuck doing it only one way."

I pushed my plate aside and banged my forehead on the table.

"Charley. Charley?"

"I'm very busy right now."

"Listen to me, favorite nephew. Mental focus, constant practice, and perfect equipment will all combine. Nine months from now, maybe less, Charley Davis will be a household word in the golfing world."

"Charley Davis is two words."

He smiled. "Come on." He reached for the check. "Let's go

back to your place and visit with your weird dog."

"Hey. She's not weird."

"No?"

"Maybe a little."

"I've seen you with that beast, Charley."

"She's grown on me."

"The weirdest thing is how instantly attached she's gotten to you."

"Attached?"

"Ever see the way those amber eyes gaze at you?"

"She looks at everybody that way, Uncle Morgan."

He dropped a few bills on the table. We stood and started toward the door. As we stepped into the parking lot, my eyes filled with tears from the cold night air.

"I'll give it my best shot, Uncle Morgan. Promise."

He opened the car door. "All I can ask, Charley. All anybody can ask."

"And...and thanks."

"For?"

"Just thanks."

He smiled.

I smiled back.

We got into the Escalade, Uncle Morgan fired up the engine, and we headed down Springfield Pike toward Bonham.

Chapter 15

By the Time We Got to Woodstock

"Hold the stick like this," Mrs. Morrison said.

I squinted through the glare of morning sunshine. It was chilly, but fairly pleasant, at least compared to yesterday. Mrs. Morrison had taken us to a small grassy clearing in Glenwood Gardens. I could see the puffs of my breath in the air. I could also see Sandy behind the viewfinder of her camera about forty feet away.

"Charley. Please pay attention."

"Yes. Sorry, Mrs. Morrison."

"Study my grip. The stick is indented in two spots. Hold the stick lightly."

She held the black stick out to me. I took it from her. Grooves in the stick were still warm from her hands. The wood had a deep, glossy polish.

"You will have two sticks," Mrs. Morrison said. "This one is for practice. A second stick you'll carry with you."

"Carry?"

"It's collapsible and spring-loaded. Both are made of Ebony Gaboon, solid black, and the hardest wood on earth. It's used to make a few musical instruments, like the clarinet and the black keys on expensive pianos." She extended her arms. "Now give it back."

I placed the stick horizontally in her open palms.

"Now, Charley, please join me." She sat on the grass, folded her legs, and gestured for me to follow her example.

I did. "So that's not my stick?"

"I wanted you to see the stick and hold it before we got started." She set the stick on the ground beside her. "Each morning we will begin with green tea, music, and meditation.

Have you ever meditated?"

"I've over-meditated a few times, in college." I knew it was a mistake to say that even before I finished the sentence. For a reason unknown to me, however, I couldn't help it.

Mrs. Morrison scowled at me. "Humor has its place. This is not that place."

"Sorry."

"I don't want to remind you of that over and over. It makes me feel like a teacher reprimanding an incorrigible student."

"You're right. It won't happen again."

She shook her head. "I know your mind works that way, Charley, but try to *focus and concentrate* here. Nothing will work unless you accomplish this first step."

"I'll hold the jokes, Mrs. Morrison. Promise."

She opened an old-looking plaid thermos and poured a steaming liquid into a ceramic mug painted with an orange peace symbol. "Here."

I gripped the handle and raised the mug to my lips.

"Green tea will aid your concentration."

I took a few sips. "This is pretty good, especially on a cold morning."

"No cold, Charley. *There is no cold.*"

I studied her expression. Her brown-eyed stare seemed to penetrate my skin. I shivered. "You're *not* cold, are you?"

Her familiar sleeveless dress fully exposed her arms and shoulders to the morning chill. She had to be into serious mind control, and it seemed to be working, at least for her.

She took a sip of green tea. "Please remove your footwear and assume this meditation position."

I pulled off my low-rise hiking boots and my socks. The air felt surprisingly good against my bare feet.

"Now, the *music*." She pressed the button on her CD player. The steady rhythm of guitar chords shattered the morning stillness.

"Is that Crosby, Stills and Nash?" I asked. "My mom listened to 60s music when I was a kid, in the car, in the house. All the time."

"Close. It's Buffalo Springfield."

I thought about music. "My dad was into *Broadway*. I used

to sit on a stack of old tires in our garage and listen to him wail away on Broadway ballads as he tinkered around with his enormous '63 Bonneville."

"Sounds like a pleasant memory."

"Yeah." I cleared my throat. "Mrs. Morrison, do you mind if I ask you something...before we start the meditation thing?"

"Ask."

"Why the hippie music?"

She placed her upturned palms on her knees. "The 60s are known for music that changed the world. Did you know that?"

"No. I mean, I don't think so."

"It wasn't the tune or melody of each song that was terribly different from songs of any other generation. But the words, Charley, the *words* were different. The words told stories of protest, freedom, and love."

"Like this one?"

"Know the name of this song?"

I thought for a second. "Don't think so."

"*For What It's Worth*. That, Charley, is the *perfect* name for a protest song. It expresses anti-war ideas with plain, simple language, without anything rude or inflammatory. Just take the words for their simple meaning. That's why this song was so hard for *the establishment* to ignore. Ordinary words, with a catchy tune and a good musical arrangement. It was genius, in its own way."

"I get that, but why are we listening to it?"

"The 60s were years of mental enlightenment. It wasn't just drugs, although that was part of it. Truth is, it was the *music* that moved the people. It was a common rallying cry. The music opened our minds and led us into productive thought. It's original. Rebellious." She gazed at me. "Do you understand?"

"Not really."

She shifted her back and took a breath. Her eyes looked a little wild. "My generation was the only group of young people who changed the world through non-violent protest. We saw our friends and relatives sent to war, not come back, and for no apparent good reason. So, and for the first time in modern history, students marched, protested, sang songs and carried signs. And we caused such a stir that Nixon finally had enough.

He couldn't withstand the daily bad media publicity. And then it was only a matter of time, after four students were gunned down at Kent State."

"That's a different song."

"Right. And that one *is* by Crosby, Stills and Nash."

"Yeah."

"I hope that answers your question, Charley."

I nodded.

"Good. Then, let's get started. First, we meditate. Then, we'll work with the sticks."

I watched Mrs. Morrison close her eyes and settle into position. My stomach felt queasy. Though I now understood the importance of 60s protest songs, I still had no idea why we were listening to them, or how they would help my golf game.

I looked across the clearing. Angelica sat with her back up against the trunk of a large tree. Her eyes were closed and I could hear the strange whining she makes when she is sleeping.

Sandy and Ray stood a bit farther away, just beyond Angelica's tree. Ray looked through the camera lens. Sandy was turned toward the blacktopped path. She dabbed at her eyes with a tissue.

"Now close your eyes, Charley," Mrs. Morrison said.

I did.

"I want you to count in your head. Count backward from forty-three to zero."

"Why forty-three?"

"Jim Morrison's draft number."

My eyes snapped open.

"Breathe," she said. "Steady, even breaths."

I shut my eyes again, inhaled, and tried to clear my mind. I knew it wouldn't work, and the whole thing seemed pointless. But I hoped my afternoon session with Pinson would make just a fraction more sense.

It was almost impossible it would not.

***

Ninety minutes passed like six hours. I counted backwards. I breathed. I tried to think of nothing, which was, of course, impossible. I listened to endless hippie music: *Get Together, Live for Today, Ohio, Revolution #9, Helter Skelter*, some song that sounded like *In I Gotta Dive India*, or something. By that time, I was ready to jump up and start screaming from the total absurdity of it all.

The meditation had done nothing for me. I tried not to feel the cold, but the air continued to chill my skin. I could not ignore a low-grade hunger and a gnawing thirst no matter how much I tried not to think about food and water. And I still felt entirely foolish sitting barefoot, cross-legged in the woods at the beginning of winter. Part of Mrs. Morrison's technique must have worked, though, since after about thirty minutes, I could no longer feel my legs. They were completely numb.

"Open your eyes, Charley."

I did. Mrs. Morrison was still there, exactly as before. Angelica, Sandy and Ray were nearby. The only thing changed was that my legs were no longer in the building.

"How did that feel to you?"

"Interesting."

"Good. Now, let's stand and face each other."

I pushed myself to my feet. It wasn't easy.

"Take the stick." She handed me the polished ebony.

I took it and tried not to wobble. My feet were tingling from the sudden rush of blood.

"We will begin this way each time. First, we stand from six to seven feet apart. Like this." She took her own fighting stick and backed up a few steps.

I saw the muscles ripple in her shoulders.

"Now, a short, respectful bow." She bowed.

I did the same. It was ridiculous.

"Grasp the stick in both hands, like this, and prepare for battle."

I mimicked her. *Battle?*

"Now, are you ready?"

I froze for a second. I suppose I could have said I wasn't ready, but instead I just said, "Yes, ma'am."

"Then, we begin."

Lightning fast, she swung her stick around and stopped it an inch from the side of my head before I had moved even a fraction. Then she backed the stick away and resumed her preparatory position. "Speed and control."

"Yeah. I can see that."

"So. Again."

We faced each other. I gripped the stick with both hands. It felt light but incredibly solid.

"Come at me first this time, Charley."

I gritted my teeth. "Okay."

"Hold the stick any way you like."

I nodded, took the stick at one end with both hands and balanced it on my shoulder. I had played baseball in grade school, was a pretty fair hitter. And Pinson had just shown me that video. Maybe I was meant to use a baseball swing kind of technique.

Our gazes met. Her face told me nothing. I spread my feet as I would if I were standing in the batter's box.

"Charley. Now."

I tried not to notice, but I couldn't help but see Sandy and Ray watching from the other side of the clearing. My stomach twitched. I took a breath, gave Mrs. Morrison the best Clint Eastwood squinty stare I could manage, and swung. The ebony stick whisked around and hit nothing but air.

"Charley. I will say something now that I will repeat a thousand times." She waited until she had my attention. "Remember. No emotion. No feeling of any kind. No thought. No planning. Just cold resolve. *Cold, frozen resolve.* Masters of Nigerian stick fighting perfect their craft by *reflex*. You must do the same, when we practice with the sticks, and when Pinson manages your golf techniques. Let your body lead the way and perform the work, both here and on the golf course."

"No planning."

"After enough practice, you will instinctively know what to do, how to attack, how to defend, without conscious analysis."

"Cold resolve," I said, and I was surprised at how much I liked that phrase. It felt good to say *cold resolve*.

"Now," Mrs. Morrison said, "I will attack, first one method, then a second, and so on. Try to defend my attacks with your stick. I want you to see the unstoppable power of Ebony Gaboon when used by someone properly trained."

I nodded.

"Ready yourself." She spun before I could even grunt, and the stick flashed about, just above the ground. It halted at the edge of my right ankle.

"Wow," I said.

"Yes."

"And I'm supposed to do that?"

"In time."

"I don't want to sound negative, Mrs. Morrison, but I can't see myself doing that, I mean, as good as you are."

"Now I will attack."

"Mrs. Morrison..."

"I have the nerve to challenge you, to threaten you. That is something you must not abide. Cannot. Harness your strength. Defend yourself."

I had just enough time to see her shoulders flex. Then the black stick rifled through space and froze at the base of my forehead, just above my eyes.

Mrs. Morrison lowered the stick and took a step back. *Turn Turn Turn* by The Byrds started on her CD player.

"Now you," she said.

I instantly gave up trying to figure out how I was supposed to master this stick fighting. Apparently, this was leading toward a method of swinging a golf club by reflex. At least, that's what Mrs. Morrison said.

I gripped the stick firmly in both hands and caught a glimpse of Sandy still watching from the edge of the clearing. Ray wrote in a notepad.

I brought my eyes up and stared at Mrs. Morrison again. Her face was blank. No emotion. *Cold resolve.*

I balanced myself into what I hoped was a correct stance, took a breath, and tried to empty my mind, or harness my strength, or whatever. This was impossible for me, and I had no expectation it would work. But Mrs. Morrison was waiting and Sandy was watching.

The stick felt warm in my hands as I lunged forward.

Chapter 16

Tuesday in the Park with Pinson

The pasture looked as though a hailstorm had just blown through. Little white jawbreakers lay everywhere.

For the first twenty minutes, my success at hitting them was awful. Most times I missed. I made occasional contact with a jawbreaker but knocked it only a few feet, and then usually at ankle level way off to the right. A few times, I accidentally connected the right way, and the small spheres went flying into outer space. The jawbreakers traveled only about forty or fifty yards, but it sure *felt* longer when I swung hard and I heard the club clink the round candy the way it was supposed to.

"Better," Pinson said.

"Thanks."

Uncle Morgan had dropped us off at the stables and then left for his office. The air was about forty degrees, but the sun made it warmer, and I felt pleasant standing in the hilly pasture.

For the last two hours, I swung Uncle Morgan's Callaway metal wood. Sandy and Ray were set up nearby, as always, filming my endless swings. White jawbreakers salted the green hillside. Angelica was asleep, flat on her back, near a sycamore tree. And the pasture was filled with 60s music from Pinson's MP3 player: Beatles, Stones, Hendrix, Cream, and many others. A relentless stream of psychedelic music. Nine months from now, I could easily host my own 60s hits radio show.

"Pinson, could we take a break?"

"Certainly, sir."

"Because I can barely grip this club. My hands are cramping."

"Let's sit for a few minutes."

I nodded.

Pinson walked with me toward Angelica. The black dog remained motionless as Pinson and I sat on the grass near the tree. He straightened his back and his face crinkled with a sudden pain. His attempt to disguise his discomfort wasn't working, but I didn't say anything.

He flattened his palms on the grass behind him and looked across the meadow toward the two barns. "Angelica is quite a dog."

"I know."

"You saved her from the end many dogs face when left in a shelter too long."

"Well, I didn't really-"

"You are lucky to have her." He glanced in her direction.

"Yeah."

"She instantly became your friend."

I nodded. "Yes."

"Did you know, Charley, dogs like people for who they are, and not necessarily for what they can get from them?"

"I didn't."

"Dogs and dolphins."

"Dolphins? Really?"

"Angelica is *your friend*, is she not?"

I tilted my head. Angelica was still sprawled on her back against the tree, her legs splayed in all directions. The girl had no shame. I smiled. "She *is* my friend."

"It's obvious. Angelica is devoted to you. The longer you stay together, the greater your devotion will be for each other."

"I can believe that."

He took a breath. "I have a friend of my own."

"You mean a dog?"

"*Rusty* is my friend," he said.

I thought for a second. "Rusty..?"

"I rescued him from the side of the road years ago on a rainy morning."

My computer research came flooding back. "The retriever."

"We were instantly bonded."

"Pinson, I, uh, I read about the bank robberies."

"I never stole anything."

"Even so."

"He was a *symbol*."

"Pinson, you've been in jail for the past four years."

"Seems longer."

"Where has Rusty been?"

"My parents were happy to keep him."

I considered that. "Maybe we could arrange a play date. Angelica might like to have a doggie friend of her own."

He straightened his back and winced again. "Maybe."

I nodded. "They might be fun to watch."

"Indeed."

My eyes tracked across the meadow where a young woman jogged through the grass.

"Charley?" Pinson said. "You're staring."

"Yeah..?"

"I don't blame you. She is pretty."

She looked strong, and she climbed the hills with ease.

"I guess."

She ran closer but didn't seem to notice us. She was the kind of girl I never stood a chance with, but was exactly the kind of girl I always wanted back in high school. I watched as she rounded a small rise, continued through the meadow, and disappeared into the trees.

"Sir, our break is over." Pinson grimaced and pushed himself up.

"Aye, Captain."

My eyes shifted. Sandy stared at me from across the meadow, hands on her hips. It was amazing; I hadn't thought of her once for the last few minutes. I'd set a new world's record.

"You coming, sir?"

I shook my head and stood up. Angelica's amber eyes followed me as I grabbed the Callaway that rested against the tree. I stepped toward the center of the meadow. The afternoon sun warmed my face. Pinson dropped a jawbreaker at my feet. I tried to empty my mind like Mrs. Morison wanted, and forget about Sandy, the girl jogger, my uncle, Angelica, and everything else. Of course, that didn't work at all.

I stared down at the candy, took a breath, brought the club back, and swung.

Chapter 17

Something in the Way She Talks

Mrs. Morrison was frustrated. She didn't say anything, but I could tell. Her blank, stony expression could only hide so much. I was doing everything wrong; I had dropped the stick, tripped on tiny twigs, slipped on any blade of grass that was even remotely wet with morning dew, and I let my attention stray to Sandy every forty-three seconds. I took a quick break and scratched Angelica's head, even though I wasn't sure Angelica liked it. And I didn't seem to be improving much, with either the stick fighting or the impossible task of emptying my mind.

But through all my failings, Mrs. Morrison kept trying. She was steady, assured, and relentless. The music played on, all Janis Joplin this morning, and we flailed at each other with the black sticks. I never could find an opening. Not once. It felt as though I were a five-year-old boxing with his dad. I had no chance. By the time Janis had given up each and every last piece of her heart, for about the sixth time, I was completely exhausted.

When our session was over, Mrs. Morrison drove Angelica and me back to the condo. I had about an hour before Pinson was to show up, so I changed out of my sweaty clothes, made a sandwich, and sat on the lawn with Angelica at my side. It was about fifty degrees, even warmer than yesterday. Weird November weather.

I finished my PB&J and started running a brush through Angelica's thick black fur. She sat motionless and watched the traffic on Springfield Pike. Her head turned toward Bonham. I followed her gaze. Sandy's van turned the corner, headed my way. My chest tightened as if a python had my ribs in a death grip.

The van parked and Sandy stepped onto the blacktop. She came toward me with that easy, confident walk that belonged only to her. "Hi."

"Hey."

"Mind if I sit?"

"No. I mean, sure. Sit."

She flashed a smile and sat beside me. "Angelica looks happy."

"You can tell?"

"You're *brushing* her."

Sandy's emerald eyes took every bit of my breath. "She might just be tolerating it."

Sandy stared at me for a moment. "You look cute."

Time stood still. The universe stopped spinning.

"What...I..."

She shook her head. "I shouldn't have said that."

"Sandy-"

"I meant you just looked so cute sitting here in the grass with your dog."

My heart raced. I caught the scent of body lotion that was definitely not patchouli.

"Look," she said, "I came here to talk. We were supposed to talk."

"I remember."

"I get easily distracted sometimes."

"It's *all the time* for me."

"I've been watching you, Charley."

"Obviously. It's your job."

She rubbed Angelica behind one ear. "The camera does not lie."

"Really? They say those films of Apollo 11 were faked."

"Charley-"

"Like the moon landing was shot in a warehouse in Roswell."

"I'm not kidding."

"Area 51 and all."

She shook head again. "You can't quit it, can you?"

"Quit what?"

"Relentless sarcasm."

"I'm...trying."

"Are you?"

"I'm sorry. I really need to stop. It's like I'm on a twelve-step plan, but the first step is icy and I can't get my footing. I know you don't like it."

She shifted around and stared at me. "*You* don't like it, Charley. *You* don't."

I considered that. "No?"

"You use sarcasm as a defense mechanism, to suppress your true feelings."

"Sandy—"

"Then it makes you feel even worse."

"No-"

"And it's because of me."

"What are you saying?"

"It's because of me."

We fell silent for a few moments. I listened to the sound of cars passing by. None of this was her fault.

"I look through the lens and can barely keep from crying. Your face...you look so tired, so *defeated*."

"That's not true."

"Yes. It is. You're only twenty-five, and sometimes...you look much *older*." She tilted her head back and closed her eyes.

"Okay," I said. "I'll try."

"Try?"

"No sarcasm."

"That's not it."

"I don't-"

"Have you even *thought about it*, Charley?"

"About what?"

"What's really bothering you?"

I slowly brought my eyes up. Bogart's voice suddenly echoed in my head, and I said, "Nothing you can't fix."

She stared at me. "That's not fair."

"Sandy, I..."

She stood quickly and turned to go. Then she twisted back around. "*The Big Sleep*. Right?"

I nodded. "Last line."

She nodded back. "Good line."

I stood. "The lines sound better coming from Bogart."

"Charley, I came here to apologize."

"No reason to, Sandy. I never wanted that."

"I'm saying it anyway."

"Okay."

"So, I'm sorry."

"Accepted."

"That I hurt you."

"Done."

She smiled. "You've always been sweet that way."

"I've changed recently. Stick fighting barefoot in the woods has changed me."

"No. You're still the same sweet guy."

"You're the director."

"Look, I've got to go set up." She took a breath. "See you later, at the stables."

I reached out and tapped the sleeve of her denim jacket. I couldn't believe I had touched her. "I was never mad at you."

Her eyes moistened. "See you in a little bit."

She bent and stroked Angelica's head one more time, then walked back to her van. I wanted to get up and run after her. But I didn't. I knew in about thirty minutes, I would see her again in the pasture. She would be looking through her camera lens as I tried to blast little white jawbreakers to kingdom come.

And now, the very thought made me smile.

Chapter 18

Putting in the Grass is a Gas

We got into a steady routine over the next few weeks. Three hours or so in the woods with Mrs. Morrison started every morning. We sat on cold ground with our eyes closed, breathed deeply, and emptied our minds. Or, at least, Mrs. Morrison emptied her mind. My mind was never empty. I didn't understand. It seemed impossible to not feel the cold, the sun, or the breeze, and to not think of anything. And, of course, the hippie music never stopped.

Then, after about forty-five minutes of useless sitting in an uncomfortable position, we started with the black sticks. At the beginning of our second week, Mrs. Morrison presented me with my very own weapon. It was a black twelve-inch baton that instantly sprung into a solid four-foot stick of Ebony Gaboon at the press of a hidden button. I had to admit, the thing was pretty nasty, and could do a lot of damage in the hands of somebody other than me who really knew how to swing it around.

At the end of each morning meditation and stick-fighting session, I usually jogged back to the condo and shared lunch with Angelica. If the weather was right, we ate outside on the grass. She would stretch out and press as close to me as she could. She never complained, never asked for anything. She would just stare at me constantly with her incredible amber eyes.

After lunch, the single peaceful, sane part of my day, I would drive up the hill to the field of horse dreams, or, as I had come to call it, Jawbreaker Mountain. Pinson dropped the little white spheres at my feet, one at a time, and I swung at them with Uncle Morgan's club. Sometimes I missed. Sometimes I hit the things. Pinson rarely said anything at all, other than, "Try again." No instruction on holding the club, standing, or how to swing.

At the end of the afternoon, I would walk down to the fitness center across the Pike and run on a treadmill for about fifty minutes. I managed to convince the trainers to allow Angelica to come inside with me. They looked into her eyes and couldn't refuse, like she was a vampire dog with hypnotic powers or something. It was spooky, even to me.

Back at the condo after my cardio workout, I was starving, but I had to complete Pinson's weight training as I ran through shoulder raises, forearm curls, thigh lunges, and a bunch of others, three sets of each. When I finished, I was almost too tired to eat dinner, but since it was time to feed Angelica, she and I ate together. It was comforting to know we somehow depended on each other. She depended on me for food and shelter, and I depended on her for companionship.

This afternoon, Pinson was apparently going to begin his putting instruction. Uncle Morgan had arranged for two putting greens to be designed and groomed at the far end of a pasture at the stables. When I got there, Pinson was waiting for me at the small gravel parking area.

"Afternoon, sir," Pinson said as I got out of my car.

I really didn't like it when Pinson called me *sir*. It was as if he were my butler, or something. "Hey, Pinson."

"Hi, Angelica." Pinson bent and scratched her head. "I have someone who wants to meet you."

I glanced at Pinson's car, a white Toyota Camry that Uncle Morgan let him borrow. I saw a furry golden head looking out through the rear window. "You brought Rusty."

"Dog introductions."

I had no idea how Angelica might react. I hoped Rusty knew how to take care of himself, just in case.

Pinson opened the rear door of the Camry. Rusty's head bobbed into view. His face was beautiful, with well-defined, masculine lines. And his fur was long and flowing, burnished a deep golden-red.

"Come on out, Russell," Pinson said.

Rusty sat quite still, his eyes fixed on Angelica.

"Russell. Come."

The Golden slowly inched one paw forward over the tan leather seat. Then, without taking his eyes from Angelica, Rusty jumped to the ground and sat at Pinson's feet.

"Good boy." Pinson stepped over to me and Rusty did not move. "Look at them."

I did. "They're just staring. Don't dogs usually sniff around at each other when they first meet?"

Pinson looked at the two dogs. "Usually."

"So, what now?"

"You learn to putt. The dogs will introduce themselves when they are ready."

The four of us trekked across the pasture, Angelica at my side and Rusty only inches from Pinson. White jawbreakers were everywhere. The dogs ignored them. We reached the end of the pasture and broke through a stand of sycamore trees.

"These are greens." Pinson made a sweeping gesture with one hand, as if he were a real estate agent showing me a new property. He held one golf club in his other hand.

"They're brown," I said.

"It's the end of November in Ohio."

"But we still call them greens?"

"Yes."

"I understand."

The greens didn't look like much to me. The grass was cut short within two kidney-shaped areas.

"Here, Charley."

I walked beside Pinson and stopped. He handed the club to me. I took it.

"Putting is different," he said.

"The *club* is a little different."

"It is quite a simple design. This club has a tapered steel shaft and a smallish titanium head."

"Sounds like an alien who stars in porn films."

"Charley."

"Yeah, I know. Sorry."

"Please listen to me very carefully, because if you grasp the vital importance of the art of putting, your journey to the top will be a great deal easier."

"Putting is an art?"

He nodded. "More games are won or lost on the greens than anywhere else on a golf course."

"You told me that."

"It cannot be overemphasized."

"Okay."

"If you can manage to get to the green in two, do you know what happens next?"

"I don't know what *getting to the green in two* means."

He put his hands on his hips. "You hit the ball twice and it lands on the green."

"Oh."

"What happens next?"

"Well, I guess I try to putt the ball into the hole."

Pinson folded his arms across his chest. "And if you manage to get the ball into the cup with one or two putts?"

"Then, I've done good?"

He nodded.

"So, what's the right way to putt?"

"Putting is mentally much harder than any tee shot or fairway drive. It takes planning, vision."

"Or, the opposite of Mrs. Morrison's philosophy."

"Not really. Yes, you will have to keenly observe the tilt of the ground, the edges of the turf, the direction the grass bends. Greens have ups and downs, curves and angles. Weather affects the speed of the ball, cold, heat, rain, and wind. The ball will travel accordingly. Your putt needs to be planned with these things taken into account."

"Sounds complicated."

"Yes, sir. That is correct."

"Mrs. Morrison wants me to live in the 60s and *empty* my mind."

"I know."

I blinked. "I'm lost again."

Pinson directed his eyes to me. "Let's try one, step by step."

"Pinson, before we start this, am I expected to putt from both sides?"

"Yes."

"Blindfolded?"

"Eventually."

I felt my stomach twist in frustration. "Well, excuse me,

but what about the grass, the angles, the curves?"

Pinson tapped the sides of his thighs with his fingers. "Come with me."

I followed him to the edge of the green.

"Stop here." Pinson stepped onto the green, and dropped a golf ball on the turf, about thirty feet from the hole. "Now. Here is where the putt starts for you. Before, sir, before you even step onto the green."

Pinson had that *Mrs. Morrison* look in his eyes.

"Your approach to the green is not a leisurely stroll where you appreciate the warm weather and greet the gallery with a smile and a casual wave."

"Gallery?"

"Fans."

"I don't have fans, Pinson."

He grinned, and it looked odd on his face. "Not yet, sir. Not yet."

"So."

"So. As you near the green, you take it all in. You observe the weather, the breeze, and all the factors I mentioned. You bend or crouch to the ground and appreciate all you can see. You reach the cup and bend to the turf again, to ensure you haven't missed anything. No putt is taken for granted, even a putt inches from the cup. Then, and only then, you stand confidently, lightly grip your putter, and..."

I waited.

He stared at me with his palms upturned, as if I should know the answer.

Then it hit me. "Close my eyes."

"Yes."

"I close my eyes."

"Yes."

"I putt with my eyes closed."

"Actually, you will be blindfolded."

"Oh God."

"And with your eyes closed, you empty your mind."

"Of course."

"The world will disappear for you."

"Mrs. Morrison will be so proud."

"And the right putt will follow by reflex."

"How did I know you were going to say that?"

"It makes sense."

"Maybe in the Bizarro World."

"So. Charley. Let's try a few."

I took a breath and let it out. Angelica was still beside me, her head only inches from my leg. I smiled down at her, gripped the putter, and stepped onto the green.

Chapter 19

A Little More Canine Conversation

It was the first of December and the weather still had not turned. The days were generally sunny with temperatures from the high 30s to the low 50s. My sessions outside with Mrs. Morrison and Pinson were reasonably comfortable, except for a couple brief rainstorms. But the bottom had to drop out eventually. The sub-zeros and snow were absolutely on their way.

That was why Uncle Morgan announced yesterday we had two more weeks here. Then, the whole gang was driving to South Carolina, where the sun would still be shining and the weather at least tolerable through the next few months. It would be a twelve-hour drive. Twelve hours from Cincinnati to Seabrook Island, near Charleston. Twelve hours of driving, restaurants, rest stops, and canine potty breaks, all with Mrs. Morrison sitting next to me.

I wondered how I could sneak a case of Coors and four bags of Doritos into my duffle bag. It was probably the only way I could get through it and retain any part of my sanity.

Today I finished my morning meditation and stick fighting routine and was back at the condo with Angelica. We sat on the lawn and silently watched the cars breeze by at the bottom of the hill on Springfield Pike. I had actually grazed Mrs. Morrison this morning with my Nigerian weapon. I faked to my left and jabbed straight ahead, kind of like a basketball move I perfected in junior high. The end of the stick touched Mrs. Morrison's left hip. She paused, smiled at me, and bowed.

I really didn't know what to think about that. I had been feeling better handling the fighting stick, but grazing Mrs. Morrison this morning was probably a fluke, a lucky break and nothing more. Or, she *let* it happen, trying to instill some self-confidence in me. God knows I could use some. Most of the time with Mrs. Morrison I felt as effective as a one-legged man in a sack race.

I was brushing Angelica when she looked to her left. I looked too. A girl limped toward us, through the grass on the condo complex front lawn. She wore a sleeveless T-shirt and jogging shorts. The solid muscles in her arms and legs flexed as she approached. She was the same girl I had seen jogging by here, and up at the stables, a few times before.

"Hello," she said.

"Hi." I stood.

Angelica did not move.

The girl smiled. "Do you live here?"

"Yep."

She gazed down at Angelica. "Oh wow."

"This is my dog."

"He is *something*."

"She."

"She? Oh."

"Yeah."

"She's still something."

"She was a code breaker during the war. Then worked cold-case homicide for Columbus PD, until recently. She's spending her retirement with me."

The girl smiled again, and then winced. "Ow." Her right ankle was obviously bothering her. "Is it okay to sit for a few seconds?"

"Uh, sure."

"I twisted my ankle back by the Civic Center. Tried to run it off, but it finally caught up with me." She sat.

I sat with her and stared. I tried not to look like I was staring but it was impossible. She was gorgeous in that athletic, always fit, always perfect, just right proportions, and lustrous eyes sort of way.

"Hey," I said. "You know, I've got some ice inside."

She looked at me. "Really?"

"It comes with the freezer."

She shook her head. "I'll be okay. I just need to sit for a

few."

"Nonsense." I stood again. "Stay here with Angelica. I'll be right back."

She winced as she rubbed the Achilles tendon on her right ankle. "Angelica?" She removed her shoe and sock.

"Right."

"You must have named her when she was a puppy, when, you know, she was *puppy* cute."

"Not really."

"Because *Angelica*? For *this* dog?"

I took a breath. "You have to get to know her. Just wait here."

"If you don't mind..." She stood and wobbled. "I'd rather come with you. I shouldn't sit for too long. It will stiffen up."

I shrugged. "Sure."

We started toward my condo door.

"This is nice of you," she said.

"Yeah, well."

"Most people wouldn't get involved."

"I'm fairly strange."

"Really?"

"My favorite meal is a Swanson fried chicken frozen dinner."

She laughed. "The kind with the apple cobbler?"

"Yes. *The apple cobbler*. It makes the soggy fried chicken almost worth it."

We stopped outside my kitchen door. I extended my hand to her. "I'm Charley."

"Oh. Scarlett."

We shook hands. Her name was *Scarlett*. I had never known anyone named *Scarlett*. "Pleased to meet you."

"Yeah."

My breathing had already stopped, so it couldn't stop again, but the idea I was at my door, shaking hands with a beautiful injured female named *Scarlett* was about enough to rocket me through the ionosphere and into orbit. "You want to wait here?"

Her eyes crinkled with a smile. "Nope."

"Okay then."

We stepped into the kitchen. With a slight groan, Scarlett sat in a chair at the table.

"One second." I folded some ice cubes in a dishtowel and handed the bundle to her.

"Thanks." She bent and pressed the chilled towel to her ankle. "Nice place."

"It's okay." I leaned back against the counter near the sink. I couldn't decide what to do with my hands. A wave of nerves hit me.

"I can't believe I did this," she said.

"It happens."

She squinted up at me and shook her head. "Not to me."

"You'll be fine."

"I feel so stupid. Big hole in the ground. A *blind* woman could have seen it."

"I smashed my finger in a car door once."

"Yeah?"

"Now *that* was stupid."

She chuckled. Then she watched Angelica pad across the tile floor toward the refrigerator. "What's he doing?"

"She."

"She's squishing herself. Backwards. Look."

"Time for her nap."

"What?"

"That's where she sleeps, between the fridge and the wall. Maybe she feels safer in there, since she's all boxed in."

Scarlett shook her head. "She looks so, well, *dangerous*. Those golden eyes glow in the center of all that black fur."

"Actually, she's quite affectionate."

"Huh."

"Goes to show it's wrong to judge a book by its cover." I chuckled at my own cleverness.

"Do you always speak in clichés?"

"You're not just whistling Dixie."

She flashed a quick grin at me, stood up and put weight on her ankle. "I should go."

"Now?"

"Yes. I need to walk."

"Can I drive you somewhere?"

"That's pretty silly since I said I needed to walk."

"Oh. Right. It's just that—"

"My car is near the library. I'll be fine."

"Okay."

She hobbled toward the door, turned and looked straight at me. "What do you think about ice cream?"

I blinked and wondered if I could have heard that last sentence right. "I like ice cream."

"Me too."

"Haven't had any lately."

"Tomorrow night?"

"What's tomorrow night?"

"Ice cream. With me."

"You...and me?"

"Yes. Gosh, do I need to be more direct?"

"No. I mean, yes. Ice cream."

She gazed at me for a second. "You know, I don't usually do this sort of thing."

"Have ice cream?"

"Ask a guy out for ice cream after knowing him for less than ten minutes."

"Yeah. That's fast for me too."

"But," she said, "you know what they say?"

"What do they say?"

"He who hesitates is lost."

I watched her eyes sparkle. "They also say haste makes waste."

"Contradictory clichés."

"I know."

She smiled. "Pick you up at 7:00."

Without waiting for any response she handed the cold towel to me and limped outside. I followed and watched her move slowly down the concrete walkway. When she reached the grass, she turned back and looked at me. "Do you have a last name?"

"Davis."

"Perry."

"Scarlett Perry?"

"Yep."

"Cool name."

"Thanks."

"Welcome."

"See you tomorrow night, Charley."

"Sounds good, Scarlett."

She smiled again, put her right hand on her hip and nodded. "Code breaker during the war?"

I shrugged.

She waved over her shoulder and limped away. I turned back inside and collapsed on the sofa. Angelica followed me into the den and sat on the other end of the sofa. Her head rested on a pillow.

Scarlett Perry. I'm going to have ice cream tomorrow night with *Scarlett Perry.*

I switched on the TV but didn't really see anything on the screen. Angelica crawled beside me and settled. Jessica Lange and Sally Field appeared, flushed and crying. Probably the Lifetime channel.

Scarlett Perry. She was a few years older than me, if I had to guess, maybe twenty-seven or twenty-eight. And I was having ice cream with her tomorrow night. I had no idea what I would talk to her about, but I still couldn't get her out of my head. Maybe I should plan the conversation, prepare something clever, so I wouldn't have to be worried about awkward silences.

I wondered where Sandy would be spending tomorrow night. I wondered if by gigantic coincidence she might see me out having ice cream with Scarlett Perry.

Something's not right.

I looked down at Angelica. "Maybe..."

Don't you?

"Don't I what?"

Get weird vibes?

Angelica was now pressed tightly against my right leg, her eyes fixed on the TV screen. Just like any other dog, except she wasn't like any other dog. *Something about that girl.*

"Scarlett?"

Scarlett.

"What about her?"

You tell me.

I thought for a moment. "She seems nice."

Pretty.

"Yes. Pretty."

Very pretty.

"Your point?"

No point.

"Yes there is."

She yawned and never took her eyes from the TV. *Think.*

"I'll try."

When was the last time an incredibly attractive female, and a complete stranger, made advances.

"To me?"

Can't remember?

"I'm still thinking."

There isn't a last time.

"Give me a second."

Never happened.

"So, it's impossible that a cool looking girl might come on to me?"

Not impossible.

"But..?"

Unlikely.

"Unlikely."

That's all.

"No it's not."

Think.

I didn't want to think about it. I didn't want to think about golf, or Zero Tagawa, or Squeaky Morrison. All I wanted to do was put Sandy Carson, Jawbreaker Mountain, and everything else far out of my head for as long as possible and only think about having ice cream tomorrow night with Scarlett Perry.

Somehow, though, I didn't think a girl named Scarlett and even a gallon of ice cream would be enough.

Chapter 20

Scarlett in Blue Jeans

Graeter's ice cream is, hands down, the best ice cream in the world, and along with Skyline Chili, the *other* best thing about Cincinnati. To be more exact, the ice cream itself is terrific, no question, but no better than many other great ice creams of the world. What sets Graeter's apart is not necessarily the ice cream part of the ice cream, but rather the *chips*: the huge, thick, incredibly spectacular semi-sweet dark chocolate chips. They are, as those who just started Weight Watchers are bound to say, *to die for*.

Scarlett picked me up in a classic 1968 Corvette. It was easily the coolest car I had ever been fortunate enough to ride in. It had been repainted with great care: a deep, shimmering red. I nestled into the black leather passenger seat, pushed aside a stack of manila file folders on the floor near my feet, stared at Scarlett as she shifted the gears, and thought I had found an early express route to heaven.

With little more than a hello and a smile, Scarlett guided the muscle car up Galbraith Road to the Graeter's in Finneytown, an old high school hangout. We ordered at the counter and took our chilled prizes to a table. Scarlett had one scoop of mocha chip in a metal dish. A solid choice. My selection was almost certainly the pinnacle of ice cream perfection: black raspberry chocolate chip. As I'd said, *to die for*. And, as a bonus, eating the ice cream gave me something to do with my hands. It kind of helped my nervousness, which was monumental, considering the way the girl across the table stared at me.

"So," Scarlett said. "Talk to me."

"Okay."

"That's it?"

"I'm still high from the ride up here."

"You're in love with my car."

"My hearing is just coming back. The power and noise of that engine..."

"My dad had that car in high school, kept it in a garage for years, then restored it and gave it to me as a graduation present."

"Wow. I got gift certificates to Walgreens."

She licked ice cream from her spoon and grinned at me. "Charley. I like your sense of humor."

"Yeah?"

"Yeah."

"Okay."

"I'm usually direct, Charley. Have you noticed that?"

"Not the first two things I noticed, but, yes."

"It's honest. And prevents misunderstandings."

"With you on that one."

She smiled. "Ready?"

"Go."

"You're not the greatest looking guy in the world, Charley. But your eyes are kind. And you have a certain gentleness that encourages trust."

"Thanks, except for that first part."

"But really? *It's the way you talk.* You're smart. And funny. It's attractive."

"Just the way I talk."

"It works."

"Want to know something?"

She edged forward a bit. "Sure."

"I've never met anyone named Scarlett."

"Not too common."

"Cool name, though."

She chuckled. "So, you like my car *and* my name."

"Are you named after a family member?"

"No. Uh, no."

"I'm sensing a tad of non-directness."

"Is that even a word?"

"Tad?"

She pushed her empty ice cream dish aside. "GWTW."

"Pardon me?"

"G. W. T. W."

"That's better. What?"

"Clark Gable. Vivien Leigh," she said.

"Wasn't he in *Casablanca*?"

"That was Bogart."

"Oh. Right. I get the classics confused, which is stupid since I watch Turner Classic Movies most of the time, when *Star Trek* isn't on."

She chuckled. "Not many confuse *Casablanca* with *Gone With The Wind*."

"Ah, *Gone With The Wind*. Believe it or not, I've never seen the complete version of that or *Casablanca*."

"I don't believe it."

"Clips here and there. Hey, doesn't *Casablanca* translate to *white house*?"

"Well, unfortunately, what we have here, Charley Davis, is an American tragedy."

"Not failure to communicate?"

"Huh?"

"Forget it."

She sighed. "You say such random things sometimes."

"Part of my charm."

She stared at me. "You really don't get it. Gable, Leigh, GWTW."

I thought for a moment and it dawned on me. "Scarlett O'Hara."

"Finally."

"I told you, I've never seen much of it. I try to steer clear of chick-flicks, most of the time."

"That settles it."

"We can be grateful for that."

She stood. "Tomorrow night."

"Tomorrow night?" I stood and faced her. The hairs on the back of my neck prickled.

"7:00. I'll be over."

"You will?"

"Don't you want to see me again?"

"Yes, I mean—"

"And I said you were smart."

"You did."

"Do you have a DVD player?"

"Yeah."

"Good. Charley, all you need to do is wear a Hawaiian shirt, make some non-microwave popcorn, warm up that DVD player, and be ready at 7:00."

"Sounds like heaven."

She touched the center of my chest with one finger. "Just you, me, and the destruction of the South."

"As I said."

She laughed. "I'm having fun." Her face flushed and she gazed at me in that way I'll never understand.

"You sound surprised."

"Pleased," she cooed.

"Good."

"It's refreshing. You're refreshing."

"Like a cold beer at an August baseball game?" I guessed.

"Just say thank you, Charley."

"Thank you, Charley."

She shook her head. "Come on."

"Where to?"

I followed her outside. The cool air was invigorating. She stepped toward the Corvette. "I need to go."

"Now?"

"Yes."

"But it's only 7:45."

We reached the car and she faced me. "It's not you, Charley. I just need to go."

"Uh, okay."

We hopped into her car. The engine rumbled to life, and we powered out of the lot onto Galbraith Road. The noise from the car was so loud we barely talked along the way. Less than ten minutes later, she pulled into the condo lot, shifted the stick into neutral, and stared at me. "Thanks, Charley."

"Welcome."

She smiled. "My pleasure."

"Scarlett?"

"Yeah?"

"I'm having fun, too."

"See you tomorrow night?"

"If the cleaners can do a rush job on my Hawaiian shirt." I pushed the door open, climbed out, and stood by the side of the car. "You were really named after Scarlett O'Hara?"

"My parents were nuts about that film."

"Imagine so." I pushed the door closed.

"Bye, Charley."

The Corvette rumbled away. I stood for a moment and watched the blood-red car streak down the Pike. It was gone in three seconds. I turned back toward the condo door and began to walk.

A tingle ran the length of my spine.

It was worse now. It had started about thirty minutes ago. Scarlett had said *tomorrow night* and an odd shiver jittered on the back of my neck.

From the moment Scarlett had pulled up in her sports car, a warning bell clanged.

Something was just not right about the almost perfect Scarlett Perry.

Chapter 21

Life is Kinda Crazy With a Spooky Samurai Like You

It was 6:15am. I was cold, hungry, and could barely keep my eyes open. Uncle Morgan guided his Escalade along Reading Road toward Sharonville. An early fog was so thick it was unsafe to go faster than twenty miles per hour, though there was little traffic. But, we had a date with destiny, and with Mr. Oh Tagawa, at exactly 6:20.

Uncle Morgan stopped the Escalade just outside Mr. Tagawa's shop. Fog swirled and I could barely see the storefront. Angelica stared up at me.

"Nice morning for a murder," I said as Uncle Morgan and I moved to Mr. Tagawa's door.

Uncle Morgan ignored me and knocked on the half-open doorframe. "Mr. Tagawa? Sir?"

"I will join you out there," Mr. Tagawa said from inside.

Uncle Morgan shrugged.

A few seconds later, Mr. Tagawa said, "Gentlemen." The fog surrounded him as he appeared in the doorway. He held a red silk blanket in trembling hands.

"Good morning, sir," Uncle Morgan said.

Mr. Tagawa gave a stiff, formal bow. It looked as if it was painful for him. He looked at me with a half-smile that vanished when he glanced down and saw Angelica. "*Inugami...*" His face paled and he backed up two steps. "*Inugami*," he said again, the single word nearly sticking in his throat.

"Her name is Angelica," I said.

He looked as though he had been severely frightened, and he didn't seem like the kind of man who had ever been severely frightened.

"Mr. Tagawa?" Uncle Morgan said. "What is it?"

"Your nephew is a *magician.* You did not tell me this."

"Sir?" Uncle Morgan frowned.

"A *powerful* magician."

"Huh?" My sarcasm kicked in. "Maybe instead of golf, it might be *fun* to be a magician. I could have a lovely assistant. And rabbits are nice."

Uncle Morgan seemed puzzled by Mr. Tagawa's strange reaction to my dog. Angelica was indifferent to Mr. Tagawa. She stood close beside me, as always.

The Japanese man gathered himself. "I am sorry, to both of you. I was taken by surprise. Your dog, you see. Your...dog."

"She does have a weird effect on people."

"Yes. Yes." He took a deep breath to settle. "Now, for why you are here."

"Are you okay, old friend?" Uncle Morgan asked.

"At my age, even the smallest shock is difficult." He took a breath. "They are ready."

"Thank you."

"As I promised."

I blinked. "Yes. Thank you."

"These blades, gentlemen, are *different.*"

"Oh?" I said.

"Special."

"Please. Explain," Uncle Morgan said.

Mr. Tagawa's face was lined with fatigue. "These weapons are my *masterwork.*" Mr. Tagawa held onto the silk-wrapped bundle with a tightening grip.

"Sir," Uncle Morgan said, "are you well?"

Mr. Tagawa squinted hard at us. "I must tell you *now.* Both of you."

Uncle Morgan and I nodded in unison.

"The weapons are fashioned for you, Charley Davis. *Only you.* Understand?"

"Yeah. I mean, yes. Sure." I didn't understand but had no idea what else to say.

"The sun will soon burn the mist away. And a new dawn will begin. For you." He focused his eyes on me. "Come here. Please."

"Me?"

Mr. Tagawa nodded.

I glanced at Uncle Morgan then took two steps forward.

"These blades are *blessed*," Mr. Tagawa said.

Blades? "Okay..?"

"With fires of the gods. Fires of *victory*."

Uncle Morgan said, "We are truly grateful, sir."

"With these weapons, you *cannot* know defeat." The elderly Japanese man's eyes widened and stared over my shoulder. I turned and followed his gaze down to Angelica.

"Good..." he stared at my dog, "does not exist without evil. It is a counterbalance. The balance of nature."

I wondered if Mr. Tagawa had been talking to Pinson. "If you mean Angelica, she's been completely gentle."

He paused for a moment. "This black beast is a *magician's* canine. She will follow the character of her companion. This one," he pointed at Angelica with a long, bony finger, "could serve either purpose. You must not allow the power of the weapons to sway you from the correct path."

My head felt as though I had been drinking cheap beer for about a week. "Sounds right. Magician's dog. Good. Evil. A little *Lord of the Rings* thrown in. Got it."

"Charley."

"Yeah, Uncle Morgan. Right." I rubbed my forearm across my eyes. "Sir, Mr. Tagawa, what is *Inugami*, if you don't mind the question?"

Mr. Tagawa cleared his throat. "Ancient Japanese lore tells of wild dog gods, summoned by great magicians. If the magicians performed white magic, their *Inugami* helped the defenseless, assisted the poor and sick. But if the magicians practiced darker magical arts, their *Inugami*..."

"I get it. They were bad dogs," I said. "But, not to worry. I'm no magician. And Angelica is a very good girl."

"Her appearance suggests otherwise," Mr. Tagawa said.

"I know. It's her eyes."

"Much more than that." He swallowed. "Now take the blades. Go. Gods of sunlight smile upon you."

I hesitated to take them, but Uncle Morgan gave me the raised eyebrow again, so I stepped a bit closer and Mr. Tagawa placed the red bundle in my arms. He seemed to deflate, as if all his energy had suddenly evaporated.

"Thanks."

Mr. Tagawa stepped back and disappeared into the murky darkness that filled the doorway. The door swung shut.

"The man knows how to make an exit," I said.

Uncle Morgan sighed. "For the first time, he looked frail to me."

"There cannot be golf clubs in here," I said.

"Why not?"

"It feels like I'm carrying nothing heavier than a shiny red blanket that looks like Superman's cape."

"Let's take them to the condo."

"Pinson will be excited to see these." I looked down at the red leather strips that wrapped tightly around the long bundle. The leather was finely stitched with thin golden thread.

I opened the back Escalade door. "Angelica."

The dog jumped inside.

"Good girl."

***

Uncle Morgan and I didn't talk much on the drive back to the condo. We rolled into the parking lot and rustled through a thick covering of fallen leaves. I opened the door for Angelica, and the three of us walked inside. I placed the clubs on the kitchen table and just stared, as if afraid to look within.

We pulled out chairs and sat. Our eyes drifted and settled on the red cloth in the center of my table.

Uncle Morgan smiled. "Curious?"

"About the clubs?"

"Yes."

"I half expect them to be made of Zero propellers."

Uncle Morgan chuckled.

We both just sat there.

"Go ahead," I said.

"Your clubs. Your favor."

"Mr. Iwo Jima calls them weapons."

"Vernacular."

"Tell that to him."

"Charley. Unwrap them."

I took a breath and reached across the table. I pulled the ties on the leather straps, and the shimmering red fabric fell away.

"My God," Uncle Morgan said.

We both stood and stared down at the clubs.

I waited a moment, caught my breath. "Beautiful."

We couldn't take our eyes from the clubs. Neither of us moved to touch them, as if we had an unspoken understanding that human hands were not meant to disturb such magnificent creations.

The six clubs were tied flat to the fabric, side-by-side, as if they were an expensive set of cutlery.

"Look at them," he said.

"I am."

"Incredible."

"Like something from the museum of modern art."

Six clubs. Three for the right. Three for the left. The burnished leather grips at the end of the clubs were deeply infused with golden Japanese characters. The shafts were impossibly thin and shimmered with what seemed to be an internal radiance.

I looked at Uncle Morgan. "Are the crab cakes good in South Carolina?"

He smiled. "They're only better in Baltimore."

"Can't play much golf in Baltimore in the winter."

"Sure can't."

Our eyes lowered to the clubs again, and for the first time since this whole weird project began, I thought maybe the recipe for success in life *required* a little craziness. The clubs *looked magical*, as if they could actually transform me, all by themselves, into a winning golfer. And at this moment, it didn't matter if I had no golf talent at all. That was probably a severe understatement, considering Mrs. Morrison, Pinson, and Oh Tagawa who knew he belonged to the land. But I did know one thing; I needed to go to the mall tomorrow and buy sunscreen and a swimsuit.

I heard the beaches near Charleston were beautiful this time of year.

Chapter 22

Georgia On Our Minds

As Scarlett peeled the wrapper from a new DVD, Angelica jumped off the sofa and backed herself into a corner across the room.

"Your dog is staring at me, Charley."

"She does that."

"I like dogs."

"Me too."

"No offense. I'm not sure I like this one."

"Need to be around her a while."

"If you say so."

"Give me a couple minutes to finish the popcorn."

Scarlett followed me into the kitchen. She pointed at the stove. "What's that?"

"*Jiffy Pop.*"

"There's popcorn in there?"

"You've never seen *Jiffy Pop*?"

"Guess not."

"You said I couldn't use the microwave."

She chuckled. "I was kidding."

"What do you think about my Hawaiian shirt?"

She eyed the orange and white flowers that covered the terribly faded shirt that had occupied a special place in my dresser drawer since junior high.

"Good job. I wasn't kidding about the shirt." She smiled up at me and I couldn't tell if she was serious or not.

"I went to a lot of trouble." I gently shook the *Jiffy Pop* foil pan across a burner on my stove until the popping started. I was glad I had something to do with my hands again because the very idea of Scarlett Perry standing beside me in my kitchen was terribly unsettling. I had practically no idea what to say to her, except for random drivel, especially since I had not been on an official date in a couple years.

"So, Charley, it occurred to me driving over here, I know almost nothing about you."

"Nonsense. You know my name, where I live, you've met my dog. You know I'm bad at movie trivia, and I have terrible taste in shirts."

The popping stopped and I removed the *Jiffy Pop* from the stove. "Come on."

We stepped into the den and sat on the sofa. I peeled open the foil dome over the *Jiffy Pop* pan and exposed the freshly popped popcorn that was not from a microwave.

"That's not really much," she said. "Name, address, weird dog. Practically nothing."

"It's something."

"Uh huh. I guess I'll just ask questions then."

"Fine."

"Do you have a girlfriend?"

"Do you?"

"Charley."

"No. No girlfriend."

"Good. That's good. Where do you work?"

"Hard to explain." I chomped popcorn.

"How hard can that be?"

"Hard."

"Code breaker for the CIA?"

"Interpol."

"I was close."

"Yeah."

"So?"

"Up until a month ago, I fixed computers. Now my uncle is paying me to, well, to play golf."

"Play..?"

"I'm in the *training* phase right now. Haven't even been on a real golf course yet."

"You were right."

"About?"

"How hard this would be to explain."

"Look, my uncle, who apparently has a lot of money to waste, has a theory that golf is totally a game of practice and not inborn talent. To prove that theory, he is paying me to be trained every day, all day, for nine months by a couple of, uh, *trainers*. I'm going to be using special clubs made by a Samurai sword craftsman. Let's see, I'll be playing both right and left-handed. Oh, and I'll play blindfolded."

"Nine months."

"The time for a normal pregnancy."

"Huh. That's it?"

"Think so."

"That's something. Odd, but *something*."

"Told you."

"Well, now I know a lot more about you than you know about me, I guess."

"Not sure that's true."

"What do you mean?"

I chewed on a few pieces of popcorn and focused on her. She wore black denim shorts and an oversized, faded red Cincinnati Bearcats hooded sweatshirt with several patches sewn onto the sleeves. A tennis bracelet with a number "1" in diamonds sparkled on her wrist. Her hair looked slightly damp, she was barefoot, and her legs were crossed underneath.

"My older brother and I used to play a game when I was, let's see, in fifth or sixth grade," I said. "We tried to use deductive reasoning to figure out things about people we didn't know."

She stared at me for a second and blinked. "I'm listening."

"If my parents had people over, we would pick one or two of them and try to guess, or deduce, their story."

"Like what?"

"Normal stuff, like their education, what they did for a living, whether or not they were married, or had kids."

"Sherlock Holmes, then?"

"Exactly. And Tim, my brother, let me be Sherlock, to his Dr. Watson. I think he was just trying to boost my self-confidence."

"It needed boosting?"

"He thought so. I did have a self-esteem problem when I

was...younger."

"Intriguing."

"Kid games. Two brothers goofing off."

"And what was your deductive batting average?"

"About twenty-five percent. Not so good."

"But I bet when you *did* get something right, it gave you two quite a charge."

"Oh, yeah."

She shifted toward me. "Go ahead."

"Excuse me?"

"Deduce me."

"I don't think so."

"Oh, no. That's what you were getting at before...you had already *deduced* everything about me."

"I didn't say that."

"Practically." She watched me, her lips pulled in a tight smile.

I couldn't tell if she was amused, or whether the look was meant as some kind of a challenge. "Okay."

"Good. I'll keep track."

"Of what?"

"Your batting average."

"I have to trust you'll tell me the truth."

"Yes. Go."

I looked at her for a moment. "This is a bad idea."

"You started it."

"I hate that excuse."

"Oh come on, Charley. Just for fun."

"As long as you remember you insisted."

"Deal."

I took a breath. "You're twenty-eight and had a birthday less than a month ago. You are committed to fitness, but jogging is new for you, and your ankle injury is completely healed. You have an older brother, just like me. You are still close to him and keep in touch. You went to Wyoming High School, right down the street near where your parents still live, and then went on to UC on a swimming scholarship. Swimming is still your preferred method of exercise, usually at the Pavilion in Blue Ash. You're not married, but you have a boyfriend, a man considerably older than you, maybe early forties. You live with him in Madeira, and you are fairly well off. You have a house with a little land, and you enjoy gardening. You work part-time, just to keep busy, or to ensure a future income, by doing medical dictation transcriptions."

Her face had visibly paled.

"How am I doing?"

She swallowed. "Anything else?"

"Sure. You play both tennis and golf with your boyfriend. You can easily beat him, but you let him win almost all the time. He's generally overweight and out of shape, and he's proud he has a woman who looks as you do at his side, especially at the club. Recently..."

I knew this was a mistake but for some reason I could not help myself.

"Recently? Go ahead."

"Yeah. Recently you've begun to question your relationship, your real feelings, and you've even thought about dumping him. Not seriously, but thinking about it nevertheless."

"Go on."

"Last night, you remembered the first time you were in love. And how it felt when..." I thought she was going to fall over.

She just stared. "Don't stop."

"How you felt when that first love of your life broke your heart. You wonder where he is and what he's doing. And if you found him again, if you could recapture the magic you had while you were together."

The air was completely silent but for Angelica's rhythmic breathing across the room.

Finally, Scarlett said, "I don't know what to say."

"One more thing? If that's okay."

"Yeah."

"Your name's not Scarlett."

She suddenly turned and pressed her hands to her face. She waited a moment, then turned back and gazed at me. "Do you want to know how you did?"

"Not really."

"I do swim at the Pavilion."

"That's it?"

She nodded. "How did you know about the swimming?"

"You're muscular, but in the way serious swimmers get. Your hair was still a little wet when you got here."

"I could have just washed it."

"Scent of chlorine shampoo?"

"And how did you know about the swimming scholarship?"

"Swimming patches on your UC sweatshirt."

"And Madeira?"

"Oil-change sticker on your windshield was from an auto shop over there."

"Gardening?"

"Traces of dirt under your fingernails, even after just swimming. That's the kind of dirt you can only get from serious gardening, preparing the autumn soil for spring seeding. Plus you have a few random scratches on the backs of your hands and wrists."

"Uh huh. The jogging?"

"New shoes. Not a scuff mark on them."

"Could be just new shoes."

"They are new shoes. But you didn't look natural when I saw you running, like it was something new for you."

"And my ankle?"

"Not a mark on it."

"Why do you think I have a boyfriend?"

"You had to go last night, at 7:45."

She waited a moment. "Less than twenty-five percent, Charley."

"I didn't say I was any good at it."

"Can I ask you something?"

"Sure."

"Why did you say that about my name?"

"The DVD is new. If your parents named you after Scarlett O'Hara, the whole family would be obsessed with *Gone With The Wind*. You would already have a DVD and wouldn't need to go out today and buy one."

She nodded. "That's just it. My *parents* have the DVD. But I don't live there anymore, according to you."

"Told you. I'm no good."

"Yeah."

She shifted position on the sofa and bit her bottom lip then pushed one hand back through her damp hair. "Well, then, shall we?" She gestured at the TV.

"Yeah. Sure."

Scarlett clicked on the TV with the remote. "Ready?"

"Ready."

I dimmed the lights. The movie started but I didn't really appreciate it, even the big *SELZNICK* that filled the entire screen in full Technicolor majesty. I couldn't stop the jittering at the back of my neck.

I knew I had been right about much more than twenty-five percent of my deductions. Yet she denied it. She was hiding something from me, but I just could not figure any motivation for such deceit. She certainly didn't have to invent a new name and hide her past to get me interested. Scarlett O'Hara? I was totally interested when I first caught a glimpse of her jogging through the pasture, no matter what her name might have been.

Scarlett sank into the leather cushions on the other end of the sofa and wrapped her arms around her midsection. She could tell I was looking at her, but she kept her eyes fixed on the TV, as if this movie was the most important thing in the world to her. Bad, bad body language.

I pushed back into the sofa cushions and tried to relax. I chewed on some popcorn but didn't really taste it. Maybe I could figure this out as the South was dancing its last waltz about five hours from now. If not, then maybe I would talk about it with Angelica again. Tomorrow. No harm in that.

That is, if Angelica was in a talkative mood.

Chapter 23

How Can You Mend A Broken Heart?

At 8:25am, the air was chilled but I didn't really mind. I had been practicing alone by the footbridge in Glenwood Gardens for more than twenty minutes. Angelica sat in the frosted grass and watched as I twirled, jabbed, and thrust through my Combassa Combelbo disciplines, called Aacutaes. Each was a ninety-second pattern of movements with the black stick. They were supposed to help concentration and agility. I had worked on these routines for almost a month, and truthfully, I looked forward to them. It felt somehow useful, as if I were actually accomplishing something.

Mrs. Morrison told me it was important to empty my mind during the Aacutaes and rely solely upon reflex. But this morning, Scarlett Perry was on my mind and I couldn't force her out. Scarlett Perry was coming over tonight. Again. And the creepy feeling at the back of my neck had worsened through a restless night. My thoughts were consumed with her as I bent and spun completely around, the stick in one hand whooshing through the air just above the ground.

We had watched the movie last night in total silence, no movement, no conversation, as if we were in an ancient cathedral watching a sacred religious rite. After my Sherlock Holmes impression, which I knew was a bad idea from the start, she clammed up and barely said ten words the rest of the evening. The film lasted forever, and when it was over, she leaned close to me and brushed the hair out of my eyes with the tips of her fingers, and said, "Tomorrow night?"

Believe me, I never claimed to have any insight into the feminine mind, and had no clue why she wanted to see me again. We had practically not touched, certainly never kissed, and she had looked at me after my deductions as if I were an exhibit in one of those Ripley's museums. But none of that mattered, I guess, because she was coming back for more. I answered, "Sure," and in twenty seconds she was gone. I listened to the rumble of the mighty Corvette as I stood by the back door and watched her drive away. It made absolutely no sense. But for some reason, maybe ego, maybe something else, I was drawn to play this out and discover the true motivations of Scarlett, or Jennifer, or Heather, or whatever her name really was. This had to be the wrong move, but frankly, I had no other ideas.

"Better."

I halted and looked around. Mrs. Morrison stood at the edge of the concrete pathway, hands on her hips.

"Thanks," I said.

"How long?"

"Have I been here?"

She nodded.

"Since about 8:00."

She smiled. "Good."

"Yeah."

"Smoother...and more controlled."

"It feels better."

"It shows."

I glanced behind her. Sandy and Ray walked down the path toward us. Each pulled a red cart full of camera and audio equipment. Mrs. Morrison just stared at me and must have seen my expression change.

"Miss Carson," she said to herself.

"And Ray," I said.

"Ray?"

"Hamilton."

Ray waved as he got closer. "Hey."

"Hey, bud," I said.

Sandy stopped beside me. "Morning." She adjusted her gloves and stared at me. Her face had not the slightest trace of a smile. "You're all sweaty."

I looked down at the wet "V" on my gray sweatshirt just under my neck. "Yeah. It's my body telling me exercise is a terrible idea."

"Wish you would have told me."

"What?"

"If you were going to start early, you should have told me."

"Sorry. Didn't decide until I got up. I felt good, it was a pretty morning, and—"

"I was up. You should have called."

"Hey. Are you mad at me or something?"

She froze for a moment. "No."

"No?"

"No." Her eyelids batted quickly a few times, and she looked at the ground. "I came by last night."

My throat was struck dry.

"About 11:30," she went on. "I wanted to talk."

I tried to focus and remember when Scarlett left the condo last night. "11:30?"

Sandy shifted her weight and glanced over at Ray. "Come on." She spun around, grabbed the handle on her cart, and stepped away.

"Sandy. Wait a sec."

Ray tilted his head at me and shrugged. Then he followed Sandy, pulling his cart behind him.

My stomach clenched. I felt terrible and didn't know exactly why.

"So," Mrs. Morrison said.

"Yeah."

"We've been together for a month."

"Forgot our anniversary," I said. "Sorry."

She looked at Sandy walking away. "I wondered when I would figure it out."

"Mrs. Morrison..."

"It's her."

"Sandy?"

"Yes." Mrs. Morrison turned from me and gazed east directly into a red-orange morning sun. "She's the answer."

My morning had started off okay and I didn't want it ruined by some in-depth hippie ramblings. "Look, I don't want-"

"I should have seen it." She touched my arm. "I've grown to care about you, Charley, as a person, more than just a student."

"Thanks."

"The stick fighting? You've improved. I'm happy to see it. And physically, the exercise, better diet, have all done wonders. But everything else? No. Nothing."

"I've been trying."

She shook her head. "This pain you carry around inside weighs you down. It stops you from accepting, from opening your mind to new concepts."

"Pain?"

"Of a broken heart, a heart burst into a million jagged pieces. It's been in your eyes since the beginning. But I never connected the dots to Sandy."

I slapped at the side of my thigh. "I'd rather not talk about this."

She faced me. "Every person has something that pushes at them, something big, important. Something that *defines* them."

"With all due respect, whatever that means, can we just move on?"

She looked into my eyes. "This defeatist attitude, you have to rise above it."

"Please. I-"

"Let's walk together, Charley, for a few minutes."

She started away, and like a lemming, I followed and caught up with her.

"Ms. Carson is an extraordinary woman," she said.

"I know."

"You loved her."

"Yes."

"And you wonder every day why you're not with her."

I stopped. "I know why."

She halted and gazed at me from a few yards away. "Tell me."

I swallowed. "I heard what she said, how she explained it, carefully, in a quiet voice. But that didn't matter."

"Why?"

"Because I knew the real reason even before she started explaining. *She didn't love me.* At least, not as I loved her."

I saw her eyes moisten a bit.

"Is that what you think?"

"Otherwise, she wouldn't have broken it off."

"Your love is still strong."

"I don't think-"

"And you want her back."

"No."

"Really?"

"I don't. In fact, I never want to get that close to anybody. Ever."

"Protecting yourself from another broken heart."

"I guess. If you say so. I don't know." I had no idea why I was confiding in Mrs. Morrison. Something in her eyes, though, something in her manner today made me comfortable.

She stepped a bit closer. "Will you take some advice from an old woman?"

I smiled. "Where can we find one?"

She smiled back. "That was nice."

"I meant it."

"I know. And I thank you."

"Welcome."

She closed her eyes tightly then opened them and focused on me. "Charley, I always think the best way to address a problem is through direct action."

"Probably right."

"But before you can face the problem, you must first decide exactly what you want. Does that make sense?"

"I don't see what you're getting at."

We reached the clearing where we practice our stick fighting each morning. She bent to the ground and sat in the grass, her palms upturned on each knee. She tilted her head at me and I followed.

"You've been trudging through your life with an unspoken pain eating at you constantly. It's affected the way you think, talk, sleep, the way you live."

"Uh..."

"The pain has to go."

"Obviously."

"What do you want, Charley?"

"I don't..."

"If you get what you want, the pain will vanish." She

stared at me. Her eyes were deep brown and filled with warmth.

I thought for a few moments, then, "I don't want her back, Mrs. Morrison, if that's what you're suggesting."

"Think, Charley. You *don't* have her back. Now."

"I know."

"And how do you feel?"

"Rotten."

"So, what does that tell you?"

"You're saying I really do want her back?"

"I saw your eyes before, Charley, when she walked up, when you talked to her, when she walked away."

"That obvious?"

She nodded.

I chuckled.

"What do you *want*, Charley?"

The truth of it, the pure simplicity of her thinking coursed through me like a sudden blood transfusion. "I want the pain to go away."

"How can that happen?"

"Either I find a way to manage the pain, a way to stuff it inside a mental locker, or..." I felt my eyes widen. "I find a way to get her back into my life."

"Yes. And it appears your uncle, strange man that he is, has started that process."

I felt my breath stop for a second. "You mean he suckered me into this mad plot *just for Sandy*?"

"He is doing this for *you*, no matter what other reason he might tell you. I've known Morgan for a long time. Behind those hawk-like lawyer eyes lurks a man with a huge heart. And there's always been a special place in that heart for you, Charley. *For you.* He's seen your pain for years, and he certainly knows its source."

"Did he tell you this?"

"Not a word. But I know it to be true."

"He was looking for an indirect way to bring Sandy back to me," I said as if it were the most amazing statement in the history of the world.

Mrs. Morrison said, "So, Charley."

"Yeah?"

"What do you want?"

"About four hundred Coors."

"Besides that."

I grinned. "I guess...I want Sandy back."

"You guess?"

"I want her back."

"Yes."

"I do. *I want her back.*"

"Good. You've jumped the first hurdle. You are able to say aloud what you want in a clear, precise sentence."

"But, there's a problem."

"Problem."

"A big one."

"Tell me."

"I'm no good at *talking* to her about this. She feels guilty already, for leaving me in the first place. But she still feels she made the right decision at the time. When we talk now, there's this strange undercurrent of pain and resentment, on both sides. And I turn sarcastic immediately. I know she doesn't like it, and yet I keep at it, as if I have a compulsion or something."

"Charley. Here's an important question, almost as important as my first question."

"Shoot."

"Does she still love you?"

"I don't know."

"But?"

"But, I think she does."

"Close enough. And that tells me what course you should take."

"To win her back?"

"To win her back."

"Well, if you can arrange that one, you can add magician to your extensive resume. Is a female magician a magicianette?"

"Will you trust me?"

I didn't have to think about it. "Yes."

She smiled. "I'll have something for you in South Carolina."

"Something?"

"Wait until then."

I looked across the clearing at Sandy and Ray setting up their equipment. I could tell Sandy was purposely not looking in my direction.

"Okay, Mrs. Morrison."

"Good. Now, let's get started with our meditation. Until today, you have not succeeded in emptying your mind. Am I right?"

"Yes."

"Today will be different."

She reached behind and pushed the button on her CD player. *In the Year 2525* came on. I truly hated this song.

"Begin counting, Charley, silently."

I started at forty-three and counted backwards. I thought about what Mrs. Morrison said, and how I had misjudged her these past weeks. She was smart, and no matter if it was drug-induced or not, she had a way of getting to the heart of the matter. Literally.

For some reason, I felt the tension in my body ease a bit. As I reached number 21, the horrible song faded into the background. Sandy, Ray, Mrs. Morrison, and even Angelica ceased to exist. For the first time since I started this, maybe the very first time in my life, it seemed things weren't as bad as I had thought.

And I felt quietly at peace.

Chapter 24

Scarlett Fields Forever

The morning Nigerian stick fighting with Mrs. Morrison was great. I couldn't get near her, but the exercise energized me. When we finished, Mrs. Morrison stared at me for a moment. Then she smiled, walked forward without a word, and hugged me. It was a long, sweaty hug. The scent of damp patchouli was intense.

I jogged back to the condo with an unfamiliar high. Maybe this was how marathoners felt when they reached mile sixteen. But whatever it was, I felt different this morning. And the difference was good.

As I neared the condo driveway, Angelica began a long, downright evil growl.

"Girl, you're creeping me out." I looked to the side. Scarlett's Corvette was parked in the condo lot. Smoke puffed from the twin exhausts. I jogged to a stop about thirty feet from the car. The red door swung open and Scarlett stepped out. She wore warm-up pants, running shoes, and a short denim jacket trimmed with a tan leather collar. "Hi there." She smiled and waved with one hand.

I swallowed. "Hi."

Angelica walked beside me as if she were part of my right leg. The dog's amber eyes were fixed with an unholy stare, straight at Scarlett.

"What are you doing here?"

"Wanna make out?"

"With you?"

"There's a good-looking clerk across the street at the Wyoming Food Mart. Maybe you'd rather make out with him."

"Are you serious?"

"Just asking."

"Scarlett, it's 12:30. Did you take a half day off from work?"

She squinted at me. "More deductions?"

"Maybe."

"I could be a bartender. Work nights."

"Could be."

"Back to my question?"

She looked fantastic and my head was spinning. I knew something was wrong, but I had to follow this through. "Yes."

"So you want to make out with me?"

"Right away, if not sooner."

She grinned, looked down at her shoes for a moment, and then back up at me. "I'll drive, Sherlock. I know a place just beyond your stables, in Winton Woods."

"Making out in the car sounds cool. The Corvette presents a problem, though." I glanced down at Angelica.

"Can't she stay here?"

"Nope."

"Why not?"

"She's in-training. We shouldn't be separated."

"More code-breaking?"

"She sniffs out dead bodies in the woods."

"Uh huh. Well, keep the drool off the leather."

"Her drool or mine?"

She laughed. "You're something. You know that?"

"I know I'm something."

"I'm serious, Charley."

"Okay."

"Can't you *try* to be serious, even for a second?"

"I can try."

Her smile vanished. "Charley. Do you like me?"

"Is this a trick question?"

"Charley?"

"Yes. I like you."

"I thought so. And you know what?"

"Tell me."

She stepped close. "I like you. I like you a lot."

"As Scarlett liked Rhett?"

She shook her head. "Not Rhett."

"No?"

"Ashley Wilkes."

"Ah."

She looked at the ground again and seemed to study the white parking stripes on the blacktop. "You know...I've changed my mind."

"You don't like me a lot?"

"That's not it." She stood there and stared.

I waited, but she didn't say anything, as if she had so much to say she didn't know how to start.

"I'm confused, Scarlett."

"Can we go inside?"

"No Corvette?"

"It'll be more comfortable inside."

"Okay. I don't have much time, though."

"Golf?"

"Pinson gets agitated when I'm late."

"Uh huh." She looked away, and made no move toward the condo. "Charley, are you still going to South Carolina?"

I nodded. "Next week."

"Where?"

"Seabrook Island."

"*Seabrook*. Wow."

"Supposed to be a couple good golf courses. Near Charleston."

"It's warm there."

"From what I hear."

She turned back around and faced me. "Charley." She moved close and took my hands.

I liked the warmth. "We're going to make out in the parking lot?"

"I have a question for you."

"I'm sorry. Question time is between 10:00 and 11:00." I caught the scent of lavender.

"I want to go," she said.

"You just got here."

"With you...to Seabrook."

"I, uh..."

She gazed at me. "Please."

I tried to put her actions together. "First you want to drive up the hill, park, and make out in your car. Next second, you change your mind and want to go make out inside the condo. Then, all that is forgotten and you announce you want to go with me to—"

"To South Carolina," she said.

"Really?"

"Please, Charley."

"You've surprised me again."

"Fooled your powers of deductive reasoning, I guess."

"Elementary, Scarlett."

"So, can I go?"

"I don't know. I have to ask."

"Still ask your mother before you make decisions?"

"My uncle. And Pinson."

"Un huh."

"There are complications."

"But Charley, what do *you* want?"

I froze. I couldn't believe she and Mrs. Morrison had said the same thing.

"Would you like me to come along?"

I stared at her. "I'll be training. Practically no time off at all."

She blinked. I could feel her mood shift. Then she turned away. "You know what? I've changed my mind again."

"At least you're consistent."

She gestured with her hand. "Come on."

"The plan?"

"Corvette. Woods. Make out." She stepped quickly back to her car without waiting for me to respond.

"Guess that answers that," I muttered to myself.

I dropped into the Corvette. Angelica jumped onto my lap. Scarlett gunned the engine, and we were off.

We raced up Bonham.

"Hey. Cops hide up here," I said.

Scarlett said nothing. The Corvette blasted up the hill. We flew by the twisting driveway to the stable and accelerated toward the entrance to Winton Woods.

Chapter 25

Walking Tall Redux

The car skidded into the gravel pull-out and fishtailed to a rocking halt. Then, she was all over me, which wasn't easy with Angelica still on my lap. I guess my canine friend sensed I was in no danger, so she leaned forward and rested her chin on the dashboard while Scarlett took my face in her hands and kissed me as though the Titanic was about to capsize.

Sandy and I used to kiss. We used to kiss a lot. But it was nothing like this. Nothing.

And then Scarlett just quit, stared at me for a second, and pulled away. It had lasted only twenty seconds, but I could barely catch my breath. "What's wrong?"

She shifted around and straightened her jacket. "Nothing." She bailed out of the car and stormed toward a small grove with a few scattered picnic tables.

"Scarlett?" I nudged Angelica off my lap, fell out of the car, and we followed her. A few drops of cold rain pelted my face. I pulled my sweatshirt hood up to cover my head and caught up with her. "Scarlett, this is weird, even for you."

She stared down at Angelica. "You live with an animal that could scare the crap out of the evil dogs in *The Omen*, and you say *I'm* weird?"

"You have a point."

"Look, just forget it."

I shook my head. "Forget what exactly?"

She turned and looked off into the distance across the park to the lake that was just visible through the trees. "I lost my head for a second," she said. "I shouldn't have kissed you like that."

I breathed. "I've never been kissed like that."

"Yeah, well..."

"It was like you wanted to give me one last kiss before being taken off to prison."

"Who's going off to prison, you or me?" she said.

"Hard to tell."

"What does deductive reasoning tell you?"

"Holmesian techniques don't work in this situation."

"No?"

"Women are insane. Thinking logically about how women think is self-defeating."

"That's what you think?"

"Maybe."

Her lips pulled tight as she focused her eyes on mine. "You don't know anything."

"I know you're a good kisser."

"Uh huh."

"I mean it."

"Thanks."

"But it had an odd sense of desperation to it."

She nodded. "What gave that away?"

"Just a feeling."

"Well, I haven't had much practice lately."

"That's hard to believe."

"It's true."

"Like everything else?"

"Everything?"

"Scarlett, do you have something to tell me?"

That got her attention. "What do you mean?"

"There's *something* you want to tell me."

"Another feeling?"

"And it didn't take Sherlock's techniques for me to figure that out."

She looked over my shoulder.

I didn't turn, but I could hear a car approaching through the gravel.

"Please remember one thing. Okay, Charley?"

I looked around. A metallic-silver Chevy Avalanche rolled to a stop in the gravel beside the Corvette.

She took a step back. "I didn't expect to fall for you, Charley. Just didn't. But, I guess, some things can't be helped."

I watched the Avalanche back doors swing open. Two men got out and looked around. They could have been twins. Both were short, built like fireplugs, and had no necks. And they both held baseball bats.

"Scarlett, who are those guys?" I asked the question even though I already knew the answer. I was just waiting for the driver's door to open.

"Charley," she said, "it's not too late."

I turned my head to her. "Too late for what?"

She backed another step, as if I were now poison and it would be deadly to touch me. "Run. Just *run*, Charley."

"Run? Why?" I turned back around just in time to see Bruce Preston step out of the Avalanche and slam the door.

"Well," Bruce said. "Charley Davis in the flesh."

A lump stuck in my throat. "Morning, Mr. Preston."

"I think it's afternoon. A lousy one at that." He pulled at the collar of his dark raincoat.

The rain fell harder.

"Odd place to run into you," I said.

"Funny how things can work out."

"Who are your friends?" I pointed to the bruisers.

"Oh, these gentlemen are J.J. and T.J. Brickner."

"Ah. The Brickner boys."

"They used to sell used cars for me ages ago. Still do the occasional odd job or two."

"I bet."

"They're twins, you know. Hard to tell them apart."

I felt my hands trembling. I hid them behind my back.

"When Crystal told me of your routine, golf training sessions and all, I thought she was making it up at first."

Crystal?

"I can't imagine why she would make up *anything*."

He took a step toward me. "Charley, this meeting is entirely *personal*."

"Glad you clarified that." It was hard to breathe. I wondered how fast the Brickner boys could run if I took off through the trees. Their eyes were the palest blue, like dead fish. The baseball bats were shiny black, the same kind Pete Rose used back in the 70s.

Scarlett stepped over to Bruce. "You promised me."

"I lied, Crystal."

"Tell them to put the bats away," she pleaded.

"I told you what he did. Remember?"

"Bruce-"

"*Remember?*"

"Yes. Yes, I remember."

"He tried to put *us* out of business."

"But he didn't, Bruce. We're okay."

"No thanks to him."

"Bruce, listen—"

"What really gripes me is *I had just promoted him.*"

He nodded at the Brickner fireplugs and they started toward me. Both wore dark blue Puma running suits about two sizes too small, as though they had been through the laundry about four hundred times.

"Hey, is that the dog?" one of them said.

Angelica had inched closer to me and started a horrible, penetrating growl focused straight at the fireplug twins.

"Mother of God," the other Brickner said.

Scarlett turned her back to Bruce and the others. "Charley. Go. Go now."

My brain was spinning.

My older brother once took me to a stupid haunted house at the Carthage fair when I was about eight. He shouldn't have taken me in there. Hell, the carnies shouldn't have let me in. That show was not for kids. I remembered how tense I felt about halfway through, how my knees buckled and a sick feeling got stuck in my throat. It happened about seventeen years ago, but I remembered that night as if it were yesterday. I was never so scared, before or since.

Until right this instant.

Panic is an odd feeling. It kind of sneaks up from behind and then shouts real loud. When it finally hits full force, I feel locked in, surrounded, and no matter which way I choose to turn, it's a horrible choice.

I could take off and run. I might make it. But then what? They knew where I lived. Obviously, Scarlett, I refused to call her Crystal, had been feeding my former boss information about my life for the past week or so.

I could face them. But I would no doubt end up in the hospital and unable to play golf. Uncle Morgan would be crushed. I didn't like the feeling of letting him down.

And then there was Sandy. What would she think if I were beaten up by two used-car salesmen, even if they used black baseball bats? Of course, she might want to join them with a bat of her own, if she found out I was here in the woods, making out with Scarlett.

I glanced around. The path to my left was clear. If I faked right, and then sprinted left, I could probably make it all the way to the ranger station about a half mile away before the National League Chevy salesmen could even get close to me. I could run pretty fast when I was afraid. And running was the only choice that seemed even partially sane. I could face the embarrassment of being called a chicken, later. At least I would still be in one piece.

"They're not going to kill you, Charley," Bruce said. "I'm no killer. Just bust your legs up a bit."

"Look, Bruce, I'm not a crook."

"But you are a snitch, son."

"That was my uncle's idea. I'm sorry—"

"Way too late for that."

The Brickners stepped closer. Angelica growled louder.

Bruce's eyes widened at Angelica.

"The gun," Bruce said. "T.J., the gun."

One of the Brickners reached into the pocket of his warm-up jacket and pulled out a wicked looking pistol.

"No," I shouted. "Put that away."

I took a wild step at the Brickner but it was too late. He aimed low at Angelica and squeezed the trigger. The gun expelled a soft *ppffftt*. I spun around. Angelica wobbled and collapsed into the gravel. I rushed to her and put my arm under her head. Her incredible amber eyes were closed, but her breathing was soft and regular. A green dart stuck straight out of her black fur just below her shoulder.

"Brought the tranquilizer gun just in case," Bruce said. "Remember that vet clinic on Galbraith? Fellow owed me a favor. Told you I wasn't a killer. Hell, I'm a *dog lover*. Right,

Crystal? Baby?"

I pulled out the dart, slid my arm away, and gently placed Angelica's head on the ground. Then I pushed myself up, and took a breath. An insistent drumming started in my temples. I turned to face Bruce and leveled my eyes directly into his. "You shouldn't have done that." My voice sounded as if it were someone else talking.

"That dog is a monster, Charley. Crystal told me. I had to be ready."

I took one step forward. I felt my thoughts washing clear, slowly, slowly, and then in a raging flood, straight out of my head and into the air. The feeling terrified me at first, but I settled into it. For some reason, I wasn't afraid, wasn't angry. All I felt was cold. *Frigid cold resolve.* I took a long breath and reached down to my side.

"You shouldn't have come here, Bruce. Your goon shouldn't have shot Angelica."

I felt the cold streaming out of my eyes, and I saw everything, all at once. Bruce, the Brickners, Scarlett near a tree, her hands covering her mouth. And Angelica, motionless at my feet.

The spring-loaded Nigerian stick popped into my hand. I pressed the button and it instantly snapped into a solid deadly weapon.

"What the hell is that, Charley?" Bruce yelled.

I lunged forward, bent low to the ground and swung the stick with full force against the left ankle of a Brickner. Still moving I spun the other direction and connected with the remaining Brickner's right knee. Both collapsed into groaning heaps, and their baseball bats thumped into the dirt. The whole thing took less than three seconds. I stood up and faced Bruce. The stick flicked under my arm as if it were a cane and I was on my way to a black-tie affair.

"Ch...Charley," he said. "Come on." He put both palms out at me in front of his chest.

"You were always good to me at work," I said.

"I know. That's right!"

I took a step toward him. He backed up a step. I could almost smell the fear in his eyes. "So, Bruce. Here's the deal." I moved closer.

"Charley, no!" Scarlett appeared at my side.

"Move away, Scarlett," I warned the traitor.

"Charley?"

"Now."

She did.

I watched her. Everything flowed across my eyes in slow motion. The rain streamed languorously across her face. She wasn't beautiful anymore, but I didn't dwell on that. I didn't think about anything. My actions were automatic somehow. All reflexes.

"You have exactly one minute, Bruce."

He stared at me. His eyes were wide and did not blink. "One minute?"

"Get yourself and your ball team into that incredibly ugly vehicle. You should take them to the closest ER." I flicked the Nigerian stick in front of me. "And I'm cutting *you* a break. But before you go..." I crouched low, and the stick lashed out at both headlights on the big silver truck. In a flash the glass shattered and splintered into the wet gravel.

Bruce paled.

I glared at him. "Your face is next. Understand?"

"When, when does the minute start?"

I looked at my watch. "Thirty seconds ago."

"Sure. Okay." He flew into action, pulled both Brickners to their feet and shoved them into the Avalanche. Then, without even a fleeting glance at Scarlett, he started the truck, swung the vehicle around, and gunned the engine. With gravel flying everywhere, the truck was almost instantly out of sight. I looked at my watch. He'd made it with nine seconds to spare.

"Charley..." Scarlett shivered in the rain across from me.

"What?"

"He *promised* me he wouldn't hurt you."

"You shouldn't have believed him."

"Honestly, he's never lied to me before."

"Honestly?"

"I'm sorry."

"He's a crook, Scarlett. You know that. Right?"

She wiped the rain from her eyes and forehead. "He wasn't

that way when I married him."

"Married?" I didn't see that coming.

Her hands covered her face. "I don't know what else I can say."

"You spied on me, pretended to like me—"

"I wasn't pretending."

"I knew something was off about you, so did Angelica, but...I didn't trust my intuition. Guess I enjoyed your company too much and didn't want to know the truth."

"Truth is..." She sniffled a bit. "I don't think I can live with him now."

"You think I care?"

"That's not funny."

"Didn't mean it to be."

"Bruce will *never* just let me leave him. He's obsessed with me. But he's been freaking me out lately. I would have to disappear, Charley. Just...disappear."

Angelica stirred.

I bent to her. "Hey, girl. Hey now." I stroked the side of her neck. She opened her eyes and focused on me.

"I'm sorry about your dog, too, Charley. I know how much she means to you."

"She's my best friend."

"You say she knew about me, huh?"

"She's a better judge of character than I am."

"Code-breaker, dead body-sniffer, and mind-reader?"

"She's special."

Angelica shifted her legs around and stood up. She was unsteady, and I pulled her against my leg. "That's my good girl." I patted her wet fur.

Scarlett tilted her head straight back and pushed her hands through her soaked hair. "I have a question."

"I don't have any answers for you anymore."

"I still want to come with you."

"Excuse me?"

"Seabrook."

"Get out of here."

"I'm going to leave him, Charley."

"You *spied* on me, Scarlett."

"He told me you were the bad guy."

"He's the bad guy...and so are you."

"I'm sorry."

"I'll never trust you." I shook my head, definitely fighting mixed emotions. My head told me I was right. This woman could *not* be trusted. "Angelica and I need to go."

"Okay. Okay, I'll drive you."

I shook my head. "We're walking."

Angelica trembled against my leg. I bent and wrapped my arms around her middle. "Girl, let me help."

She whined.

I scooped her up. She wasn't heavy. I wrapped her around my neck, standard fireman's carry. "We're leaving now." I started down the drive through the gravel.

"Charley, please."

I didn't turn around. "Goodbye, Scarlett."

"I'll leave him."

"Good for you."

"Charley-"

"I said *goodbye*."

"Charley, stop. Please listen."

I turned. Her arms were wrapped around her middle and she was shaking.

"Okay," I said. "I'm listening."

"I'll leave him for you."

I watched her for a second, turned back around and started walking.

"Charley!"

"Forget it."

"After I leave him, I'll come to you. I want to be with you."

I stopped and turned to look at her. "You've only known me about a week."

"Yes."

"And after just a week, you want to be with me?"

"Yes. Yes."

"You're crazy, you know that, right?"

"Crazy about you. It's true."

"Well, frankly, Scarlett..."

"Oh God, no, don't say it."

"...*I don't give a damn.*"

I turned and continued down the hill toward the access road to the park, extremely embarrassed I'd allowed myself to be fooled, but extremely proud I was able to think fast enough to deliver the most effective exit line of my life.

Part II

Chapter 26

Cracker Barrel Restaurant

Angelica took to Mrs. Morrison right away. Even before we reached the Brent-Spence Bridge that crossed the Ohio River into Kentucky, Angelica rested her head on Mrs. Morrison's thigh. She smiled and rubbed the thick black fur around the dog's neck.

From the opposite side of the back seat, I turned and looked behind the Escalade. Sandy's van followed a few hundred yards back along I-75. I was sure Ray sat next to her, looking through the latest *Esquire* or other men's fashion magazine, as he usually did. I wasn't sure why Ray was fascinated with men's fashion since his attire consisted of the inevitable torn blue jeans and surfer shirts, but I had never known Ray to be without one of those slick rags, usually folded and stuffed into a rear pocket.

I hadn't taken the time to really think about what happened the other day with Bruce and his goons. Afterwards, I had walked for nearly thirty minutes to the stables with Angelica wrapped around my neck like an exotic Russian fur. Pinson waited in his car as we approached. He didn't say anything about Angelica as he stepped out into the cold drizzle and handed me a golf club. Maybe he had thought this was a new way of exercise Mrs. Morrison had developed.

I'd bent down and lifted Angelica off my neck. She stood firmly on the grass and stared up at me, as if to thank me for the ride. I had rubbed my neck, and then taken the club from Pinson. We'd practiced for two hours, and I didn't remember a thing about it. My mind had been back at the picnic grove, re-living the one moment of my life where I felt truly in control of my own destiny, and where nothing could stand in my way.

"Cracker Barrel alert," Uncle Morgan said.

Jarred back to the present motorcade, I looked ahead. We were just past Lexington, Kentucky. The traffic on the Interstate was fairly sparse.

"Breakfast," I said.

"Yes."

"Where?"

"See the sign?" He pointed through the windshield.

Sure enough, a Cracker Barrel billboard loomed ahead on a grassy hillside. We pulled off I-75 and rounded a short bend into the Cracker Barrel parking lot.

"How I've missed this," Pinson said as he stepped from the front seat onto the blacktop.

I scratched Angelica's head. "Be right back, girl."

The four of us walked inside and sat at a table near a huge, roaring fireplace. We settled down. Nobody spoke. Maybe it was too early in the day to make idle conversation. It occurred to me as our hostess handed out menus, this morning was the first time the four of us had been together. I looked around the restaurant and wondered why Sandy and Ray had not come inside.

I scanned the menu. "The Smokehouse breakfast looks good."

Uncle Morgan folded his menu and placed it on the table. "Maybe this is a good time to fill you in on your schedule."

"Good a time as any," I said.

"I've arranged tee times five days each week."

"What about the other two days?"

Uncle Morgan smiled. "Off-course practice."

I pictured sitting across from Mrs. Morrison, cross-legged on the beach, emptying our minds for forty-five minutes, and then swinging black sticks at each other. "I have a question."

"Sir, I personally recommend the Old Timer's breakfast," Pinson said. "You get two extra side items for only a dollar more."

"What's your question, Charley?" Uncle Morgan said.

"I have more than one, now that I think about it."

"Ask."

"This is *real* golf we're talking about, right?"

"Yes."

"Not me hitting jawbreakers, but me on a real golf course playing real golf."

"Yes."

"Golf isn't played solo, Uncle Morgan. I mean it's not like basketball where you can go out and shoot a few hoops by yourself."

Uncle Morgan nodded. "You want to know who else will be playing."

"Yes."

"I will be playing."

"You."

"And Leslie Rae. Mrs. Morrison."

"Do they allow 60s music on the course?"

"I was a fine golfer once, Charley," Mrs. Morrison said. "Golf did wonders for managing my stress level."

I chuckled. "From what I've read, I think most golfers would disagree."

"What's your other question?" Uncle Morgan asked.

"What about Angelica?"

"I don't understand."

"We'll be on the golf course most of the day. Right?"

"That is the plan."

"Where will Angelica be?"

Uncle Morgan blinked. "I don't know."

"I do."

"Where?"

"With me."

"On the course?"

"The course, the beach, the gift shop."

"You know dogs are not allowed on golf courses."

"I *don't* know that. I've never played golf."

"Well, they're not."

"Then find a way."

"What?"

"This can't be the first time someone has tried to bring their dog along for eighteen holes."

"Charley—"

"Find a way."

The waitress appeared with coffee and a wide smile. "Have we decided?"

"I have." I looked directly at Uncle Morgan. He probably wondered where the assertive side to my personality had come from.

"What can I bring you?" the waitress asked.

"Old Timer's for me," I said.

"Yes, sir. And your sides?"

The waitress finished taking our orders.

I glanced toward the door. Sandy and Ray had still not entered. Maybe Sandy had some long-standing dislike of Cracker Barrel. Or maybe she was just avoiding me.

Pinson sat across the table and played a table game, jumping golf tees into rows of holes in a wooden triangle.

"How you doing, Pinson?"

"This game infuriates me."

"Uncle Morgan," I said after a few seconds of watching Pinson, "playing golf for five days a week, all day long, is a lot of golf."

"Charley, the more you practice..."

"I know the theory, but I meant for *you*."

"Me?"

"And Mrs. Morrison. I'll always need a partner. One of you will be on the course, and playing, all the time."

"Yes."

"That's a lot of golf."

"Charley, are you worried Mrs. Morrison and I won't be able to handle the physical exertion?"

"I just thought it might be better if we had *three* people taking shifts, you know, instead of two." My eyes settled on Pinson across the table.

He stared back at me as if trying to fully process the implications of my last sentence.

"Let's see how it goes," Uncle Morgan said, "before we start recruiting more players."

"Yeah," I said, still staring at Pinson. "Let's see."

Our food came about two minutes later, and it was delicious. We finished, and Uncle Morgan hustled us outside. He wanted to get back on the road.

A number of prospective diners waited in rocking chairs on the front porch. As we stepped onto the parking lot, I saw Sandy sitting in her van about three parking spaces from the Escalade. "Why didn't she come in?" I said, more to myself than anyone in particular.

"Ask her." Mrs. Morrison nudged me toward the van.

"Good idea."

I approached the Carson Industrial Films van and stopped at the driver's door. Sandy's head lay back against the headrest. Her eyes were closed. Ray was in the passenger seat, looking at a magazine.

I tried to quiet the flutter in my stomach, bent, and looked through the window. "Hi."

"Hey, bud," Ray said.

No matter what I used to think about Ray, he never ceased to surprise me with his friendly, agreeable manner. "Hey, yourself."

A furry head poked through between the front seats.

"And hi to you, too, Rusty."

Ray rubbed Rusty's scruff. "Awesome dog, man."

"You getting along?"

"We had a long talk back around Versailles."

"Yeah?"

"Yeah, well," Ray said, "I was doing most of the talking. Dog's a good listener. Think he's got a thing going for your Devil Dog."

"Hey. My angel is sensitive." I squinted at Sandy. "She easily takes offense to things she doesn't understand."

Sandy opened her eyes, glanced at me, and then closed them again.

"Not hungry?" I asked.

"No, man. Sandy and I had some Skyline at 2:00 or 3:00 last night after we left the studio."

"Chili?"

"Yeah. Besides, we got Twinkies, for, you know, in case we get the munchies on the road."

"Twinkies."

"Food of the Gods, man."

"Haven't had a Twinkie since grade school. My mom used to pack them in my lunch."

"Ever had them fried?"

Sandy had not moved.

"Sandy, are you okay?"

"Just tired is all," Ray said. "We were both up late, editing some stuff together."

"Uh-huh." I frowned. "Missed a good breakfast, though."

"We hated to pass up the free food and all, but, well, you know." He shifted his eyes at Sandy for a second and then over at me.

I stood there for a moment. "Sandy?"

She opened her eyes but stared straight ahead out the windshield. "Yes?"

"Something wrong?"

"No."

"Because if something's wrong, I think it's best to talk about it."

She shifted around and locked her eyes on mine. "Do you really?"

"Yes. I do."

She blinked. "I'm too tired to talk about this now."

"About what?"

"*I'm too tired*, Charley."

"I heard you."

"Didn't seem like it."

I said, "Be nice to have you with us when we eat."

"Us?"

"Me."

"Really."

"I miss talking."

She huffed. "Maybe next time."

"Sandy, we can't live on Skyline Chili and Twinkies alone," Ray said. "Not after college, anyway."

"Ray is a wise man," I said.

"You better go," Sandy said.

"Why?"

"Your uncle is waiting."

"We're all going to the same place."

"So?"

"I should ride with you guys for a while."

"Hey, great idea, man."

She glared at Ray. "No."

"Sandy-"

"No."

"I'll sit in the back."

"I told you no."

"Why not?"

"I'm too tired."

Ray chuckled. "You guys sound like an old married couple."

"Fine," I said. "Then I'll see you at the next stop."

Sandy started the van before I stopped speaking. I stepped back and she swung the van around toward the parking lot exit. The van halted there and idled. I supposed she was waiting for the Escalade to take the lead.

"Sir? Charley?" Pinson said from about twenty feet away. He looked at me through the open window of the front passenger seat.

I continued to stare at the Carson van. "Yeah. I know." I turned before Pinson could say anything else and I walked back toward the Escalade. I had a feeling I knew why Sandy was mad at me, but I had no idea how to fix it. It took every last bit of strength I had to remain calm and not run screaming the other way when I came close to Sandy. I felt foolish avoiding a person who meant so much to me. Yet I felt equally petrified to chance being rejected again. No words could explain the sick, empty feeling of rejection.

I moved a step closer to the Escalade and stopped. I thought I'd seen the flash of a red Corvette move behind the Cracker Barrel on the opposite side of the parking lot. It was a classic Corvette from the 60s. It was exactly the kind of Corvette I had recently seen at home.

I decided not to mention the Corvette sighting, even though I got another twinge of a sick feeling when I thought about Scarlett. No good could come of mentioning it, especially with Sandy in the immediate vicinity. So, I climbed into the Escalade, closed the door, and pulled Angelica against my side.

She welcomed my hand stroking her shoulder.

Uncle Morgan guided the big SUV out of the parking lot and to the on-ramp to southbound I-75. I glanced around. Sandy's van fell in behind us.

I took in a long breath and let it out slowly. "Mrs. Morrison. Music?"

Her eyebrows lifted. "Why yes." She reached under the seat and found a dark blue CD case. "Something you want to hear?"

"*Whiter Shade of Pale* sounds just about right."

She beamed. "Procol Harum it is."

"Great." I settled back into the black leather. Pinson turned and stared at me again from the front passenger seat. I stared back for a moment, and then closed my eyes.

As Mrs. Morrison searched through the CD case, I tried to empty my mind and ignore the sound of the Escalade rushing along the pavement, the touch of Angelica on my bare arm, the penetrating vision of the red Corvette, and every last thought, feeling, or reminder of Sandy Carson. I needed to stop obsessing about her. It was unhealthy and pointless. If ever there was a true test of Mrs. Morrison's techniques, this was it.

My goal was to not think about Sandy until we reached the Tennessee border. I could make it until then, with Angelica's help. And Procol Harum's.

If a song like this one, with totally nonsensical lyrics, couldn't flush out my mind, nothing ever could.

Chapter 27

Sweet Home South Carolina

I took the wheel near Asheville, North Carolina. Uncle Morgan replaced me in the back beside Angelica. A while later, I glanced around and saw Angelica's head resting across Uncle Morgan's chest. Both of them were asleep. If I wasn't driving, I could have taken some primo blackmail photos.

We drove straight through without another meal stop and arrived near the outskirts of Charleston at about 4:30. The temperature had steadily risen since we left Ohio; I guessed it was 60 degrees or so. And the air was clogged with humidity. To me, it was odd weather for the beginning of December. Guess it showed I didn't get around much.

We stopped for gas and Uncle Morgan switched places with me.

"We made good time," Uncle Morgan said.

"And we're having a good time," I added.

"Are you?"

"Am I?"

"You're impossible."

"Thank you."

He pointed out the window. "Look at the Spanish Moss."

We traveled down a two-lane country road covered by a near-continuous canopy of enormous trees. Thick shrouds of moss intertwined through the branches and hung down over the road like a tattered green blanket.

"Looks like the surface of another planet," I said.

Pinson said, "My childhood home in Valdosta looked just like this."

A few minutes later, the trees thinned and the canopy disappeared. We passed a small plaza with a food market on the right. Closed wooden fruit and vegetable stands dotted the roadside. And then everything changed again. The grass became even, lush and manicured. The sun hovered low in the sky as we neared a fork in the road. A sign to our left announced *Kiawah Island*. A sign to our right read *Seabrook*. We angled right and entered a two-lane access road surrounded on both sides by thick green vegetation. We passed Bohicket Marina. Sailboats and powerboats of all sorts were tied to a small dock. Rows of condos painted in muted pastels lined the shoreline, light pink and powder blue. The entrance road to Seabrook wound to the front of a small office.

I waited in the car while Uncle Morgan walked inside to retrieve our keys. I rolled down my window and watched Sandy get out of her van and stretch her legs, low to the ground the way joggers do. She finished, stood straight, and shielded her eyes with both hands from the glare of the setting sun. She scanned the surroundings in every direction except mine, as though it would be painful to even chance a glimpse at me.

We started onto the main Seabrook boulevard toward our condos. It was obvious while part of the island catered to tourists, the Seabrook community was largely residential. Magnificent but tasteful homes were nestled in the trees at every turn. About a mile later, a series of beachfront condos appeared on our right. A sign read *Pelican Watch Villas*. Uncle Morgan pulled in the entrance drive and parked near the front of the condos. Only three other cars were parked here. Must have been the slow time of year.

We all stepped out of the car. Sandy and Ray parked two spaces away and then joined us.

"Here." Uncle Morgan pulled keys from his jacket pocket. "Three condos, two people to a condo. Mrs. Morrison and Sandy, Pinson and Hamilton, Charley and me."

Uncle Morgan had gone over the living arrangements before, so this was no surprise.

"Before we go inside for the night," he said, "there's something I want you all to see."

He turned and started away on a wood-plank walkway. We all followed him to the dunes behind the villas that bordered the beach. The sun just touched the far horizon, sending steaks of red across the water, and painted the air with glistening pink.

Uncle Morgan sighed. "It doesn't get any better than this."

We waited silently until the sun had nearly disappeared, and then turned back to our vehicles to claim our belongings.

"Refrigerators are stocked," Uncle Morgan said on the way back to our cars. "Morning call at the beach for Mrs. Morrison and Charley at 8:00. Then, 10:30 tee time. Charley, Pinson and myself."

"And Angelica," I said.

"Charley-"

"*And Angelica.*"

He squinted at me and nodded. "And Angelica."

"Good."

Angelica was close to my side, as always. I reached down and scratched the fur around her neck.

"Well, let's get inside," Uncle Morgan said.

The six of us, with Angelica and Rusty, retrieved bags and settled in to our respective condos.

I stepped inside. "Pretty nice." I fed Angelica and made a quick sandwich for myself.

Our second floor unit had a balcony overlooking the ocean. I slid the glass door open. "Wow. The air is full of the sea."

"That's poetic, Charley." Uncle Morgan joined me on the balcony, an open box of Wheat Thins in hand. He munched on a few crackers, then: "Maybe you should consider being a writer."

"Yeah, in my spare time."

He leaned his arms on the railing and looked out at the darkness over the water. "You could write a journal."

"Journal of..?"

"Might be inspirational to others."

"Uncle Morgan..."

"I'm serious. Write about your insecurities, your faults."

"Well, that shouldn't be hard."

"And then how the practice, the discipline, turned it all around."

"Turned..?"

"Your life."

I tilted my head at Uncle Morgan. He stared off into the dark blue shadows that hung across the beach.

"Uncle Morgan, I have no idea how this is going to turn out."

"Yes you do, Charley."

"No, I—"

"You feel it already, how things are changing."

"I don't. Not really."

"Change is hard to accept. Even good change."

I thought about it. "You may be right."

"Good."

"Yeah."

"So, do you want something else to eat?"

I shook my head. "Nah. I'm pretty tired."

"Are you going to turn in early?"

"Yeah. Okay?"

"Sure. Set your alarm. I won't be here to wake you."

"Early date?"

"Driving to Charleston, first thing."

"For?"

"It's a surprise."

"For me?"

"Can't tell you."

"Can't or won't?"

"Charley, listen. There is one thing in this life you *can* count on."

"What?"

"You *can* trust *me*."

"I know, Uncle Morgan."

He smiled and placed his hand firmly on my shoulder. "Good. And don't forget it."

"I won't."

"Now, there's a pastrami on rye with a slice of raw onion that's calling to me from the fridge."

"You eat that and you'll never fall asleep."

"Ah, yes. The trade-offs of good deli food."

"Night, Uncle Morgan."

"Good night, Charley."

I carried my bag into the single condo bedroom. Uncle Morgan insisted I have the bed. He said he would be comfortable on the pull-out sofa. I knew that wasn't true. No one is ever comfortable on a pull-out sofa. But there was no arguing with him when he set his mind.

I pushed open my bedroom window and invited the sea air inside. I set the alarm, started to pull off my shirt, but stopped and just crumpled onto the bedcovers. Angelica hopped onto the bed and pushed her body against me.

It had been a long drive, and I had a lot to think about. But that could wait. At 8:00 in the morning, Mrs. Morrison would greet me on the beach with one of her enigmatic smiles. And for some unknown, irrational reason, I was looking forward to it.

Chapter 28

Twist and Shout and Stick Fighting

The sun warmed the top of my head as I walked barefoot down the wooden walkway. I had smeared sun-block on my face and neck and looked ahead at the movement of the tide, the water washing to the edge of the dunes. The air carried the scent of salt on a soft morning breeze.

I stepped down the last step onto the sand. I carried my fighting stick and a large bottle of water. Angelica walked behind me and stopped at the end of the last step.

"It's okay, girl, look." I pushed my bare feet through the sand. "See?"

Angelica gazed at me, as if to question my sanity, but finally stepped down into the sand and stood beside me.

"Come on. You'll like it."

I turned and walked out farther across the sand. The beach was deserted except for Sandy and Ray.

"Morning, Charley."

I looked back over my shoulder. "Hi, Mrs. Morrison."

How had she followed me so silently? Must be her Ninja training.

"Beautiful, isn't it?"

"New for me."

"You're not a beach person?"

"My family never took beach vacations. Went to Disney World a few times. My dad took us to Yellowstone, but never to the beach. And after my dad died, well, we pretty much stuck close to home."

Mrs. Morrison smiled and looked out at a few huge pelicans as they strafed the surface of the water, looking for breakfast. "Good. Then this will be even more special for you."

"Yeah."

Sandy and Ray were set up on the beach about a hundred feet from the walkway. They were shooting with telephoto lenses, so they wouldn't intrude on our space and inhibit *natural behavior*, as Sandy had described it. She acted as if she were in the mist filming gorillas with Jane Goodall.

"Shall we?" Mrs. Morrison was barefoot and wore loose-fitting khaki shorts. She set a CD player and a bottle of water on the sand.

"Sure."

We sat in the sand across from each other.

"Hey," I said. "Where's Angelica?"

Mrs. Morrison glanced around and pointed. "There."

I looked toward the shore. Angelica had stretched out in the sand at the base of the tide. She stared into the endless movement of the green water.

"Looks like she's found a comfortable spot," Mrs. Morrison said.

"Guess so."

I placed my hands on my knees, glanced down the beach at Sandy for a second, and closed my eyes.

"Charley."

I opened my eyes. "Yeah?"

"You know, Sandy and I are rooming together."

"I know."

"She was pretty quiet last night. Kept to herself."

"Probably tired."

"I sensed more."

"Like?"

"Something is bubbling just under the surface."

"Did she say what?"

"No."

"Mrs. Morrison, she's really mad at me."

"I don't think so."

"No?"

"I'm fairly intuitive, Charley."

"So what do you think?"

"She's mad at herself."

"I don't think so."

"I do."

I gazed down the beach at Sandy and Ray. "Let's get started."

"Sure." She stared with those brown eyes again, as if she could see under my skin. I took a breath and shivered, even though the morning sun was heating the air quickly.

Mrs. Morrison pressed a button and the music started. This time, it was The Animals, *Please Don't Let Me Be Misunderstood.*

"Close your eyes, Charley."

I did.

"And clear your mind."

That was harder. I tried not to feel the sun, the salt-water breeze, or the sand under my legs. I tried not to hear the water break onto the shore, or the sound of the seabirds passing overhead. And I tried not to think about Sandy Carson, staring at me through her camera lens from a hundred feet away, probably still furious because she happened to see Scarlett Perry exit my apartment and roar away in her fantastic red sports car.

But I was getting better at Mrs. Morrison's methods, and little by little, it all faded, the heat, the breeze, all the sounds, and even the golden image of Sandy down the beach. I took a breath, another, and let the deep drumbeat of The Animals carry me away.

Chapter 29

Blind Ambition

Later that day, we drove the short distance to a golf course in Sandy's van. Uncle Morgan had still not reappeared from his journey into Charleston, and we decided to start on the practice tees until he arrived. Ray drove, Sandy in the front seat, and the rest of us in the back with all the clubs and camera equipment.

The entrance to the course was stately, with stone columns and endless green. The brochure I read described the course as being designed by Robert Trent Jones. I didn't know anything about Mr. Jones, but he sure knew how to build a golf course entrance that pleased the eye.

Ray stopped the Carson Industrial Films carriage and we all piled out. Sandy stepped to the rear, opened the twin doors, and started to remove her equipment. She still had not said a word this morning.

"I have a golf bag for your clubs," Pinson said to me.

"Better than a gaudy silk blanket."

"Yes. It might attract undue attention."

"Wouldn't want to do that."

The Escalade pulled around the corner and slowed into a parking spot. Uncle Morgan stepped out of the SUV and stepped toward us. He carried a white plastic bag. "Sorry. I'm later than I thought."

"Not a problem," I said.

"Yes," Pinson said. "We just this moment arrived, sir."

"That our lunch in there?" I pointed at the plastic bag.

He fished inside the bag and pulled out a set of dark sunglasses, Ray Bans, I assumed.

"Here," he said to me. "Take these."

I took the sunglasses. "Worried about my eyes?"

"Put them on."

I looked at Pinson. He shrugged.

"Okay." I slid the glasses onto my face. The lenses were really dark. "Now what?" I tilted my head from side to side. "Some Stevie Wonder songs?"

"Where's Angelica?" Uncle Morgan asked.

"Still in the van, Mr. Kinshaw," Ray said.

"Charley, let her out."

I moved a step to the back door. "Come on, girl."

Angelica jumped down, came close and looked up at me.

"Now, put this on her." Uncle Morgan reached into the plastic bag, pulled out something green, and handed it to me.

"What's this?"

"A vest."

"Uh, okay." I crouched and set the green vest over Angelica's sides. The back of the vest had a dark-brown rubber handle sewn into the material. Then I saw the words embroidered in the center of an official badge. "Oh my God."

Pinson narrowed his eyes. "What is it, sir?"

I thought for a moment and tried to let the words and the whole concept sink in. "I don't know whether it's twisted genius or, or..."

"It's twisted genius," Mrs. Morrison said.

"Yes, sir," Pinson agreed. "I believe it is."

"A...a *service* dog?" I said.

"Yes." Uncle Morgan grinned.

"A dog for the *blind*?"

"Yes."

"And, correct me if I'm wrong, Uncle Morgan, but now I'm supposed to pretend to be blind?"

"Yes."

"On the golf course?"

"Yes, Charley."

"It's brilliant," Mrs. Morrison said.

"And you think Seabrook won't care if a service dog follows me around out, out there." I pointed to the gently rolling fairways.

"She won't be *following* you, Charley," Uncle Morgan

said. "She will be *guiding* you."

"Oh, right. *Service* dog."

"Yes. We planned for you to play blindfolded anyway, Charley. Remember?"

"I wasn't going to pretend to be *blind*, Uncle Morgan. I thought the plan was to put on the blindfold only at the moment before I was about to shoot."

"That's true, sir," Pinson said.

"But *here*, Charley," Uncle Morgan said, "since you insisted Angelica accompany you on the course, this is the only method that might work."

"And the golf course crew won't care?"

"Can't see how. No pun intended."

Mrs. Morrison nodded. "If they protest, your uncle will raise a number of discriminatory legal issues."

Uncle Morgan smiled. "Could be."

"You mean, the blind have a right to play golf as well as the sighted?"

"That's one way of stating it."

"Seems fair."

"Are you okay with the idea, then?"

"Sunglasses. Blind. Service dog. Samurai sword golf clubs. Sure. Why not?"

"Good," Uncle Morgan said. "Let's give Carson Films a few moments to set up, and then we'll get on the course."

I took hold of the hard rubber handle on Angelica's back, and we walked toward the stone columns that framed the entrance to the golf course Robert Trent Jones designed. Angelica pulled me along, as if she had been guiding the blind her entire life. I chuckled to myself. I felt a bit like Rosa Parks, paving the way for downtrodden blind golfers everywhere. Maybe I was starting a new trend, blind golfers, blind tennis players. The possibilities seemed endless.

We passed through the stone columns and I set foot on a real golf course for the first time in my life. I took a breath. It felt oddly good, but scary too, as if I were perched in the front car of a rollercoaster at the very top of the first hill. I let out a long breath and hoped I felt half this good later, after playing golf using my Samurai clubs, with a guide dog at my side.

I looked across the even grass to one of the vacant practice tees. It was perfect, quiet, and peaceful. This was the spot where Sandy and Ray had planned to set up their equipment. I pictured Sandy by her camera later, gazing my way, one hand on her hip. She would undoubtedly have the look on her face that belonged only to her.

I just had to talk to her. *With* her. I could not go on this way, especially since we were all bunched together on Seabrook, barely a blink from each other all day long. Maybe after a few weeks in the South Carolina sun, she might change her mind and be willing to talk. I hoped so.

I stopped at the practice tee and looked at Pinson.

He handed me a driver from the golf bag. Then he nodded.

I turned, looked down at the small, dimpled sphere that looked back up at me from atop a golf tee. I wrapped my fingers around the magnificently formed grip on the Samurai club. It was time for my first shot.

Chapter 30

I Can Visualize Clearly Now

"It's time, sir, for a few pointers," Pinson said.

"Pointers?" I said. "But I was just about to swing."

"Technique. *Practice* techniques."

"Now?"

"Yes."

"After five weeks of slamming *jawbreakers* into the grass with no instruction, other than to play *by reflex*, now I get instruction?"

"Yes."

"Not to mention the putting."

"Not to mention."

"I'm on a *golf course* now, Pinson."

"Obviously."

"I'm on a golf course with a guide dog."

"I see her, sir."

Uncle Morgan stood about twenty feet away just watching. I wondered whether he was as excited as I was. I hung my head for a second. "Okay. Go."

"Simplification, sir. Economy of action."

I shrugged.

"If you focus correctly at the beginning, it will make easier everything that follows."

"Easier. Right."

"You need to be serious, Charley."

"I can be serious."

He set the golf bag on the grass. "No. You cannot."

"I can try."

"Please do."

"Okay."

I glanced over Pinson's shoulder. Ray adjusted his camera on a tripod from about a hundred feet away. Sandy was missing. Uncle Morgan had not moved.

"We will alternate sides with each hole," Pinson said. "You will shoot right-handed first."

"Got it."

"Now, when you shoot off the tee right-handed, your left arm is the key. When you shoot left-handed..?"

"My right arm is the key?"

"Yes."

"Okay."

"Now, this is very important. You must remember this."

"A kiss is still a kiss?"

"Well, sir, that didn't last long." He shook his head and gave me his most grim look. "You must get serious and stay serious."

"I know. I know. I'm really sorry."

"Are you paying attention to anything at all?"

"Pinson, I couldn't help it. The opportunity for me to say that line may never come again. But, let's go. Serious now. This time, I promise."

"I have no confidence in your promises, sir. But we will continue."

"Great."

He let out a long breath. "Your *key* arm guides the flight and direction of the shot. Your *key* arm, then, must remain straight. If your *key* arm remains straight, ninety percent of all your possible technique problems will never surface."

"Keep my arm straight."

"It is all I want you to think about. Remember, you have trained to shoot by reflex. That will not change. We've worked on directing the force of your shot from your legs, hips, and shoulders. But now, I want your mind to focus on the straight line of your key arm. You will not think about your grip, your stance, your follow-through, or anything else. *Focus entirely on the line of your key arm.*"

I thought about it. "Sounds easy."

"We shall see."

"Okay."

"There's something else."

"I'm still listening and I'm still serious."

"Visualization."

"What?"

"Visualization."

"I heard you. I don't know what you mean."

"You must *visualize* the flight of the ball."

"Imagine where I want the ball to go?"

"More than that. You visualize the exact flight path of the ball, from the moment the ball leaves the tee or the ground, through its upward arc, its peak, downward ride, ending with its contact with the ground and final roll."

"Sounds harder."

"Yes. And it is a technique few can master. In fact, few even try."

"Why?"

"Most golfers, or more specifically, most *unsuccessful* golfers become inundated with too much instruction, too much to think about. It constantly swirls around in their heads like an August tornado. And they sink under the weight of it all."

"Economy of *thought*?"

Pinson smiled, his full mustache tilted up at its ends. "Yes."

"And visualization of the flight path."

"Yes, again."

"Pinson, I have a question about that."

"Ask."

"We've never talked about how to plan a shot. Or which clubs to use."

"Second question first."

"Okay."

"You have three basic clubs, so club choices are extremely limited."

"Well, I have three clubs for each side."

"True, but essentially, three clubs. One club to drive off the tee, one for fairway shots, chip shots, and the like. And a putter. That's it. So, being your caddie might be the easiest job in golf, from a club usage perspective."

"And the shots themselves?"

"Much, much harder. And this is something for which I cannot train you."

"Can't?"

"No."

"Maybe Angelica can help."

"Charley."

"I just don't get it."

"It will come to you after playing, after walking the courses. It will come to you eventually, or..."

"Or?"

"It will not."

"Cheery."

"Please understand, Charley, the *feel* of a course, your perspective, your inherent judgment, cannot be taught. It can only be gained through experience. And, of course, right now you have none."

"True."

"So, a good caddie will try to assist his golfer by sharing insights into the course and each particular shot."

"I'm getting a caddie?"

"I will caddie for you, at first."

"You."

"Yes. I do have some golfing experience."

"I know."

"And at some point, your uncle has arranged for a professional caddie of some repute."

"What a surprise."

"So, Charley, should we get started?"

"Yes."

"Then go ahead," he said. "Your honor."

"Was I promoted to judge?"

"It means, sir, it's your shot."

"Kind of exciting."

"Just remember, focus only on your key arm."

"Key arm. Got it."

I glanced over his shoulder. Angelica moved to me and pressed the top of her head into my right leg. I tilted my head from side to side. "She is the sunshine of my life."

Uncle Morgan shook his head at me. "Let's begin."

"Sure," I said. "Angelica? Move over, please. Please?"

She pulled her head away, walked to the edge of the taller grass, and plopped down.

"Thank you."

"She *listens* to you, sir. And it appears she not only listens but also *understands*."

"She took a canine Mensa test when she was in the dog orphanage. She aced it."

"Of that, sir, I have no doubt."

I took my Samurai driver and positioned myself in a right-handed stance beside the ball. The club felt weightless but incredibly solid. "Is everybody ready?"

Pinson and Uncle Morgan nodded.

I gazed down. The little white ball was suddenly not so little. It seemed enormous compared to the jawbreakers I had been swatting. Maybe Pinson had been right. The practice at Jawbreaker Mountain might pay off after all.

I tried to shut everything out and focused on my left arm. I hoped it was straight, brought the club back over my shoulder, closed my eyes, and swung at the huge white ball on the ground.

I shielded my eyes and followed the ball as it sailed into the sky, angled a slow left, then crashed through a canopy of trees and splashed into a marsh. "Great."

"Focus," Pinson said. "Your arm must be straight."

"I'm trying."

"Try again."

It was going to be a very long day.

Chapter 31

When Charley Met Sandy

The next three days flew by. I ran on the beach each morning before my meditation and stick fighting sessions with Mrs. Morrison. My reflexes were faster than they seemed in Cincinnati. I felt stronger, too, as if I had swallowed a gallon of vitamins. I knew the improvement was due to all the exercise. Or, maybe it was the South Carolina air. At the end of it, late morning, I wasn't even slightly winded. I had to face it; I was getting into terrific shape.

This morning I jogged down the beach with Angelica before the sun was up. I don't know why, but I was particularly jazzed to set my body in motion. From the beach, the rising sun sparkled pink across the bobbing surface of the ocean water. Angelica trotted at water's edge and avoided the skittering sea birds. I guessed she liked the feel of salt water splashing up around her legs.

The sound and feel of the morning beach were fantastic. I was never an outdoors-type person, and usually preferred to stay inside watching bad sci-fi videos instead of walking, jogging, hiking, or doing *anything* outside, especially anything that required exercise. I guessed that part of my personality was changing, too.

About twenty minutes into our run, I reached my spot where I usually reversed course and jogged back to the beach behind Pelican Watch. The halfway point rested at a wide stretch of beach where no homes were visible from the sand. I liked to think of this spot as a deserted tropical hideaway where I might sit with Sandy, stare at the water, and talk about movies, old TV shows, or anything else, day after day, until we got sleepy, thirsty, or just fell unconscious together atop a heap of warm sand.

I was about to turn around and start the jog back when I saw a flicker of movement on the beach ahead. I slowed to a stop and tried to focus through the morning glare. It took three seconds before my stomach twisted into a knot. The broad shoulders and the ball cap gave it away, even from this distance: it was Sandy Carson, herself and in person, jogging directly at me.

I had about ten seconds to decide. I could turn around and run back to Pelican Watch as fast as I could possibly run, hoping she didn't see me, or I could simply stand here and wait. I was frozen, but maybe by being frozen, and by just standing here, I had actually already decided.

Sandy saw me, slowed, and stopped. "Hi." She bent forward to catch her breath.

Angelica trotted up from the water and stood beside me.

"Hi, Sandy."

She straightened and stretched her back. "Your dog is staring at me again with those yellow eyes. She's not normal."

"She was traumatized as a pup. Her parents abandoned her outside a French restaurant. Never got over it."

"Traumatized."

"My poor puppette."

"You're a long way from home," she said.

"About eight hundred miles, I think."

She adjusted her cap and stared at me. "From the condo."

"I know what you meant."

She took a cloth from her back pocket and wiped her face. "Charley, we can talk on the way back, if you want. We would have to walk, though."

"Walk."

"It's tough to talk while running."

"Walk and talk," I said.

She put her hands on her hips as she always did when she was aggravated. "Charley..?"

"I know. You're right."

"Uh huh." She stared down and shook her head, as if silently scolding herself for stopping to talk with me. "Well, let's go then. Mrs. Morrison will be waiting. Ray should be there setting up."

She started and I fell in beside her. She walked with a steady, even stride, her eyes focused straight ahead.

"How's it been rooming with Mrs. Morrison?"

"She doesn't say much. Keeps to herself mostly."

"Really."

"Yeah."

"Uncle Morgan dated her once," I said.

"When?"

"Decade of peace and love."

"Back in the 60s?"

"Yeah."

"Explains her choice of music, I guess."

"There's a lot more to it."

"Do you think he was in love with her?"

"I don't know. I don't...I just don't know."

"Is he sorry that they broke up?"

"Sandy, he never told me about her, until recently."

"Well, if he loved her, then he wasn't sorry."

"No?"

"Because being in love is defined as never saying that you're sorry."

"God, Sandy. That quote..."

"You know, she *likes* you, Charley."

"Huh?"

"I've watched her face, close-up through the telephoto lens, and I've seen how she looks at you."

"Like how?"

"Like a proud parent."

"Really."

"Or maybe like you're her star pupil."

"Last time we took attendance, I was her *only* pupil."

About a minute passed and we didn't say anything. Then, Sandy said, "You're not pasty anymore."

I thought before I answered, trying to curtail the sarcasm. "I've been out in the sun."

"And..?"

"And nothing. I've just been out in the sun for the past month. Out. In the sun."

She nodded as she walked. "Yeah. Guess you have."

"Yeah."

"And all that exercise shows."

"I used to do nothing but sit around."

"Not back in college."

"Long time ago, Sandy."

"You were working out every day back then."

"I remember."

She stopped and took my arm. "We've been talking for thirty seconds."

"Yeah?"

"And you haven't tried to be funny."

"Told you."

"I'm proud of you."

"You too?"

She smiled and my heart wrenched to a halt.

"I'm sorry we haven't been friends lately, Charley."

"I thought love meant—"

"Charley."

"Yeah, I know."

"Couldn't last, could it?"

"I lost focus."

She chuckled.

I grinned at her.

"Come on," she said. "We've got to get going."

"It's nice to talk with you. Feels good."

She looked at the sand for a second and then up at me with her sparkling emerald eyes. "It does."

"So..."

"We really need to get going."

"I know."

A jogger approached from the beach toward Pelican Watch. I glanced at her and then back at Sandy. "Can we talk about this later?"

"I suppose we should."

"No pressure. Just, whenever."

She nodded. "That's fine."

I tried to suppress the enormity of my oncoming smile. "Well, Mrs. Morrison awaits."

I caught sight of that beach jogger again. She was much closer, about a hundred feet away, and would be next to us in a few seconds. I watched. She had brown hair, wore ear buds, looked sleek and athletic. My eyes fixed on her and I couldn't help but stare as she passed by and continued up the beach.

"See something you like?" Sandy asked.

"What? No, she just-"

"I don't know what I'm thinking sometimes." Sandy pulled the brim of her ball cap down hard and broke into a run.

"Sandy!" I started after her, but she was moving fast. After about twenty seconds I slowed to an easy jog. That was all I could really manage for any distance anyway.

Sandy had an extremely short fuse. Always had. I should have known better than to stare at an attractive female on the beach. Nothing would excuse that kind of behavior from me, as far as Sandy was concerned, even though Sandy and I were not together. We're not even *dating*. Plus, *Sandy* was the one who broke up with *me* in the first place.

I tried to even my breathing so I could pick up the pace. I had to catch up with her before she started hating me again. Sandy's mood could turn instantly dark, and I knew thoughts of hating me were swirling in her head as she pushed herself up the beach even faster. If I didn't catch her and explain, it might take another three weeks before she would forget I had stared at the girl on the beach. And I didn't want three weeks of being around Sandy every day with her eyes avoiding me. When her eyes avoided me, it was physically painful.

The problem, though, the actual *center* of the problem, was even if I explained everything to her, it might make matters worse. She might hate me for more than three weeks, maybe forever, and never speak to me again. Maybe I should say I was just a *guy*, and guys *stare* at attractive girls who run by on the beach. Maybe that would be the better explanation. She couldn't be mad at me for being a *guy*. That was something I couldn't help. It was the nature of...nature.

I slowed my pace and stopped. I looked out at the water and tried to catch my breath. Angelica stepped close to me and rested her head against my leg.

I had no idea how I would explain the real reason I stared

at the girl jogger, and why I couldn't look away. I had no idea how I would explain the girl was someone I recognized, someone I recently kissed with more passion than I ever thought possible.

All at once I thought of the Technicolor red clay of Tara, swirling orchestral strings, and of two ill-fated lovers kissing in silhouette, the red-orange tint of Atlanta in flames in the background.

I had no idea how I would tell Sandy the girl on the beach, the girl I couldn't help stare at, was Scarlett Perry, a girl whose name was not really Scarlett Perry, and a girl who apparently would not accept *no* as an answer.

Chapter 32

Mother Nature's Dog

Uncle Morgan parked across from the golf course entrance for our afternoon eighteen holes. We got out of the Escalade, and stood by the car for a moment. Ray stepped out of the van and joined us.

"Shall we?" Uncle Morgan said.

I adjusted my sunglasses. "I'm supposed to be blind?"

"That's the plan for today."

"Just wanted to clarify."

"Consider it clarified. Let's get started." He circled his right arm in an arc by his side as we walked to the tee.

"Warming up?"

"Sore. Haven't played this much golf in a long while."

"Sorry to hear that."

"Let's take a few swings."

"Maybe you should take the afternoon off."

"Mrs. Morrison played yesterday."

"She can sure drive that ball," Ray said. "Lots of power in such a little package."

"You don't know the half of it," I said. "But I wasn't thinking of Mrs. Morrison."

I shifted my gaze to Pinson. "I have an idea."

"Out with it," Uncle Morgan said.

I kept staring at Pinson.

"Pinson, what's he getting at?" Uncle Morgan said.

"His implications are clear," Pinson said.

"Not to me."

"He is suggesting, sir, that I play."

Uncle Morgan turned to me. "Is that right?"

"Yes."

"Wow," Uncle Morgan said. "A straight answer."

"Remember the date. We'll have a party next year."

Uncle Morgan turned to Pinson. "What about it?"

"Sir, may I have a moment with your nephew?"

Uncle Morgan shrugged. "If I say yes, is there the slightest chance we'll start playing golf sometime within this month?"

"Just a few minutes, sir."

Uncle Morgan wiped his sunglasses with the bottom of his golf shirt. He shrugged, stepped away, and sat on the even grass.

"I think he's really mad this time," I said.

Pinson squinted at me. "Believe it or not, I think you mean well. You have a good heart."

"Thanks."

"But I don't understand this."

"Pinson—"

"It's almost cruel."

"Not meant to be."

"Then what are you after, Charley? Why even raise the *issue* of me playing golf?"

"I'm not sure."

"You sure are making a point of it."

"It would help me."

"Help?"

"If *you* could *show* me. Swings. Putts."

"Charley, I have not played golf in—"

"So? Play *now*."

"I cannot."

"Bet you can."

He shook his head. "There are two reasons why not."

"Tell me."

He turned and looked at white gulls as they skittered on spindly legs across the grass toward a water hazard on the fairway. He held his gaze for a few moments, and then turned back to me. "An old injury."

"Maybe it's better now."

"I wear a brace."

"You sure you still need to?"

He waited a second before he answered. "And, Charley, a *pact*."

"Pact?"

"An exchange. An even exchange."

"Involving..?"

"Nature, sir. *The balance of nature*."

"Like in your manifesto?"

He raised an eyebrow. "There's a Golden Retriever back in the condo. He's waiting for me. Patiently. He loves to play on the beach and let the waves crash into him. He *smiles* on the beach, Charley. I've seen him *smile*."

"He's a good dog."

"He trusts me. Completely. Blindly."

"No comment."

"And part of the reason he is so loyal, so trusting, is the *pact*. He *knows* about the *pact*. He knows I gave something, I exchanged something, to save his life."

"You mean your *back*?"

He nodded.

"In exchange for Rusty's life," I said, "the balance of nature required you exchange your ability to swing a golf club?"

"You have to remember, Charley, at the time, my ability to swing a golf club was what made my life special."

I wrapped my fingers around my driver over and over. "Pinson, maybe the balance of nature wouldn't be so upset if you tried to play golf again."

"No."

"It's been years. Maybe your debt is paid."

"I owe it to Rusty not to test that theory."

"You owe something to yourself, too."

"I don't think so."

"In fact, it seems to me the balance of nature could not be in total alignment with the sun, moon, and all the planets, if you ignore a skill you'd learned. It's not the natural way of the world."

He stared at me. "That sounds like Mrs. Morrison."

"And love shall steer the stars, my friend."

"Yes." He smiled. "Yes it shall."

"So?"

"I don't know."

"I've seen it in your eyes since the beginning, Pinson. You

watch me swing away and it kills you that the club is not in your hands."

"I trained myself not to even *think* about playing."

"And you miss it."

"Yes."

"Every time we get clubs out of the car, you miss it."

"Every time."

"Uncle Morgan has a set of clubs with him."

He stared at me. His eyes narrowed. "You know, Rusty has been asking me to let him run down on the beach with Angelica."

"Yeah?"

"We haven't arranged for them to be together and play since we've been here."

"Rusty speaks to you, does he?"

"Certainly."

"Well then, how about tomorrow morning?"

He smiled. "When?"

"7:00. I'll bring the burritos."

"Charley, you say the strangest things sometimes."

"Takes one to know one, pal."

He chuckled. "You have a point."

"So?"

He took a breath. "Your uncle's clubs are sub-standard."

"There's a really nice pro shop here."

He stepped ahead and put his hand on my shoulder. "Thank you."

"Don't thank me yet."

"There's more to you than meets the eye, Charley."

"Uh, Pinson, I just say things that sound meaningful. But they're really not."

"We'll see." He laughed again.

We stepped across the grass to Uncle Morgan. I couldn't wait to see his face when we told him.

Chapter 33

Start Her Up

I was totally exhausted.

After four straight days of running, stick fighting, and eighteen daily holes of golf, my eyes burned with fatigue. It was only 7:30, and the sky had a last tint of red, but I was ready for ten hours in the sack.

I was afraid to admit it, even within the confines of my own skull, but my golf, and everything else, was improving. I could tell from the look on Uncle Morgan's face when I swung one of my Samurai clubs, even though more than half my drives ended in the trees, the water, or just somewhere in the undiscovered country. But I was progressing, little by little, especially my putting, which had become my new favorite golf activity. At least I didn't have to endlessly scour the grounds looking for my Titleist after a putt.

Mrs. Morrison took greater care with me when we fought with the sticks. She knew I was becoming a force to be reckoned with. And I could tell from the lower, respectful tone in Pinson's voice whenever I attempted to putt. He even smiled, once or twice.

It was also rewarding to know I probably made a difference in Pinson's life. Once he made his decision, he charged ahead. He borrowed Uncle Morgan's clubs, and, with just a couple warm-up swings, he absolutely attacked the ball. When we finished our game this afternoon, he walked straight up to me and held out his hand. I took it, and he nodded. I knew what he meant.

I shuffled into the kitchen to make some green tea, to which I was now completely addicted, and saw Angelica sitting beside her food bowl. She was motionless and her eyes were closed. I guessed she wanted to make sure she didn't miss a meal, but was just as tired as I was, and couldn't stay awake.

"Okay."

She opened her eyes. Even after all this time, her amber stare was unsettling.

"What'll it be tonight, girl? Turkey or turkey?"

She didn't answer.

"Turkey, then. Coming right up."

I picked up her bowl and put it on the countertop. Then I opened the fridge, found the plastic bag of shaved turkey breast and dropped a handful into Angelica's bowl. Finally, I added all the other ingredients of a special Petsmart nutritional recipe, just to make sure Angelica was not malnourished because of her extremely limited diet.

"Here you go." I set the bowl on the floor.

She ate quickly as usual, in four or five gulps. Then she sat beside her bowl, closed her eyes, and licked the turkey remnants from her chops.

"Okay then. I'm going to heat some tea in the microwave, then go into the other room and put on some music."

I walked into the main living area, took the new CD Mrs. Morrison gave me about an hour ago, and placed it in the CD player. I switched the power on, and a Bob Dylan song played, the one with *How does it feel?* in the chorus.

I stepped into the kitchen as the song ended and another began. *Born to be Wild*, by Steppenwolf pumped from the speakers. This had to be one of the top-ten bar song favorites. I've heard it four hundred times. Sandy always liked the contradictory nature of the name of the group. She said it was both hard rock and literary. I agreed with her each time she said it, even though I didn't understand.

Then, Steppenwolf finished singing about never wanting to die, and The Beach Boys began harmonizing. If ever there was a group or a sound that contradicted Steppenwolf, it was The Beach Boys. They were asking Rhonda in four or five-part harmony, to help get her, whoever *her* may have been, out of their mind. Or minds.

Next, I heard a familiar electric guitar line - *Satisfaction*. Classic early Stones, Mrs. Morrison had instructed. She liked the

Stones for their *bad boy* British rock image, and not necessarily for their music. Her favorite Stones' song was *Mother's Little Helper*, which was, according to Mrs. Morrison, as close to a protest song as the Stones ever recorded.

The *Satisfaction* lyrics started, and Angelica's eyes snapped open. Her back straightened, and her body started a non-stop shiver, as if she had just stepped into a mountain lake of icy water.

"What's the matter, girl?" I took one step back from her.

Angelica stared at me, as if to let me know she was waiting for just the right moment. Mick Jagger sang on and got to the chorus for the first time. Then, Angelica threw her head back, and as soon as Mick started the "I CAN'T GET NO..." lyrics, the black dog let loose with a bloodcurdling "AWR AWR AWR AWRRR, AWR AWR AWR AWRRR." Mick screeched, "I CAN'T GET NO...," and Angelica sang along.

I flattened my back against the wall and stared with intense fascination. *I had a singing dog.* My head immediately flashed to that classic Warner Brothers cartoon about the singing and dancing frog, and the poor slob who spent his days trying to convince anyone of the frog's peculiar talents. In a way, Angelica's talent was even greater than that of the singing frog. Not only could Angelica sing, but *she had quite a specific taste in music.* Apparently, this was the only song that prompted her to sing.

Satisfaction ended. *Spooky* by the Classics IV started. This song always reminded me of Sandy, since Sandy was spooky, and I never really knew where I stood with her.

Angelica relaxed her rigid stance as soon as Dennis Yost began singing. She yawned and padded across the kitchen tile. She backed herself against a cabinet near the fridge, her normal spot for a nap, and collapsed onto the floor. The abbreviated concert was over.

Uncle Morgan stepped into the kitchen. "What was that?"

"She *sings*, Uncle Morgan."

"That...howling?"

"Uh huh. It must be the only song she knows."

"Did you train her to-"

"No."

He stared at me. "Angelica and Mick."

"Only song I've heard her sing. Maybe she's trying to tell us something."

"What would that be?"

"I started thinking about it, but my head began to hurt."

"You do look kind of beat."

"Long day. Long few days. Think I'll turn in. Early start tomorrow."

"Early?"

"Angelica has a beach date with Rusty. Thought we would walk down to Oystercatcher Bay."

"Are you doing some canine matchmaking?"

"Pinson's request."

"Do you mind if I join you?"

"Sure. I mean, of course not."

"I could use the exercise." Uncle Morgan flexed his arms. "Didn't get much today." He stared at me.

"I understand."

"I know you do."

"I'm meeting Pinson out back on the beach at 6:30. We're walking from there."

"Sounds good."

"Great."

Uncle Morgan walked back into the living area, turned off the music, and switched on the TV. Angelica followed me as I stepped by him, out onto the balcony. I slid the door closed behind us.

The air had cooled instantly once the sun disappeared below the western horizon. It felt good. I felt good. Sandy had not spoken one word to me all day, but for some reason, at this exact moment, that didn't matter. I could tell little by little, things were changing. I could try to sort out my twisted emotions about Sandy later. At least for tonight, and maybe *only* for tonight, most things were right with the world.

Chapter 34

On the Beach Near a Horse With No Name

It was chilly on the beach the next morning, and I was glad I wore my battered Miami Redhawks sweatshirt. I pulled up the hood and stepped along the wooden planks as if I were Rocky Balboa ready for his ultra-training beach montage, running with Carl Weathers.

Pinson and Rusty waited on the Pelican Watch beach, as promised. Uncle Morgan and I removed our shoes and placed them in the sand near the end of the wooden walkway. All of us started at the edge of the tide.

Angelica stayed at my side, almost attached to my leg. She kept her eyes straight ahead, as if Rusty were not even there. Rusty trotted in the water with his head turned toward the rest of the group.

It took about twenty minutes to reach Oystercatcher, an enormous beach I found while on a morning run a few days ago. Clouds kept the rising sun from breaking through, and all of us puffed whiffs of steam as we exhaled. The entire walk, Angelica ignored Rusty completely, even though the Golden made a few attempts to get her attention. Finally, Rusty gave up and trotted back to the edge of the water.

We talked about golf, the weather, southern living, and all sorts of things. It was almost as if we were the best of friends, or long-separated family members suddenly reunited. And it felt good. Uncle Morgan talked to me like a father, and Pinson felt like a brother.

The walk to Oystercatcher took a bit longer than I thought, but it was worth it. The tide was low, and the beach ran hundreds of feet from the shore to the water. There was plenty of room for the dogs to play, if, of course, they even got close to each other, and if, of course, Angelica even knew how to play.

"Look at that." Uncle Morgan pointed south, down the beach. "What a beautiful sight."

Pinson and I turned. A horse and rider pounded through the surf directly at us and then slowed. The water splashed just above the horse's hooves as the animal jittered to a halt. The shapely rider wore gray sweats with the hood pulled up over her head. She sat angled toward the water, as if she were watching the sun rise.

"I suppose we should start back," Uncle Morgan said after a moment. "It doesn't look like Angelica and Rusty have much playtime in mind."

I nodded at him as I watched the rider dismount into the sand. She turned toward me, stood still for a moment, and then pushed her hood back. I felt my breathing stop. "I don't believe it."

Pinson and Uncle Morgan followed my gaze. "You know her?" Uncle Morgan asked. "Charley?"

My stomach clenched in a sick, twisted grip. "Sort of."

Angelica started a deep, menacing growl.

Pinson cleared his throat. "I sense an oncoming complication."

"Hi, Charley," the woman said.

I waited as long as I could. "Quite an entrance, Scarlett."

"Not as good as your last exit."

"If you say so."

"I do."

"The jogger," Pinson said.

"The jogger," I said.

"What jogger?" Uncle Morgan said.

Scarlett took the reins and led the horse toward us. "I didn't expect to see you, Charley."

"You followed me down here, Scarlett. *From Ohio.* Exactly what did you expect?"

"I meant this morning."

"Uh huh."

"Who are your friends?"

"Oh, this is Uncle Morgan. My Uncle Morgan." I couldn't believe I was introducing the spy to my uncle.

"Hello," he said. "Scarlett is it?"

She smiled. "Nice to meet you."

"And, this is Pinson Dill."

He extended his hand to her in his best southern gentleman style. She took his hand and smiled.

"My pleasure, miss," Pinson said.

"You teach Charley how to play golf, right?"

"Sometimes I wonder just who is teaching who."

"Your dog is here," Scarlett said to me.

"And her friend Rusty." I pointed at the Golden who was desperately digging a hole at the edge of the water.

"Your dog still hates me, Charley," she said. "Her eyes are like death rays and they're aimed straight at me."

"Scarlett, I'm not too fond of you myself."

"My name's not Scarlett, you know."

"You're not Scarlett?" Uncle Morgan put in.

"Long story, Uncle Morgan. She's a pathological liar."

"Charley," he said, "maybe Pinson and I will meet you back at the condo."

"Yes," Pinson said.

"Don't you want to hear the long story?"

Uncle Morgan said, "Tonight at dinner, maybe. We're going out. Local spot."

"Fine. Go, then," I said. "But I'll be about thirty seconds behind you."

"Uh huh. I'll tell Mrs. Morrison you might be late."

"I won't be late."

Pinson looked down at Angelica and clapped his hands at her. "Angelica. Come on. Come with us."

My four-footed friend glanced up at me, as if asking for approval, and then stepped over to Pinson.

Uncle Morgan turned away. He and Pinson walked across the sand back in the direction of Pelican Watch. Angelica stayed close to Pinson, and Rusty trotted along at the edge of the tide.

Scarlett looked out at the water. "So."

My stomach felt sick. "This is ridiculous."

"Me?"

"Did *your husband* and his minions come down here with you? Maybe I should see if the pro shop has a catcher's mask they can sell me."

"Bruce doesn't know where I am."

"Uh huh. And where did your horse come from? You didn't tow him down here behind the Corvette."

"She. She's a mare."

I gave her my best Eastwood squint.

"I'm leasing her for the month," she said. "Seabrook has an equestrian center near the entrance to the island."

I shuffled my feet in the sand and searched for any words that might make sense. The only one I could think of was *goodbye.*

"She just arrived a few days ago, and she needs a new name."

"She's orange like a pumpkin," I said.

"Pumpkin." Scarlett smiled. "I like that." Scarlett leaned back against the side of her horse. "You look good, Charley."

I shook my head. "What are you doing here, Scarlett?"

"Why don't you call me by my right name?"

"What are you *doing here*?"

"I missed you."

"And followed me across the country."

"It's not that far."

"You into stalking now?"

She looked down at the sand. "We have a place on Kiawah, Bruce and I."

"The criminal mastermind."

"We came down here a few times a year. He moors his yacht at the marina. But this trip, I'm here by myself. On Loggerhead Way. I spend most of my time over here, though."

"Stalking me."

"No."

"You actually expected I'd be thrilled to see you on my sand-filled doorstep?"

"Maybe a little happy."

"I'm *annoyed.*"

"I left Bruce, Charley. I packed my things and left. Drove right down here. We can still be together."

"Not going to happen, Scarlett."

"I'm not going back to him."

"Enjoy your horse and the beach."

"I will."

"Don't wear sunscreen. See what it feels like to get burned."

"Charley, won't you think about it?" Her tears shimmered in the morning sun.

"Like I said, that's ridiculous and you know it."

She stepped into me and wrapped her hand around the back of my neck. Before I had time to react she pressed close and kissed me. Her lips were intense and desperate. She held the kiss for a moment and then pushed me away. Guess she didn't like the fact that I didn't kiss her back. She turned to her horse, pulled the reins up and over the mare's head, stepped into a stirrup, and swung up into the saddle. "I won't be far away, Charley."

Scarlett held a stare for a few seconds. Then she blinked, and reined her horse around. "Not far at all," she said to the air.

She pressed her heels into the mare's sides and the horse trotted away.

I felt sick to my stomach but started moving the opposite way down the beach. I tried to use Mrs. Morrison's meditation techniques as I slogged through the sand. I needed to forget about Scarlett Perry, or Crystal Preston, or whoever she was. I needed to forget about her hair, her smile.

And her lips.

She could not be trusted.

I rounded a curve in the shoreline and spotted Pinson and Uncle Morgan ahead. I needed to talk this out with Angelica right away, because everyone would ask me questions when I got back. They would want to know everything about Scarlett, especially why she was here in South Carolina.

And I had no idea what I was going to say.

Chapter 35

Eating Near the Dock on the River

Cappy's was about a thirty-minute drive from Seabrook. The local seafood restaurant bordered the Stono River, a quiet tributary that must have been a gateway to larger waters. The boats moored to the small dock at the edge of the restaurant grounds were serious fishing craft. The late evening sun washed across the ripples in the water and up into the parking lot, touching a family of ducks that greeted guests along a ramp leading to Cappy's front door.

We were seated at two tables that looked out at the water through wide windows. Pinson, Ray, Sandy and Uncle Morgan sat at one table. Mrs. Morrison and I sat nearby. The waitress appeared immediately and brought drinks.

"This is nice," Mrs. Morrison said to me.

"Smells good."

"Low country cooking. Can't beat it."

"Don't know much about it."

"Maybe I should order for you."

"Sure. If I can trust you with a deadly weapon in your hands while my eyes are closed, I guess I can trust you to order seafood for me."

She laughed. "Charley?"

"Yeah."

"I've been smiling lately."

"Is Bob Dylan coming to town?"

"Seriously, Charley."

"Why have you been smiling?"

"Because of you. Your improvement has been amazing."

"Thanks."

She shook her head. "Nothing you have attempted is easy

to master. Successful meditation is difficult. Nigerian stick fighting is more physically demanding than many other martial arts. And yet, starting from nothing a few months ago, you can hold your own with either discipline."

"Because you're a good teacher, Mrs. Morrison."

"Not to mention the golf. You are already playing with a skill many golfers would trade ten years of their lives for."

"It's the magic clubs. Samurai Tagawa coated them with Japanese fairy dust. Soy based."

The waitress, who had dark red hair and skin so translucent I could see the outline of veins across her forehead, took our orders, smiled, and walked away.

After a moment, Mrs. Morrison leveled her eyes at me and folded her hands on the table. "Talk to me, Charley."

"Subject?"

She angled her eyes toward Sandy.

"Mrs. Morrison, I've had a long day already."

"Have you tried to talk to her?"

"You mean...about my feelings?"

"Yes."

"I'm not courageous enough for that."

"So you haven't tried."

"No."

"Then..?"

"My words get twisted. Everything would end worse."

Mrs. Morrison smiled. "Charley?"

"Yes?"

"I would like to sit with Ray."

"Why?"

"He's interesting."

"*Ray?*"

"And cute."

"Mrs. Morrison, we have to talk about those funny cigarettes I've seen you smoke on the beach."

She reached over to her small denim bag decorated with topaz and emerald beads. Her hand fumbled in the bag, and she pulled out a clear CD case. She held it out to me.

"What's this?"

"I told you I would have something for you when we got to

South Carolina."

I took it from her.

"Now," Mrs. Morrison said, "listen very carefully."

The waitress appeared with plates of food.

"This looks wonderful," Mrs. Morrison said. "Our talk can wait, for now."

We ate. My blackened catfish was great, and the southern hushpuppies were even better.

"So," Mrs. Morrison said about fifteen minutes later as she pushed her plate to the side. "Good?"

"Oh yeah."

"Are you ready to talk seriously?"

"Ready to listen very carefully."

She stared at me and waited, maybe to make sure I was really paying attention. *"The power of music."*

"Music?"

"A great three-minute record can express more real, immediate emotion than a seven hundred page award-winning novel."

"Never thought about it."

"The words, the melody, and boom! The connection is instantaneous, if the song is just right."

"I assume we're talking 60s here?"

"True romantic songs that grab the heart just as strongly the first time you hear them as the thousandth time. These songs don't whine or complain. They are pure. They are infused with love."

She stood and took her small beaded purse from the padded leather chair beside her. "I'm going to go sit with Ray. Sandy will be coming over here to sit with you."

"Mrs. Morrison-"

"Talk with her. No agenda. Share dessert and twenty minutes together. When we're all finished, go outside with her. Walk to her van. Get in with her. And when you step out in front of the condos, give her the CD."

"It's for her?"

"Say nothing about it. Wait until you have her attention, hand it to her, smile, and walk away. Go straight inside and don't look back."

"Melodramatic."

She nodded. "And I guarantee success."

"Do I get a full refund if it doesn't work?"

"Just make sure it's what you want."

"What do you..?"

"Be certain you want her back, want to be with her, before you give her the CD."

"The song on the CD is *Love Potion Number 9*, isn't it?"

"I wouldn't call that song a great romantic hit."

"Mrs. Morrison, the problem is, I'm so screwed up I'm really not sure what I want."

"That's why I mentioned it. Think it through. Be sure. Because once you give the CD to her..."

"It will be too late?"

She flashed a quick smile at me and walked away to the other table.

I looked at the CD and my mind flashed to Scarlett Perry. Scarlett was beautiful. Scarlett wanted me. I wouldn't need to give Scarlett a CD, or quote lines from Shakespeare. Scarlett would be mine if I just winked. Too bad she was crazy and not to be trusted.

I watched, completely fascinated as Mrs. Morrison and Sandy exchanged words. A moment later, Sandy stood, gave Mrs. Morrison a half-smile, and then stepped toward me.

I didn't want dessert. I wanted to be somewhere else. Anywhere else. In a few seconds Sandy would be sitting across from me. I needed to spring up from the table before she got here, before Sandy sat down, before I said the wrong thing and pissed her off again, maybe more than she was already pissed off.

But, instead, I sat frozen in place. I tried to look calm and cool, but I knew that would never work. So, I concentrated on Mrs. Morrison's favorite mantra: *cold resolve*. I tried to wash my fear away, wash everything away. I just got started when Sandy arrived at my table.

Chapter 36

I Can't Stop Loving You

"**H**i," Sandy said from the edge of my table.

"How was dinner?" I tucked the CD under my leg.

"I ate a couple hushpuppies. Didn't have much of an appetite."

"Ah." I indicated the empty seat.

Her eyes locked with mine for a second, as if she couldn't decide what to do next. Then she shook her head and settled into the seat across from me. "Mrs. Morrison wanted to talk with Hamilton. Ray."

"I know."

"What in the world could they talk about?"

"Ray may be deeper than you believe."

"No. He isn't."

I looked into her flashing emerald eyes, and suddenly Ray was the farthest thing from my mind. "You look great, Sandy."

Her mouth dropped open. "I don't get many compliments."

"Because you're tall, maybe."

"Tall?"

"Intimidates some guys."

She looked at my folded hands on the table. "Do I intimidate you because I'm tall?"

"You intimidate me for other reasons."

She adjusted her black ball cap. "It's just the opposite, you know."

"What?"

"It's you who intimidates me, Charley."

The waitress appeared again. "Dessert?"

"I didn't eat much dinner," Sandy said. "Some kind of chocolate sounds pretty good."

"Oh, yes. Our Mountain of Chocolate Magma."

I smacked my lips. "Sandy? Sound good?"

"Sure." She turned in her seat and stared out the window at the shadowed outline of fishing boats in the water.

"Bring the Magma," I said. "Three spoons."

"Three?" The waitress frowned.

"I eat dessert with both hands. Bad habit since I was a kid. Miss Mondavi at the orphanage screamed when I shoveled it in with two spoons."

I saw the corners of Sandy's mouth slightly curl up. I could tell she wanted to laugh but was holding back.

"Coffee?" the waitress offered.

"No thanks," Sandy muttered.

"Pass. Early start tomorrow."

The waitress spun on her heel and was gone in an instant. Sandy nodded as she gazed out the window. "Miss Mondavi?"

I pointed at the wine bottle on the table. It held a lighted candle. Ages of melted wax coated the dark glass. The label on the bottle read, *Mondavi.*

"I see."

"I was trying to be funny."

"I know."

"To make you smile."

"Charley, do you know why you intimidate me?"

"That cannot be true, Sandy. You are a *force of nature*. I'm nothing. I don't intimidate anybody or anything."

She shook her head. "You underestimate yourself."

"I try not to think about myself. I get depressed."

She shifted in her chair. "Mrs. Morrison didn't want to talk to Ray, did she?"

"If you say so."

"Uh huh. You two were plotting."

"No. Just her."

"Mrs. Morrison cares about you, Charley. I've seen that look in her eyes."

"She smokes funny cigarettes."

Her expression darkened. "I'm sorry we haven't been closer lately, Charley."

"We haven't seen each other in years, Sandy. Hard to be

close when we don't see each other."

She bit her bottom lip, then: "I think back to college sometimes. We were good together, Charley. We had fun."

"You were the best time of my life."

She reached across the table and placed her hand on mine. "You loved me so much, Charley. So much."

"Sandy-"

"It was strong and pure. I saw it filling your eyes every time you looked at me."

"Not sure I want to hear this."

She waited a moment. "I *want* to tell you."

"Told you. Force of nature."

"Charley, I could never *return* that kind of love. Never. It's something that just isn't in me."

My stomach pulled tight. "I can't believe that."

She took a breath, exhaled, and stared at me. "I'm *shallow*, Charley. I spend my life filming *other* lives, without living a real life of my own. I've been immersed in movies since ninth-grade. Movies aren't real, Charley. And I keep at it, keep drowning in it, so I never have to face any kind of reality."

"Sandy. Stop." My hands trembled.

She pressed down harder and breathed a soft chuckle. "Remember what I used to say to you, nearly every day?"

"What?"

"You're killing me, Mr. Smalls. Remember?"

"Yeah. It's from *Sandlot*. But, Sandy, the quote isn't exactly—"

"What I meant was, I knew I had to eventually break up with you. And that thought, Charley, that thought was killing me."

"You never told me."

"I'm sorry."

"The idea you are incapable of love is ridiculous."

"You don't know that."

"Wrong. Wrong, Sandy. I know all about you."

"Oh?"

"Have you even watched your own films? They radiate emotion. Fear. Loneliness. Love. Majestic, magical *love*. That's what sets them apart. That's what makes them special, what makes *you* special."

"They're just films."

"Everyone who sees them is moved."

"People are easily motivated by film."

I took a breath. "Look, I know we made a deal. Either of us could call it off at any time, without any explanation."

"I remember."

"But when you said *the words*, they almost didn't register. It felt exactly like the end of the world. And I wanted to turn the clock back a day, a week, and arrange things so you would never say those words."

"Like *Somewhere in Time*?"

"Is that the one where Christopher Reeve has a broken heart over Jessica Lange and he starves to death in a hotel room at the end of the film?"

"That's the one. But it was Jane Seymour."

"Yeah. Like *Somewhere in Time*."

"Wouldn't have worked," she said. "Eventually, the same thing would have happened, past, present, or future. I'm too afraid."

"Sandy—"

"And I am struck numb with jealousy when I see other women looking at you."

"You are?"

"I came over to talk that night, and I saw a girl coming out your door."

"Oh."

"She drove away in a hot Corvette, and I was *steaming*."

"Sandy, look—"

"*I have no right to do that*. None."

"I don't know what to say."

"Just that we'll both move on with our lives. That you won't be angry with me. We can't go back to the way it was in college."

"I was never angry."

"And you'll try to stop loving me."

I choked back my words as the waitress reappeared with a plate of volcanic chocolate. I knew before she was gone, I would never touch a single bite.

Chapter 37

The Rhythm of the Falling Rain

I sat paralyzed. She *knew* I still loved her. But she wanted me to stop, just like throwing a switch.

Part of me remembered Mrs. Morrison's master plan, so I walked with Sandy out into the parking lot. I didn't say a word on the way.

We approached the cars. I retrieved Angelica from the Escalade, and we slipped into the back seat of Sandy's van. She gave me a sideways look, but didn't say anything. Ray nodded to me from the passenger seat. I didn't say a word either, the entire drive to the condo.

Exactly what did I want? The question was eating at me. Mrs. Morrison was right. I had to sort this out before I made any kind of move.

I was never one who craved female companionship. I liked girls, sure. I was attracted to a few. And now, Scarlett Perry, aka Crystal Preston, was figuratively on my doorstep, and was literally throwing herself at me. I was a fool for even thinking her name.

But when I looked beyond any initial attraction I had for any girls, Scarlett included, nothing ever compared with the way I felt when I first set eyes on Sandy. Something registered, something sparked and then clicked, as though a frayed, electrical circuit inside me was somehow repaired and finally surging with power. While I was with her, everything made sense, I could do no wrong, and the world was a truly wonderful place to live.

Angelica pressed close to me as we motored along the dark, tree-covered access road that led to Seabrook. A light drizzle began and the wipers streaked droplets across the windshield. I scratched the top of Angelica's head. Her eyes were closed, and her paws started to twitch. I wondered if she might be dreaming about chasing sea birds on the beach.

We turned into the condo lot. Sandy parked the van in a large space and switched off the engine. The rain fell harder and pelted against the van roof with a steady rhythm. Ray and Sandy pulled their hoods up, opened the doors and stepped out onto the wet blacktop.

I waited a moment, and then pushed the door open. I straightened up outside and stood in the shower of warm raindrops. "Sandy?"

She stopped and looked back at me. "Yeah?"

"Ray, could you give us a minute?" I gestured at Sandy and myself.

"Oh. Sure, man."

"Take Angelica inside?"

He smiled. "Sure. Dog is cool."

"Thanks, Ray."

He patted the side of his thigh a few times. "Come on, girl."

Angelica followed him toward the condos as if this were nothing out of the ordinary.

"Charley, it's raining." Sandy peered at me from under the shadows of her jacket hood.

"I know." I fished inside my jacket pocket, pulled out the single CD case, and held it out to her. "Here."

"What's this?"

"Please take it."

She took the CD. "What's on it?"

I looked at the ground. "Night, Sandy."

"Good night?"

I angled by her and stepped toward the condo door.

"Charley?"

I didn't look back.

"Charley..?"

The rain ran into my eyes as I climbed the stairs to the landing. I turned the doorknob and walked inside.

***

Uncle Morgan arrived a few minutes later. He found me sitting in the kitchen, bent over Angelica, rubbing her black fur with a dry towel.

"I made a stop on my way back." Uncle Morgan set a six-pack of Coors longnecks on the countertop in front of me.

"What's this for?"

He removed his wet slicker and hung it over a hook on the back of the pantry door. "Maybe this is none of my business."

"What?"

"The look on your face when we were leaving Cappy's."

"How did I look?"

"Like you needed a Coors."

"Really?"

"Yes."

"Isn't this breaking training?"

"Maybe this is an *important part* of your training."

I stood, took a bottle from the carton and twisted off the cap. The frosty bottle felt reassuring in my hand. "Thanks, Uncle Morgan."

"Don't mention it."

"Have one with me?"

"Absolutely." He opened a bottle and we both took long swallows.

"My gosh that's good," I said.

"Charley, do you want to talk about what's bothering you?"

I took another swallow and shook my head. "I don't think my brain can take the torture."

"Okay." He stepped back from the countertop. "If you change your mind..."

"Thanks."

"I'm going to watch some TV, Charley. You?"

"I want to finish this beer first. Let my brain settle."

Uncle Morgan nodded and walked out of the kitchen.

I blinked. Sandy was still in my head. Sandy was *always* in my head.

I gave her the CD. Part of me couldn't believe I had done it. I didn't even know what song Mrs. Morrison had recorded. If I had to guess, it was probably a Bob Dylan song. Dylan had been her hero since her junior year of college when she was part of a committee that arranged a Dylan concert at Antioch. She told me how the single day she spent with Dylan changed her life forever.

Angelica walked beside me through the living area and out onto the balcony. The overhang covered us from the rain. It was unusually warm, even for South Carolina, and the soft, summer-like sprinkle created an odd atmosphere for late January. I took another swallow of cold beer, looked over the railing at the darkened beach, and listened to the soft splashing of the tide. The sand was deserted in the evening rain, and a curtain of silver mist hung motionless along the shore. It was a scene totally foreign to me. I liked it, though. It was peaceful.

A door slammed below and I caught a flicker of movement from under the balcony. Angelica gave a quick, startled, "Woof." A figure burst outside from the first-floor condo. She ran down the wooden walkway, past the small dunes and toward the beach. My breath caught in my throat. The beer bottle slipped through my fingers and clattered across the wooden floorboards.

"Charley?" Uncle Morgan called.

I took a breath and turned. "Yeah?"

"You okay?" He stepped out onto the balcony.

"I don't know."

"Thought I heard a door slam."

I turned back to the railing and stared into the air. "So did I."

"Something I can do?"

I shook my head. "I gotta go, Uncle Morgan. Watch Angelica for me?"

"I'll turn the TV on Animal Planet for her."

I opened the outside balcony door and flew down the two flights of steps. I hit the sand and raced to the beach walkway. My shoes barely touched the wooden planks, and I crossed them in seconds. At the end of the bridge, I jumped over the steps that led down to the beach and tried to focus.

Sandy stood at the edge of the water. Her form was unmistakable, even in shadow.

I rushed to her. "Sandy?"

She did not turn. One of her hands was wrapped in a white

towel and hung at her side.

"You okay, Sandy?"

She turned slowly and started toward me. Her eyes were glistening with tears.

"Sandy, what's the matter?"

She stopped just beyond my reach and held her wrapped hand out to me. The white terry-cloth towel was stained a deep burgundy. "I cut my hand."

Rain trickled into my eyes. "How..?"

"The CD case."

"What the..?"

"It splintered. I was in a hurry to close it. My hands were shaking so...from the song..."

"Seriously, Sandy. It's bleeding."

She gazed at me, her eyes swirling pools of green. "It's nothing you can't fix."

"What?"

"You *can* fix it, Charley."

"I don't..."

She stepped close. Her face was inches from mine. "I want you to fix it."

Her head tilted back a fraction; her lips parted. "Please, Charley. Please."

My hands found their way to the sides of her face. I pushed my fingers through the soaked blonde curls behind her ears. Her ball cap shifted back, bounced on her shoulder, and fell to the sand.

She touched me with one finger and gently stroked the water from across my forehead, just above my eyes.

And then she kissed me.

She kissed me.

She.

Kissed.

Me.

The warm rain soaked our faces. I held her shoulders and pulled her close. She trembled against me. Then our lips drew slowly apart. She wrapped her arms around my back and rested the side of her head against my chest. I felt her exhale.

We silently held each other. Sandy remained still and

pushed her face harder against my chest, as if she couldn't get close enough.

After a moment, I opened my eyes and looked toward the shore.

A figure stood at the end of the walkway.

I blinked rain from my eyes.

The figure looked like Mrs. Morrison, a woman I had recently grown to admire and respect.

I squinted and tried to focus on her face. It was nothing more than a dark silhouette, but I was sure she was smiling.

Part III

Chapter 38

Weird Vibrations

About 7:45 the next morning, I stumbled down to the beach to meet Mrs. Morrison. I had no idea how I made it to our designated spot on time, or even how I made it from the condo down to the beach at all. I had no clear memory of any part of my trip to the beach. Seven hours of absolutely no sleep was to blame.

Sandy and I had held each other last night, and held each other, and held each other, until it felt as though we might not be able to physically separate. Eventually we relaxed our embrace and slowly walked up to the narrow wooden bridge and back to the condos. She stared at me for a few seconds when we reached the end of the walkway, squeezed my hand and smiled. I watched her turn and walk inside, her hand still wrapped in the bloodied towel. We had not spoken a single word since she first kissed me.

I blinked against the morning sun and focused on Mrs. Morrison. She squinted at me with her arms folded across her chest and nodded.

I said, "You look like you want me to say something."

"Is there anything *you'd* like to say?"

"Maybe."

"And?"

I lifted my palms into the air. "You are a genius."

"Genius?"

"A freaking genius."

"No need to go that far, Charley."

"Oh yes there is, Mrs. Morrison. There's a very great need to go that far."

"The power of music. That's all."

"No argument from me."

"But, you know, Charley, there's nothing mystical about it. The music would not have worked if she didn't already love you."

"Mrs. Morrison, you saw her kiss me."

"Yes."

"Did you see her hold me?"

"Yes."

"Want to know what she said to me less than an hour before our scene on the beach? Before I gave her that voodoo CD? 'Stop loving me, Charley. I'm shallow and can never return that kind of love'."

"She said that?"

"At Cappy's. And roughly sixty minutes later, she listens to your magic music, and...and..."

Mrs. Morrison smiled. "So I guess it worked."

"You just won the prize for understatement of the century. Don't even try to tell me it wasn't the song. And by the way, what song was it?"

"Sandy will tell you, in time."

"Well, I know for sure it wasn't *Eve of Destruction*."

"Are you two a couple now?"

I thought for a moment. "I suppose we are."

"Does that make you happy?"

"I didn't get three consecutive minutes of sleep last night. I started to nod off, smiled again, and woke myself up. About four hundred times. So, I guess that means I'm happy."

She nodded at me. "Good."

"Yeah."

"But please remember one thing for me, Charley."

"Sure."

"Keep your focus."

"Meaning?"

"Sandy and Ray will be setting up down the beach just before we begin our stick fighting."

"I know."

"She will be seventy-five feet away."

"I know."

"Focus on what we are here for. *Focus*."

"Yes. I will. No problem."

She bit her lower lip. "Then, let's begin."

***

Mrs. Morrison ended our session after ten minutes. I suppose she could tell my head wasn't in it. I couldn't stop thinking about Sandy.

I shifted my gaze toward the condos. Uncle Morgan, Pinson, and Rusty walked toward us along the wooden bridge. Lately, Pinson and Uncle Morgan had been coming to watch the stick fighting.

"Problem?" Uncle Morgan asked.

"We're taking a break," Mrs. Morrison said. "Charley has been having concentration difficulties this morning."

"Let's go inside then, and sit in the air conditioning for a while."

Pinson led the way, and we all walked back to the condo with Angelica and Rusty trotting beside us.

***

Ray came out of the kitchen with two bottles of beer in each hand. "Drinks?"

"It's not even 9:00, Ray," I said. "In the morning."

Ray looked blank. "Seemed later."

Sandy and Mrs. Morrison sat beside each other on a small sofa. Uncle Morgan and I crowded around Pinson who held a book in his hands.

Pinson said, "My folks gave this book to me for Christmas one year when I was playing on my high school golf team. I suppose I've read it a hundred times. It's updated every year or so, but this edition is my first...and my favorite."

He turned the book around for us.

I read the title. "Weird Golf Legends."

Pinson handed the book to me.

"I have this book," I said as I scanned the pages. "A later

~209~

edition."

"What's in it?" Sandy asked.

"I can tell you," Mrs. Morrison said.

I looked at her. "You can?"

"I have a copy of that book, as well."

"Mrs. Morrison, why would you have a book about odd golf stories?"

"Remember, I was quite a golfer in my younger years. Golf stories fascinate all golfers."

Pinson added, "The stories about great golf successes are just as important as the greatest golf *failures*."

"I suppose, Pinson." I waved the book. "Just not as entertaining and funny."

"My point, Charley, is I foresee a time when *your* story will appear in a new edition of this book."

I stared at him. "Disaster story or success story?"

"That's right," Pinson said. "That, sir, is right."

We all looked at each other silently, as if waiting for someone to really answer the question.

"So," Uncle Morgan said, "back to the beach?"

"Yes," I said. "Break time's over."

I led the way outside.

Chapter 39

Three Dog Day

The afternoon sun hid behind a cloud, and the air was positively chilly as I approached the first tee. Angelica seemed content, stretched out in the shade of a nearby outcropping of shrubbery. Her service-dog vest blended in with the perfect green of the lawn.

Pinson teed off first. His drive was straight and powerful. Over the past week or so, Pinson's performance improved with each round. He never talked about it, but I could see his confidence growing. His putting was especially dead-on. He could infallibly read the curves and angles of each green. I watched his every move. I hoped maybe I would absorb some of his skill through the air along the way.

Uncle Morgan walked the course with us this afternoon and gave me occasional words of encouragement. He was good that way, always highlighting the positive. I wasn't sure I ever really appreciated the true nature of his *friendship* until recently.

I adjusted my dark sunglasses and lined up a putt on the eighth green. I visualized the path of the ball, from the exact moment of contact with my putter, to the rolling curves of the immaculate grass, and finally into the small, empty circle at the far edge of the kidney-shaped green. I was playing right-handed on this hole, and it didn't feel much different than when I shot left-handed. It was hard for me to accept sometimes, but Pinson and Mrs. Morrison were right. Visualization and reflex were proving to be the keys. I couldn't believe I'd ever doubted them.

The sun emerged when we reached the tee at 16, and finally the light was strong enough to make my midnight-black sunglasses useful. I selected my left-handed driver, and waited as Pinson placed a new Titleist upon the furred edges of a Brush-T, an ingenious device that cradled a golf ball atop a surface of filaments.

Pinson closed his eyes for a second, before he took a breath and said, "Charley."

"Yeah?"

"A moment, please."

"Sure."

"Your clubs have fascinated me from the beginning."

"They are cool."

"May I try your driver?"

"Go ahead."

Uncle Morgan joined us on the tee as Pinson gently slid the club from its leather bag. He caressed the finely stitched grip with both hands and balanced the weight of the gleaming metal shaft. Then, without even taking time to adjust his stance, he brought the club back over his shoulder and swung. The head of the driver barely touched the tips of the smooth lawn.

"Great God in heaven," Pinson said.

We gazed up as the Titleist rocketed into the ionosphere.

"Yeah," I said. "I know."

"But it doesn't feel quite right."

"Remember, The Last Samurai made them to fit just me."

"Still, quite a shot," Uncle Morgan said.

Pinson locked his eyes with mine for a moment then held my club out to me. "These clubs are special, Charley. Your body has responded to our exercise program, and your mental focus continues to improve."

"Thanks."

"One item is still missing, however."

"What item?"

"We need to know how much all the training and exercise really means."

"Just tell me, Pinson."

"Competition."

I stared for a moment. "Competition, like..?"

"Your training is all theoretical until you stop practice and really begin to play. Nothing takes the place of a real game against a real opponent."

"I suppose that makes sense."

Uncle Morgan said, "He's right."

"You need a match," Pinson said.

"Against..?"

"One of the Seabrook pros," Pinson said.

"A pro."

"Yes."

"Who?"

"There are several."

"Well, if that's what you think, Pinson. I trust you."

He smiled. "Then, sir, I shall arrange it."

"One thing, though."

"Yes?"

"It's one thing to practice out here with you and Uncle Morgan and pretend to be blind, but playing a real game against a pro, blind, am I ready for that?"

Pinson considered that, and glanced over at Angelica who was sprawled in the grass in a nearby patch of shade. "I believe the charade must be maintained. The course management will not react kindly if they discover they have been duped over a dog."

"Duped?"

"He's right again," Uncle Morgan said.

"I'm still a little nervous about it."

Competition. Me against a pro.

Down the beach, Sandy stood by her camera with one hand on her hip and the other hand shielding her eyes. Ray was slumped in the sand beside her, his head angled down at his hands folded on his lap. I took a breath, gripped my magic left-handed driver, and stared down at the ground.

Without taking time to think, I closed my eyes.

I closed my eyes.

I squeezed them tight...and exhaled a long breath.

I knew the white Titleist at my feet was about to be launched into orbit by a club made from Japanese steel. I *knew* this, even though the shot would come from reflex and be driven by cold resolve.

The shot would be long and straight.

And I knew this with absolute certainty.

Chapter 40

Do You Believe in Magic?

I skipped dinner, managed to sneak away, and drove Angelica to Bohicket Marina, right down the access road on the way over to Kiawah. I parked Uncle Morgan's Escalade near the Bohicket clubhouse, and Angelica walked beside me along the boardwalk. The fishing boats came into view behind the shops and restaurants as we rounded a bend. The vessels were painted in combinations of stark white and deep blues, and they were moored in long, neat rows. A few scattered visitors walked beside the boats, holding hands, or just taking a quiet stroll after a dinner of authentic low country cuisine. Just the place for a private canine heart-to-heart.

"Come on, girl," I said. "This is that special place I told you about."

Angelica padded beside me as I led her to the far end of the pier. I sat on the edge of the wooden boards, and Angelica stretched out next to me. She rested her chin on top of my thigh.

"So. Look at that sunset."

An enormous red-orange ball hung low in the sky and framed the colorful boats.

Suppose it is beautiful.

"Suppose?" I said.

Dogs are color blind, after all.

"You know, I've always wondered how people know that."

Not sure, but it is true.

"Yeah. Well, that's too bad."

A good trade off.

"Oh?"

You know, super hearing and super nose?

"Maybe you're right."

Would be nice though, if for once, the colors...

"I bet." I rubbed Angelica's neck through her thick fur for a few moments.

She looked up at me. *You need to talk, right?*

"True."

Not Sandy this time.

"No."

Go ahead.

"Pinson says I need some real golf competition."

Pinson speaks quietly. And he's smart.

The sun inched lower and touched the far edges of the water with sparkles of orange. Angelica took her chin from my leg. Her paws extended out across the weather-beaten pier.

"I'm a little nervous about it, Angelica."

A little?

"Maybe more than a little. Maybe I'm terrified."

Playing for real is different than practice.

"Yes."

When it's practice, there's no chance of failure.

"Of course, at some point I have to play for real."

Without question.

"But what happens if I choke? What happens if I really stink? I don't think I can deal with disappointing Uncle Morgan."

I gazed down at the red-orange light reflected in her eyes.

Angelica licked the top of her front paws. *Try harder, practice harder. That's the only way to succeed at anything.*

I nodded and patted her side. "You are the smartest girl I know."

Your relationships must be quite limited.

"Even so." I watched a few gulls flutter across a sky streaked with purple, and I absorbed the beauty of everything around me.

Angelica took a breath and sighed. *Do you believe in magic moments?*

"What do you mean?"

When everything aligns perfectly.

"Like..?"

We sit here together, in this beautiful place, and share

friendship. This special moment may only happen this once, exactly this way.

"Yeah. I know."

Do you?

I nodded again and smiled. "We are *true friends*, Angelica. I think it hit me when you first appeared in the woods and walked right over to me, as if somehow our meeting was destined to happen, written in the stars somewhere."

Angelica stretched completely out and rested the side of her muzzle against the wooden pier. *Remember this special, magic moment, and think about it if any little bit of sadness begins to creep up.*

I blinked a tear away, leaned over and wrapped my arm around Angelica's thick black coat. "Yeah, girl. I will. I truly will." I leaned my head against her side.

We both watched silently as the sun disappeared into the quiet ripples of the early evening tide, and all the reds, oranges, and purples faded to gray.

Chapter 41

Dust in the Wind

The clouds started to move in just as we got to the first tee of the Crooked Oaks course. The forecast called for scattered rain, so Pinson, Uncle Morgan, and I all wore our light rain gear. Mrs. Morrison, of course, who could obviously *will* her skin from getting wet, chanced the elements with her usual shorts and sleeveless shirt.

"I'm still not sure about this," Uncle Morgan said.

I fidgeted with my golf bag as I watched Sandy and Ray set their camera equipment about sixty feet away on the far side of the tee.

"I'm sure," I said.

"Pinson," Uncle Morgan said, "what about it?"

"I have not changed my mind. Everything changes with competition. I see no reason Charley shouldn't learn that now."

"And I suppose you agree, too, Leslie Rae?" Uncle Morgan said to Mrs. Morrison.

She nodded. "Practice is just practice. Pinson is right. Charley needs this. I see no reason to wait."

I tilted my head to the fairway. A young woman, about thirty-two and dressed for golf, stepped toward us. The morning breeze caught her flowing dark hair and swept it around her neck. A sleek red golf bag balanced motionless, neatly over one of her shoulders, as if it were part of her body.

"Uh, Pinson?" I said.

"Sir?"

"*She's* the course pro?"

"P.J. Varelli. She has played on the women's tour many times and finished well."

"I realize, Pinson, if Ms. Varelli played on the *tour*, it

would be the *women's* tour."

Pinson shook his head. "Sir, I do truly wonder how you get through each day without someone punching you as hard as they can."

P.J. Varelli stopped beside us and I had a hard time not staring for two reasons. First, P.J. Varelli was so startlingly attractive I could easily see her as a cover girl on a golf magazine, or, really, *any* magazine. But second, I was supposed to be *blind*, for God's sake, at least for the next eighteen holes, and I could not afford any hint I could actually see her.

"Gentlemen, lady," she said. "I am P.J. Varelli."

"Ms. Varelli, I am Pinson Dill."

He offered his hand and P.J. Varelli shook it once.

"This is Charley Davis, your opponent," Pinson said.

"Hi." I was careful to aim my head a bit off and to the side.

"Let's be clear," P.J. Varelli said, without offering her hand to me. "I am not here today to socialize, tell golf stories, give lessons, or pose for photographs with you or your children."

"Uh huh." I said.

"And just for the record, and no offense to you, Mr. Davis, playing against a blind man seems as though I'm supposed to be the victim of an elaborate practical joke, and at the end of our round a surprise reality-TV crew is going to pop out of the rough."

"Uh huh."

"Not to mention the dog."

I could barely breathe. This woman was stunning, and, ironically, Sandy's polar opposite. She was much shorter, and her long dark hair fell about her shoulders. She was richly tanned. Her brown eyes sparkled with flecks of red.

Without thinking about it for even a fraction of a second, I asked, "What does P.J. stand for?"

Pinson glared at me through the next few moments of silence.

"Let's begin, gentlemen?" P.J. Varelli said. "Unless there are any other *important* questions."

"Certainly. Let's begin." I handed my small bag of clubs to Pinson.

He removed my left-handed driver and held it out to me.

"Who goes first?" I asked.

P.J. Varelli eyed my club with one raised eyebrow, and pulled a driver from her golf bag. "That honor is yours, Mr. Davis."

Pinson stepped close to me with his back to the others, and spoke quietly. "This course is no different today than when you played on it yesterday, sir. 6780 yards, par 72."

"I know, Pinson. And please stop calling me *sir*."

"Remember to plan your shot, close your eyes, and visualize your shot in explicit detail."

"That's exactly what I have been doing for weeks."

He nodded. "Yes. But now someone is here to beat you, to *distract* you, to ruin your technique and concentration. You must remain focused."

"Okay."

"And stop staring."

"Huh?"

"You know what I mean."

"I can't help it. *Have you seen her?*"

"Yes."

"Well, she is quite distracting."

"Partially why I requested her."

"You're killing me, Smalls."

"Cold resolve, Charley. Frigid, cold resolve."

"I need a frigid cold *shower*."

"Look, I'll be right here. And I'll do what any good caddie should do."

"Why couldn't she be a pot-bellied, middle-aged guy from Georgia? He would definitely not be so distracting."

"Mr. Davis, are you inferring that people from Georgia are unattractive?"

"Of course not."

Pinson glared at me. "First hole is par four. Hit it straight off the tee, as far as you can."

And with that, perhaps ironically, the sky cleared and a full sun beamed across the turf. Pinson stepped to the tee. Uncle Morgan and Mrs. Morrison watched from behind us. Angelica stretched out in the grass in a small patch of shade.

Pinson crouched and gently set my Titleist atop the tee on

the incredibly even turf. He took my arm, guided me a few steps to the tee, and stepped away. I adjusted my total-eclipse sunglasses, which were so dark they nearly blinded me. Maybe that was the point.

I gripped my Samurai club with both hands, and stared down at the ball. The air was totally silent, and that seemed weird. I glanced in Mrs. Morrison's direction. "No music?"

She smiled. "Music can still fill your head, Charley."

"Thought I was supposed to *empty* my head."

"Call upon the music and it will come to you, inspire you. Call to the music as you approach the tee."

"Uh huh."

Even though that made as little sense to me as anything Mrs. Morrison had ever said, for no particular reason I thought of *Sunshine of Your Love*, by Cream, a 60s rock song with an infectious beat, carried throughout by Ginger Baker, one fantastic drummer, as I had been instructed by Prof. Morrison in her daily *History of 60s Rock Music* class. Ever so slowly, I brought the club back up and around my left shoulder, exhaled a deep breath, closed my eyes, and swung. I stared off into the horizon and looked for the ball, even though I was supposed to be sightless.

"Where is it?" I said under my breath.

"Sir," Pinson said as he appeared beside me.

"Yeah?"

"Try again."

My eyes sneaked a peek down to the white, dimpled ball on the ground, right at my feet. "Oh."

"Still your go," P.J. Varelli said.

"Yeah."

I couldn't believe I missed the ball entirely.

Wind suddenly sprang up as I readied myself again. Plan the shot. *Don't stare at P.J. Varelli.* Think of the music. Clear my mind. *Don't stare at P.J. Varelli.* Close my eyes. Swing.

This time I thought of *If I Fell*, by The Beatles, a song quite high on my list of possible songs that could be on Mrs. Morrison's voodoo CD I had given to Sandy; I eventually needed to ask Mrs. Morrison about that, if Sandy never decided to tell me. It also suddenly occurred to me I was subconsciously choosing songs like *Sunshine of Your Love*, and *If I Fell*, because of the brunette who was standing a few yards from me with a golf club in her hands. I closed my eyes before I brought the club back. I swung again. The bottom of my club head sliced a layer of turf from the tee. The wind caught the clump of sod, and dust swirled everywhere.

"You caught it, sir," Pinson said.

My Titleist landed halfway down the center of the fairway.

"Good shot, Charley," Uncle Morgan said.

"It was actually two shots. And two shots to get halfway to the green is not good, Uncle Morgan."

I moved back as P.J. Varelli stepped to the tee. She casually dropped her ball to the ground. Then, with no stretching, no practice swings, no adjustment of her grip, she planted her feet, brought back her club, and swung.

"Crap-o-rama," I mumbled.

The ball rocketed into space. P.J. Varelli did not watch at all. She simply turned to retrieve her bag while her shot was still airborne. I tried not to notice the muscles flex in P.J. Varelli's calves.

The ball finally descended about thirty yards from the green, dead straight on target. Pinson and I exchanged quick glances of disbelief.

"Nice shot, Ms. Varelli," Pinson said.

"Thank you, Mr. Dill," P.J. Varelli said, even though she still had not looked. She strolled by me on her way to the fairway.

I waited until P.J. Varelli was out of earshot, and then I said, "Can you even believe that?"

"She *has* played on the *tour*," Pinson said.

"No warm ups," Uncle Morgan said. "Amazing."

Mrs. Morrison said, "It illustrates a point, does it not?"

"Probably." I said.

"I've been teaching how much of the game is mental."

"Yes you have."

"Think about that before your next shot."

It took a few minutes to reach P.J. Varelli who waited near my ball. She stood off to the side and stared at Angelica who was sprawled in the grass beside her.

Pinson handed me my right-handed *everything else* club, as I liked to call it. This music thing was obviously not working for me. Instead, I tried to simply clear my mind of *everything*, as I had practiced since we began this journey into madness. I flicked a glance over at the green almost two hundred yards away, even though I was barely able to see it through my dark lenses. I thought about it and visualized my shot. Then I squeezed my eyes shut, brought my Samurai club back, and swung.

The Japanese steel caught another clump of sod, and dust sprayed everywhere in the rising breeze. I watched my ball as it flew fifty yards or so, and landed a good distance from the green. I must have gotten way under it.

"How was it, Pinson?" I said, preserving my blind persona.

"You were a bit under the ball."

I gritted my teeth. "Did I raise a divot so big the dust from it could fill a scene from *The Grapes of Wrath*?"

"Sir, it was not that bad."

"And please stop with the *sir* already. I can't take it."

"Okay, all right." Uncle Morgan stepped close to me. "We've been at this for months now, and we've all kept our tempers under control. Mostly."

I exhaled. "Sorry, Uncle Morgan." I looked at Pinson. "Sorry, Pinson."

"No harm done, si... Charley."

Uncle Morgan looked me straight in the eye. "Shall we continue?"

I nodded, and the four of us walked down the fairway toward my ball. Angelica had followed P.J. Varelli, and finally plopped flat on her side in taller grass near a small pond. Pinson led me directly over my Titleist.

I decided to allow less time for my mind to wander, gripped my club and swung. I didn't need to peep downward to realize the club had merely grazed the top of the ball. From behind my dark sunglasses I watched the ball roll and come to a stop, still about thirty yards from the green. After three shots, on a par four hole, I wasn't even close.

I remained in place as P.J. Varelli chipped her ball onto the green. The ball stopped after a slow roll, about ten yards from the cup.

"Pinson," I said, keeping my voice down, "I don't freaking believe you set me up to play against this woman. *Competition?* It's as if I was just learning basketball and you put me on the court against Magic Johnson."

"Magic retired a long time ago, sir."

"Then it's even more true."

"Watch her and learn," Mrs. Morrison said.

I shook my head, allowed Pinson to walk me to my ball, and tried another shot. And another. After seven strokes I was miraculously about eight feet from the cup. I glanced behind and noticed a foursome gaining on us. I must be setting a course record for the slowest round.

This game needed to be over, the sooner the better. I casually touched the ball with my putter and watched the ball stop on the lip of the cup. I wanted to shake my head in disbelief, but couldn't since I was a blind person. I bit my bottom lip hard, Pinson guided me, and I tapped the ball in. The first hole was finished.

And the score on this par 4 hole: P.J. Varelli, who didn't warm up and who took less than one second to hit the ball: Three. Charles Marriott Davis, expert at ratting on former employers and not clearing his mind: Nine.

We continued, and nothing much changed, except, perhaps, I got worse. My concentration totally evaporated, and with each errant shot, I felt my grip grow harder and my stance become more unbalanced. We had waved the foursome behind us through, and by the end of the eighth hole, I was about finished.

"Uncle Morgan, can I have a word?"

He walked over, and we stood off to the edge of the eight green. "Yes?"

"A favor?"

"Go on."

"I'm not sure what's wrong, but enough already."

He considered that. "For just today?"

"Yes. Just today. Face it, I cannot hit *anything*. I'm playing like I've taken four steps backward."

Mrs. Morrison and Pinson joined us.

"What is the problem, Charley?" Mrs. Morrison said.

"If I knew that, Mrs. Morrison, maybe I could fix it. I can't believe I suddenly stink even worse because I'm playing for real."

Uncle Morgan took a breath and gazed at me. "I agree."

"You do?"

He nodded. "But let's give it one more hole. We will have completed nine. Then we'll break for the rest of the day, meet for dinner, and talk it through. No pressure, no admonitions, just discussion and analysis. Okay?"

I tapped my putter on the turf. "Sure. One more hole."

I noticed Angelica in the grass on the pathway to the ninth tee. Something struck me, and I turned to face my uncle. "Uncle Morgan, I need a few seconds."

"Sure. But another group is fast approaching from behind."

I nodded and handed my putter to Pinson. "Pinson?"

"Sir?"

"Lead me to Angelica, if you please."

"Oh. Certainly."

We reached Angelica in about twenty seconds. I sat in the grass beside her as Pinson stepped away.

She looked right into my eyes.

Not so good today?

"Total screw up. I've forgotten everything."

Why? She snapped at a grasshopper close to her nose.

"Not sure, but now that I'm out here, now that it's not just practice, with everyone watching and expecting so much, my concentration has gone to the junkyard."

Apparently. The dog's mottled tongue hung out of her mouth. She stretched her front paws out on each side of her muzzle.

"That's all you have to say?"

What do you expect?

"Not sure. I don't know. Something."

Clear your head, the way you are supposed to.

"It's way harder than it sounds."

Is it P.J. Varelli?

"Part of it."

Approach it differently.

"I'm listening."

Difficult to concentrate on emptiness.

I nodded. "Yes."

Instead, clear everything except for one image.

"I tried this once with Mrs. Morrison. She thought it might help."

One scene that brings a smile. Nothing to do with golf, of course.

"That won't be a problem."

Give that a try.

I took a breath. "I will. Thanks."

What are friends for, after all?

I gave Angelica a pat on her side and stood up. "Pinson?"

He retrieved me and we started our walk to the ninth tee.

"Mr. Davis?" P.J. Varelli said.

"Yes?"

"Are you ready to continue?"

"I believe so."

Without any hesitation, P.J. Varelli set her ball on the tee, took a fraction of a second to center herself, and swung. As always, her ball flew straight and true.

"Good shot?" I asked.

"Fair," she said.

I took a breath, crouched, carefully placed my ball on the short turf, and exhaled as I straightened up. I gazed down the fairway at Angelica as I took my Samurai driver from Pinson.

"Par three," Pinson said. "198 yards." He took a step closer to me. "Fire at the ball, Charley. Forget that anyone else is here."

"I'll try."

"Good." He patted me once on my shoulder and stepped off to the side.

I positioned over my ball and stared down the fairway at the distance to the green. I took another look at Angelica, and slowly closed my eyes.

She trots in slow motion at the tide's edge, the water splashes about her face, drops of salt-water land on her dark, blotchy tongue that flops from side to side. She smiles. She is happy. She is my friend.

I exhaled and gazed down. The ball came into focus with an impossible clarity. I closed my eyes, brought my driver back, and with only the image of my four-legged friend swirling in my brain, I gathered my energy, and swung.

The Japanese steel sliced through the air in near silence, and connected with the Titleist with a tiny *clack*. I opened my eyes.

The ball zoomed into the air and kept going, higher, farther. I was numb as I watched, unsure if I was really seeing this. It seemed to take forever, but finally, the ball descended, and rested on the far edge of the green.

"My God," Pinson said.

I looked over at him. "Good?"

"Yes, sir. Yes it was."

Mrs. Morrison walked up to me with the look of a proud parent, wrapped her arms around me and squeezed the breath from my body. Patchouli filled my head. She released me, and without a word, stepped back to the others.

We walked to the green in silence and watched P.J. Varelli finish out the hole in three. As usual, her seemingly casual putting amazed me.

With Pinson's completely unnecessary assistance, I stepped to my ball at the very edge of the green and eyed the cup. For some reason, the hole did not seem so far. Mrs. Morrison, Uncle Morgan, Pinson, and P.J. Varelli must have been standing nearby, but I blocked them out. Angelica plopped down near some trees just off the side of the green. I gazed at her for a moment, and pictured the ocean in the background.

My hands moved the putter.

I watched the ball avoid the edge of a sand trap and angle straight to the hole. The Titleist rolled forever. I stared, mesmerized.

And the last sound I heard was the satisfying finality of the ball plopping into the cup.

I glanced across the turf at Sandy. She stepped away from her camera and slowly clapped her hands together. Ray caught my eye and bowed to me at the waist.

Uncle Morgan started toward me with an incredulous look on his face. "Charley."

"Yes?"

Uncle Morgan's smile broadened. He gazed at me for a moment. "It's coming together."

I looked over at Angelica. "Finally."

"Yes," he said. "Those were two magnificent shots."

"Let's hope they weren't two lucky flukes." I turned from him. "Pinson? I'd like to hug my dog."

Pinson took my arm and we quickly stepped to Angelica. Before I could bend to her, P.J. Varelli was right in front of me. The breeze caught the scent of a soft fragrance. "Mr. Davis."

"Yes, ah, P.J.?"

"Pamela Jean."

"Oh. P.J. Pamela Jean. Right."

"I understand this was our last hole for the day."

"Not my idea. I could play ten more."

She chuckled. "I bet you could."

"Maybe another game sometime?"

She took my hand and grasped it. "Without a doubt." She turned from me. "Mr. Dill, it was my pleasure."

"Thank you, Ms. Varelli."

I stared after P.J. Varelli as she retrieved her golf bag and walked far down the fairway, until she faded into the muted colors of an impressionistic painting. Then my eyes shifted toward Sandy. She stood beside her camera with a hand on one hip. Her eyes gazed across the grass at me, and I instantly realized I had made another huge mistake.

The official dating rules clearly stated: *Never stare at another beautiful woman while your girlfriend is in the vicinity.* In fact, that is dating Rule Number 1.

And I had just shattered it...again.

Chapter 42

Ray's Lonely Hearts Club Band

Spring in Charleston was spectacular. The days warmed quickly and flowers bloomed everywhere.

On a Sunday morning, Sandy and I managed to sneak away and visit *Magnolia Gardens*, a nature retreat of incredible blossoming splendor. We walked, held hands, and appreciated the warm sun. The air was thick with the fragrance of new flowers. We smiled like we were thirteen-year-olds. It was one of the best mornings of my life.

Our group had fallen into a solid routine for the past few months. In the morning, I usually ran on the beach with Angelica at my side. I tried taking Rusty with us, but the retriever still was more interested in digging in the sand than running with me.

Mrs. Morrison's meditation sessions had taken on an entirely new picture. Pinson joined our sessions. Most surprisingly, so had Uncle Morgan. It was impossibly strange to see Uncle Morgan sitting barefoot, cross-legged in the sand with his eyes closed. If ever there was an image I never expected to see, that was it. Still, Uncle Morgan seemed to be getting something from it. He was calmer, more peaceful. A few times, I even caught a quick smile he flashed to Mrs. Morrison. But what really caught my attention were the quick smiles I caught Mrs. Morrison flashing back. Now that was strange indeed.

Ray had been showing up late in the morning. At first he ran onto the beach just a few minutes after our scheduled meeting time. Sometimes the few minutes stretched into ten minutes. Fifteen. And his eyes had dark brushstrokes underneath, as if he had missed a great deal of sleep.

He also started disappearing right after our afternoon games. I assumed he was running off to meet a girl, specifically *the girlfriend*, as he called her. But Ray never gave us any details. None of us had seen her or even knew her name.

One morning in early May, about two weeks before we were to leave the southern charm of the Charleston area and drive the long trek back to Cincinnati, I decided to ask Ray about his new and mysterious relationship. He came trotting from the condos onto the beach, right on time for once.

I waited for him with Angelica at the water's edge near Sandy and her camera. "Hey, Ray."

"Hey, Charley." Ray took sun-block from his pocket and rubbed it into his cheeks, nose, and forehead with his fingers.

"Morning, Ray," Sandy said.

Ray gave her a brief salute. "Morning, General."

"I asked Mrs. Morrison to give Ray and me a few minutes to talk," I said, "before we start."

"Talk about what?" Ray asked.

"Mind walking with me?"

"Did I do something wrong?"

"No. Oh no. You're not in trouble. Just want to talk."

"General?" Ray said to Sandy. "Your boyfriend wants to talk with me."

"So go."

I led Ray down the beach for about thirty seconds, until I was sure we couldn't be overheard. Angelica stopped with us and gazed at the pelicans gliding overhead.

"What's the big deal, Charley?"

"Haven't seen you around much lately."

"I'm here every day, man."

"Ray, you've been *late* nearly every morning."

"I thought you said I wasn't in trouble."

"No trouble, Ray. Not in trouble."

"Then what?"

"You're gone every evening. Tired every morning. What's up with that?"

"Yeah, well..."

"I wouldn't be much of a friend if I didn't ask you about it."

"I appreciate that, man."

"It's your new girlfriend, right?"

Ray nodded. "I suppose."

"Why haven't we met her? You keeping her a secret?"

"What? No."

"Ray, you don't normally clam up about a girl. Usually you can't wait to talk about her. At least, that's the way it used to be."

He looked out at the water. A fishing boat bobbed on the tops of the waves. "I don't want to jinx it, is all."

"You really like her. I get that, but—"

"Might be more than that."

"I don't believe in a jinx, Ray."

"Are you sure?"

I nodded. "Yeah. I'm sure you can't jinx your relationship just by talking about her."

Ray looked down at his bare feet. "We're friends, right? You and me?"

"Yeah, Ray. We're friends. I mean it."

Ray nodded. "What do you want to know?"

"Start with her name."

"Melanie."

"Where did you meet her?"

"I ran into her down at Oystercatcher while walking the beach one morning."

"It's cool down there."

"Way cool, man."

"She pretty?"

He chuckled. "Dumb question."

"Details?"

"When she smiles I can't breathe."

"Sounds serious."

"As a Black Friday sale at Home Depot."

"I don't understand what that means, Ray."

"I don't understand why the last couple seasons of *Lost* were so confusing."

"So, Ray. Hair? Eyes? Something?"

"Eyes like a blue sky after a morning storm."

"You had to have heard that one somewhere."

"She's shorter than Sandy and a little older. Maybe twenty-eight."

"A little old for you, don't you think?"

"She's an athlete. Looks like she could do some grim damage, man, if she got angered."

"Works out?"

He nodded. "Runs. Swims. Rides horses."

"Sounds like she's a cowgirl."

"She has a horse named Pumpkin."

I felt blood rush to my face. "Pumpkin? You sure?"

"Yeah, man. Pumpkin. Not a good horse name, I know. Sounds like a *cat* name."

I knew it. All I could do was stare at him.

"Hey, you okay, Charley? You look like you just saw a fat man do a cannonball at the pool."

"I'm okay. And Ray, You really need to work on your metaphors."

"Is that where you signal with flags from the deck of a ship?"

I studied his face. "You're kidding."

"You always underestimate me, man."

"Does Melanie have a last name?"

"Wilkes. Melanie Wilkes."

"Oh my God."

"Yeah. She has a place over on Kiawah."

I inhaled. "Ray, can I ask you something?"

"We're friends, aren't we?"

"Do you know if she's married?"

His eyes darkened. "She told me she was, man."

"And where's *Mister* Wilkes?"

"Ohio. They're separated."

"Oh?"

"But she's getting divorced."

"Sure about that?"

"As sure as a-"

"No more, Ray."

"Good. I couldn't think of one anyway."

My head was filled with a thousand things to say, but I couldn't force myself to say any of them and wreck Ray's world. "Well, great. I'm glad for you."

"So, is that it?"

I nodded. "Sure. Mrs. Morrison is on her way down. We better get back."

Ray turned and watched Mrs. Morrison step across the wooden bridge. "Charley, I've got something to ask you, now that you mention it."

"Mention what?"

"It's just an expression, man."

"Right. Go ahead."

"Do you think the hippie queen would mind if I joined in some of your stick fighting sessions?"

"Why would you want to do that?"

"Need to work out more, man. Build up my strength."

I smiled. "I don't think she'll mind. Maybe it would help having another body to swing at."

"I'll ask her right now, then."

"But Ray?"

"Yeah?"

"I wouldn't call her the hippie queen."

"Hell no, man. Lady's dangerous with that stick."

I turned from him and looked out at the ocean. Angelica shifted with me and stretched her front paws out in the sand. Three dolphins sliced through the water near the shore. Sea birds flew just above them, on watch for any stray scraps of fish.

My stomach twisted into a thousand knots and the front of my head pounded. I couldn't decide whether I felt sick or angry. I barely knew I was still standing on the beach. I didn't know if Scarlett was really interested in Ray or just *using* him to get to me.

But one thing was certain.

Ray *was* my friend.

I was sure of that.

And I would do everything I could to keep Ray from getting hurt.

Chapter 43

Lyin' Eyes

I knew it wouldn't be hard to find Loggerhead Way. Maps of Kiawah were available in the Seabrook office lobby. The next morning, at 6:00, I borrowed the Escalade and cruised the short distance to Kiawah.

Loggerhead Way was a no-outlet street with ten or so houses. By Kiawah terms, these houses were modest two-bedroom bungalows on a half-acre of land. The red Corvette was displayed at the curb, halfway down the street as a silent monument to when Chevrolet ruled the world. I parked around the corner and switched off the engine. The air was filled with the clicks of morning insects.

I sat and watched like a TV detective on a stakeout. The only things missing were donuts and bad coffee.

At about 6:30, a front door opened at a house near the Corvette. Ray strolled out and retrieved a bike from the front lawn. He got on the bike, put in some ear-buds, and pedaled down the street, right at me. I ducked down and waited until he passed. He was focused on the music and didn't notice the Escalade. At least, I don't think he did. I waited a few moments, pushed the car door open and stepped out into the street.

"Scarlett," I called as I neared the yard in front of the house. "Scarlett."

The door opened and she appeared. She was barefoot, wore a wrinkled t-shirt and denim shorts. "Charley?"

"I can't believe this, even from you."

"What are you talking about?"

I stopped in front of her. "I don't have many friends, Scarlett."

"Want to come in?"

"Tell me about Ray."

"Who's Ray?"

"Hamilton."

"*Ray*. Is that your pet name for him?"

"Scarlett-"

"I *like* him, Charley. That's all. We met on the beach and hit it off."

"But you knew he was working with me."

"I do now."

"But *Melanie Wilkes*?"

"It's the first name that came to mind."

"Crap, had you even seen *Gone with the Wind* before we watched it together?"

"Now that's insulting."

"But why use a fake name? Why lie to him?"

"Look, Charley, I guess I should have told Hamilton my real name."

"You have so many. What is your real name?"

"Norri. Eleanor, really. Eleanor Harding."

"Not Crystal?"

She shook her head. "Nope."

"Why do you need a secret identity?"

"I'm a celebrity's daughter."

"Celebrity?"

"Yeah. Just like Hamilton."

"Ray's dad works at the G.E. plant."

"He's the son of Indiana Jones."

"Is that what he told you?"

"He promised me a visit to Harrison's ranch in Jackson Hole."

"He told you that?"

"Well...not in so many words."

"That Ray. He's something."

"I think he's interesting."

"Who thinks he's interesting? Scarlett? Crystal? Melanie? Norri? Eleanor? Mrs. Bates?"

"All of us."

"So, who's your celebrity parent?"

"She's...Tanya."

"Tanya...Harding?"

"She's my mom."

I felt something get stuck in my throat. A memory of one of Uncle Morgan's *weird athlete* stories stirred in the back of my brain.

"The Tanya...*Harding*?"

She took a breath. "Only a few people know."

"I don't believe you."

"It's true."

"Your track record with the truth is zero."

"I told you the truth about the way I feel, Charley."

"Look. Scarlett—"

"Norri."

"Whatever. Don't hurt my friend."

"That's not my plan."

"Good." I turned to leave.

"Where are you going?"

"Back to playing golf."

"Don't go."

I stopped. "Didn't take long, did it?"

"What?"

"To get over me."

She blinked. "It's not that way."

I walked to the street. "Bye, Scarlett."

"I didn't plan this, Charley."

"I'm not convinced."

"All you had to say was yes, and we could have been together."

I stopped again and looked back at her. "You're nuts."

"I could have been yours, Charley. And I would have loved you forever."

I frowned. "What movie is that line from?"

"*The Big Chill*, I think."

"Never seen it." I stepped away again.

"I've got the movie. Inside. Great score. 60s music."

"Is there any other music?"

"Why do you keep walking away from me?"

"It fits the scene," I said without turning around.

"Charley..."

I walked until I reached the Escalade. I opened the door and looked back toward the house. Scarlett was still outside, staring in my direction. I started the engine and drove out onto the main road. My head was spinning again. I didn't know whether to trust Scarlett with Ray; he was bound to get hurt when he discovered the truth.

Scarlett was still after me; I knew it, and it was unbelievable. The thought of having *Tanya Harding* as a mother-in-law was somehow chilling. And Scarlett being Tanya's daughter was probably true. Norri, or Eleanor, Harding wasn't random enough to have invented it on the spot.

The toughest thing on my mind, though, was whether I should tell Ray about Melanie's history of lying. And the more I thought about it, the harder it was to decide. I didn't want to be the one to break Ray's heart.

I neared the entrance to Seabrook and realized I would soon have to face Mrs. Morrison, and probably Ray, with Nigerian fighting sticks. That would take total concentration, and I could not afford to have Scarlett on my mind. So I decided I would think about Scarlett tomorrow, tomorrow at the beach, when I went for my morning run.

Maybe I could figure out what to do then.

Chapter 44

Then You Can Tell Me Goodbye

We were set to leave Seabrook tomorrow. I was in no hurry to go. The last two weeks were extremely productive, not just for me, but for Pinson, as well.

My game was still improving, even after I started to shoot with my eyes closed. I almost never failed to connect with the ball. Mrs. Morrison repeated her mantra of emptying my mind. Pinson told me to trust my instincts, visualize, and let reflex take over. I'd been trying, but my drives had been way off course. My putting, however, actually got better. Go figure.

Pinson had been slamming the heck out of the ball. I smiled every time he rocketed one far into the sky. Pinson closed his eyes, too, just for an instant, before he connected with the ball. I didn't know if he was doing that intentionally, but his drives had been magnificent. Lately, Pinson had been smiling practically all the time.

Uncle Morgan and Pinson joined us for meditation nearly every morning. I knew Pinson took meditation seriously, but I thought Uncle Morgan was there just to spend time around Mrs. Morrison. I saw his expression change each time he looked at her. I was nearly certain Uncle Morgan was trying to rekindle a romance that ended more than forty years before.

The real shock, however, was P.J. Varelli. About a week ago, she just showed up, glided down to the beach like some mythical sea bird and meditated with us. I was surprised, since she certainly was far from a creation of the 60s. But she sat silent and immobile, eyes closed, upturned palms on her knees. She listened to Mrs. Morrison almost reverently, as if Mrs. Morrison were Gandhi.

Angelica always stretched out beside P.J. on the warm

sand, never leaving her side. For some reason, Angelica was quite taken with P.J. Varelli, which was the opposite of the way Sandy felt about the pro golfer who had played on the *women's* tour. Whenever P.J. Varelli was around, Sandy seemed surrounded by a simmering heat about to explode into a nuclear fission cloud.

P.J. Varelli also joined us regularly on the Seabrook courses, swatting the ball straight and true. And her putting was even better. She became deadly serious, and her total focus and concentration were riveting to watch, even though I still had to pretend to be blind whenever P.J. was around. She had a knack of just barely touching the ball with her putter and then looking off into the distance in the other direction as her ball rolled unerringly toward the cup.

Ray stick-fought with us, and had thrown himself right into it with no hesitation. He'd played basketball in high school and was a pretty fair athlete, but it was his steely-eyed assertiveness that unnerved me a little. Ray was such a peaceful soul. Watching him stick-fight as if he were a gladiator in the arena was a bit unsettling.

Sandy and I spent nearly every free moment with each other, and that was unsettling for an entirely different reason. Each day with her, each minute with Sandy at my side, was nearly as magical as our kiss on the beach. How did the song go? *Every day with you, girl, is sweeter than the day before.* I thought that was right, and even if it wasn't, that line described my recent life with Sandy

***

I called to Angelica, and my black canine friend followed me onto the balcony and down the wooden steps to the beach. I carried a small CD player along with a CD that Sandy had surprised me with just before dinner. It was still warm outside, and the sounds of the waves were comforting. I was expecting to be a little sad when we left here tomorrow morning. Southern living was just too easy to get used to.

We walked out across the sand and I saw Pinson sitting under the early stars with Rusty at his side. Rusty spotted us as we approached and gave a few sharp *woofs* of welcome.

"Pinson."

He looked at us. "Come to enjoy a night at the beach one last time?"

"I didn't expect to like it here this much."

"Sir, I will miss this immensely."

I sat in the sand near Pinson. Angelica plopped beside me. I opened the CD player and inserted the CD.

"What do you have there?" Pinson asked.

"Don't know. Sandy just gave it to me."

"Is it a special occasion?"

"Not sure."

I pressed the play button and music began. The song was *Never My Love*.

"The Association," Pinson said.

I wanted to say something, but my throat tightened.

"Charley, are you okay?"

I nodded to stop the tears from building. I tilted my head back and squeezed my eyes shut. "Yeah."

"Truly?"

I smiled and looked at him. "Truly."

"A woman who gives that song also gives her heart."

"Mrs. Morrison...she's been busy matchmaking."

"I sense her hand in this love affair."

I looked at the CD case. "Pinson, I have a question."

"Proceed."

"What do you really think of my chances for an appearance in *Weird Golf Legends*?"

Pinson smiled. "Your legend will be more inspirational than all the other stories put together."

"How's that possible?"

"From *nothing* to shooting *below par* in nine months. Remarkable."

"We'll see."

"No doubt about that at all, sir."

"I'm going to miss the ocean."

"Ohio has good things as well."

"Graeter's."

"A beautiful autumn."

"At least friends will be there," I said. "That's a good thing."

Pinson scooped a handful of sand and let it sift through his fingers.

We sat for a while and stared out at the rippling shadows on the water. I took deep breaths of the salty night air. Maybe some of it would stay in my lungs after we all got in our cars and drove away in the morning. I knew it wouldn't work, I knew it was a stupid thought, but I was already missing this place more than I ever thought possible.

Chapter 45

Me and You and a Dog Named Angelica

Angelica and I waited outside Pelican Watch with our luggage when Sandy and Ray pulled into the condo lot. We had arranged to ride together on the first leg of the trip back. Sandy stepped out onto the blacktop, pushed open the van's side door behind her, and smiled at me.

Her smile still made my heart stop.

"You look ready," she said.

"You are master of the obvious."

She walked straight to me, put her hand behind my neck, and kissed me. Then: "Where are the others?"

"Just left. We'll meet them at the gas station down the road."

"That means Angelica is coming with us.*"*

"She likes to go for rides with me."

Sandy bent to Angelica and scratched the top of her head. "I liked her from the beginning."

"You mean after she scared the crap out of you?"

"I wasn't ever scared of her."

"Course not."

I grabbed my bags, threw them in the van, and got in shotgun. Angelica stretched across the back seat beside Ray. Sandy settled behind the wheel and started the engine.

The van swung onto the main avenue and motored slowly through the Spanish Moss and canopies of flowers. I turned and looked at Angelica. She stared out the side window. It felt good to have her with me.

That ball of black fur in the back seat was my friend from the first moment she came out of the woods and pressed her head into my leg. If I had changed in the past few months, part of the reason was about two feet from the back of my head right now, staring out the van window with her incredible, all-knowing amber beacons.

"Oh, Sandy, how about some music?"

"Sure."

"I brought something." I pulled a CD from by bag, removed the disc, and reached toward the radio controls. "Stones."

"Charley, you've clearly succumbed to Mrs. Morrison."

I nodded. "She's a wise woman."

"Dangerous with that black stick, man," Ray said.

"Your uncle has the hots for her," Sandy said.

"I think you might be right."

"Something's going on, Charley."

"Uh huh." I pressed my finger to the radio button. "So, Sandy, if you feel like singing along..."

"Charley, what the hell are you talking about?"

"Nothing."

"You've turned weird on me again."

"You see right through me, Sandy."

I took a breath, pushed the button, and clicked through the CD cuts to track number four. Then, I grinned so hard it hurt my face.

The electric guitar buzzed through the speakers.

I checked behind me. Angelica snapped to attention.

Sandy saw my expression. "What?"

Mick sang, *"...and I try, and I try..."*

Angelica's nose pointed at the ceiling.

And then Mick shouted the chorus: *"I CAN'T GET NO..."*

Angelica threw her head back and howled.

"Oh you have got to be kidding me!" Sandy shouted.

"I CAN'T GET NO..." Mick growled again, with a furry, female canine howling back-up. *"SATISFACTION."*

I looked at the back seat. Ray draped one arm around Angelica and howled with her.

"Oh my God, Charley. This is too much. Mrs. Morrison's gotten to your dog, too."

I turned the radio volume higher. Sandy kept shaking her head.

Cappy's was about thirty minutes away. Maybe we could stop there, and I could order a big steak. Then I could save a nice juicy bone for my British Invasion dog in the back seat.

She would like that.

"I CAN'T GET NO..."

Part IV

Chapter 46

Six Degrees of Garland Quick

The day after the gang of us returned to our Cincinnati digs, Uncle Morgan asked me to report to Mr. Garland Quick, in Mt. Adams, a crowded village on a steep hill overlooking the city. It was a cool place to visit, if one liked winding streets crowded with bistros and art galleries. In the winter months, though, it was nearly inaccessible, either in or out, if even one inch of snow fell. The streets ran at ninety-degree inclines, or at least it seemed that way.

I was lucky to find a parking spot about two blocks from the address on Hatch Street. It was always impossible to park around here, and that was enough to keep me away from Mt. Adams, unless I had no choice. Like today.

The address turned out to be a condo. It was small and squeezed between two other condo complexes on a steep avenue packed with ancient buildings, all recently rehabbed. The condos were small, sat on a narrow, congested street, and overlooked the river through big picture windows, and each had a wide balcony with a hot tub for twelve out back.

Garland Quick was supposed to be a *caddie of special talents*, according to Uncle Morgan, and I apparently now needed a caddie of special talents, since I was about to start playing real, regular golf. His nickname was *King Looper*, but I was not to call him that for some reason. Uncle Morgan also told me Garland Quick was a celebrity caddie of sorts, flown regularly to California by Tom Hanks and the like.

I was tired, didn't want to be here, but walked with

Angelica up the brick walkway and stopped at King Looper's door. The doorbell was shaped like an electric guitar. I looked at my watch, glanced down at Angelica, then reached out and pushed the doorbell.

The tune from inside the condo was an electric guitar riff, low and fast. And it sounded vaguely familiar, like maybe an old Doobie Brothers song. The door was dark, solid wood with no window, so I couldn't see if Mr. Quick or anyone else was inside. I looked at my watch again and waited another moment.

Nothing.

I pushed the doorbell, harder this time, even though I knew it wouldn't make any difference. Same guitar. I couldn't place it, but I knew I had heard that riff somewhere before.

"Yeess?" The voice came through a speaker near the doorframe.

"Mr. Quick?"

"Yeess?"

"My uncle, Morgan Kinshaw sent me."

"And who are you?"

"Davis. Charley Davis. I'm the...golfer."

"Full name?"

"You mean...I'm, I'm Charley, uh, Charles M. Davis."

"What does the M stand for?"

"Look, Mr. Quick, I just got back from a long road trip, I'm kind of tired, and—"

"The 'M'!"

I shook my head and wondered if Uncle Morgan had set me up with one of his devious practical jokes. He was good for one a year, but it was usually around my birthday, and that wasn't for months. Maybe this weirdness was just how my life was destined to be from this point forward.

"Sir, the M is for Marriott."

There was a brief silence, and then, "Like the hotel people? Are you one of those *hotel people*?"

"No. No, it's just a name my parents gave me. That's all."

"What's your full name? I will not allow you into my house unless I know your full name!"

I blinked. "I told you. Charles Marriott Davis."

"And the *Marriott* story behind that name?"

I bit down on my tongue and took a breath. "My, my mom was pregnant. Okay? She was pregnant with me. She and my dad were out for a Sunday brunch at the Marriott in Blue Ash. Her water broke and she had me right there in the lobby. Took forever for the ambulance to get there, my mom says. So they named me Charles Marriott Davis."

I heard the voice chuckle through the speaker. "Good story."

"My dad used to say it was a good thing the brunch wasn't at the Best Western."

"I see his point."

"Now, Mr. Quick, should I come in?"

"I need a few minutes."

"What?"

"I forgot you were coming over and I just got out of the shower."

"Oh my good lord."

"Enjoy the sunshine and come back in five minutes."

I looked at my watch for the third time as if asking it to reveal the answers to a thousand questions. "Okay. Sure."

I shrugged, turned from the door and walked with Angelica back to a small grassy area beside the street. It was sunny and relatively warm for an early April morning in Cincinnati. And the nice weather was just about the only thing nice about it.

Garland Quick. This guy had to be a nut. I should call Uncle Morgan and ask for more details before I allow myself to be subjected to whatever craziness Mr. Quick had in store. *A caddie of special talents.* Right. How hard could it be to caddie for someone who uses only three clubs? I took another breath, scratched the top of Angelica's head, and tried to appreciate the smell of new grass in the cool, spring air.

A few minutes later, I stepped up to the door and pushed the button again.

The door instantly swung inward even before the electric guitar doorbell had finished its up-tempo tune. "Hello!" Mr. Quick said.

"Good morning."

Garland Quick was in his late fifties, about five-feet-four. His face was freshly scrubbed and his dyed blonde hair was spiked with gel. He reminded me of what Joe Pesci might have looked like had he been in *Birdcage.*

"Charles Marriott Davis?"

"Yes."

"Ah, good. I am Garland Quick."

"Pleased to meet you."

I was still standing outside on the front step. Garland Quick stared at me as if I were a Halloween trick-or-treater. He wore white shorts and a pink satin vest with nothing else underneath. "You're quite prompt."

"Thanks."

"And who is this with you?"

"Angelica."

"Angelica is a dog?"

"Mr. Quick, golf? Caddie?"

He nodded. "There was a dog in *Stir of Echoes.*"

I stared at him. "What?"

"Do come in. Both of you. I *like* dogs."

I walked inside. The morning sun streamed into the room through huge picture windows and reflected off a highly polished hardwood floor. Music and movie posters hung everywhere.

"Welcome, welcome."

"Nice place."

"I certainly do try."

I noticed a poster of the movie *Footloose,* the original version, hanging on a stone wall near a fireplace. I could see a signature in the bottom right corner of the poster. And suddenly I realized where I had heard that doorbell guitar riff. "You a *Footloose* fan?"

A smile washed across his face. "You remember?"

"Remember?"

"Some do, some don't. Depends how devoted the fan is."

"Uh, I'm not sure-"

"You know there's a convention in July."

"Okay, uh..."

"In Boulder."

"Boulder."

"That's in Colorado."

"I know where Boulder is, Mr. Quick."

He smiled and took my arm. "Let me show you around."

"Sir-"

"Do you have a little extra time?"

"Extra?"

"I donated books about my single film appearance to my high school about ten years ago. Did you know that?"

"Uh, no."

He pointed across the hall at the *Footloose* poster.

"You were...you were in that film?"

He wrapped his arms around himself. "Yes."

"*Footloose*? The original version, I guess?"

"Oh, yes."

"I watched that with some friends in about ninth-grade. Who were you?"

He grinned. "Want to see a clip?"

"I would, Mr. Quick, but I'm on a tight schedule."

"Too bad. And please call me G.Q."

"You know Kevin Bacon?"

"Since the 70s. In fact, his band, The Bacon Brothers, is playing at Bogart's this weekend."

"Really."

"Would you like to go? I have a few extra tickets."

"Mr. Quick..."

He raised an eyebrow.

"I mean, G.Q., I can't take—"

"Bring a friend. Or several. I have quite a few tickets. I have extras to the convention, too. Kevin is almost certain to be there."

I no more wanted to go to Bogart's with Garland Quick than I wanted to sit in my dentist's office for three hours reading old magazines. I did like Kevin Bacon, though. He was especially effective in *A Few Good Men*, where Tom Cruise supposedly couldn't handle the truth. "Well, okay."

His eyes sparkled. "Just okay?"

"I'd love two tickets." I needed to get out of Garland Quick's condo before I had a psychic breakdown.

"Wonderful," he said. "Excellent. I'll have the tickets before you leave."

"Great."

"And the convention?"

"You mean there's a *whole convention* for that film?"

"It has quite a following, Mr. Davis."

"Call me Charley."

I had no idea why I said that.

He nodded politely. "Charley."

"Who were you in *Footloose*?"

"One of the dancers at the end of the show. You know, the big dance. Total screen time, forty-eight seconds."

"Less than a minute is all?"

"I had wavy, black hair then. Look for me in the credits."

"Mr. Quick, G.Q., I appreciate the tickets, the conversation and all, but how about caddying? Even though I'm not sure what there is to talk about."

He shrugged. "Oh, well. This way."

I followed him down a short hallway. Framed photos of Kevin Bacon lined the walls.

He guided me into a large bathroom. Mirrors surrounded the room from all sides. And five identical blond spiked wigs sat atop five faceless mannequin heads.

"We're in your bathroom," I said.

"Yes."

"We're talking in your bathroom."

"It's quite convenient."

I was afraid to ask for what. "Okay. Whatever. I'm ready to listen."

There was nowhere to sit, except, well, the one obvious place, so we both just stood there. Angelica sprawled out on the cool marble floor.

"Good," he said. "Diligent listening is the beginning. You have to be willing to listen to all of my instructions, *no matter what logic might tell you.*"

"Believe me, Mr. Quick—"

"G.Q."

"Yes. Sorry. G.Q. Believe me, after seeing what Mrs. Morrison and Pinson have been able to teach me over the past six or seven months, listening to people with special talents is the best thing I do."

He smiled. "Do you want to know a secret?"

"That's a Beatles tune."

"Why, Charley. I sense a streak of rebellion in you, just barely under the surface."

"Rebellion? *Me*?"

"No matter. I have been a caddie for both Leslie Rae and Pinson. Different decades, of course."

"I'm shocked to hear that."

"Rebellion and *sarcasm*."

"So I've been told."

"Okay. First things first." He left the room for a few seconds, returned with two Bogart's tickets and a small book.

"Take this book home. Read it. Study it."

I looked at the cover: *The Language of Golf.* "Okay. I'll read it tonight."

"Good."

"What is it?"

"Just read it. You will understand later."

I nodded. "You know, I'm sure I've heard that mantra somewhere before."

He took me by my arm and led me out of the bathroom, down the hallway, and back to the front door.

"That's it?"

"Read. Study."

"Okay. I will."

Garland Quick, or King Looper, CEO of the Kevin Bacon fan club, grinned. "Charles Marriott Davis, you are a princess among men." With that, he nearly pushed me out the door and back into the sunshine. The door closed quickly behind me, no pun intended.

I shook my head, took in a deep breath of cool morning air, and broke into a jog back to the Civic. Angelica trotted beside me. I tossed the book and tickets into the front seat, dropped inside the car, and gunned the engine. I needed to shake the vague sense of claustrophobia that had slowly descended around me ever since I rang Garland Quick's doorbell.

Another nut. Uncle Morgan had shoved another fruitcake into my life. *Where does he find these people?*

I guided the car around the twisting streets of Mt. Adams at speeds the best NASCAR driver would have found unsafe. I never thought I would say this, but I needed to sit on the ground and meditate with Mrs. Morrison. I needed to immediately empty my mind of my early morning visit with Garland Quick, *Footloose* extra, possible Joe Pesci stand-in, and caddie with special talents to the stars.

Chapter 47

The Quick and the Strange

I wasn't positive how Uncle Morgan had arranged it, but Angelica was permitted on the Kenwood Country Club course we were starting today, as long as she stayed in the golf cart. And I didn't even have to sing any Stevie Wonder songs.

I did overhear Uncle Morgan explain to Kenwood management how the Carson film was going to put the Kenwood course in the national spotlight. If not for that promise, and a hefty donation to the annual Kenwood pro-am tournament, I thought management would not have agreed. But they did, and for the past two weeks, Angelica tagged along for every hole, while Sandy lugged her camera and Ray all over the course.

We had been playing nearly every day on other Cincinnati courses, and worked out a rotation that included Mrs. Morrison, Pinson, and Uncle Morgan. Pinson constantly offered criticism of my shots, whether he was playing or watching from the sidelines. He had a sharp eye for any small detail that might have been affecting my grip, my stance, or the way I might study the density of the grass.

Typically on my first shot, I shut my eyes before each stroke. The drives became fairly easy. I set my stance, scanned the fairway, and planned the strength of my swing. For a bit of luck, I would glance over at Angelica, who was usually asleep on the back of the golf cart. Then, with my eyes closed, and Angelica's image still in my mind, I swung away. The last day or so, I'd even wrapped the black silk scarf around my head and covered my eyes, just to increase the darkness and to ensure I really couldn't see a thing.

My reflex shooting was paying off; it was hard to accept but true. And Mrs. Morrison's meditation technique of emptying my mind really seemed to work. Whatever it was, my scores were lower than Uncle Morgan's, and not far above Mrs. Morrison's, even though she was also improving with each round. As far as Pinson was concerned, I had a lot more to learn before I could expect to get even close to his scores. Pinson seemed to be on a dedicated mission when he was on the course, and he had a look in his eye that was all business. This was quite a change for a man, who months before, was a half-crippled prisoner without prospects and no clear vision for his future.

None of this was really a surprise to me; it was reasonable to expect improvement from all of us, considering the amount of time we were playing. My only real surprises came from being in the surreal company of my new caddie, Garland Quick. It was hard to fully describe the *Garland Quick Experience*, except to say the best director to film G.Q.'s teaching methods might have been Mel Brooks. In fact, a younger Mel might have been the best person to *play* G.Q. Or maybe Joe Pesci. I went back and forth on that one.

G.Q. arrived here on our first day at Kenwood at least thirty minutes early, all jittery and frenetic, freshly showered, with blond hair appropriately spiked. After a snip of a "Hello," he raced an electric golf cart around the course to inspect each hole. He did this even though he had caddied on this course hundreds of times before.

I asked him why he needed another course inspection. He stared at me for a few seconds, and then answered, "Casual water."

I said, "Oh," and that was the end of the conversation. I didn't need to question G.Q. any further, because the answer King Looper gave to this, and, as I discovered, to most of my questions, was found right in the *Language of Golf* book he had asked me to read when we met at the Shrine of Bacon.

Yesterday, when I was on a green, G.Q. spent moments of intense concentration judging the curves and contours of the incredibly smooth grass. He stretched flat on the surface of the green, his eyes even with the turf. Other times he would bend slowly into a deep squat and hold a putter at the very end of his fingertips, straight in front of him, vertical to the ground. He held that position, studying the floating club for what seemed like hours.

Sometimes these greens looked so perfect it seemed a sin to even stand on them. Even so, I put that thought aside as I closed my eyes, or blindfolded myself, just before putting my Titleist across the pristine sod. I had no trouble making contact with the ball, or correctly analyzing the power needed to propel the ball toward the cup. My problem, however, continued to be determining the *course* of each shot. For my money, putting was much harder to perform successfully than any other golf swing. At least for me it was. And this was where G.Q.'s very special talents were supposed to come in handy. He hadn't said much to me yesterday, but I suspected all that was about to change this morning.

The weather was perfect when Angelica, Pinson, Mrs. Morrison, and I stepped out of Uncle Morgan's Escalade. Sandy and Ray parked in a spot next to us, got out of the van, and began unloading their film equipment. Ray shielded his eyes from the morning sun and spotted G.Q. trotting toward us from the direction of the Kendale course.

"Charley," Ray said. "Your caddie is in the building."

G.Q. jittered to a halt beside us at the edge of the parking lot. He was dressed conservatively in khaki chinos and a white short-sleeved golf shirt with an embroidered green alligator over the left breast.

"Gentlemen. Ladies," he said in his faded New Jersey accent.

I said, "Morning, G.Q."

He held his arms out in front of him. "Clubs?"

"Oh, hey, G.Q., I can carry my own clubs. They weigh less than a loaf of Wonder Bread."

His eyes squinted into a mask of incredulity. "I am your *caddie*." His arms were still outstretched.

"Oh. Okay."

I removed the clubs from the Escalade and placed the sleek leather bag into his hands.

"Mr. Davis," he said, "we will *walk* the course today and every day. Golf carts are not used by true golfers."

"Like true mountaineers don't use oxygen?" I put in.

G.Q. ignored that one and turned toward the course. "Who

is playing this round with Mr. Davis today?"

"Me," Mrs. Morrison said. "I have that honor."

G.Q. nodded at me. "I will stay close."

"Okay."

"This will not be about club usage," G.Q. added, "since you only have three."

"Six."

"Yes. But this is about the course itself, and how to play each shot *on this particular course.*"

"Hey, G.Q., I'm truly in your hands."

He turned and abruptly started a deliberate walk in the direction of the first tee. Sandy and Ray joined Mrs. Morrison and me, with Uncle Morgan, Pinson, and Angelica following in the cart close behind.

As we walked, G.Q. began to speak, and stared straight ahead as if lecturing to an invisible crowd.

"The Kendale is the championship course here. Major tournaments are played on the Kendale. The first hole, at the championship level, is 424 yards, par 4. You want to try for just right of the fairway bunker off the tee. This will set up a chip onto a fairly well protected green."

"Uh, okay," I said.

We reached the *teeing ground*, as G.Q. called it. I bent, placed my Brush-T in the turf, and set a gleaming new Titleist atop the amazingly tiny filaments.

"Today is the last time for those things," G.Q. said, pointing at my Brush-T.

"Let me guess," I said. "Not traditional?"

He stared with impenetrable beady eyes. "Last day."

"Sure. Last day."

"Now," he continued, "it matters little to me on this hole, or practically any other, whether you play right or left-handed off the tee. It will be up to you. But choose you must. And you must tell me before you shoot, because my guidance may change depending upon your shooting angle."

"Well, I swing better right-handed, so today I'll start left-handed."

He stared at me. "I have one rule, Mr. Davis. Do you know what that rule is?"

"Uh, don't watch the Academy Awards until Kevin Bacon is nominated for best actor?"

Garland Quick held his breath and glared at me.

"No," I said. "Sorry, G.Q. The rule is I'm to listen carefully to what you say."

"Yes. And today I'm saying when we are on the course, there is no place for humor, attempted humor, or misguided sarcasm."

I glanced across the grass at Sandy who watched me through her telephoto lens.

"I'm sorry, G.Q. I'll be serious."

"Mr. Davis, assume your address position."

"What's with the *Mr. Davis*?"

"You will be Mr. Davis when we are on the course."

"If you say so." I shrugged and settled myself over my Titleist.

G.Q. withdrew my left-handed driver from its leather case, held it gently in his hands and gazed at the glittering, finely crafted metal. "This is a truly amazing instrument."

"Everyone says that."

G.Q. gazed off to the eastern horizon. "Remember, on this hole, aim for just right of the fairway bunker." He pointed out and beyond, as if I could see what he was pointing at hundreds of yards away.

He handed the club to me.

I rested it against the front of my thighs and pulled my black kerchief from a back pocket. I bound it around my forehead, covering my eyes. Then I wrapped my fingers around the driver in a ten-finger, or baseball grip, as Pinson called it. I held the club steady as I tried to empty my mind...to empty my mind...*empty my mind...*

...Angelica trotted through water at tide's edge...

I let the spirit wind take control, brought the Samurai club back, felt the breath squeeze from my lungs, and I *swung.*

The Japanese steel sliced the air in near silence, and my club head struck the Titleist with a solid *snick*. I pulled the scarf from my eyes and stared into the sky.

"My good lord," I heard Pinson say from the sidelines.

The ball soared high and straight. I followed its flight until it fell into the glare of sunshine.

After a few seconds, G.Q. stared straight at me. "Who made these clubs?"

"War hero," I said. "Ask my uncle to introduce you."

"That was a fine shot. Flush. Pure."

"Thanks."

"But it was *stronger* than I advised. It didn't land where I asked you to shoot."

"What?"

"That was a *lights out* drive."

"But you said—"

"I said to aim for just right of the fairway bunker. Instead, you cleared the bunker by forty yards."

"I, uh, oh."

"You simply cannot just wail away and drive for show. This isn't a home run competition."

"Okay. Okay. I get it."

G.Q. considered my response for a moment then took the club from me. "Leslie Rae?"

Mrs. Morrison placed her ball atop a white wooden tee. "That was a great swing, Charley."

"Thanks."

Mrs. Morrison readied herself. She gripped and re-gripped her club, a Callaway driver with a gleaming black head. She concentrated for a moment. The muscles rippled in her tanned shoulders, exposed to the air by her sleeveless denim top. She took a breath, let it out slowly, brought her club back, and swung.

The ball streaked up into the cloudless sky. All of us followed its flight until it descended and came to rest somewhere ahead.

"Shall we?" G.Q. said.

Without waiting for an answer, since none was required, Garland Quick stepped forward into a swift pace down the fairway. The three of us reached Mrs. Morrison's ball a few minutes later.

"You are away, Leslie Rae," G.Q. said.

Mrs. Morrison nodded and withdrew some kind of iron from her golf bag. "Uphill lie here, Garland." She extended her club to show him. "What do you think?"

He nodded at the club. "That's fine. You do need a less lofted club here."

She nodded back, rested the bag on the ground, and stepped to her ball.

"Hey, Mrs. Morrison. G.Q. is *my* caddie."

She smiled at me. "We should all take advantage of the opportunity to learn from Garland Quick while we have the chance."

With that, Mrs. Morrison gripped her club, settled for a moment, and swung. The white sphere jumped into the air and flew toward the green.

The three of us walked ahead without words. The grass was still frosted with spring dew. We stopped when we reached my Titleist.

G.Q. withdrew my *everything else* club and handed it to me. "This is a par 4. You're twenty yards from the green. Lob it. No power needed. Just set it dead still on the green in two. Hard to do better than that."

I positioned myself in front of the ball and squinted into the sun as I visualized the flight path. Then I blindfolded myself again, exhaled, and swung.

The solid *clack* told me I'd made contact. I pulled off the blindfold and watched my ball ascend into the sky.

"Mr. Davis," Garland Quick said. "Have you ever played basketball?"

"Basketball?"

"A game played usually on a court with two baskets, ten players, who—"

"Yes, G.Q. I've played basketball."

"Good. I wanted to be sure. Because if you have played basketball, you certainly are familiar with *lobbing* the ball to another player."

"Sure. Usually, the lob goes to the guy under the basket, who leaps up, catches the lob and dunks it."

"Right." G.Q.'s lips drew tight. "Then why is it, Mr. Davis, that you fail to grasp lobbing a *golf ball*?"

"I know what it means."

"Yet to be proven, Mr. Davis."

"Oh?"

"Your ball traveled over the green, on the fly. Landed in the rough on the other side."

"Oh."

"Yes. Oh." G.Q. twisted around and walked on. I exchanged glances with Mrs. Morrison, and we followed obediently just behind. We caught up with Mrs. Morrison's ball. She withdrew a club from her bag and hit a soft chip shot about fifty feet into the air, then right down on the edge of the green.

"Nice," I said.

"Thank you, Charley."

We walked together and found her ball. G.Q. was already perched in the middle of the green. I waved to Uncle Morgan and Pinson on the sidelines. Sandy and Ray were far out in the grass, still watching with their ever-present telephoto lens.

I pointed across the green. "I think my ball is way over there, Mrs. Morrison. You go ahead."

Mrs. Morrison smiled at me. She took a putter from the bag and stepped to her ball. She stared so hard I could almost feel her waves of concentration. Then she drew the club back just a fraction, brought her putter forward. Her ball rolled right toward the cup, but angled off about seven feet to the side during the last few seconds.

"Finish it out, Mrs. Morrison."

She bent, studied the path to the cup, and touched her putter to the side of her ball. It rolled unerringly forward and dropped into the hole.

"Wow," I said. "Five. You got there in five. That's one over par."

"Actually, Mr. Davis," G.Q. said from about fifteen yards away. "Women's par for this hole *is* five."

That floored me. "Par is different for women?"

He nodded.

"Why is that fair?"

"Charley," Mrs. Morrison said. "Women are just not as strong as men." She winked at me.

"Your play, Mr. Davis," G.Q. said.

"Uh huh." I shook my head and walked across the green. Again I was amazed how perfect the grass was, as if it were plastic and came out of a box of Legos. G.Q. pointed to my left and I followed his finger into some tall grass.

"Now softly, Mr. Davis. *Softly.*"

"Okay. Like Charmin tissue." I stopped over my ball, tied the black scarf around my head, and without much time or thought at all, I chipped the ball into the air. Surprisingly, it lifted straight up and landed lightly about twenty feet from the cup.

"Mr. Davis," G.Q. said, "play on."

"What, no advice from you?"

"Play on."

"Okay, then."

I steadied myself over the ball, wrapped the blindfold around my head, and touched my putter to the ball. I pulled the blindfold off just in time to see the ball roll to a stop about twenty feet to the other side of the cup. "Not so good."

"Once again," G.Q. said.

"What am I doing wrong?"

"Just shoot."

"Whatever you say."

Without another word, and without using the blindfold, I stepped to my ball, glanced from my ball to the cup, and putted, right-handed this time. The ball rolled to the other side of the hole again, and came to rest about eighteen feet from the hole.

"Sorry."

G.Q. stepped toward me with a purposeful look in his eye. "Wait." With that, he dropped flat on the green with his chin touching the very tips of the grass. He remained there for about fifteen seconds, and then pushed himself up. He grabbed a club from Mrs. Morrison's bag, dropped to one knee, and held the club in front of him with two fingers.

"Mrs. Morrison, what is that club?"

It was certainly a working putter at one time, but now had a club head about twice the size as normal. And, most curiously, it had a *human* head, hands and feet.

"Garland's plumb bob," she said.

"His plumb bob."

"Yes."

"Please correct me if I'm wrong, but is that a bobble head

on the end of the clubface?"

"That's right."

"I'm almost afraid to ask this, Mrs. Morrison, but who is the face on the bobble head?"

"John Travolta."

"Ah."

"In *Saturday Night Fever*."

"Disco movie, lots of dancing?"

Mrs. Morrison bit her bottom lip. "Garland's other film appearance, but his scene was cut before the final release. He's never forgiven the producers."

I considered that and gazed over at G.Q. as he magically cradled the club dead still in front of him. He was frozen, like some golfer's lawn gnome.

"Mrs. Morrison, what is G.Q. doing with his John Travolta plumb bob club?"

"He's plumb bobbing."

I stared at her for a few seconds. "I have a great deal of respect for you, Mrs. Morrison."

"I appreciate that, Charley."

"Then please tell me, before I turn mercilessly sarcastic, what exactly is plumb bobbing?"

"Oh, no one really knows. It is supposed to give insight as to derivations in the surface of the green. I don't believe there is really any scientific proof it works. It is kind of like when prospectors search for water with a bent stick, a...divining rod."

G.Q. suddenly sprang to his feet.

"Mr. Davis." G.Q. pointed to a spot on the green. "The turf curves into a slight depression right here. Angle your putt just *over* the curve. Understand?"

"I don't see a curve, but I may be getting depressed."

Before G.Q. had a chance to berate me for my breach of seriousness etiquette, I lined up my putt, took my best guess, and shot. I watched the ball roll gracefully on a slight curve and drop lightly into the cup.

"Charley, very good," Mrs. Morrison said.

"Yeah, well, not so good since I didn't blindfold myself for that one."

Pinson came trotting over. "Sir, that entire hole was, well,

I'm not sure what to say."

"Good?" I said. "Was it good?"

Pinson smiled. "Yes. Yes, sir, it was."

"A six. I shot six. Two over par."

"Believe me, sir, six is excellent, even for a well experienced player. You are not well experienced. And you played four of your shots blindfolded."

I glanced at Uncle Morgan who was sitting in the front of the cart with Angelica. He smiled at me and nodded.

G.Q. said, "I wanted you to realize the difference a good caddie's advice can make."

"Okay. I can see that."

"Do you, Mr. Davis?"

"Yes. You roll around, fool with your Travolta club, figure out how I should putt, and tell me."

He looked at the ground for a second. Then: "I will ignore the attempted humor, Mr. Davis, but just this one last time." With that, G.Q. walked away on a steady track.

"You played a great hole," Mrs. Morrison said. "Really. Garland will take some time getting used to."

"I'm used to him. I watched *Goodfellas* last night."

"You lost me, sir," Pinson said.

"I truly doubt that. Well, shall we?" I said to Pinson and Mrs. Morrison.

They both smiled back at me, and we started together toward the next tee.

Chapter 48

We Can't Work It Out

The next weeks flew by, and I felt great. My golf was good one day, not so good the next, but at this point, none of that really mattered to me. I had a new four-footed best friend, always a comfort by my side. And Sandy Carson was back in my life.

Sandy and I spent evenings together, maybe twice a week. That was all the time she had to give me, since she was busy editing her film after practice. And on those magical two nights each week, we invariably sat in each other's arms on the sofa and just talked. I supposed we were making up for all the years we'd lost, but we talked endlessly about important stuff and about the most mundane trivia. It never seemed to matter, as long as we were together, occupying the same space, and sharing our lives.

It was wonderful.

I knew a lecture from Mrs. Morrison about this was approaching on the event horizon. I saw the look in her eyes a few times when my focus wavered and my shots lofted into the trees. We both knew it was mostly because I could not empty my mind before I swung; my brain was constantly swimming with thoughts of a long future with Sandy.

P.J. Varelli appeared about ten days ago with no announcement or warning. We were playing on the front nine on the Indian Hill Country Club course, when I noticed Pinson pointing to the sidelines near a shady area in the rough. P.J. Varelli stood there.

She smiled and nodded to me.

From time to time in the following weeks, P.J. Varelli would join me for a round or two. She volunteered practically nothing about herself, or about how she came to be in Cincinnati; I didn't ask and she didn't say. It didn't seem to matter to me, for whatever reason. And she was amazing to watch, both because of the way she played, and because she was just, well, amazing to watch.

We covered a number of courses around town, but kept coming back to Kenwood. Both Pinson and G.Q. felt that the Kendale was best for my golf education, at least at this point in my training. On one stunningly beautiful and bright morning on the Kendale, when my mind was elsewhere and my shots were flying all over the course as if we were in a violent windstorm, I just holed on the 8th green in seven, when I noticed a tall tanned man with a tall pale young woman by his side. They were walking my way.

"Uncle Morgan?" I said.

He lifted his golf bag. "I see them."

"Who's that goober?"

G.Q. said, "Oh no," from the nearby grass that led to the 9th tee.

Pinson stepped over to me. "Rutt Labouhn," he said, as if announcing the twentieth straight day of losses on the New York Stock Exchange.

I squinted at Pinson. "Is that his name or a new type of influenza virus?"

"Pro here," Pinson said. "Quite a good golfer, sir. Made it through Q School twice."

"Isn't that a Broadway musical with The Muppets?"

Uncle Morgan gritted his teeth. "Had me *disqualified* during the pro-am last year."

"He *what*?"

Uncle Morgan tapped his hands against the sides of his pants. "Labouhn is an old-school proponent of strict rules interpretation." He shook his head. "He's like my third-grade teacher. Old Mrs. Kinch prosecuted each and every school rule as if they were lifted from The Dead Sea Scrolls."

I watched Labouhn and his companion approach, steadily closer. Labouhn waved to Uncle Morgan.

"So, what rule did you break?" I asked.

"Improper footwear. I was recovering from a pulled

Achilles tendon after a hiking mishap, and I was wearing that boot contraption. Labouhn said *strict interpretation* was required. I must wear proper golf shoes or I could not play. If the rules were not strictly construed, according to him, then all golfing hell would eventually break loose."

Rutt Labouhn and his companion reached us and strode casually onto the green. Labouhn was maybe in his early forties, wore impeccably pressed golf pants, and a pristine white golf shirt with a royal blue horse embroidered on the left breast.

"Morgan," Labouhn said. "Certainly haven't seen you out on the course here in a while." His voice had a slight British accent.

"Rutledge."

"This is Carla Taft, my fiancé. Carla, Morgan Kinshaw."

"A pleasure," Uncle Morgan said to her.

"For me as well."

She was beautiful, but cold and sterile as a department store mannequin. She smiled politely and extended her hand. Uncle Morgan took her hand for a moment.

Labouhn looked at Pinson, raised one eyebrow and stared. "Pinson Dill. *Good lord*, it's been years."

"Good morning, sir."

"I was truly sorry to hear about your *difficulties*. I, for one, am a dog lover, too, as you are, certainly. Awful business a few years ago. Bloody awful business."

"Behind me now," Pinson said.

"Yes. Good."

"Oh, Rutledge," Uncle Morgan said, "this is my nephew, Charley Davis."

"Of course." Labouhn's hand came in my direction and I shook it. He smiled at me with perfectly even, white teeth.

"Mr. Labouhn," I said.

"It's Rutt. Please call me Rutt. Short for my great, great-uncle William Riker Rutledge, Confederate colonel in the Civil War. Are you familiar?"

"Big battles in the 1860s, right after Lincoln freed the slaves?"

Labouhn chuckled and grinned insanely at me.

"Wait a second. William *Riker* Rutledge?"

"*Don't* Charley," Uncle Morgan said.

"But, Uncle Morgan. William *Riker*?"

Labouhn turned from me and shifted his gaze to G.Q. as if he was examining a body in the morgue. "Garland."

"Mr. Labouhn."

"Last I heard you were living in Hollywood."

G.Q. shook his head. "Back now."

"Did you really caddie for Madonna?"

"Rutt, we need to keep moving." He gestured down the fairway. "Backing up."

"Oh. Certainly."

Labouhn caught sight of P.J. Varelli across the fairway. His jaw dropped and his eyes stretched wide. "Oh my good lord. *P.J. Varelli*."

He continued to stare at P.J. Varelli, and I said, "Mr. Labouhn, winter will be here soon."

He snapped out of it. "Mind...do you mind if we walk with you, then? Carla and I? Just to the next tee."

"Sure," I said. "Let's walk."

We started a brisk pace through the manicured turf. Uncle Morgan gave me one of those *keep-it-together* looks, but I was really unsure what he was so uptight about. Rutt Labouhn seemed a nice enough guy, even though no normal human male should look this well groomed.

"So, this is quite the gathering you have here, Morgan," Labouhn said.

"Just leave it alone, Rutledge."

"Certainly, *quite* the gathering."

Uncle Morgan stopped dead, turned and faced Labouhn. "If you've got something to say..."

"Morgan, I am not a golf snob. I welcome any and all who wish to play."

"That's good to hear. Right, Uncle Morgan?" I gestured at the air with my putter.

Labouhn said, "May I take a look at your club?"

"Uh, sure." I handed my putter to him.

"Magnificent."

"Thanks."

"You have a left-handed putter also?"

"Yes. Six clubs, three left and three right."

Labouhn seemed to consider that. "Six clubs."

"Six."

Labouhn turned to Uncle Morgan. "When I heard about your nephew, Charley, weeks ago in the clubhouse, before I flew across the pond for *my monthly rules meeting in St Andrews*, I thought some of our members were possibly too fond of Grey Goose, since I could accept no other rational explanation. Imagine. Playing both right and left-handed. Blindfolded, Morgan. *Blindfolded.*"

"Specialized training methods," Uncle Morgan said. "Seven months ago, Charley had not played a round of golf in his life. Since then, Charley has been shooting from both sides, and with his eyes shut or blindfolded."

"Interesting. And apparently effective. I watched your last few holes, Charley. Impressive, even for a golfer who has played many years."

"Thanks."

"As I said, I researched the rules here at some length. As you must know, Morgan, there is no rule against playing from both sides."

"Yes. I know," Uncle Morgan said.

"Nor is there any rule against playing blindfolded."

"Rutledge, we need to play on."

"But *there is a rule*, Morgan, a certain, definite Kenwood Country Club rule, about *dogs* on the course."

With that, I blinked and turned my eyes to Labouhn.

"I know the rule, Rutledge," Uncle Morgan said.

"Ruttie," Carla Taft said, "I have a fitting in Hyde Park."

"In a minute, Carla."

She pointed at P.J. Varelli who stood off course to our right. "And just who is that...*girl* over there you keep staring at?"

Labouhn ignored his fiancé. "Somehow, Morgan, you have managed to circumvent that rule. *The dog rule.* You have, indeed, *certainly* circumvented it."

Uncle Morgan took a breath. "Look, Rutledge, the committee approved the rule exception only for a few months. Soon you won't need to worry about it."

"I'm just wondering how you did it, Morgan."

I said, "Rutt, how about leaving it alone?"

"Maybe you *bribed* someone," he said to Uncle Morgan.

"Rutt, enough."

"Or maybe he found a loophole," Labouhn said to me.

"Loophole?"

"The rule specifically prohibits *dogs* on the course."

"So?" I said.

"Perhaps that black monstrosity in your cart isn't even a dog at all."

My faced flushed, and my right hand flashed to my Nigerian weapon.

"No, Charley," Mrs. Morrison said.

She hopped off the cart and placed her hands around my clenched fist.

"Morgan," Labouhn said, looking at Mrs. Morrison, "I don't believe I've had the pleasure."

Mrs. Morrison turned and glared at Labouhn. "I advise you to watch what you say because in five seconds, I am going to release Charley's hand."

Labouhn turned from her. "I don't like bending the rules, Morgan."

"I'm glad you cleared that up."

"A price must certainly be paid for *rule bending*, to prevent such *bending* in the future."

"Look, I told you, Rutledge, at the end of July, it will no longer be an issue."

"And I intend to see the price is paid."

Uncle Morgan sighed. "Okay, Rutledge. What price do you have in mind?"

"Why complete and utter banishment, Morgan."

"Banishment."

"The stakes must be high so it *means* something. So, Charley and I will play eighteen holes. *Stableford* system. Should I win, you will resign your membership at Kenwood."

"What? You want to play *me*?" I couldn't believe it.

"Eighteen holes?" Uncle Morgan said, considering it.

"Yes."

"When?"

"Second Sunday in June, ten days from now. I'll reserve

our tee time."

"Second Sunday..."

I had to stop this nonsense right now. "No, Uncle Morgan."

"And what if *you* lose?" Uncle Morgan interjected.

Labouhn smiled. "Why you know, I hadn't thought of that."

"I have," Pinson said. "Marleigh Benford is a personal friend of mine."

LaBoughn paled. "Marleigh..."

"Benford. Yes. Current editor of *Weird Golf Legends*."

Labouhn straightened his back. "I understand."

"She's always looking for new stories," Pinson said. "How about, *Blindfolded Golfer Beats Kenwood Country Club Pro.*"

Labouhn glared at Pinson. "I said that I *certainly* understand."

I jumped in. "Understand this. You lose, my dog gets free run of this golf course."

"I'll have it picked up by animal control."

"If you get within fifty feet of my dog, your knees will need titanium braces."

"Charley," Uncle Morgan shouted and pulled me aside, just out of earshot. "Don't stoop to his level."

"He's a bully."

"You don't have to play against him."

"You're saying I can't beat him. Right?"

"Right. Sorry."

"So, when I lose..?"

"Then I'll resign. Besides, I should never have joined a club that would have me as a member."

"Who said that?"

"I just did."

"He can't disrespect you like that, Uncle Morgan."

"It's up to you, Charley. I just want you to decide for the right reasons."

"He threatened Angelica. Is that reason enough?"

He smiled and placed his hand on my shoulder. "Yes. That's more than enough reason."

I grinned at him. "Then let's go tell Number 1 to make it so."

Uncle Morgan shook his head. "I knew you wouldn't be able to stay away from that line indefinitely."

"Certainly not," I said, as we both turned back to tell Labouhn the news of his impending demise.

Chapter 49

Kind of a Drag

"She's already eaten," I said to Katie Clifton, the thirteen-year-old daughter of one of Uncle Morgan's friends. We had to find someone to watch Angelica since Kenwood officials suddenly withdrew permission for Angelica to be on the course for my match with Rutt Labouhn, even if she just sat in the golf cart. Apparently, Labouhn had pressured the Kenwood staff and they finally caved.

Katie's eyes could not open wider. She stared at Angelica who was sprawled out on my kitchen floor. "So, I don't have to worry about him getting hungry?"

"She."

"Because I don't think I want to be in the *same county* if he gets hungry."

"She. Angelica is a *she*. And she has a regimented feeding schedule. She's already had breakfast."

"Are the neighbors missing any cats, or dachshunds?"

"Katie, Angelica is gentle as a panda bear."

"I saw a nature show about pandas. They will rip your throat out if given a chance."

"Okay, bad example. Think *Teddy* Bear. I have to go, Katie."

Katie glanced down at Angelica and scowled at me. "I think this job is worth more money than my usual fee."

I frowned at her. "How much?"

"No one really explained everything about Angelica."

"Katie—"

"Cause with that name, Angelica, well, I pictured something much...smaller."

"*How much*, Katie?"

"Twenty dollars an hour."

I nodded. "Fine. That's fine."

"Maybe twenty-five."

"Now it's twenty-five dollars?"

"Yes."

"Okay. Done."

"Do you have Netflix? Hulu?"

"Her leash is by the door. She likes to sit in the grass and watch the cars go down the road."

"Will she try to chase the squirrels?"

"The squirrels keep their distance."

I reached down and scratched Angelica's head. "Later, girl."

She tilted her head up and gazed at me with her amazing amber eyes.

"Wish me luck."

***

No one spoke as Uncle Morgan guided the Escalade down Kenwood Road on this clear Sunday morning. The tension inside the car was so thick I don't think it could have been cut with a knife, not even with one of those Ginsu knives I'd seen advertised on late-night TV. I tried to focus on the passing scenery, to distract my brain from my looming confrontation with First Officer Labouhn. But nothing worked. My hands trembled so hard I stuffed them in my windbreaker pockets.

We found a spot and parked at the country club just as we had done many times before. We all got out and gathered by the rear of the big SUV.

"Breathe, Charley," Mrs. Morrison said. "Remember your breathing."

G.Q. eyed me as he took the black leather golf bag and strapped it over one shoulder. "She's right. And I'm going to remind you before we start each and every hole."

"Hey, guys, I'm okay."

"Sir, that is not correct," Pinson said.

"You are definitely not breathing," Mrs. Morrison said. "We should have meditated this morning."

"I would like to talk with Charley for a minute," Uncle Morgan said.

G.Q. turned and started toward the clubhouse. "Talk with him about breathing." Pinson and Mrs. Morrison followed close behind.

"I know this is ridiculous to say," Uncle Morgan said after a moment, "but I don't want you to be shaken by this whole production today."

"You're right."

"I am?"

"It's ridiculous to say it."

"Yes. Even so, win or lose today, it doesn't matter to me. If the worst that happens is I resign from this establishment, well, it won't be the worst thing that ever happened to me in my life."

"I know that."

"More than anything, this is a chance for you to measure how far you've come."

"Pretty far."

"Yes. And don't forget that."

"Seven months ago, a golfer like Labouhn would not have asked me to play a match."

"True."

"Seven months ago, I had never meditated or understood how much it helps with everything in my life."

He smiled. "I recently began to understand that myself."

My eyes focused on the Carson van, already parked at the other end of the lot. "And seven months ago, the chances of Sandy Carson coming back into my life were about the same as Sean Connery starring in the next Bond movie."

"I wouldn't rule that one out."

I laughed. "Thank you, Uncle Morgan.

"No reason to thank me, Charley. You are the one who is doing this. You've absorbed all your instruction faster than I thought possible, and now, well, you just said it. You're about to go toe-to-toe with a golfer who has played on the professional tour. *The tour*, Charley."

I nodded. "I meant about *Sandy*. Thank you for bringing Sandy back in my life."

"You did that yourself, too, Charley."

Lane Cohen

"No, Uncle Morgan. I had a lot of help."

***

I pushed my sunglasses on as I walked from the clubhouse. G.Q. carried my bag of Samurai clubs. I had read about playing the Stableford system right after I had accepted Labouhn's challenge. Stableford involved a different way of scoring than usual. Instead of the lowest score being the best, the *highest* score wins. Points are awarded, or deducted, after each hole. Par on a hole equals zero points. One shot under par is worth one point, as one stroke over par deducts one point. There are some special scoring opportunities as well: an eagle is five points, a double eagle adds eight. My plan was to leave the computation of my scoring to my *caddie of special talents*.

I looked ahead and noticed a fair number of people on the sidelines near the approach to the first tee. "G.Q., what's going on up there?"

"Observers."

"Who would want to watch this?"

"From what I can see, about fifty people."

"Fifty?"

"I believe many are attending to see Mr. Labouhn. They want to see him lose."

"Popular guy?"

"He's a terrific golfer, but he is also obnoxious and disliked."

"So, they're not here to root for me, they're here to see someone stick it to Labouhn."

"Some. But not all."

"They're going to be disappointed, G.Q. I have as much chance of beating Labouhn as I do of blocking a Magic Johnson jump shot."

G.Q. stared at me. "Magic retired many years ago."

"Then it's even more true."

G.Q. faced me. "In all my years in the course, no matter who I've caddied for, I've learned something equally important as how and where to hit the ball."

I squinted at him. "I'm listening."

~274~

"When a player *believes* he is going to lose, then..."

"Yeah."

"Understand?"

I nodded. You're right. I get it."

"Just keep that I mind, please."

We started off and reached the first Kendale tee. Labouhn was already there, and taking smooth, fluid warm-up swings, as though he was born with a driver in his hands. He wore a powder blue shirt and creamy-white pants so clean a speck of dirt would be afraid to touch them.

Pinson, Uncle Morgan, and Mrs. Morrison stood nearby in the gallery. P.J. Varelli stood alone, away from the crowd, partially obscured by a small stand of trees.

"Ah, Charley." Labouhn stepped to me and extended his hand. I shook it. Labouhn's grip was solid, the skin on his hand so smooth and soft he must soak his hands in Nivea lotion overnight.

"Good morning, Rutt."

"Beautiful morning for a round of golf."

"Let's hope so."

"I'd like you to meet my caddie." Labouhn gestured at the opposite side of the tee.

An older, gaunt man was standing upright, as if at attention. He held a maroon leather golf bag.

"Garland, do you know Hardy Dinmont?"

"I've seen him before. We've never met."

Labouhn looked at Hardy Dinmont. "Dandie, come on over here, please."

"Dandie?" I said.

Labouhn nodded. "My nickname for him."

Hardy "Dandie" Dinmont stepped toward us slowly, as if he was walking to his assigned spot as a pallbearer.

"Sir?" Dinmont said.

"Introductions," Labouhn said. "Charley Davis, my honored opponent."

Dinmont tilted his head down at me. "The pleasure is mine, sir." He spoke in an upper class British accent.

Dinmont looked to be in his 60s, with hollowed cheeks and long gray hair. He could easily play the crazy butler in a horror movie, haunted house spoof.

"And Garland Quick," Labouhn said.

"Mr. Quick."

"Dinmont."

Labouhn said, "So, shall we?"

"Yes," I said. "Let's."

"Charley, your honor," Labouhn said. "You are the guest here."

G.Q. looked at Labouhn. "A few seconds."

"Certainly."

G.Q. pulled me aside. "Charley."

"Is this where you give me an impassioned motivational monologue?"

"Do you know who I've caddied for?"

"You want to give me your resume *now*?"

"The best. I've caddied for a long time, and for the very best. Some names I can't even tell you."

"I didn't ask."

"Point is, Charley, golf is hard, and much harder than it looks. That is why we idolize the truly great players. They have *it*, Charley, and that elusive *it* is quite difficult to acquire."

"I don't have anything, G.Q., and certainly not the *it* you're talking about."

"Are you sure?"

"Granted, seven months ago I couldn't hit a jawbreaker thirty yards."

He looked off into the distance beyond the first tee. "And now?"

"Well, now, I can hit pretty well, sometimes."

"Not possible, Charley, not without the *it factor*. You've got it. I've seen it."

"Uncle Morgan would disagree. This whole thing, my playing golf in the first place was always about his theory, that golf is a game of *practice*, not talent."

G.Q. leveled his eyes at me. "I'm fairly certain, Charley, this challenge has been about a great deal more than that."

I glanced into the rough at Sandy behind her camera. "Yeah, G.Q. You may be right about that one."

He followed my gaze. "More than her, too."

"G.Q., since we're on that subject, and since we have all the time in the world over here to just stand around and gab at each other while the whole world is watching, I have something to say to you."

"It's not necessary."

"Even with all my meditation, reflex shooting, and magic Samurai clubs, I would not have been able to sink half my putts these last months without your guidance."

"*Putting is where the games are won.*"

"Yeah, you and Pinson agree on that."

"Mr. Dill and I agree on much more than that."

"Your plumb bobbing is amazing. Huh, now *there's* a sentence you don't hear every day."

He smiled. "Bacon Brothers are coming to town in a couple weeks. Playing at Riverbend."

"Oh, yeah?"

"New CD coming out, too."

"I like concerts at Riverbend."

"Me too."

"Want some company?"

He smiled again. "You're on. So now, let's concentrate and play some golf. It's time."

He withdrew my right-handed driver from its black leather home. "Swing away, Mr. Davis. You've played off this tee four hundred times. You know what to do."

"Four hundred times? You're starting to sound like me."

"Take the club."

I nodded, took the club, and turned toward the tee. I stepped across the immaculate grass, slowly bent and placed the new Titleist atop my new, but old-fashioned, wooden tee. The only sounds I heard were a few birds chirping in the distance. G.Q., Rutt Labouhn, and Hardy Dinmont, stood by, all motionless, respecting my space, careful not to interfere with my concentration. Labouhn may be obnoxious and disliked, but he was a true pro and conducted himself accordingly when on the course.

I planted my feet near the tee and stared down at the small while sphere at my feet. G.Q. was right. I knew where to hit the ball off this tee, and how hard to hit it. Now the trick was to envision the path I wanted the ball to take, concentrate on the force needed to propel the ball, then close my eyes, empty my mind of everything, let reflex take over, and power away.

I have done this four hundred times.

The problem today, though, the real difference, was a whole bunch of people were watching, riveted to every movement I made. And some of these observers were the most important people in my life. Plus, the results of this match *actually mattered*; this wasn't just about my improvement as a golfer. There were *consequences* today, should I lose.

As countless times before, I steadied myself, wrapped on my Zorro blindfold, washed away everything in my brain, and let my arms do the rest, all on their own, without any conscious direction from me.

I swung.

***

It didn't take long to figure out Labouhn was the class of this match, since I was stinking up the joint from my first putt on the first hole. My tee shot was awesome, and I made it to the green in three, accompanied by a crescendo of vocal appreciation from the onlookers. But after that, despite everything I tried, I simply could not find a way to roll that little sphere into the four-and-one-quarter inch hole. After eight strokes, I quit, since three over, and the resulting negative three points, was the maximum allowed by Stableford scoring. Labouhn was par on 1, and so after the first hole, Labouhn was three points ahead of me. Great beginning.

On 2, an impressive par 5, 537 yard hole, it was pretty much more of the same. My first drive was perfect, between two fairway bunkers, right where I aimed. But after that, the whole world fell apart. I wasn't sure why my concentration dissolved, but it vanished right after my tee shot. I finished the second hole with another negative three. Labouhn was one over. So, after hole 2, I was behind Labouhn by five points.

Number 3 was even worse for me. It was a short hole, only 234 yards, par 3. G.Q. advised me to aim carefully and to hold back on my usual power drive, since the hole was not that long, and bunkers on each side of the fairway allowed for a very narrow landing area. Of course, I overshot off the tee and landed in the far edge of the rough. Once on the green, I could not deal with a severe slope, and each shot deteriorated, despite G.Q.'s plumb bobbing. I finished in seven, another negative three points, and I decided right then to stop wearing the blindfold.

The way Labouhn handled this hole, however, was beautiful to watch. He had a magnificent combination of power and control, and practically finessed the ball mentally to succumb to his will. He finished at par. Three holes, and I was already down eight points.

"Charley," G.Q. said, "Leslie Rae approaches."

Mrs. Morrison walked quickly out of the rough and joined G.Q. and me on our way to the fourth tee. "So..."

"I know."

"And if you know, then you can fix it."

"Maybe it's the lack of music on the course. Mrs. Morrison, is your CD player in the car?"

"Charley—"

"Maybe the soundtrack to *The Graduate*?"

She laughed. "Can't empty your mind, right?"

"Seems not."

"From the sidelines, you appear to be concentrating, or *not* concentrating, like the day we met by the creek and you tried meditating for the first time."

"Yeah."

She shielded her eyes with one hand and gazed ahead. "I want you to be sick."

"Sick?"

"You need to go into the trees." She stepped closer to me, and removed her Nigerian fighting stick from a clip on her belt. "Take this. Go into the trees. Practice your first Aacutae."

"Now?"

G.Q. asked, "What's he going to do in the trees?"

"Go," she told me. "I will make your excuses. Golfers are sick on the course all the time. The others will respect your privacy."

I took the stick. "Why am I doing this?"

"It will help you focus, realign your Chakras."

"My Chakras."

"Go, Charley."

"Maybe I should see a chiropractor."

"Charley?"

"Sure. Into the trees."

I started toward a nearby clump of trees.

"Charley?" Labouhn said from about twenty yards away.

"Sick," Mrs. Morrison called to him. She pressed one hand against her stomach.

Labouhn nodded. "Ah. *Certainly.*"

I tried to ignore all the eyes from the observers as I trudged into the thick greenery. A million thoughts spun in my brain, which was, of course, the problem today.

I looked back toward the crowd and could not see a soul through the vegetation. I hoped that meant they could not see me, as well. The patterned Combassa Combelbo exercises Mrs. Morrison had taught me seven months ago were terrific for training reflexes, sharpening hand-eye coordination, and general physical conditioning. I've performed these Aacutaes hundreds of times, practiced them each morning, sometimes twice. I pressed the release button on the fighting stick and it instantly extended. I took a breath, and began.

The past few months I'd watched tons of golf on TV, and I just couldn't figure how the pros did it. Being a talented golfer was one thing, but how on God's green earth did those people concentrate and keep it together with an audience of millions at home, and hundreds, if not thousands, actually on the course?

Shooting by reflex with an empty mind had worked for me before. *But it only worked when I could actually empty my mind.* Today, besides a bunch of strangers who were absolutely agog that I was playing from both sides, I'd gotten two real pros, including Rutledge Labouhn, obnoxious and disliked, watching and mentally critiquing everything I did. He was the guy who had Uncle Morgan banished from a tournament *that Uncle Morgan helped organize.* For that reason alone, I wanted to beat Labouhn in the worst way.

And *P.J. Varelli* was here, haunting the sidelines with a dark beauty that could drop most any guy with blood in his veins at twenty paces. Plus, I knew the day was coming when Pamela

Jean would confront me about pretending to be blind in South Carolina. I was not looking forward to that conversation.

Sandy watching me through her lens was something I should have been used to, but lately, Sandy had lingered constantly in the very front of my brain, and getting Sandy Carson out of my head was a goal I had yet to accomplish.

I completed my Aacutae, bowed to the air, and started back. I minimized the fighting stick and stuck it in my back pocket. G.Q. and Mrs. Morrison greeted me.

"Better?" Mrs. Morrison said as I handed the Nigerian stick back to her.

"We'll see."

We met Labouhn at the fourth tee. "Charley?"

"Your go, Rutt."

"Certainly. Glad you're feeling better."

He steadied himself above his ball, took no practice swings, and swung. His ball went into orbit, well on its way to the green on this 584-yard, par 5 hole. I heard an "Ooohh" from the gallery.

The Aacutae must have helped, because my concentration actually was better on this hole. But that made little difference; I finished at one over, yet another negative point. Labouhn managed par. After four holes, I was down nine. Even though both Pinson and G.Q. attempted to encourage me, since 1 over on this hole was a score most weekend golfers would kill for, it did little to improve my spirits.

I felt my focus slipping again on 5, after landing my drive to the right of the fairway instead of the left, as G.Q. had instructed. Even so, I managed 1 over again, but to Labouhn's par, I'd lost yet another point. Down ten.

I held my own on 6, 7, and 8, and managed to slip behind only two more points. After eight holes, with all my months of specialized practice, playing eight to ten hours a day, and practically no beer, I was behind eleven points to the great, great nephew of Confederate Colonel *William Riker* Rutledge.

G.Q. was unusually silent on our walk to 9. Then he took me by my forearm and stopped. "Mr. Davis."

"Yeah."

"How can I help?"

"Nothing you can do, G.Q. Not your fault."

He considered that. "You're erratic. Some shots are great. Some are off into strange lands. What's different?"

"Meaning?"

"Your concentration has been much better than this. What's different today?"

"The crowd. Nothing else, really."

"I think you're wrong."

"I've been wrong before."

"Your coal-black friend is missing."

"She's with Katie Clifton who is making some serious cash."

"She's your *friend*, isn't she?"

"Katie Clifton? No."

"Angelica. I've seen you and her together. You're very close."

"Your point?"

"I have an idea."

"Okay."

"Good. I want you to go into the trees."

"Of course."

"Be sick again."

"Shouldn't be hard to do."

"I'm going to have Pinson bring your friend to the course."

"What about Katie Clifton?"

"Her, too."

"Make sure she calls her parents."

"Right."

"And, well, then what, until Angelica gets here?"

"I don't know. Play out the 9th hole. Pinson should be back here with Angelica before you begin the back nine."

I stood for a moment and stared at him. "You know, G.Q., according to Pinson, you are a natural genius reading the greens. What he didn't say, is how good you are at reading *people*."

"I've been around you and Angelica every day, all day, for months. I would have to be a fool not to notice how devoted you are to each other."

"Okay. Well then. *Engage*."

"*Star Trek?*"

"I'm going to beam into the next stand of trees."

***

G.Q. made more excuses for me as I shuffled into the rough. I peeked through the branches, watched Pinson nod a few times and then step briskly off the course. I waited a few more minutes, and emerged from the greenery as if I just completed hiking the Appalachian Trail, now supposedly better from my persistent, yet undefined, stomach ailment. I joined the group at the 9th tee.

"Charley, I am concerned," Labouhn said.

"You should be. I'm eleven points behind. This is where I suddenly rise from the ashes and beat you at the last stroke, instantly becoming a golfing legend."

"I meant I am concerned for your *health*."

"Had a chili pizza from Empress Chili last night."

"Ah. So then, are we ready?"

I extended my hand to the tee. "Go."

Labouhn set his ball on his tee and straightened up. He placed his hands around his driver in what Pinson described to me as an interlocking variation of the Vardon grip. Basically, the little finger of Labouhn's left hand hooks together with the index finger of his right hand. He began to ready his swing, when he stopped himself, and focused his eyes on the gallery.

"I say, Charley," Labouhn said.

I followed his gaze. P.J. Varelli stood in plain view at the edge of the course amid the rest of the onlookers.

"Yes, Rutt?"

"P.J..?"

"Fresh from South Carolina."

"Do you know why she is here again?"

"We're friends."

"Friends. Quite. Has she been here all morning?"

"Yep."

"Is Ms. Varelli planning to join the gallery at...*every hole*?"

"I don't know, Rutt. Does it matter?"

His face paled. "Why no. *Certainly* not."

"No?"

"We do have a history, Charley."

"Well then, maybe Pamela Jean is here to see *you*."

He swallowed. "Pamela...Jean..."

Labouhn snapped out of it, cleared his throat, and took a practice swing. He took a second swing, and then a third. He brought his club back a fourth time, gathered his strength, and swung.

Labouhn's ball skied into the heavens to the left of the bunker.

"Good try, sir," Hardy Dinmont said.

I looked back at G.Q. who joined me as Labouhn stepped off the tee.

G.Q. whispered to me. "A good drive here is to the *right* of the bunker. He now has a totally blind shot to the green."

"Gotcha."

I placed my new Titleist, took only a few seconds, and at the last moment I tied my shiny black blindfold around my head. Then, I swung away, right-handed. I pulled off the black cloth and watched my shot loft nicely on the par 4, and plop down directly where I had aimed, just to the right of the bunker.

G.Q. said, "You shot the lights out."

"I don't know what that means, but it sounds good."

"Oh yes. It's good. But beyond that..."

"What?"

"A chink has appeared in Mr. Labouhn's pastel armor."

"P.J., maybe?"

"Something has him spooked."

My second shot, from the left this time, spun up in a nice arc, and found its place on the far edge of the green.

"Nice again, Mr. Davis," G.Q. said.

With G.Q.'s direction, I 2-putted, and left the hole with a par. No points awarded, but none deducted, either.

Labouhn managed to settle, fine player that he is, and finished at par as well. After the front nine, I was still behind by eleven. At this point, I needed much more than a motivational monologue to catch Rutt Labouhn.

Chapter 50

Leader of the Pack

I saw the golf cart roll slowly along the cart path as G.Q., Rutt Labouhn, and Hardy Dinmont reached the 10th tee. Mrs. Morrison and Uncle Morgan sat in the front. Pinson and Katie Clifton sat in the rear. A large plaid blanket covered Pinson's legs.

I said, "G.Q., look."

"I see them."

"Make my excuses for a second, okay?"

"I'm an expert in making excuses."

I chuckled. "Be right back." I left G.Q. and trotted over to the cart.

"Hello, Charley," Mrs. Morrison said.

I stared at the huge lump under the plaid blanket "What's the plan?"

Uncle Morgan stepped off the cart. "Here's the deal. Leslie Rae, Pinson, Katie, and I will stand together, beside the cart, about ten yards toward the tee. If we bunch together, we should block the view of anyone nearby. You should have a few minutes with her, Charley. But that's about it."

I nodded. "Let's do it."

Katie asked, "What am I going to do?"

"You'll come with me," Mrs. Morrison said.

"I've never been on a golf course before."

"It's like a walk in the park." Mrs. Morrison smiled. "Come on."

"Am I still getting paid?"

The four of them stepped away and stood in a closely grouped line. I got into the back of the cart and lifted the blanket. Angelica's amber searchlights stared up at me.

"Hey, girl."

Hey.

I sat beside her and rubbed her neck through her thick, shiny fur. "Missed you."

Me too.

"Look, the thing is, well, nothing much different than normal, really. I'm pretty good for a shot or two, and then I hit the ball here, there, and everywhere."

Focus fades easily.

"I suppose so."

You think bringing me here might help?

"I'm supposed to empty my mind and shoot by reflex."

Not until you shut out all the distractions.

"It *means something* today. It's not just a test for me, a measuring tool, to gauge my improvement as a golfer."

Yes.

"Plus, Pamela Jean Varelli is a distraction of an entirely different kind."

Listen to Garland Quick. He is a smart man.

"I know."

Seven months ago you could barely walk eighteen holes. Now look at you.

I smiled down at her. "So, what do I do? Between the two of us, you're the smart one here."

Cold, frozen, arctic resolve.

"I keep losing it."

Remember the coldest you've ever been?

"Right after that early winter storm on Jawbreaker Mountain. Thought my hands and feet would never get warm."

All you can see, all you can feel, is the cold. Cold resolve. That's what Mrs. Morrison says. That's the key.

"Right."

Understand?

"When I start to lose resolve, I need to remember how cold I was that day."

Worse thing is you'll be cold, then take a hot shower later.

I bent to her and wrapped my arms around her neck. "Thanks."

Anytime...

I pulled the blanket over her fur and stepped back toward Uncle Morgan.

"Are you okay?" he asked me.

"What's the temp today?"

"The temp?"

"Fahrenheit, if possible."

"Mid-70s maybe."

"I don't know," I said.

"What?"

"Feels colder than that."

I watched Pinson drive Katie and the cart away with Angelica completely covered by the plaid blanket. G.Q. and I made it to the 10th a few minutes later, and for the first time today, Labouhn hadn't beaten us to the tee.

"It's Rutt's go," I said to Hardy Dinmont. "Where's Mr. Labouhn?"

"In the trees, sir. Breakfast evidently disagreed with him."

G.Q. said, "Must be something going around."

"And I believe Mr. Labouhn is, well, otherwise concerned," Dinmont said.

I frowned. "With..?"

"Well, sir, I probably should not be saying this, since it is a private affair, between Mr. Labouhn and Kenwood."

"Maybe if you told us, we could help."

"It's just that, and please take this the right way, sir, but Mr. Labouhn's contract with the club expires in the fall."

G.Q. said, "Take *what* the right way?"

"Three gentlemen from the committee are on the course, and watching today."

"Committee?"

"Yes, sir. The hiring committee."

The light dawned on me. "And it wouldn't look so good if a former tour player, namely Rutledge Labouhn, lost to a goofy guy who plays blindfolded."

"Sir, that might just be the case," Dinmont said.

A few seconds later, Labouhn came out of the rough and stepped up to the tee.

I said, "You good, Rutt?"

"Charley, that last hole was even. Why don't you have first

go at it on 10." His fingers trembled as he gripped his club.

"Okay, Rutt."

I placed my Titleist on the tee.

***

For the last five holes, it was a complete reversal of fortune from the front nine. Labouhn started shaken on 10, and practically shaken and stirred by the end of 14. He bogeyed 10 and 11, double-bogeyed 12 and 13, and steadied himself at par on 14.

Before each hole, and before each shot, I blindfolded myself and pictured a blizzard in a land so barren even the penguins wouldn't live there. And since my head was filled with frozen tundra, there was room for nothing else. My shots flew exactly as I'd visualized. I was par on 10 and 14, but *birdied* 12 and 13. So, as we approached 15, the scores had moved closer: I was down only three points.

Hole 15 was a monstrous 600 yards, with trees on both sides of the fairway, and a severe dogleg. G.Q. advised me to keep my drive off the tee at moderate power, to avoid driving too far through the dogleg and into trouble.

Labouhn looked even worse at the 15th tee, if that were possible. Sweat streaked down his face, and his powder blue shirt was more wet than dry.

"Hey, Rutt," I said. "You okay?"

He stared at me, and his entire body straightened. "*Certainly*. Why shouldn't I be?"

"No reason."

"We all have good shots and bad."

"I do. You don't."

"Today I do." He took a long breath and let it out. "Charley, would you mind if I...tell you something?"

"Uh..."

"And you as well, Garland."

G.Q. said, "What's he talking about?"

Labouhn took a step toward me. "I shall *certainly* explode if I tell no one."

"Well, go on, then," I said.

"It's, it's P.J."

"Really?" I glanced at G.Q.

"Since I noticed her, I *cannot concentrate*."

"Yes, she is beautiful, in a feminine sort of way."

Labouhn shook his head. "Do you know how a first love can affect a man, Charley?"

A slight shudder ran through me. "Yes. Yes I do."

"I was starting out, just making a name for myself in the game. And then..."

"She dumped you?"

"*Yes*."

"For her *career*, I bet."

Labouhn's sculptured jaw dropped. "How did you know?"

"Guys can tell sometimes."

"Yes. She dumped me for her career. We haven't spoken in nearly five years."

"Look, Rutt-"

"And now to see her, for *P.J. Varelli* to appear on the turf like some David Copperfield illusion, is just so...unsettling. I don't know whether to try to talk with her, or to sprint away as fast as I can run."

"Do you want to call it, then?"

He shook his head. "No. Let's play on."

"You sure?"

"Yes."

He stared at me for a few seconds. I suddenly felt a little bad for the guy, since I knew exactly what he was feeling. But then again, maybe his sudden mental breakdown was just what I needed to stand any kind of chance against him in this match.

"Okay. Well, your go."

Labouhn gritted his teeth, pulled his club back, and fired. His ball rocketed directly through the dogleg and into the trees.

At the end of 15, we were both two over, and lost two points each. I was still down three points to Rutt Labouhn.

Hole 16 was a relatively short 365 yards, par 4. Rutt's concentration wavered, and he finished 16 at one over. I managed to par 16, and I gained one point. I was now only two points behind.

Labouhn redeemed himself with a wicked drive on 17, and

he birdied the hole with a beautiful, brilliantly played final putt. He gained two points for that one. I managed to par 17, gaining a zero. After seventeen holes, I was four behind Labouhn, with just one hole to go.

As we walked together toward 18, G.Q. said, "You've played extremely well today, Mr. Davis."

"Thanks, G.Q. I hope I haven't let Uncle Morgan down."

"I am sure that's not the case."

"Labouhn looks like he just got out of detox."

"Emotional troubles can be physically exhausting."

"So, now, tell me about 18."

"465 yards. Par 4."

"And..?"

"That's all you need to know. Play this one by instinct."

"Instinct."

"Sometimes, instinct is as good as anything else."

We reached the tee. I saw P.J. who stood closer, just behind the tee. She smiled and waved in our direction. Labouhn saw her too, and his face suddenly paled. Maybe he thought P.J. had waved at him. It was hard to be sure. He looked at me, with stress-filled eyes. "Up to you, Charley."

I nodded and bent to place my ball. I stood and noticed how quiet the course was. The gallery was still there, had actually grown, but was completely hushed.

Blindfolded, I internally called upon all the gods of winter. The frigid arctic winds howled in my ears. My skin was covered in an icy spray of near-frozen water.

I swung.

I instantly pulled off the blindfold but couldn't find my ball, so I watched the crowd for a reaction. After a few seconds, the gallery turned toward me and cheered.

"What?"

G.Q. smiled. "On the dance floor, Mr. Davis."

"Middle of the green. Wow."

Labouhn placed his ball on his tee, waited a second, and said, "That was a championship shot, Charley."

"Lucky, I think."

"No luck about that one."

He turned toward his ball, brought his driver back behind

his shoulder, and brought his club around. His ball flew true, and landed on the fairway, about thirty yards from the green.

I said, "Nice one."

Labouhn found the strength to smile at me for an instant, and then we walked together through the grass. We reached Labouhn's ball first. He clubbed it skyward, and it landed on the edge of the green.

"Rutt, go ahead."

"Your ball is closer to the pin, Charley."

"I don't care. Your shot."

He hesitated a moment, then took his putter, bent on one knee, and studied the green. Satisfied, he stood, planned his shot, and brought his putter to his ball. It rolled toward the pin, missed the cup by about an inch, and came to rest a foot away.

"Afraid of the dark," G.Q. said.

Labouhn tapped in his ball, and his round was over at par on 18.

"Good round, Rutt," I said.

"You are a gentleman, Charley." He extended a handshake to me. "And a fine golfer."

I shook his hand. "Thanks."

"In fact, I see a bright future for you."

"I hope...things...work out for you."

"Yes."

"And, really, if you want to talk?"

He glanced across the grass at P.J. Varelli. "Charley, I am ahead four points. You can't possibly win."

I glanced at G.Q. "Give us a second, Rutt."

Labouhn nodded. "Certainly.

"Mr. Davis?" G.Q. said.

I angled close to G.Q. and whispered, "He's right. I'm four points behind."

"He's wrong, trying to rattle your nerves. You can win."

I squinted at him. "A par or a birdie does me no good."

"Correct. And it's too late for a hole-in-one. So an *eagle* needs to land?"

"An eagle would be worth 5 points playing Stableford."

G.Q. nodded. "If you sink this putt, and finish this hole in 2, then you win."

"By 1 point."

"Anything else, then you lose." Without another word, G.Q. fell to the surface of the green, flat on his stomach, and eyed the turf from ground level. He stood up and held his plumb bob. The he came to me. "I've examined the shot path. Let me tell you—"

"Charley?" Labouhn called.

"One more second," I said back to him. Labouhn looked unsteady and terrible, as if he desperately needed a double-shot of tequila.

"Mr. Davis," G.Q. whispered, "an eagle is possible here. This putt is doable. Very doable, especially for you, using your special techniques."

I peered back at Labouhn. He looked like I must have looked like back in college right after Sandy dumped me. Not the most pleasant sight. I actually felt sorry for him now, one shot from disaster. "G.Q., what happens if I don't shoot?"

"Don't shoot?"

"Yes. If I don't finish the last hole, what happens?"

"You must finish it out. Otherwise...you forfeit."

I again glanced over at Rutt Labouhn, one time touring golf professional, about to get beaten by a goofy blindfolded amateur. Stashing his old feelings for P.J. aside for the moment, he'd not only be embarrassed here, today, but he'd most likely lose his contract with the Kenwood Country Club.

"G.Q.?"

"Mr. Davis?"

"Thanks."

"For what?"

"You've been great."

"Thank me later. Just sink this putt!"

"I hope you understand, G.Q. I know it sounds a little crazy, but if I sink this putt, I'll ruin the man."

G.Q.'s eyes widened. "Excuse me, Mr. Davis, but *are you nuts*? He wishes to ruin your uncle."

"Hell, I hope Uncle Morgan understands." Before G.Q. could say anything else, I stepped off the green and walked to Labouhn. "Rutt."

"Yes, Charley?"

"I quit."

"Quit?"

"Yes."

"You *can't* quit."

"I can forfeit the game."

"But with the way you've been playing the back nine..?"

I stared at him and our eyes locked. "The match is yours. Congratulations."

"Charley, you need to shoot this out."

"Nonsense, Rutt. I wouldn't make that last putt anyway. My concentration is gone. The girl who dumped me five years ago, the love of my life, is over there, staring at me right now, through the lens of her camera."

Labouhn blinked at me. "You can't do this to me."

"Goodbye, Rutt. Thanks for a great game."

"Is...is *this* the kind of man you are, Charley, a *quitter*?"

I halted and turned back to him. "What was that?"

"I didn't figure you for a *quitter*, after all you've been through, all that time, all the effort and money Morgan has put into you, supporting you, training you. That's all I'm saying."

My eyes started to burn. "I'm no quitter, Rutt."

"Didn't you just quit..?"

"I don't want to embarrass you."

"Well, you can't just quit," Rutt spluttered. "I'd rather lose to a miracle putt than win by voluntary forfeit. It's, well it's...humiliating."

I clenched my fists tightly. G.Q. appeared at my side and pressed the putter against my arm. He tilted his head close to me. "Listen to me, Mr. Davis. You offered to do him a huge favor. And he has refused. So, play this out, Charley." He locked his eyes with mine. "You can sink this putt. Give Rutledge Labouhn *exactly* what he deserves."

I looked over at Labouhn. "You sure about this, Rutt?"

"I've never been more certain about anything."

I took a breath.

"G.Q.?" I said.

"Mr. Davis?"

"I'll have my putter now."

G.Q. nodded.

I took my Samurai putter with both hands and strolled confidently to the edge of the green then angled my head at G.Q. "So, tell me."

"Slight curve to the left," he whispered, "just before the cup. There's no wind or moisture. Shouldn't require much more than a straight touch with good power. It's a long putt, quite long in fact, but you've made putts like this a few times before. You can make this one as well. No tricks, no special planning. Just line it up, remember to apply proper force, clear your mind, and shoot directly."

I nodded and stepped onto the green. G.Q. faded back and stopped beside Mrs. Morrison and Uncle Morgan. I positioned myself over the Titleist and gazed from the ball to the cup, which seemed a continent away. I've made putts this long before? G.Q. must be remembering a *different* Charles Marriot Davis, or perhaps he was thinking of a celebrity golfer from his past caddying victories.

No matter. I was committed now.

Think. Line up the putt. Gauge the strength needed to propel the Titleist this monumental distance.

I realized the complete silence all at once. I glanced to the sidelines and saw Uncle Morgan, Mrs. Morrison, Pinson Dill, Garland Quick, P.J. Varelli, and about two hundred strangers who were all staring straight at me.

Okay. No pressure.

Then, a familiar idea hit me. I rested my putter against the front of my legs and pulled my blindfold from my back pocket. I wrapped it around my eyes; if I was to beat Rutt Labouhn, I may as well go all the way with it. I hoped being beaten by a blindfolded amateur would ruin the egotistical goat.

I gripped my club, steadied myself, and took a long breath. I let it out slowly. I could feel Mrs. Morrison's thought-waves penetrating my skull straight into my brain. *Empty your mind, Charley. Reflex. Feel the bitter cold, and shoot by reflex.*

The arctic winds pushed everything from my mind, and all I could see behind my blindfold was the bitter cold surface of the moon. My hands readied the shot on their own, as they had done by reflex hundreds of times over these past months. And then...

Labouhn cleared his throat and muttered under his breath,

"That dog of yours, if it really is a dog, may be the ugliest in all canine creation. A black canine horror. It belongs in a carnival freak show."

My eyes popped open under the black blindfold.

Black canine horror..?

A severe molten heat thumped at my temples.

Freak show..?

I bit down hard on my bottom lip and pictured Rutt Labouhn being carted from the course on a stretcher after I had battered him with my Nigerian fighting staff.

My heart pounded.

My fingers squeezed the life from my putter.

I gritted my teeth and pushed my Samurai putter forward with both hands, only to greet the ball with a dull *plink*.

Chapter 51

Happy Together

One week after my match with Rutt Labouhn, we all gathered in Sandy's screening room, in her Victorian two-bedroom bungalow in Glendale. I stood with a can of Diet Cherry Dr. Pepper in my hand, waiting for the movie to begin. G.Q. seemed fascinated by the movie posters hung on every wall, especially the poster for *The Right Stuff*. Ray sat on the sofa beside Angelica, speaking close and quietly into one of her ears. Uncle Morgan and Mrs. Morrison stood beside each other, quietly talking.

Sandy told us she had put together a four-minute sample of her film, just to give us some idea of what she was going for. I wasn't looking forward to seeing the film, since I have never liked the way I looked in photos. As the lights dimmed, I took a seat beside Ray and Angelica, and settled back as the video screen faded to black.

Music started low and began to build. It sounded familiar, like a soundtrack from a gladiator movie, heroic, and moving. Sandy always used real film scores when she put together a film sample. The short film was just for her, really, and great music set the tone.

The screen slowly fills with a close-up of me sitting cross-legged in a meditation position on the ground in Glenwood Gardens. My eyes are closed, the camera pulls back, and...

...I am stick fighting in slow motion with Mrs. Morrison. She whirls all around me, and I am obviously lost. She connects with my shoulder, I turn, and throw my stick to the ground. The music rumbles ominously, as...

...a meadow is peppered with small white specks. We are at Jawbreaker Mountain. A horse whinnies. I swing my club. A jawbreaker takes flight, the screen fades, comes up again, and...

...the majestic entrance to the Robert Trent Jones golf course at Seabrook fades up. I concentrate on a putt and touch the ball with my club. The camera follows the ball as it rolls slowly across the green, until...

...Angelica's furry head is seen in profile, as she sits in the rough, and later...

...Angelica trots along the beach at the water's edge. The camera pulls back and I run beside her, again in slow motion, the sun reflects brilliantly on the surface of the ocean, until...

...the verdant green of the Kendale course surrounds me. The camera focuses on my face, follows me as I blindfold myself, take my club, and swing.

The screen faded to black and the lights came up in the room. Everyone applauded. Sandy stepped over to me and sat on the edge of a coffee table in front of the sofa.

I said, "That music sounds like it's from a superhero movie."

She nodded. "Yeah."

"Painting me as a superhero?"

Her hand found my knee. "Of course not, dummy. I've never learned how to paint." She smiled, stood and walked across the room.

I got up as well, just as Angelica hopped off the sofa. She followed Ray, her new confidant, into the kitchen.

Uncle Morgan reached the sofa. He held two bottles of Coors. "Sit back down for a second."

"Sure." I took the bottle from him and sat.

"Know what I'm thinking?"

"How I made you resign from one of the most exclusive country clubs in the state. It has a two-year waiting list just to get in."

He shook his head and took a swallow from his bottle. "Wrong."

"Oh?"

"Two things."

"First thing first," I said.

"There are two months left to go, Charley. Look how well you are playing."

"Sometimes it's there, Uncle Morgan, but sometimes it just evaporates into the clouds."

"Charley, last week you played an incredible match against an excellent golfer, and you played while under extreme pressure."

"Yeah. I'm trying to forget about all that pressure."

"As I told you before, not one pro in ten could have sunk that putt."

"Uncle Morgan, I missed that last shot by a good twenty yards."

"More like ten. The shot was just a bit too strong, and off to the right."

"Okay. Ten yards. Whatever. I wasn't close."

"We should learn from our failures, Charley."

"Meaning..?"

"A huge part of golf is mental, as we have stressed to you from the beginning. All Rutt Labouhn did was use the mental part of the game against you. Successfully."

"Uh huh."

He eyed me carefully. "The Kenwood club just signed Rutledge to a new contract."

"Well, good for him."

"Really?"

I chuckled. "I started to feel bad for him. Can you believe that? He was afraid of losing his job at the club, and P.J., his ex-girlfriend, was unexpectedly haunting the course. But he eventually showed his true colors, mental aspects of the game or not. Uncle Morgan, I think maybe years ago Labouhn was removed from the litter too early."

Uncle Morgan smiled. "So, do you want to hear the second thing?"

"*Certainly.*"

"I was *right.*"

"About what?"

"Golf is not a game of talent, but truly a game of practice."

"You sound surprised."

"Not surprised at what you've been able to do."

"It's not that much."

"But a little surprised at the *immense* changes I've seen in you."

"I'm the same guy, Uncle Morgan. Just a little happier."

"You're a good person, Charley."

"Oh?"

"Charitably good. And that takes more heart than slamming the heck out of a golf ball."

I held out my Coors bottle and touched it to Uncle Morgan's bottle. "Here's to the next two months, Uncle Morgan."

"So say we all, Charley. So say we all."

***

Angelica gave a short *woof* from somewhere at the front of the house. I pushed myself from the sofa and followed the sound. Angelica was poised in the front hall, one paw raised and her snout aimed at the door.

"What is it, girl?"

She *woofed* again.

I stepped to the closed door and looked outside through a side window.

"Oh," I said. "Uh...I...oh."

"Charley?" Sandy said from behind me.

"Charley's not here," I said to her. "I'm his twin brother, Rafael."

She chuckled. "And where are the rest of the turtles?"

"Sandy, I had *nothing* to do with this."

Sandy Carson flicked one of her patented you're-a-silly-idiot looks, nudged me to one side, and stepped to the door. She pulled it open.

Sandy waited a few seconds and looked back at me. "You had nothing to do with this?"

"I swear."

"Hello, Ms. Carson," the female voice said from the front walkway.

"Hi," Sandy said. "Ms. Varelli, right?"

I moved beside Sandy.

P.J. Varelli watched us from the cement walk about twenty feet away. "Please pardon my intrusion."

"Oh, no problem." Sandy bumped me aside. "Would you like to come in? We're having sort of an informal R and R."

"No. Thank you. I can talk out here."

"Come sit on the porch then."

P.J. Varelli didn't move.

Uncle Morgan, Pinson, and Mrs. Morrison appeared in the hallway.

"What's going on?" Uncle Morgan said then noticed P.J. Varelli outside. "Oh. Huh?"

"So, P.J.," I said. "What brings you here on this fine, early summer evening?"

"Mr. Davis, can we speak alone?"

"Uh, sure." I could sense Sandy's laser-like stare burning through my clothes and into my skin. I stepped outside and walked to P.J.

She turned so that her back was to the house.

I said, "So."

She was stunning in the streetlights. I took in each and every detail as I willed myself to breathe. Her hair framed her face in sweeps of dark brushstrokes, and her face was so perfect she could easily grace the cover of any upscale fashion magazine.

"Mr. Davis, I want you to understand I am not here to satisfy any romantic notion."

"No romance? Right. No romance."

"And I apologize for not joining you and your group inside, but I value some privacy. I have so little of it in my life."

"I understand," I said, even though I didn't.

"We've played a few games together, and you've seen me at some of your recent matches."

"I have. Thanks for coming."

"I hope you haven't gotten the wrong idea."

"Hard to tell until I know the right idea."

"I've been scouting you...and a few others."

"Scouting me for..?"

"A partner."

I swallowed. *Partner?*

"I do about three pro-ams each year. There's one at the end of next month."

"A pro-am, where pros play against amateurs?"

She shook her head. "Pros and amateurs play as a foursome, *with* each other and *against* each other. Each team in this particular tournament has one pro and one non-pro."

"And you want *me* on your team?"

"I do." She bit her bottom lip, turned her head, and glanced toward the house.

I felt my heart beat faster. "I'm flattered. But I don't think I've played enough golf to even qualify as an amateur."

Her eyes locked onto mine. "Mr. Davis, I've been playing golf since I was eight years old. I've seen them all, good, bad, overrated, underrated, *and* the ugly. Believe me, you more than qualify. You are among the select few who I would describe as a special player."

"Well, thanks. And please call me Charley."

She closed her eyes for a moment. Then she stared at me. "You know, there's also something extremely likable about someone who loves dogs as much as you do."

"You mean Angelica."

"Someone who would pretend to be sightless in order to bring his dog along on the golf course."

I blinked. "Oh. Back at Seabrook."

"Yes."

"I meant no harm. Just wanted her with me."

"I know."

"Thanks for understanding."

"Forget it."

"This may sound ridiculous, but sometimes I feel lost without her."

"It's likable."

"I...I...thanks."

She gazed into my eyes. "You and Ms. Carson are together?"

"We were five minutes ago. Now, I don't know."

"Uh huh. Well, I hope she doesn't get the wrong idea about me coming here like this."

"Oh, there's no chance of that."

I realized I was staring at her like a five-year-old stares at his presents under the Christmas tree. I snapped myself out of it.

"The end of July will be nine months."

"Nine months?"

"From when I started playing golf."

Her eyes widened. "You mean to say you've been playing golf for only *eight months*?"

"More like seven months. Training started last November. Never played before that."

"Incredible."

"I quit my job, and trained all day, every day, with Pinson and Mrs. Morrison."

"Just eight months?"

"A little less."

"Unbelievable."

"It's been quite a journey."

She stared at the ground and placed her hands on her hips, as if carefully deciding what to say next.

"Guess I was more right about you than I imagined."

"If you say so."

I knew this incredible woman was not hitting on me, at least I didn't think she was, but she was so *stunning*, I couldn't stop my hands from trembling. I shoved them into my back pockets. "So, P.J., listen-"

"Pamela. Please, call me Pamela."

"Okay. Sure. Pamela, I have to check with my uncle about...*playing with you*...but assuming he has no problem with it, where is the tournament to be held?"

***

Uncle Morgan blinked several times, then settled himself and stared at me. "She wants you to play at Pe...Pe...Pe..."

"Pebble Beach," I said. "Yes, Pebble Beach."

Uncle Morgan lowered himself and sunk into the sofa. He seemed unable to speak.

"What's the big deal?" I said.

"*Pebble Beach* is a big deal," Pinson said.

"Why? Did the Flintstones play there?"

"Among the finest courses in the world," Mrs. Morrison said. "And constructed so elegantly it has been considered by many as an art form."

"I went there with my dad when I was a kid," Sandy said. "I think the blue water splashing up against the rocks at the edge of all that smooth green might be the most beautiful setting I've ever seen."

Uncle Morgan stood again. "We planned for you to play in a major tournament, eventually. And you've already proven yourself, as far as I am concerned. This pro-am is totally optional. Is it something you really want to do?"

I thought for a few seconds, and really couldn't come up with a positive answer to that question. This was a truly bad, bad idea. I shouldn't do *anything* to encourage being around P.J. Varelli; the last thing Sandy wanted was for me to be partnered with such an attractive female. The past seven months or so have not only molded me into a respectable golfer, but also allowed Sandy and me to mend our tattered relationship. I should stay far, far away from P.J. Varelli.

"Yes," I said. "I want to play Pebble Beach."

There really wasn't any question about it.

Uncle Morgan said, "Then, let's inform Ms. Varelli tomorrow."

"Uncle Morgan, P.J. is still outside."

"Outside?"

"Waiting for an answer. She values her privacy, she said. Wouldn't come in."

I saw Sandy stare at the door, looking out.

"You know, I forgot to ask. Where is Pebble Beach?"

"Monterey," Pinson said. "Monterey, California."

"Sounds nice."

"It is, sir." And sir..?

"Yes?

"The Flintstones?"

"Oh, I thought maybe Pebbles played there at, you know, *Pebble* Beach."

"I see."

"Pinson, do me a favor?"

"Certainly."

"Would you go outside and tell Pamela...P.J. for me?"

"I will."

I sat on the sofa next to Angelica. "I need some quiet time with my friend here."

"My pleasure."

I rubbed Angelica's neck. Pinson left the room. Uncle Morgan and Mrs. Morrison spoke excitedly about my unexpected and fortunate opportunity to play on one of the world's finest courses right at the end of my nine-month training period.

And Sandy Carson stood silently across the room, and stared out the front window at a shadowed female figure on the walkway. Sandy absently sipped from a can of Diet Coke, thoughts of the incredibly gorgeous P.J. Varelli and me playing together at Pebble Beach undoubtedly spinning in her curly blond head.

I knew she was already fuming, connecting the dots, and wondering exactly what this future partnership in California might lead to.

**

Angelica's growling woke me at 2:00am. Then I heard the knocking at the kitchen door.

"Charley," Sandy called from far away. "Charley, it's me."

I fumbled out of bed and glanced at the clock to make sure I read the numbers right the first time. It took just a few seconds to rush into the kitchen, and I pulled open the door. "Sandy, what the hell..?"

She looked terrible, no makeup, eyes bloodshot, as if she had been in bed, thrashing about, for hours. Her ball cap was gone, and her hair was a mess. "Charley..."

"Is something wrong?"

She narrowed her gaze at me. "Can I...come in?"

"What kind of question is that?" I moved to the side.

Sandy shuffled to the kitchen table, touched the top of a chair, and sat.

"Is Ray all right?"

She gathered herself. "Ray's fine."

I waited a few seconds while Sandy stared up at me.

"Sandy?"

Angelica padded over and plopped down at my feet.

I considered whether I should sit in a chair beside Sandy or remain standing. I decided to just stand there.

She blinked a few times. "I know this is going to sound crazy."

"That's what someone says just before they spill their guts about the UFO that landed in their backyard."

"We are back together, Charley, and I am happy about that. No, I am *thrilled* about that."

"That doesn't sound crazy."

"Ms. Varelli," she said.

"P.J."

"Yes."

"What about her?"

Sandy shook her head. "I saw the way she looked at you."

"P.J.?"

She shook her head again. "Don't play dumb, Charley."

"So, P.J. looked at me. And..?"

"I knew what that look meant. Girls can tell."

I sat in a chair across from her. "It's 2:00 in the morning, Sandy. You seriously came over here to-"

"And you were looking back."

"Looking back?"

"Yes. Girls can tell about that, too."

I took a breath. "I didn't ask P.J. to come over."

"Doesn't matter. The connection was obvious, Charley."

"What connection?"

"You know..."

"Okay. P.J. Varelli came over. I *looked* at her. She was standing right there, Sandy, we were talking, and she is pretty. What's that got to do with us?"

Sandy rubbed her eyes with the palms of both hands. "I want you to tell her *no*...Pebble Beach."

"Tell her no? You're right. That is crazy. It's just a golf tournament."

Her lips grew tight. "You'll be with her for nearly a week. P.J. Varelli, cover girl, and sex goddess of the golfing universe, you'll be with her all the time."

"Sandy, I don't get it. Nothing is going on with her."

"Nothing?"

"Nothing."

She looked off to one side, and then back at me.

"I believe you. I do. And I trust you, Charley. I know how much you care about me."

"So, there should be no problem. Right?"

She chewed on her bottom lip. "I want to avoid any *potential* problem."

I stood and took a step back from the chair. "Pebble Beach is important to Uncle Morgan."

"Playing there wasn't his idea."

"True, but-"

"He had no plan to enter you in the tournament."

"I know."

"Pebble Beach was *P.J. Varelli's* idea."

"Sandy-"

"The same P.J. Varelli who was talking in the dark with you, just a few hours ago, in my front yard."

I didn't speak for a moment. "What about what *I* want?"

She stood. "That's all I came here to say, Charley."

"What about *my* feelings, Sandy? Don't they matter?"

"Of course they do."

"Well, I *want* to play this tournament. It would be a huge public forum for Uncle Morgan to see the actual results of all his planning."

"Charley-"

"And I want to do it for *me*, Sandy. *For me.* I'm a different person today than I was months ago. Playing at Pebble Beach would be a symbol of how far I've been able to come since we started this madness."

She started toward the door. "Look, I can't stop you, if that's what you want to do. I just don't think it's too much to ask, that's all."

I lightly took her wrist and stopped her. "You don't trust me?"

"I need to go home, Charley."

"You think I'll dive into bed with her at my first opportunity?"

"Please let go of my wrist."

I did. "That's insulting, Sandy."

"Didn't mean to insult you."

"Well, you're saying, I guess, even though I'm in love with you, I eventually will not be able to resist falling all over P.J. Varelli."

She didn't say anything.

"Isn't that right?"

"You're a *guy*, Charley."

"That's breaking news."

She shook her head. "I've got to go." She started away again.

I stepped in front of her. "Sandy, everything in this world is not about you."

"I'm tired, Charley."

"Just listen to me for a minute."

She stood rigid and watched me.

"I used to stay up all night wondering why you left me. *Dumped* me. And I was convinced it was not really what you said, that you needed to concentrate on your career. I was convinced it was because you just didn't love me. And something must have been wrong with *me*."

She turned toward the door and touched the doorknob.

I placed my hand on her shoulder. "But you know what? I think I was *wrong*. All this time, I was dead wrong. You *absolutely* dumped me for your career. Because no matter how much I loved you, *worshipped* you, *your* feelings and desires were just plain more important than mine. Because Sandy Carson comes first in this world."

"That's not fair. And that was long ago, Charley. We were different people then."

I stepped away from her and shifted my weight until I felt secure. *Cold resolve* crept up involuntarily and swirled in my brain. "I hope you don't do this, Sandy, but leave if you want to. Walk out my door and disappear into the night, just like you did five years ago. You will leave knowing I have no plans to be with P.J. Varelli on any level, other than on a beautiful golf course in California for a few days. If you believe me, and want to stay together, I'm willing to give it a try. If you don't..."

She covered her mouth with her hand for a moment.

"Sandy?"

Her eyes moistened. "I can't help how I feel, Charley."

I looked at the floor for a few seconds, and then raised my eyes to her. "Neither can I."

She swallowed. Her hands were clenched and trembled at her sides. "I think it's best if we take a break from each other for a while."

"A break..?"

She nodded. "I'm hot-headed. If I've learned anything, I know that. And I know it's bad to make big decisions while I'm stressed out. I just need a little time to think."

I shrugged. "Well, I guess that makes sense, even though taking a break from each other is a big decision all its own."

She looked at the wall. "Even so."

"Yeah. Even so."

Sandy looked into my eyes, blinked, and looked away. "Goodbye, Charley."

She turned the doorknob and was gone in an instant.

Chapter 52

Double Vision

I went to the library and borrowed videos about Monterey and Pebble Beach the day after Pinson accepted P.J. Varelli's invitation. I learned about the three courses I was to play. Our foursome would play seventy-two holes in four days, rotating from three different courses, the MPCC Shore Course, Pebble Beach Golf Links, and Spyglass Hill. I thought the Spyglass Hill course was the one Sandy was talking about. The views of the intense blue water just below the greens were so amazing the photos looked digitally enhanced; nothing could actually have been so beautiful.

I watched some online travel videos about Monterey, as well. I suggested to Uncle Morgan we arrive in California five or six days early. There was so much to see and do in Monterey I wanted to take advantage of the situation. The Monterey Aquarium was first on my must-see list of tourist attractions. Uncle Morgan thought this was a bad idea, though, since he wanted my attention focused solely on golf and the tournament. He suggested we stay in California for a few days *after* Pebble Beach was history, and, naturally, Uncle Morgan made sense.

***

I felt especially energized this fine July morning, as I anticipated stick fighting with Her Ladyship of Yellow Springs. The air was awash with the fragrance of summer flowers. I felt wonderful, and I was sure this was going to go down in history as one of my favorite *magic* days.

I threw myself into the exercise and attacked Mrs. Morrison almost joyously, unfettered by my past or anything that may have filled my life before eight months ago, before Sandy had come back into my life, and then walked out of it again, and before P.J. Varelli, one of the most beautiful women on the planet told me she thought I was good enough to play golf as her partner. That's right, P.J. Varelli from the May 2013 cover of Maxim, thought that I, Charles Marriott Davis, was a good golfer.

Makes the head spin.

I took a breath and readied myself again then swung at Mrs. Morrison with electrical intensity. She edged aside and my Nigerian fighting staff of Ebony Gaboon sliced through the air beside her; she didn't even raise her own weapon to block me. I slashed at her again, one-handed from the other direction, faster this time. Mrs. Morrison leaned slightly away, with a relaxed ease. The stick touched nothing but the morning sunshine.

Mrs. Morrison took a step back, bowed, and straightened. She narrowed her gaze straight into mine. "Tell me, Charley."

"Tell you what?"

"What is *different* today?"

I shrugged. "I don't know. It's a really nice day."

"You are strong, swift, but unfocused."

"Oh. Sorry."

"Sorry doesn't cut it."

"Mrs. M., what do you want me to say?"

"You've suddenly regressed. Physically, your strength and speed are truly amazing. But your *control* this morning, Charley, your *control*...you've lost it."

"I'm not coming close to you. I know."

"Think about *why*, Charley."

I thought about it. Mrs. Morrison was right, of course. All my disjointed thoughts about Sandy's sudden departure, P.J. Varelli, and how absolutely amazing it was that Scarlett Perry hadn't shown her face lately, were probably all good reasons why I couldn't empty my mind and channel my full concentration to Mrs. Morrison's exercises this morning. Not to mention how I let Rutt Labouhn get to me and how I'd mentally imploded that day.

"I get it, Mrs. M. There's just so much going inside my pea-sized brain lately."

She relaxed her *ready* position. "Let's take thirty seconds or so, Charley. Empty your mind, as you have been doing for many months, and then let your body take over by reflex."

"Okay." I tapped my fighting stick against my thigh. "Okay, I'll try harder."

"Let me know when you are ready to start again."

I closed my eyes and focused on my breathing. I tried to sweep away every last scrap of thought or feeling. After about a minute, I still could see Sandy's eyes and how they glowed straight at me on the beach that night in the South Carolina rain; I'd never had any romantic moment in my life that could compare with that one. And just to think about it, *just to think about Sandy being back with me*, as a true couple, and then being gone again...confused me royally.

I opened my eyes. "Okay, Mrs. Morrison."

We settled into our *ready* positions.

I waited for her first move. Maybe it would be better to be on the defensive at first.

Mrs. Morrison swung. Her deadly Ebony Gaboon baton came flashing toward me. I ducked to my right–

The stick struck me above the bridge of my nose, at the base of my forehead.

The world exploded...

"Oh, God!" Mrs. Morrison said. "Charley!"

Her words seemed muffled, as if I were underwater.

"Mrs. Morris..?" I blinked, saw light flickers...

"Are you okay? Charley?"

I could form no words. My face felt wet. A few seconds later, I heard Mrs. Morrison call 911.

Then I passed out.

Chapter 53

Tell Me Why

It was difficult to describe the feeling in the pit of my stomach when I got called out of class in sixth-grade, walked into the principal's office, and saw my mom sitting there trying to contain her tears. Before she said a word, I knew something must have happened to my dad; nothing else I could think of in that split second could explain the look on my mom's face. The only other time that same feeling just completely pressed down all around me, was when I opened my eyes in the hospital a week ago and was greeted by nothing but darkness. It was unreal, dream-like, and horribly unsettling. As I finally came to grips that I was really awake and not dreaming, I instantly felt like my life was over.

My vision had always been perfect. That was one reason I was even more disturbed to open my eyes now and see only formless gray shapes.

The doctors said my optic nerves were likely swollen. Or compromised. That was the word they used. *Compromised.* I didn't know what that really meant, but I knew it couldn't be good. They said the concussion from Mrs. Morrison's baton struck me square in the center of my optic chiasm, the place where the optic nerves cross in front of my brain. I was taking steroids to help the swelling go down, but as of this morning, nothing much had changed.

I heard a knock at my hospital room door.

"Hey, Charley."

"Come on in, Uncle Morgan." I had been sitting up in my bed listening to the TV. All I could see were blurred outlines and those same gray blobs.

"Good morning." His voice sounded strained. He moved a

chair near me and sat by the bed.

I gritted my teeth. "How's the bruise look?"

"Deep purple."

"Chicks dig deep purple bruises. And 70s rock bands."

He didn't say anything for a few moments. Then: "So...any better?"

"Not really."

"What's the latest from your doctors?"

"Nothing they can do, just monitor the swelling of my optic nerves. My vision is supposed to return when the swelling goes down. But, so far...nothing."

He didn't say anything.

I felt his hands cover mine. "Hey, Uncle Morgan...are you all right?"

"I'm sorry." His voice cracked. "I haven't slept two hours this whole week. I'm a stupid, egotistical old man."

"No, Uncle Morgan. It was nobody's fault."

He removed his hands and scooted back in his chair. "I should have known better."

I heard him sniffle and clear his throat.

"Look, Uncle Morgan, I don't blame you for this. It's not Mrs. Morrison's fault either. Heck, I was distracted and too slow. Zigged when I should have zagged."

"You know Charley, I used to tell you some pretty wild tales when you were younger. You and I would go fishing, or to a ballgame, and I had the greatest time entertaining you, or..."

"Yeah?"

"Maybe it was more that I was entertaining myself. For nearly fifteen years I had the most fun rambling to you about crooked politicians, how artificial sweeteners were a Russian plot to poison us, and my stupid golf theory. Golf theory. *Right*. I should have never believed that ridiculous idea, Charley. Never.

"I think maybe crooked politicians is redundant, Uncle Morgan."

He ignored that one, and I gave up trying to lighten the mood.

"But one day an idea struck me. I knew I had to do *something*, Charley. I wasn't your father, I understood that, but I couldn't just sit by and see such a wonderful person, with so much potential, just wither away, broken-hearted. Couldn't do it. So, our old golf theory arguments came to mind, and I thought, let's all quit everything we are doing and play golf for nine months. Sure. Why not? I was bored. It was new and different. What did we have to lose? Maybe it would even give you a purpose. And if it didn't, what's the worst that could happen?"

I heard him take a tissue and blow his nose.

"Right," he said after a moment. "What's the worst that could happen?"

"A lot of good has happened, Uncle Morgan."

"You are right about that, Charley. You've grown as a person. And physically, you're in the best shape of your life. But considering the fact you are right across from me and can't see the color of the shirt I'm wearing, well, it's not been worth it."

We were quiet for a moment.

"Maybe the most positive note from this disaster is, well, I'm happy for your relationship with your dog."

"Angelica? How is she?"

I heard him wipe his nose again with a tissue. He took a breath. "Remember Jasper?"

"Your Border Collie. Sure. I used to play with Jasper when we came over to your house when I was little."

"Jasper was smarter than any kid on the street. He could identify each of his toys by name, was trained to sit, stay, shake, roll over, and was a champion at chasing and catching a Frisbee or any kind of ball. He was so intelligent, I absolutely knew Jasper would just start talking one day, tell us to remove the nasty dog food from his bowl on the floor, and to bring him a real steak, or at least some burgers, cooked medium rare. We loved that bundle of black-and-white fur, and he went everywhere with the family. And I still miss Jasper, every second of every single day."

I heard him take a long breath.

"When I watch you with Angelica, Charley, I remember how much of a friend Jasper was to me, especially in those days of your aunt Melissa's long illness. I *talked* to him. He *listened*. His soulful, understanding expression, and just his company, always made me feel better. You needed somebody like Jasper, Charley. Somebody to be your friend, someone for you to talk with, and someone to share this adventure with you."

My eyes moistened. "Mind handing me one of those tissues?"

Uncle Morgan put a tissue against my fingers. I lifted it and wiped my eyes.

"You okay?" he said.

I nodded and cleared my throat. "I suppose I was lucky she found me that cold day on Jawbreaker Mountain."

"I think you found each other."

I covered my face with my hands. "How is she doing with Mrs. Morrison?"

He chuckled. "I'll be shocked if Leslie Rae will voluntarily part with her. They are constantly together."

"I wonder if she can teach Angelica how to swing a Nigerian fighting staff?"

"Wouldn't surprise me."

I cleared my throat. "The doctor said he'd release me if I could find a ride home."

"Of course, Charley. Of course I'll take you home."

"Uncle Morgan, please call Pinson and Mrs. Morrison. I'd like to get back into practice as soon as we can."

"Are you sure?"

"I'm not going to just sit around and feel sorry for myself."

Uncle Morgan took a step back. "I'll go check at the nurse's station."

"Okay. And hurry. The food in here is terrible. And I can't stand this antiseptic smell for five more seconds."

"I'll move at Warp-9, Charley."

I laughed. "Thanks, Uncle Morgan."

"No problem." He hurried from my room and ran down the hall.

Chapter 54

Saturday, In the Park

The next morning, I was sitting on the sofa in my condo with Angelica when I heard a knock at the kitchen door.

"I'll get it, Charley," Uncle Morgan said from the kitchen.

Angelica *woofed* and jumped off the sofa.

"I'll be right there," I said.

I had been sitting with my arm around Angelica as we listened to the local 60s music radio station. It was comforting to sit there, safe, with my friend beside me. I knew the condo well enough to get up and carefully step into the kitchen, even though all I could see were blurred outlines.

"Morning," Uncle Morgan said. "I was just making breakfast."

I felt for a chair and sat. I folded my hands and rested them on the table. "Who's here?"

"It's Ray."

"Hey, man," Ray said.

"How's the weather?" I asked.

"Good."

They both were silent for a few moments.

Ray said, "We're not going to a golf course today, man."

"Are you sure you want to go, Charley?" Uncle Morgan asked.

"Better than sitting here."

"Pinson and Mrs. Morrison are outside," Ray added.

"I'm psyched to go. When I'm outdoors practicing, I won't have to think about...much."

"We're going to that horse pasture again," Ray said. "Right up the hill."

I gazed in his direction. "Good old Jawbreaker Mountain."

"Pinson said something about going back to the beginning. He said it real slow."

I thought about smacking jawbreakers around. "Whatever Pinson wants."

"The man knows what he's doing."

"I'll get my clubs." I stood. "Go ahead outside."

Uncle Morgan said, "Charley, what about breakfast?"

"Later, Uncle Morgan."

"Before we leave..."

I felt something atop my hands. I moved my fingers and touched what felt like thick paper. "What's this?"

"Tickets."

"Tickets for..?"

"The Reds. Season tickets behind the plate. They were damn hard to get."

I smiled. "You remembered."

I heard him sniffle again. "Yeah, nephew. I remembered."

"Thanks, Uncle Morgan."

I wondered what it would be like to attend a game at The Great American Ballpark while being unable to...

"So, you need any help?"

"No. Go on. I can fumble around pretty good by myself and get my stuff ready. Besides," I reached down and scratched Angelica's furry neck, "my friend is here if I need help."

"Okay."

Someone put a hand on my shoulder.

"I'll be right there, if you need something," Ray said.

"Thanks."

Ray patted my shoulder once and moved away.

***

It was amazing how my other senses magnified since my sight went bye-bye. As soon as the Escalade started up the winding drive that led to Jawbreaker Mountain, the aroma of horses and summer meadow grass completely overwhelmed me. We slowed to a stop, and I heard every slight crunch of the car tires rolling through the gravel in the parking area. The soft whinny of horses in the distance sounded as though they were welcoming me back home. I tried to appreciate my heightened senses instead of feeling sorry for myself.

"Charley," Mrs. Morrison's hand found mine.

I stepped out onto the gravel.

"No meditation today," she said. "In fact, I suppose we are finished with our meditation sessions."

"That makes me a little sad, Mrs. Morrison."

"I know. And, once again, I apologize—"

"No. I told you four hundred times, it was my fault. Just forget it. Please."

I heard her sniffle once. "I will still be here, Charley, if you, well, want to talk about anything."

"Sure."

Her arms were around me. Fresh patchouli was all I could smell. I felt her hands tremble against my back, and then she pulled away.

I shuffled my feet in the gravel. It sounded really loud.

"Garland Quick will meet us in California," Uncle Morgan said. "I informed him of, well, what happened."

"I bet it will change nothing. G.Q. has a special way of reading greens. It doesn't matter to him whether I can see or not."

Pinson said, "Charley, let's walk up the hill ahead of the others."

"You're the boss."

Ray, Mrs. Morrison, and Uncle Morgan's voices faded behind me as I took hold of Angelica's vest handle and walked beside Pinson into the grass. I never really understood the true meaning of *irony* until I reached down and grasped the handle on Angelica's service dog vest for the first time, after I got out of the hospital. Fiction to fact in a heartbeat.

I heard Ray struggling with the camera equipment, alone now that Sandy had fled the scene and left the rest of the filming to Ray. She told Uncle Morgan she would still follow through and edit the film, but it would be unlikely we would ever see her again. That fact still made me feel sick to my stomach.

Pinson stopped and so did Angelica. He placed his hand on my forearm. "This is an amazing situation, sir. After all, you have been shooting blindfolded for months. Why should an actual loss of vision matter now?"

I had it figured that way, too. "It shouldn't matter."

"No, sir. It should not. But when you first realized your sight had vanished, my bet is your head filled with an immediate terror."

"Anybody who wakes up blind would have the same reaction."

"You seem to be dealing with it pretty well now."

"Only on the outside, Pinson. Inside, it's barely restrained panic. If I let myself lose control, if I think about it too much or lose my ridiculous sense of humor, I'd go insane in about four minutes."

"Understandable. But you cannot lose control. If you're going to continue to play golf, I want your mind now focused on just one thing."

"Yeah, golf."

"I want you to go back to the beginning, and remember what Mrs. Morrison taught you that very first day in the woods. Clear your mind, Charley. Let a shroud of cold resolve surround you, let reflex take over, and focus all your attention, all your power, on each and every shot."

"Cold resolve."

"You harnessed that power when you played Rutt Labouhn. Blindfolded. Playing from both sides. You can do it again."

"My play against Labouhn wasn't entirely successful."

"I disagree, sir."

I nodded in his direction. "Well, right now, on the top of this hill with you and my furry friend here, I'll be okay. But in California, amid a crowd of strangers and playing in the dark the entire time, I'm not so sure."

"Angelica is not your only friend on this hill."

I reached out with an open hand.

Pinson grasped my hand and I shook it warmly. "Shall we begin, sir?"

"Sure. And please stop calling me sir."

I heard a loud rattle. "What's that?"

"That, sir, is a bucket full of jawbreakers."

I laughed. "I suppose the theory is, if I can hit a

jawbreaker..?"

"I will place the jawbreakers and guide you to the proper position. The rest will be up to your training."

"Fine. But do we have any music on this hill?"

I heard a click. *Black Magic Woman* by Santana played from Pinson's MP3 player.

I huffed. "She's got me *so blind I can't see...*"

"Are you ready, sir?"

I heard a jawbreaker hit the ground. "Back to the beginning, Pinson. Let's start."

Chapter 55

Leaving on a Jet Plane

All I could think about on the airplane was what Angelica must have been feeling imprisoned in a crate in the baggage compartment. More than anything, I wanted this plane to land so I could get her out of there. There was no telling how she might react to something this peculiar.

As the hours passed, I had a lot of time to think, especially since I couldn't read or watch the in-flight movie. One thing that struck me was how expensive this whole mad project had become for Uncle Morgan. This trip alone, flying to California, and housing six or seven people in a 4-star Monterey hotel, must cost him a small fortune. Certainly, nine months ago, Uncle Morgan could not have predicted a trip to Pebble Beach for a whole cadre of people.

I also thought about Sandy marching out of my life again, although this time, that familiar death grip of rejection didn't seem as bad, since marching out wasn't entirely her idea; I'd made a choice she couldn't live with.

My blindness didn't seem to matter much on the plane. But when I let my brain wander to the possibility this lack of sight might be permanent, an icy shiver coursed through my entire body. When that happened, I wished Angelica were seated beside me, more than ever. I needed her company.

We landed, rented a minivan, and drove to our hotel, which turned out to be right on the beach. I could smell the salt water as soon as we pulled into the parking lot. We were whisked inside to our adjoining suites almost instantly by an incredibly efficient hotel staff. And the entire time, Angelica was with me, guiding me to wherever I needed to be.

Later, I settled by the pool with the sounds of the ocean in the background. Ray sat next to me and brought me a V-8 over ice.

"Thanks."

Angelica sprawled out beside me as usual.

"Your dog loves you, man."

"You might be right."

"Without a doubt."

Ray was quiet for a moment.

"What's up, Ray?"

"I'm leaving in a couple weeks, man. Thought I should tell you face to face."

"I appreciate that."

"Because the two of us are friends, and all."

"Where are you going?"

"Got an offer couple weeks ago. Interning with Thomas Mangelsen."

"The nature photographer?"

"In Alaska."

"Well, that's great, Ray. I'm happy for you. Sounds like a wonderful opportunity."

"Thanks, man."

"Does Sandy know?"

"Yeah. She knows."

Ray was silent.

"What else, Ray?"

"I know all about you and Jenn."

I squinted at him. "Who?"

"Melanie. But her name's not Melanie."

"She told you, huh?"

"She came over while I was editing and spilled the whole barrel of worms. About how you both were an item, but it was way before she met me. And she was happy to be with me. She was crying, man."

Dread set the butterflies free in my stomach. "So, what's her real name?"

"Jennifer. Jennifer Quaid."

"Let me guess...the daughter of—"

"Dennis Quaid's step-daughter."

"No joke?"

"I know. Surprised me, too."

"She going to Alaska with you?"

"Said she was, man."

"Well, good luck to you up there, Ray."

"Sounds really cool. I'm looking forward to looking at the stars. They're closer to the ground in Alaska." Ray was silent for a moment. "Charley, who you will be playing against tomorrow?"

"Don't know much about them, except for what P.J. told me. The pro is Cushman Wakefield, from Australia. The amateur is Wallace Jay. He's from Colorado Springs."

"P.J. Varelli. Wow."

"I know."

"Magazine covers."

"Is there something you're trying to say?"

"Just good luck to you, Charley."

"Yeah. Playing golf truly blind will be tough."

Ray took a breath. "I wasn't talking about golf, man. P.J. *Varelli.*"

Someone wearing flip-flops walked towards us.

"See you later, Charley," Ray said. "Hey, G.Q."

"Hamilton," G.Q. said from close by.

"Ray," I said, "before you go..?"

"Yeah, Charley?"

"Do me a favor?"

"Anything."

"Be careful about Melanie...Jennifer."

"Careful?"

"Before you fall much harder for her. I know she's beautiful, I get it, but lying about her name to you might not be the best way to begin a relationship."

"Sure."

"Might be a red flag, Ray. All I'm saying."

I felt a hand on my shoulder.

"Thanks for caring about me, Charley. Means a lot."

I heard Ray step away.

"G.Q.," I said.

"Yes."

"Just get in?"

"Caddied a round for Will Smith on a course in Sausalito. Will is quite the golfer."

"Caddie with special talents to the stars."

"Angelica looks peaceful."

She was sprawled on the concrete across my feet.

"I think she's tired. Probably didn't sleep much on the plane."

G.Q. waited almost thirty seconds before he spoke again. "Quite the situation we have here, Charley."

"An understatement, G.Q."

"I've been giving this a great deal of thought."

"And?"

"Both our jobs just got about four hundred times harder."

I chuckled. "We are definitely rubbing off on each other."

"Before each swing, I will not only need to *plan* each shot, but I will also need to *describe* everything to you in detail. If I do not, then you will not be able to visualize your shot, and visualization is crucial."

"I've thought about that."

"But we'll get through it."

"Thanks for your confidence."

He gave a short laugh. "Here's the way I look at it: Your job is essentially the same as before. You will listen to my instructions, *pretend* you've blindfolded yourself, then gather your inner strength, and shoot. Not that much will be different for you. My job, however, is much harder, because you need to *see* the course only by listening to my words."

"That's nothing we haven't done before either."

"Actually, it might be an advantage."

"How?"

"The Pebble Beach courses are so drop-dead gorgeous, Charley, being able to actually see them might count as a true distraction to some golfers. It is impossible to gaze at these courses without being somewhat moved by the beauty that surrounds you. But now..."

"I won't have that distraction."

"Correct."

"Yeah. I'll be walking blind, led by a guide dog that isn't really a guide dog, stumbling around eighteen holes of the world's most spectacular real restate. Sounds like one in the plus column for me."

"You also will not be distracted by those in the gallery, your friends, family. Celebrities." G.Q. placed a hand on my shoulder. I caught the scent of floral body lotion. "I don't know if he will truly show up."

"Who?"

"Each of us in the tournament, caddies as well, have two free gallery invitations. I sent one to Kevin by special messenger."

"Ah. *Mr. Bacon.* Did he respond?"

"His assistant said Kevin would be thrilled to attend one of the rounds."

"G.Q., that's...great."

"Surprised me, Charley. I haven't spoken to Kevin for many years."

"But it's a nice surprise, G.Q. It will give you a chance to catch up."

Someone touched my forearm. "Charley?"

"Hi there, Mrs. Morrison."

"Do you have a second?"

"For you, sure."

"Excuse us just for a minute, G.Q." She took my wrist, helped me out of my deck chair, and led me a few steps away from the poolside hubbub. "Guess what I have in my hand."

"Ahhh...tickets to the Jefferson Airplane reunion tour?"

"A tennis ball. A tennis ball with a long rubber band attached."

I chuckled. "And I bet you also have a broom handle."

"I do."

"And you want the blind man to take the broom handle and swing at the tennis ball?"

"I do."

"Okay. Sure. I can't do any worse than last time."

"I thought it would be constructive for you. A demonstration of going full circle."

"I'm up for it. Let's go."

She placed the wooden handle into my hand. I gripped the handle as if it were a baseball bat, and rested it on my shoulder.

"All set?"

"Yep."

"When you're ready, Charley."

I assumed Mrs. Morrison was holding the rubber band away from her body and the tennis ball was just hanging there. I pictured the ball, the rubber band, and Mrs. Morrison just as she stood in the woods like this nine months ago. Then I called upon the frigid arctic tundra and it rushed straight through my skull. I lightened my grip until I was barely touching the handle, and I swung.

The wooden handle struck the tennis ball with a dull thump.

"I knew it," Mrs. Morrison cried out. "Just remember this moment tomorrow, Charley."

"Okay."

"You can do anything if you really want to." She hugged me and stepped away.

I had no idea if I had really connected with the ball, or if Mrs. Morrison had moved the ball so it would connect with my bat. But I thought it was cool that Mrs. Morrison was doing her best to boost my self-confidence.

G.Q. remained silent for a few moments. I tried to guess his expression.

"Now." G.Q. stepped closer to me and cleared his throat. "Charles Marriott Davis, let's talk about the three courses themselves and our overall strategy."

Chapter 56

Down in Monterey

The first thing I noticed on the course was the unearthly quiet. I held Angelica's vest handle and we walked together beside G.Q. who told me the approach to the first tee was lined with hundreds of spectators and news crews. The numerous pro-am teams were gathered, preparing to begin their games. And yet, with all that potential commotion, all I could hear was the tide rippling against the shore, sea birds softly chattering above, and California seals howling at each other in the distance. It was as if everyone kept silent, out of solemn respect for this pristine golfing establishment.

The air brimmed with the scent of the ocean, and if I didn't know better, it felt as though I was back on Seabrook, just out for a morning stroll down the beach.

"So, would it be a bad idea if you told me who is here watching?" I asked G.Q.

"It won't hurt as long as you keep it together."

"Can't promise that."

"Well then..."

We walked on. Angelica led me at just the right pace, the grass beneath my shoes as smooth and soft as thick wool carpeting.

"We are nearing the first tee, a few hundred feet to go," G.Q. said. "P.J. Varelli is inspecting her clubs at the tee. Mr. Dill is there, as well, with your clubs. Mr. Ford is across the fairway with his camera equipment."

G.Q. didn't say anything for a few seconds.

"And Mr. Ford has help," G.Q. said.

"Help?"

"A certain curly-headed blond female wearing a ball cap."

I felt my breath stick in my throat. "G.Q., are you kidding me?"

He stepped closer. "She's walking this way."

I remained still and waited.

"Hi, Charley," Sandy said a few seconds later.

My eyes opened wider even though it wouldn't make her gray form any clearer. "Sandy, what are you doing here?"

"Sorry I didn't let you know I would be here."

"Ray needs the help, I know."

"He called me. Told me what happened."

"That's odd. Didn't tell me he'd called you."

"I was hoping we could talk later, Charley. Maybe tonight."

I took a breath. "Yeah. Tonight."

She took a long breath and exhaled. "Well, I've got to help Ray set up."

"All right.

She touched my arm. "Knock the heck out of the ball, Charley."

"I sure will try."

"I'll be watching."

I heard her step away. "Sandy?"

"Yeah?"

"I'd say it was good to see you, but..." I shrugged.

She chuckled. "Some things never change, Charley."

The air was quiet.

"G.Q.?"

"Right here."

"How does she look?"

"Charley, remember to keep focus. You can't let Sandy distract you."

"I'll be fine." I took a breath knowing that was a lie. "Who else is here on the course today?"

"National radio, TV, and print media are everywhere. Your uncle and Leslie Rae are behind the tee. Oh, and Charley..."

"Yes?"

"They are holding hands."

"I knew it."

"Now, what you have to do is to empty your mind of every

last particle of information I just told you."

"When I am at the first tee, my mind will empty faster than my high school at the last bell of the day."

"Our competition approaches."

"Mr. Quick?" a male voice said in a heavy Australian accent. "I am Cushman Wakefield."

"My pleasure," G.Q. said. "This is Charley Davis."

"Hi." I offered my open hand.

G.Q. guided my arm.

Wakefield and I shook hands.

"And I'm Wallace Jay," a different male voice said.

I shook his hand as well.

"Mr. Davis," Cushman Wakefield said, "may I introduce myself to your remarkable canine?"

"Sure."

Wallace Jay said, "Look at those eyes."

"She sees deep into your soul."

G.Q. said, "Ms. Varelli is coming this way."

"Thanks."

Wakefield said, "So, best of luck to you, mate. If what I've read is true, you are a true inspiration."

"Me?"

"I've heard rumors about your clubs."

"Oh?"

"May I see them?"

"Pinson?" I shouted. "Bring a club."

"Right here, sir." He placed a driver in my hands.

I held it out in Wakefield's direction. "Here you go."

A few seconds later, Wakefield said, "God save us."

"Like it, Mr. Wakefield?"

"The rumors did not tell half the story."

"May I?" Jay asked.

"Certainly."

"Magnificent," Jay said. "Like a relic from another time. Or planet."

"Well then," Wakefield said, "the rumor also running about is you practiced and played blindfolded...before your accident."

"True."

"And you trained to play both left and right-handed?"

"Also true. But not here. I'm better from the left, and left it shall be. I've got enough to worry about."

Jay said, "It can't be true that you never played golf until nine months ago."

"I had good trainers. They're around here somewhere."

"May I ask," Wakefield said, "how your trainers took a non-golfer this far in such a short period of time?"

"Three or four hours of meditation each morning, hitting jawbreakers into a horse pasture, and swinging like crazy with Nigerian fighting sticks."

"Cushman," P.J. said from beside me.

"Ah, P.J. A pleasure to see you again," Wakefield said. "My partner, Wallace Jay."

"Ma'am."

"Mr. Jay."

"We go in five minutes," G.Q. said.

Wakefield said, "The best to you, P.J., and to you, Mr. Davis."

"It's Charley. The only one who calls me Mr. Davis is G.Q. here, and I've nearly broken him of that."

"Charley," P.J. said as she touched my arm. "Let's talk for a minute." She led me a few steps to my right. "How are you doing?"

"Okay, I guess."

"I don't know about you, but I am nervous as hell. This tournament is always well attended by the press and celebrities. This year, though, because of your growing fame, the whole place has gone crazy."

"Because of me? I'm not used to being the center of attention."

"Better get used to it quickly."

"Oh, that's something G.Q. could do quite well."

"What's that?"

"Get used to it 'quickly.' You know, Garland *Quick*?"

I felt her move closer to me.

"Charley, when this is over, will you keep playing?"

"Golf?"

"No. Tiddlywinks."

"I haven't thought that far ahead."

"Your deal with your uncle was to train for nine months, to see if you would be good enough to play with the pros at the end of it. And you trained blindfolded. Left and right handed. With sword clubs."

"It sounds just as ridiculous now as it did when Uncle Morgan first proposed it."

"Nine months are up. We have this pro-am. Then what?"

"I don't have a job anymore. And, of course, there's this small problem with my vision."

"Listen, Charley, I'm a pro part of the year at The Homestead, in Hot Springs, Virginia. The club manager heard I was playing Pebble Beach with you this weekend, and, well, he's been following your progress in the press."

"Word gets around."

"Whatever happens in this tournament, if you continue to play, I can arrange a position for you."

"In Virginia?"

"Yes."

"With you?"

"Yes."

I took a long breath. "Are you positive I'm good enough to work with you in Virginia? Hard for me to imagine. And now, P.J., with my visually challenged condition and all..."

"Non-golfer nine months ago. Today, playing the Pebble Beach Pro-Am. Blind. It would be an honor to work with you."

"Thanks."

"And a pleasure."

"I'm kind of irritating sometimes."

"Plus you make me laugh."

"My curse."

She squeezed my hand. "Show the world today, Charley. Prove you can do it, for yourself."

I smiled. "Yeah. I'll give it my best shot."

***

G.Q. handed me my Titleist. I bent, pushed a tee into the turf, and placed the ball on the tee. I straightened, shut everything out, cleared my mind except for an acre of ice cubes, brought my Samurai club back left-handed, and swung. I heard nothing but the club slashing through the air.

G.Q. said, "You okay?"

"Missed it, didn't I?"

"You've driven off the tee blindfolded a thousand times, Charley. This is no different."

"I can't say why, but this is *seriously* different."

"Let it fly again."

I did it right this time.

G.Q. said, "Nice shot."

We walked on.

According to G.Q., my third shot went careening into the trees.

I managed to sink my seventh shot into the cup.

If I could see my uncle's face, I'm sure he would be smiling to hide the fact I was shooting horribly. P.J., on the other hand, shot a three, and earned the applause of an appreciative gallery.

Angelica led me to the second tee. I bent close to one of her ears. "I'm stinking up the joint again, girl."

Jitters. Normal.

"And how do I de-jitter?"

You know.

"I do?"

Clear your mind. Reflex takes over.

"It's not that easy surrounded by all this attention."

It is easy. You know it is.

I straightened up.

G.Q. took my arm and centered me over my ball.

"G.Q.?"

"Mr. Davis?"

"Better get your binoculars."

"What on earth for?"

I took a breath. "I'm knocking this ball to Sacramento."

"That, Charley, I would truly like to see."

***

After the first round and a quiet dinner with Uncle Morgan,

Pinson walked with Angelica and me to my room. Mrs. Morrison had excused herself to an early bedtime. G.Q. wanted to walk tomorrow's course before complete darkness, and Sandy, well Sandy was off to fiddle with her camera equipment, in a room she shared with Mrs. Morrison. Nobody really said much. I suppose it was still hard for anyone to feel especially celebratory about today's round, considering the state of my vision.

"Good match today, Charley," Pinson said.

"Thanks."

"Tomorrow then. Anything you need?"

"I'll be fine, Pinson. I am going to speak with Sandy."

Pinson put his hand on my shoulder. "I told you before my friend. That woman loves you."

"She has a funny way of showing it." I nodded. "Good night, Pinson. Thanks again."

"You are welcome, Charley. Good night."

He walked away.

"Sandy?" I said. Her room was next to mine. I rapped lightly on her door. "Sandy?"

A door clicked open.

"Hi," she said from the doorway.

"Is this a good time?"

She took my hand. "Come on in."

She led me inside. Angelica walked in beside us.

"Mrs. Morrison is already asleep," Sandy whispered, "so we should keep our voices down."

We stopped and sat on a sofa together. Angelica plopped on the carpeted floor near my feet.

I waited a few seconds for my heart to stop pounding. "Surprised you're here...in Monterey."

She shifted her position, moved closer and squeezed my hand. I smelled fresh soap.

"Do you feel like talking?" she said. "I don't want to pressure you, the tournament and all."

"No, this is fine. For some reason, since my accident with Mrs. Morrison, the pressure of playing golf has seemed less...distressing. Maybe it's a question of perspective. Not sure."

She was silent for a moment.

"Okay."

Lane Cohen

She squeezed my hand harder. "Since I walked out of your condo that night, walked out on *you*, I've done nothing but stew about it, over and over, backwards and forwards."

"And?"

"Then Ray called me and told me what happened, how Mrs. Morrison—"

"No." I shook my head. "It was *me*, Sandy. Not her fault."

"Charley..."

I heard her start to cry.

"Hey, Sandy?"

"Ray also told me how you were still planning to play Pebble Beach. It was then, right at that moment, when I realized I had to come find you, to talk with you, as fast as possible."

"You thought P.J. would steal my heart."

"Nothing about P.J. I just had to talk to you."

"Then...go ahead."

She rested both hands atop my knee. "Charley, you've been right all along."

"I have?"

"I've done nothing my whole life except follow a step-by-step course, so eventually I could be great at what I do. I was seriously single-minded about it. I fashioned my whole existence around filmmaking. And you know what? It worked. My films show it. I've won awards. My name is respected in the documentary film industry."

"I'm happy for you, Sandy. What else can I say? You've got it all."

She took a breath and exhaled. "But you know what I don't have? None of it has brought me *happiness*. I've run from you, twice, the only person who has ever brought me joy, because I was afraid to take a risk with anything that might be a serious distraction. But here you are, a person with no golf talent nine months ago, who took a risk, and changed his entire life. I've never risked anything, Charley. That's why I pushed you away back in college. I thought it had to be a choice, either work or you. But not both."

"Sandy—"

"No, Charley. Let me finish."

I found her hands and covered them with my palms.

"You've taught me that taking a risk is what life is about. You were struck blind, Charley, and you know what? You haven't quit. You continue to take risks. You just plain refuse to give up."

I shook my head. "You make me sound heroic or something. In fact, I started this golf mission by default. I couldn't figure how anything could be as bad as what I was already going through."

"You're more than any old hero, Charley. You're my hero."

"I don't know what to say."

"Say you'll forgive me."

"Sandy, are you saying you want us to get back together?"

She started a soft cry. "You don't know how many times I wish that I had told you..." She burst into tears.

All at once I couldn't breathe, and all at once I realized what song Mrs. Morrison had recorded on the voodoo CD I had given to Sandy back at Seabrook beach: *Cherish* by The Association.

"Sandy. My God, Sandy, stop crying. Please."

"I'm sorry. I'm sorry." She sniffled. "How do you feel about it, Charley? I mean you and me."

My brain was spinning. "I love you, Sandy. I truly love you. But considering what's happened, several times, I don't know *what* to say. I don't know if I should fall head-over-heels for you again, just to have you eventually...run away." I took a breath. "I'm not sure I have enough strength to recover from another heartbreak like that."

She gently pulled her hands away. "I know. I guess we should both give it a lot of thought before we decide anything."

"I suppose."

"Okay."

"Sandy, there is something I would like to tell you."

"What's that?"

I gazed directly at her. "I can see the shape of your face."

"Charley..?"

"Started improving on the course today."

"Oh my God."

"Not great, still blurry, but getting better."

She leaned closer and took my hands. "That's wonderful."
"Yeah. I just hope it continues."
She squeezed my hands again. "Can you forgive me, Charley?"
I blinked as a few tears burned my eyes. She started to cry again, took a deep breath and pulled me close before I could answer. I rested my head against her chest, tears streamed from my eyes onto her shirt, and I listened to the muffled beating of her heart, maybe for the last time.

***

It was 1:00am but still warm outside. Angelica was stretched out in the grass near the pool. I joined her and lay on my back. My head nestled in the very center of her black fur. "Quiet tonight, girl."
Yes.
"Peaceful."
Nice.
"I just saw Sandy."
I know.
"She wants to get back together."
Will you?
I took a deep breath and let it out. "No."
Oh?
"What's that old saying, the definition of insanity is repeating past mistakes hoping for a different outcome?"
Something like that.
"Anyhow, I've been thinking seriously about P.J.'s offer. I really think I might like to work with her in Virginia. Sounds cool. And if I did that, well, Sandy would be gone anyway."
Angelica yawned.
"The first round was pretty good today."
74. Below par. Nothing to be ashamed of.
"I have a lot of people to thank for that."
Certainly.
"My eyesight is clearing up."
Yes.
"Started on the back nine."

Good news indeed.

I sighed. "Thanks, Angelica."

For?

"Being there for me. For being my friend."

We'll always be friends. I told you; it was destined from the beginning.

I chuckled. "Maybe after the pro-am, we can magically help the defenseless, and assist the poor and sick, you know, like Mr. Tagawa said."

You're no magician, and I am not a magician's dog.

"There's magic involved here somewhere."

I stared straight up into the foggy heavens. "Look at the stars, girl. I think Ray might be wrong about Alaska."

Oh?

"The stars are pretty close to the ground, even here in California."

Angelica stretched her front paws in front of her.

Early meditation in the morning?

"Yep. I told Mrs. Morrison I needed it. Our tee-time for the second round isn't until 10:30."

Can we sleep in just a little later?

I yawned and patted the fur around her neck. "Sure, girl. For you, we can sleep in."

I put my hands behind my head and pushed my fingers through Angelica's fur. I took one last blurry look at the star-filled sky, smiled, and closed my eyes.

Lane Cohen

Author's notes:

Sincere apologies for my 400 pop-culture references, including *Star Trek*, the Indiana Jones films, Harrison Ford, Sean Connery, Kevin Bacon, Joe Pesci, Chris Harrison, Calvin Klein, Swanson Frozen Dinners, the musicals *Oklahoma! West Side Story*, and *1776*, the bands The Rolling Stones, Procol Harum, Crosby, Stills & Nash, Buffalo Springfield, The Classics IV, and The Association, Antioch College, Chevrolet, and the films *The Big Sleep*, *The Big Chill*, *Gone With the Wind*, *Casablanca*, *Sandlot*, *Somewhere in Time*, *Pearl Harbor*, and *The Princess Bride*. I can't help myself.

The locations in this story are real. In Cincinnati, all the streets mentioned, the Skyline Chili restaurant, the Graeter's ice-cream parlor, the locations of Charley's apartment and condo, Garland Quick's Mt. Adams residence, the horse stable Charley refers to as *Jawbreaker Mountain*, and the Kenwood Country Club golf course still exist and are described as they truly are. Likewise, the details of the specific holes at the Kenwood Country Club course are accurate. In South Carolina, Seabrook and Kiawah are real places, as are the named beaches, Pelican Watch Villas, Bohicket Marina, and the Robert Trent Jones golf course. Cappy's was a real restaurant, but closed a few years ago after a long run. The details of the Pebble Beach holes are described as accurately as possible, and are truly some of the most beautiful wonders on the face of this Earth.

And, for those of you who have met Angelica, for those of you who have whispered close into her ear on a seriously magic day, you already know that Angelica is, and always will be, absolutely and completely real.

About the Author

Lane Cohen attended the University of Cincinnati, studied musical theater, and has appeared in West Side Story, Bye-Bye Birdie, Funny Girl, Footloose, Jekyll & Hyde, and more. His favorite authors are Robert B. Parker, Carl Hiaasen, and Stephen King. His favorite rule of writing: "Write drunk. Edit sober." - Ernest Hemingway. He's authored several short stories and novels: **Protection**, the story of two brothers who face an ancient evil in Protection, Kansas, and **A Matter of Time**, a time-travel race to catch a serial killer in the future. A civil lawyer by day, he lives on a rural ranch in Parker, Colorado, with his wife, Barbara. Here he's pictured with his friend Leo, a dog who rescued him not long ago.

More books by Lane Cohen

Protection (TWB Press, 2014)
A horror novel by Lane Cohen
www.twbpress.com/protection.html

A Matter of Time (TWB Press, 2020)
A time-travel thriller by Lane Cohn
www.twbpress.com/amatteroftime.html

Find links to more books at

www.twbpress.com